Waiting for Zoë

A Novel

James R. Ament

Hugo House Publishers
Englewood, Colorado

Waiting For Zoë
© 2011 James R. Ament
All rights reserved

Disclaimer
This book is a work of fiction. The characters, incidents, and dialog are drawn from the author's imagination and are not to be construed as real. Any resemblance to actual events or persons, living or dead, is entirely coincidental.

ISBN: 978-1-936449-05-7
Library of Congress Control Number: 2011933905

Hugo House Publishers
Englewood, Colorado
Austin, Texas
877.700.0616
www.HugoHousePublishers.com

Design by NZ Graphics

For Margaret Miller Ament

"A man is likely to mind his own business when it is worth minding. When it is not, he takes his mind off his own meaningless affairs by minding other people's business. This minding of other people's business expresses itself in gossip, snooping and meddling, and also in feverish interest in communal, national and racial affairs. In running away from ourselves we either fall on our neighbor's shoulder or fly at his throat."

Eric Hoffer
The True Believer—
Thoughts on the Nature
of Mass Movements (1951)

Part 1

Chapter 1

Russ awoke early, before sunrise, switched on a light and then opened the vertical blinds covering the sliding door to the back porch, noticing that there was no visibility. The house was completely socked in. He turned off the light, crawled back into bed, and dozed in and out of dream states.

He loved this house, a friend's beach house in San Clemente, because Sara had been here with him. Once when they had stayed here, they had left the bedroom door to the back porch open so they could hear the pounding waves—the primal rhythmic sound that soothed them to sleep. On that cool May night, the clouds had rolled in and filled the bedroom with wet mist, spilling into the great room, snaking its way into every corner, dampening everything it touched. They had giggled as they stumbled about, looking for the light switch and turning on the gas fireplace to bring warmth to the room. Russ knew better than to leave that door open overnight in subsequent visits.

Their favorite season to visit was winter, when the San Clemente beaches were quiet, although this particular location was almost a private place, even in the summer. They'd eat dinner out early and then return for a dark walk on the beach wearing their sweats. Or, on a cold night, Sara would wrap a wool blanket around her from the ready supply stored in an antique trunk in the house.

Russ often remembered the night, about four years ago, when she had asked him to bring a second blanket. She'd stopped during their walk, laid down her blanket, reclined, and pulled him to her. They made love on the beach that night, laughing like teenagers at their caution to avoid getting sand in the wrong places. Russ had always been pleased that it had been her idea, her initiative. Then they did what they often did after a walk: they went back to the porch for coffee, a glass of red wine and some rich chocolate dessert, while wrapped together under wool on the chaise lounge built-for-two. Resting in the cold damp air, listening to the ocean, they would read, talk about their plans for the future, their wishes, or their daughter Grace, until sleep lured them into the bedroom. These were precious moments easily recalled.

It was a three thousand-square-foot, single-story house located on a high bluff overlooking the beach, well south of the San Clemente pier. The Amtrak train ran on tracks between the bluff and the beach, and there was a dirt path at the end of the short gated street that led across the tracks down to the beach. The three-bedroom, two-bath house had a big, open family, dining, and kitchen area—the great room—facing the ocean, with a back porch that extended the full length of the structure. Like many beach houses, it was constantly battered by the weather, or simply the salt mist, which had a deleterious effect on whatever anyone might build there.

The house was well maintained and tastefully decorated in a modern California Beach House style. It was a summer home used frequently by its owner, Robin Kite, but was unoccupied by him often enough so there was plenty of time for guests to stay there…at least, those who had the good fortune to be invited to use the house. The place was stocked with all the necessary supplies—with the exception of fresh food—so a visitor could easily move in for a three-day weekend. And nobody in their right mind would think of drinking Robin's carefully selected wines from his temperature-controlled, built-in wine cellar in the garage.

The people lucky enough to use the house, and who wanted to ensure the privilege of doing so again, replaced that which was consumed and brought their own alcohol. The fact that Robin wouldn't care about some used laundry soap or consumed canned asparagus wasn't the point. Enjoying a mini-vacation here was Robin's occasional gift to a select group of friends, and Russ and Sara never abused his wonderful generosity.

The couple would have loved to buy this house, or one like it, but beach property being what it was, common souls just couldn't afford it. Although they lived a comfortable life, not having to stress over a defunct washing machine, for instance—they'd just buy a new one—they never felt like they were any different than they had been during their humble beginnings. When Russ was a man on the rise in the corporate world, there was no real possibility of owning a beach house, and when he had his own company, they were both appropriately cautious about pursuing such a move, given the risks and uncertainties of entrepreneurship. As a teenager, his father had told him, "There is an advantage to working for someone else. You won't necessarily get rich, but if you live with prudence, all you have to lose is your job. If you have your own business, and it doesn't work out, you can lose everything."

Attached to this concept of prudence, Russ and Sara went house hunting in Laguna Beach once, just for fun, and while everything was beyond their price range, they wanted to see one of the cheaper homes anyway. It was a nine hundred-square-foot, run-down shack above an arroyo offered at $495,000…actually, a tear-down. But who could afford to spend that kind of money and then build a new house on the same property? Obviously some people could. It sold three days later.

Russ and Sara also looked at an eleven hundred-square-foot cottage on a hilly street a couple miles away from Robin's house, advertised as having an "ocean view," which was true. If you stood on the second-floor bathroom toilet and looked out the high window, you could see a tiny corner of the Pacific Ocean. The price was ridiculous. They gave up even thinking about beach houses, and moved on to other shared dreams.

———

For a number of years, Russ ran a small division at Dunstan Industries, a manufacturer of aerospace products. But in 1997, the company divested itself of that division. Dunstan had paid a consulting company $1.2

million to help develop a new strategic plan. After a year's work, the consultant's report concluded that Dunstan needed to get back to its core business, shedding peripheral, though interesting, subsidiaries and divisions, and focus on maximizing their fundamental volume aircraft and helicopter supplier businesses. The CEO and Board of Directors considered Russ's small research division one of the obvious choices for divesting, so it became the signal event in implementing the consultant's strategy. The transition was smooth, though it entailed a lot of work, and the spin-off benefited Russ's new company by securing equipment at lower than book value, maintaining existing government contracts, and negotiating favorable, long-term supplier contracts with Dunstan.

Russ also had room to grow his business, particularly in foreign markets, but an unwritten gentlemen's agreement included a non-compete clause with Dunstan. Russ had plenty to do without ever touching Dunstan's business, and he had a good working relationship with management as a supplier, so competing with them in the marketplace never became an issue. However, some employees wanted to leave Dunstan to work for Russ. This became a delicate matter, since stealing employees was frowned upon, ultimately handled without hardship. Russ got some quality staff engineers out of it, which was a good thing since hiring new ones was problematical. Russ was an old-school engineer and was often surprised to hear that many of the new graduates never built anything. He would ask them, "Did you ever rebuild a car engine?" And in answering "no" they would look at him as if to say, "Why would that be important?" He was frustrated that there were too many computer geeks with no hands-on experience in the business. He nonetheless found the project managers he needed and the business became a success. It became his life.

Russ had intended to leave the beach house at 6:00 A.M., just ahead of the worst of the traffic. Although he would be heading east, where in the past, traffic flow would have been minimal, now it could be busy in any direction and on any day of the week. The early morning news confirmed that the fog bank that had greeted him upon waking, covered the whole L.A. basin, so he decided to wait until it lifted before he departed. He wasn't on any fixed timetable anyway, and he didn't want to deal with the possibility of being a participant in another forty-car pile-up, as had happened last week on Interstate 5.

Russ took his time. He made coffee from fresh roasted beans, Irish oatmeal, and wheat toast, sitting down to his breakfast in front of the television, hardly paying attention to the news except for the weather report.

Robin had said that his housecleaner, Maria, was scheduled the next day, so Russ shouldn't worry about doing the laundry, dishes, or anything else before he left. Indeed, Robin had the house cleaned every week, even when no one stayed there, since windows always needed to be washed after being attacked by the ever-present salt mist in the air. Nevertheless, after Russ shaved, showered and dressed, he stripped the bed, and washed the dishes, towels, and bedding. With the chores done, he finished the last forty pages of Jon Krakauer's, *Into the Wild*, and waited for the sun to burn off the fog.

Russ wrote a warm thank-you note to Robin, folded it into an envelope, put his name on it, and left it on the kitchen table, knowing that Robin was planning to visit his home-away-from-home in a few days. Russ also wrote a short note to Maria, informing her that her chores would probably involve washing windows rather than cleaning up his mess. He wasn't at all sure she would appreciate his gesture.

He made the bed, finished packing, took one last walk through the house to insure the place looked like it had when he had arrived, finished loading the truck, locked the front door, and dropped the key into a lock box outside as planned.

Russ departed California, marveling how easy it was to begin the process of running away from his former life.

Chapter 2

Zoë Valiente wasn't sure what the next few weeks would bring: whether it would be a life-altering experience, a mere footnote, or something in between. She suspected a footnote. She had this tendency to speculate possibilities and reactions to potential outcomes, particularly when something new was scheduled. The grinding of teeth was the occasional manifestation of such moments, but mostly, she thought herself tough, street-wise, and able to get through almost anything.

Having just finished her third year at Columbia University's School of Journalism in New York City, Zoë had committed to a short summer internship working at the *Demming Gazette* in Demming, Wyoming. Her favorite professor and guidance counselor, the enigmatic Dr. Wilhelm, had attended undergraduate school with Martin Coleman, the editor of the small town paper in Demming. Over the years, the two men had become good, though physically distant friends. Their contact had been primarily by e-mail or infrequent phone calls; most of the time they spent solving the world's problems and then intellectualizing every topic chosen. These exchanges were less than scholarly, according to Dr. Wilhelm, but rather, characterized by a conversational tone that wouldn't have been much different had they been sitting in front of each other at a Starbucks.

It was Dr. Wilhelm who suggested that "a life experience, different from that with which you are familiar" might be just the thing needed prior to Zoë's senior year. This was after she had broached the idea of an internship, possibly in Europe. It needed to be a short one, however, because she had to get back to New York to her part-time job as a waitress at an upscale restaurant, and she wanted to devote her "every other waking hour to helping elect a Democrat President." Unless she just wanted a vacation or an excuse to play, Dr. Wilhelm couldn't find any place in Europe that would offer an internship for just a few weeks. Since he had a professional connection in Wyoming, the Demming internship seemed to be the likely choice. Besides, he had reasons, unexplained to Zoë, why working for his old friend might be good for her. So, he arranged for her low-paying job and living arrangements with his old friend.

Zoë had her own reasons for wanting to depart New York for a while, having to do with her recently failed relationship with Darrel. She chose not to include any comments about Darrel in her discussions with her professor. She needed a diversion, and she hoped this little opportunity in unfamiliar territory would give her just that. Indeed, when Dr. Wilhelm offered that he knew the owner and editor of a small town newspaper, who also owned a book store, and he was willing to offer her an internship, she eagerly latched on to the idea. Besides, she'd never been to that part of the country.

The good professor had all the right answers to her questions…he was in salesman mode and he did a good job. She would have room and board expenses to cover, but it didn't appear these costs would be too burdensome. She had to organize her travel and her ongoing expenses. Then, she just needed to show up, a point Dr. Wilhelm stressed by quoting Woody Allen: "Eighty percent of success is just showing up."

Chapter 3

It was in March 2008 when Bud Wilhelm called Martin Coleman in Demming. After the introductions, the "long-time-no-talk" comments, and inquiries about family, Bud said, "Marty, I have a favor to ask. It's another request for you to look after one of my students during an internship at your paper. Late May into early July is the perfect time, if you can do it."

"Well, I'm not going anywhere. Having the newspaper, a bookstore and a ranch keeps me planted. Perhaps I can encourage a couple people to schedule their vacations around that time. It could work out. You're not going to send somebody like the last one, are you? That boy had no idea what he wanted to do with his life. He lasted about two weeks out here. Sometimes I think you're using me to weed out the undesirables. That was a while ago…seven years, if I remember correctly. Haven't heard from you about an internship since. Did I upset you, Bud?"

"No, it's just that most of my bright students have other ideas about how they want to spend their time during an internship, and Wyoming isn't high on their list. You're talking about Joel. He's a lucky kid. He changed careers as soon as he left your place. What did you do to him? He became a flunky of sorts working somewhere at the World Trade Center until the end of August 2001 when he moved to Philadelphia, to a real job at some financial institution…I can't remember the name. He didn't last there, either. I think he's now a monk in some obscure monastery in Upstate New York."

"I remember that now. You called me a few days after September eleventh. I didn't know the monk part, though. I guess he has good reason to be praying without ceasing. So what's this new guy's problem?"

"It's a girl this time, a very pretty girl. She looks a little like Halle Berry."

Smiling, Martin asked, "Bud...who's Halle Berry?"

"Martin, ask some younger men around town, people who go to the movies, people who pay attention to our dynamic American culture."

"Here we go again, huh?"

"I thought I'd get in the first dig. Besides, I know you're waiting for an opening."

"Really pretty women—the kind that know it—aren't much fun to be around, Bud. I'm getting a bad feeling here."

"Don't worry. She has a very warm personality and isn't a primping narcissist at all. She doesn't ask for special treatment, a very natural young lady. You'll like her, Marty.

"Okay. I'll believe you for a while. What am I to fix this time?"

"I'm not sure that there is anything to fix. I'm operating from a hunch, really. She's just so certain about how the world works, or should work—although I know students often act that way to test their own arguments in a safe environment. Also, she is floundering in her own life, or so it seems. She's a good student, a good person. I want her to succeed."

"What's her name?"

"Zoë Valiente."

"What's she so certain about? How can I help?"

"Regarding the first question, she's a political junky, an amateur policy wonk, with a partisan commitment to the Democrats. She's—"

Interrupting, Martin said, "Certainty about Democrat policies shouldn't bother you, Bud, big government statist that you are."

"That's what I love about you, Marty. We've been talking for over forty years, and you always try to pigeonhole me. Anyway, Zoë and I do agree on some things although I avoid telling her that. I occasionally have to caution her about her warfare model—the 'them vs. us' attitude.

"Here's a quick example. A few weeks ago in class, we were all discussing the quality of recent reporting about the feds raising the minimum wage, and she referred to the more conservative perspective as 'morally outrageous.' I took it as an educational opportunity for the class, so we defined our terms and then I talked about the self-righteousness one assumes when referring to an opinion with which one doesn't happen to agree. I suggested that we need to be careful about defining ourselves by judging the character of those with varying opinions from our own. You'll no doubt recall our similar conversation some years ago. You see, Martin, I do learn things from you…rarely, but every once in a while."

"I learn from you as well, Bud. For instance, I've learned that age hasn't diminished your desire to be a smart ass one bit." Chuckling, Martin added, "I thought you were teaching journalism, not psychology or philosophy?"

"Well, understanding human nature is pretty important in most professions. My summarizing point was to question the contempt for those with whom one might disagree. Think about how a story might read if the reporter decided beforehand that the person they're interviewing has nothing credible to contribute so they should simply be dismissed. I questioned my students how such an attitude would affect their reporting. I asked them, 'How are you going to be objective if you are filled with outrage?' Zoë came around, as did most of the class, but she needs to spend some time with more moderate thinkers. The tone in her writing is actually quite balanced, as it needs to be, if she wants to graduate."

"Sounds like a fundamentalist leftist. Or is it just youthful exuberance I hear in your description of her?"

"If she were eighteen, I'd think the latter," said Bud. "But, she's twenty-six. She spent a number of years trying to be a professional tennis player. When that didn't work out, it took her some time to figure out what she wanted to do with her life. She came here as a freshman fairly apolitical, but over the last couple years she's developed a passion for left-of-center positions. It looks like it's what gives her meaning, but I still can't figure out if she's like most twenty-somethings: they take on the ideology-*du-jour* without really delving into it, you know what I mean?"

"Ah, yes, in the minds of the passionate, passion is the source of wisdom about the meaning of life."

"Passion was no doubt necessary in her tennis career. There are certainly good kinds of passion, but it can also go too far. We read it in the news all the time." Bud paused, then added, "By the way, did you come up with that phrase, 'fundamentalist leftist'?"

"No, I stole it. But you know me…thievery of words and phrases is the greatest form of flattery." Martin laughed softly. "Your concern, I take it from what you've said so far, is an apparent lack of objectivity which could creep into her reporting and affect her journalistic credibility. So what else is new in the journalistic world?"

"Come on Marty…."

"Okay, let me rephrase that. Is your department still drilling the concept of objectivity into the students the way we got it drilled into us when we were in school?"

"Well, I just gave you an example of what I do in that regard. We flunk those who don't get it. Any student that submits a news report containing editorial bias gets a low grade. We're relentless with teaching people not to make the news, not to be the news, not to slant the news, not to report a story with an agenda in mind, or only report the stories that fit one's agenda while ignoring those that may hurt it. We're not teaching a methodology of how to advance an ideology. That's for public relations people, think tanks, and people running political campaigns."

"I'll bet that's a tough sell."

"Marty, did you know that right now, journalism schools are jammed with students? And we're preparing them for work in an industry that's compressing…that may be in trouble."

"I've sensed that, too, in the industry…certainly the trouble part. Why do you think students are still attracted to it?"

"Just like in our day, people who go into journalism are idealists. They want to change the world," said Bud.

"There is a lot of that going around. They're going to be terribly disappointed when they can't find work. The competition for jobs must be fierce in the big markets."

"That's why internships are important, unless somebody wants to study journalism as a kind of liberal arts education or go into public relations. If somebody really wants to be a reporter, they'll need connections to insiders to secure employment."

"Well, I don't see any prospects for a job here. I might have to make cuts."

"But you're connected, Marty. You know people in places like Denver."

"Bud, you know I can't offer any guarantees about a job. Let's get back to the idealist part. I'm curious…how do today's students respond to the drill?"

"Actually, quite a few work hard at trying to develop objectivity, to know what it looks like, and maintain it after they leave. Personally, I'm very proud of some of my former students. However, some of them just sit there glassy eyed, like they're humoring the old fart, thinking that I have to say such things to keep up appearances. The smart ones play the game. They submit quality work that meets the requirement, but inside of them, they have other ideas."

"I assume they can and do read the news," replied Martin. "Perhaps they see how it works in the real world. 'It's only news when *we* say it's news.' The story on which *The New York Times* wants to elaborate, is on page one. The story they want to hide isn't covered, or it is a bland notice on page seventeen. '*The New York Times*; all the news that's fit to tint.'"

"Are you still angry at your old employer?"

"Not really. I've just become abjectly cynical about them. You remember, they wanted to bury my submission because it didn't fit the narrative, and I argued too loudly about it and got fired. Like a lot of things in life, call it fate if you will, it was a blessing in disguise. But back to your intern, which kind of a student is this Zoë?"

"I think she's one who plays the game, and she plays it well. I'm not a mind reader, but I'm guessing somewhere in that good brain of hers, she sees the profession of journalism as a means to an end."

"It's not much different than getting an MBA or a law degree. For many, it is a means to an end, the end being a promising career, giving the bosses what they want. If you want to please Pinch Sulzberger, you had better give him and his readership what they want, although as a business, the *Times* doesn't seem to be doing too well. I've always respected you, Bud. You're a rarity at Columbia. You've always cared about the integrity of the profession more than a career in the business. And you're always the realist, too. Let's get back to, 'How can I help?'"

"Let me put it this way. You and I have been talking and writing each other for a long time. We mostly argue, but we've always been civil, and our words have always had an underpinning of humor and mutual respect. I give you credit for that. Thinking back, I see a lot of my young self in the way Zoë is now. I've changed over the years. I like to think that you and I have both learned something as we've conversed in this way… at the very least, clarity of thought. Zoë has something of a crusade mentality, and I think exposure to a different culture with some very different discourse out there in the wilds of Wyoming would be good for her. Like I said, I want her to succeed."

"Oh yes, the 'wilds of Wyoming.' You know, just last week, we put in a flush toilet at the house?"

"Yes, yes, okay." Bud laughed. "Listen, Zoë is just trying to figure out who she is, and as I suggested, exposure elsewhere might reinforce a sense of balance in her thinking. I could be wrong. A few weeks in Wyoming may harden her. My gut says otherwise…because I know you. My concern is that most all the people she hangs out with here are in general agreement. They have essentially the same attitude—they're in-your-face leftists. And I hear—strictly rumors—that a few of her acquaintances have done some bad things. Nothing serious—things like throwing dog feces at pro-life picketers and minor property damage to cars with Republican bumper stickers on them."

"Really? There are Republican bumper stickers in New York City?"

"Evidently, they are out-of-towners; and the Wall Streeters don't drive themselves. To the best of my knowledge, she hasn't been involved in that kind of thing. But her friends are still around influencing the conversations, and her friends enjoy participating in dissent. It's their right of passage."

"Ah, yes. The romance of dissent. Fashionable pseudo-rebels speaking twaddle to power. And in all the excitement, maybe getting laid. The U.S. has never quite gotten past the sixties, has it? It's just a new generation, perhaps even more spoiled than we were in our day, trying to be relevant in a tired old way."

"There is some of that. There are surely better ways to affect policy than carrying a sign and yelling at people. And to that point, with Zoë's crowd, where they disagree is in the aggressiveness required to make the world fit their ideal. Over time, that is an unhealthy environment. It's just reinforcement of your bias with the most zealous being the drivers. My hope is that some time with you and your people could be a counterbalance for her."

"Groupthink…with the emotionally incontinent in charge."

"You know that there are all kinds of groups, both left and right, engaging in it."

"Yes, I know, Bud. We're living in a world full of true believers who lack humility and hopelessly disagree about what is true. Back to your earlier point about our discussion—thanks for the compliment, but I always reckoned that I received more than I gave. You taught me what the smart folks from the dark side think. Are these friends of hers studying journalism? Anything else I should know?"

"Reckoned? Oh, she'll just love the country colloquialisms. A couple of her friends are journalism students, but they are mostly political science or social studies majors. Some are hangers-on, but they don't go to Columbia, and I don't know them. As for anything more you should know, yes, there probably is, but after that 'dark side' comment of yours, I'll derive pleasure knowing that you will find out on your own."

"Thanks a lot, Bud. You seem to know a good deal about this student."

"I'm her guidance counselor, Marty. She talks—she's a very open girl—and I listen. Then I come up with wise aphorisms that she's supposed to take on board in order to impress me. You won't have any trouble getting to know her fairly quickly. She's no shrinking violet. I don't think you'll turn her into a Republican. I wouldn't send her to you if I thought that, but I do think you'll be good for her."

"Bud, I'm still a registered Libertarian, which means I have no influence whatsoever with the political forces running this country. As for Zoë, it remains to be seen how good I'll be for her. Any influence imparted may have little to do with me and more to do with my staff or other locals she meets. What are the specific dates of this internship?"

"From the weekend of May twenty-fourth until the weekend of July twelfth. She gets out early, but has to be back here for her job. And she's volunteered to work for the DNC to get Obama elected."

"Okay, by my calendar that's seven weeks. Let me work on the details. I'll call you next week, and we can iron out the plan. I always enjoy people who work here for practically nothing."

Chapter 4

In years past, Russ had joked that he could put all the material possessions that he truly cared about in the trunk of his old 911SC, a car he no longer had. It turned out to be untrue.

He always remembered back when the big Laguna Beach fire storm hit in October 1993. Over sixteen thousand acres burned in that one fire—there were many fires in Southern California that month fueled by the hot dry Santa Ana winds, which destroyed almost four hundred homes in Laguna alone.

Watching the news one evening, after the fire was put out, a local TV station interviewed an old gentlemen standing with his wife near the rubble of his home piled on its cement slab foundation. The newswoman asked him how he felt about the terrible events of the previous week. He said, "Well, my wife and I and the dog got out safely, and we're okay. That's the most important thing. And after all, it's just stuff." The news station cut away to another story about the fire. Russ always thought they did that because the old guy wasn't following the storyline they wanted; or perhaps they just didn't know how to end the segment.

Russ always liked the philosophical attitude of the interviewee—he was a stoic, like Russ's mother and father. He also figured that the guy must have had plenty of insurance. Nonetheless, "It's just stuff" stayed with him as an underlying theme whenever discussing or thinking about material possessions. Russ marveled how odd it was that someone you don't even know could say something and it resonated. It affected your outlook forever. To this day, that old man didn't even know the impact he'd had on Russ. But there was the scarier proposition: something you said resonates with another person forever—and what if you got it wrong?

Now, Russ drove a 2003 low-mileage, four-wheel-drive Ford F-150 with a full bed cover. He'd bought the truck after trading in his four-year-old, high-mileage Toyota Camry. He got a very good deal since few people were buying full-size pickups with gas prices the way they were in 2008. He figured he needed a four-wheel drive where he was going and also reasoned that he could buy a lot of expensive gas for several years compared to the payback from buying a new hybrid. He also rented a small U-haul to pull behind the truck.

Russ loaded those few things he truly cared about into the truck, but also included practical items that he would have been foolish to get rid of: power tools, wood-working tools, and a small set of Snap-on mechanic's tools. He also included a top-shelf coffee maker, his Mac Pro laptop, his library, two bicycles, his financial and tax records, a Bose, CD's, a box of old pictures and picture albums, essential clothes, and numerous other things he thought would provide utility. He carefully boxed many of the items and efficiently loaded the truck and trailer, himself, placing some of the more delicate things in the extended cab with him. He had a cooler containing water, Gatorade, a few stalks of celery, and a smoked turkey sandwich he had prepared, plus ice. He planned on taking it slow since the truck was weighted down with the tools and many books. He was in no hurry.

The house sale had gone well. It sold five weeks after going on the market and at a decent price considering the state of the housing market. But then, he lived in Irvine, CA, and while the market had declined from the high prices of 2005, it had not done so significantly since he lived in an area of good schools. His house was a typical, California stick-and-stucco with a tile roof, located on a pleasant, tree-lined street in a desirable neighborhood in which almost everyone had remodeled and modernized their homes from their nineteen-seventies origins. Considering that he and Sara had lived there for twenty years, the house had certainly appreciated in value and, in the end, he did well financially—not that he cared all that much.

He had sold or given away most of his possessions through an estate sale and many trips to their church, which was preparing for its annual bizarre. There were nice items of good quality involved, but none of them had any meaning to him, and some things were downright impractical, like the fancy dining room set with the huge china cabinet and the massive, L-shaped couch—great in the right house and for entertaining but not for him, alone. As he didn't know how this journey might turn out, he didn't want to be saddled with anything that offered little utility or that held no emotional attachment.

Russ was becoming a minimalist by—which was it, necessity or design? He admitted to himself that he was not a collector. Lacking the instinct, he chuckled to think how that one trait of his must have driven hundreds of salespeople crazy. No, what he was doing this time was consciously purposeful. He was reducing his world of possessions. He was withdrawing, going inside himself, with new self-imposed boundaries, and he knew full well that it wasn't a healthy thing to do. Russ was accepting his lot in life. He was accepting the cards that had been dealt. He was fifty-three years old.

Chapter 5

When Zoë first met Martin Coleman, it was mid-afternoon on Saturday, May twenty-fourth at the Jackson airport where he picked her up for the long drive to Demming. She immediately noticed his Roman nose resting on an otherwise square, aging face. She observed noses, a topic in her home as her mother was an expert on nose jobs. Zoë was fortunate to have a classic Spanish nose, inherited from her father. She believed her mother resented her for it.

Martin looked to be in his sixties, maybe five-feet, eleven inches tall, and balding severely, a fact she noticed when he had removed his hat. Martin was a little overweight. He wore jeans, a plain dark blue shirt, brown cowboy boots, and tan cowboy hat. She thought that he would be easy to pick out of a crowd, but then, she hadn't yet learned that where she was going, numerous men dressed like Martin, and there were no crowds.

He drove through Jackson, obviously irritated with the tourist traffic. Once he could relax, he confirmed that she would be staying in a house within walking distance from the paper. She would be living with a Mrs. Elsie Granger, a women in her seventies who seldom took in boarders. Of course, Demming seldom had anyone looking for a room in a boarding house, but when there was someone, Mrs. Granger surely didn't want any smokers, a point clarified prior to Ms. Valiente's arrival. For Zoë, it was easy. She hated cigarette smoke, couldn't understand smoking, and had little sympathy for smokers.

As she examined the beautiful surroundings during the drive, Zoë felt a sense of excitement and a desire to make the most it. Turning to Martin, she asked if there were good places to jog around Mrs. Granger's place.

He simply smiled and said, "Ms. Valiente, there are mostly wide open spaces." He then informed Zoë that she'd have access to the newspaper's circulation van when on assignment, or if she personally needed transportation. Otherwise, walking would be the normal way of getting around. "In the summer," he told her, "this won't be an unpleasant experience, except for the wind."

Zoë had known this going in. Actually, she was quite comfortable being without a vehicle in New York. However, this wasn't New York, and it was now hitting her that her ability to move about could be hampered seriously if there wasn't a liberal policy on the use of the van. With gas prices being what they were, she wondered just how liberal this would actually be. As she tried to absorb the scenery and listen to her new boss describe the area, she realized that she was tired from the trip.

Zoë spent Saturday night getting a tour of the house from Mrs. Granger, then organizing her room. She wasn't hungry enough to have dinner, but Mrs. Granger insisted that she have a piece of fresh apple pie, which was the best she had ever eaten. Mrs. Granger liked to talk, so Zoë was filled with stories about the town, most of which she had trouble absorbing. On Sunday, she oriented herself to the area by taking a long walk around the deserted town—everyone was at church—followed by a six-mile jog, taking in the beauty. The rest of the day she read, visited with Mrs. Granger, and found a café nearby to have dinner. The few people there looked at her as though to say, "Stranger in town."

Martin picked up Zoë early Monday, asking her, "Did you have a pleasant Saturday night and Sunday?"

She told him she did. "It's a lovely town." Laughing, she added, "Life is certainly slower here than in New York, though."

"Does that concern you?"

"No, I didn't expect city life, and I know how to make good use of downtime."

"How so?"

"Reading, writing and exercise, which is what I did mostly."

They arrived at the newspaper before anyone else. Martin said, "Look around my office if you like. I'll be back in a minute. Oh, do you like coffee? I'll get us some."

"Yes, I do. Black please."

"Coming right up."

Zoë noticed how neat everything was. Martin's office included a main desk and a separate one for his computer, a small couch, two end tables with lamps, a small meeting table, two comfortable chairs in front of his desk, and a credenza. She noticed that the only books present were journalism's essentials: the *AP Stylebook*, *The Chicago Manual of Style*, *The New York Times Manual*, and about a dozen other style manuals including the famous Strunk and White, *Elements of Style*. There were no personal books whatsoever, not even some of the great books on journalism like *Not So Wild a Dream* by Eric Sevareid, or *The Front Page*, or *Sarajevo Daily*. There were personal pictures on the credenza and on the wall, which she assumed were of family.

She also saw two framed quotes vertically placed on one wall and she quickly scanned them. One was from the preface of *The Great Conversation*, about citizens being reduced to objects of propaganda… that there's an assumption that people cannot develop their intellectual powers, but they can be bamboozled and that the people must strengthen their minds so that they can appraise the issues for themselves. The second one was from philosopher Eric Hoffer's book, *The True Believer*, about a man being likely to mind his own business when it is worth minding. When it isn't, he takes his mind off his own affairs by minding other people's business. Zoë thought, "So he's into the philosophy of dead white males."

Martin walked in with two cups of coffee, handed one to Zoë, and moved toward his seat. She wanted to ask about the pictures, but he immediately started explaining how things worked. As other people drifted into work, they peeked in while walking by his open door. He was very business-like as he talked to her.

"First of all, let me tell you about our mission. We're a community paper trying to support and uplift the community. Being the only game in town, we have a sense of responsibility about that. When I first started, when I bought the paper, it was in bad shape, odd when you consider the owner had a monopoly, and the cost structures were entirely different then. Of course, they did their own printing with some pretty old equipment. The previous owner, Charles Demming, the son of the town's founder, was an old Scrooge-like grump, pretty stuck in his ways. He thought he was running the town like his dad. He did what he wanted with the paper and didn't care what his customers thought. Needless to say, this was not a formula for success. He was also in a rut editorially. He seldom had any...and he kept changing his advertising rates. If he had a bad month, he'd raise them and lose business. He had a weak staff—underpaid, tired old newsmen that were going through the motions and making mistakes—and growing equipment problems because he wouldn't spend the money to maintain it. He lost his best people, through retirement mostly, and wouldn't replace them.

"The paper was spiraling downward, losing revenue, about to go bankrupt. I saw it as a business that could make decent money if managed right, although that's in the past now. Anyway, I bought it at a good price, to the delight of his creditors, and he retired to his bourbon. Charles died a lonely man about fifteen years ago."

Zoë soaked in all that Martin had just told her and then asked, "Making money is in the past?"

"I expect you already have some insight into the problems in this industry from school. In a town of about ten-thousand, if you include a broad swath, we're getting a circulation of three-thousand, so we're doing reasonably well—for now. But from the perspective of a small town paper, even a monopoly paper, the threat looks like this: The Web is eventually going to dominate the way news is disseminated. Young people, in particular, get their news from Yahoo or MSN.com or Drudge. They don't read newspapers. Secondly, classified ads are drying up because of free services like Craigslist. Thirdly, newsprint prices have been skyrocketing due to increased wood, recycled paper, and transportation costs. In fact, our newsprint prices are increasing by twenty percent next year. In such a setting, ad revenue becomes paramount because you can't make up the cost increases with the subscription price. We work hard to maintain very close relationships with our advertisers because without them, we'd be in deep trouble. In general, small town papers, won't last, particularly those close to big market newspapers in places like Salt Lake or Denver. We'll be one of the last to go because we're isolated. I won't speculate on when that will be, but some people I know around the country in different markets figure they have, at most, ten years left."

"How do you keep the firewall between your sales people and your news people, so your advertising customers don't have undue influence over how you report the news?"

"Good question. It's a very delicate balance, weighing the commercial side with the integrity of our reporting. I'd be interested in your perspective after you've studied us and worked here a while. I do know this. If we tick off some people on both sides of an issue, we're probably striking a balance. I know that's an old saw, and sometimes it's just BS, but—look, I don't want to go off on a tangent. I think everybody's arrived. Let's go meet them and then we'll resume our conversation."

They went into the main office, and Martin started making his rounds, introducing Zoë and asking each person to tell her what they did. She met the reporters/editors, Rick and Betsy; Tom, the photo editor; Connie, the advertising manager in charge of two sales people, Adela and Kathy; and Phil, the sports editor.

After she met Phil, Martin said, "I cannot emphasize how important local sports reporting is to a community like this. Sports activities are where a lot of the kids spend their time. Families want to see their kid's name in print and their pictures."

Zoë was introduced to Anna, the human resources manager and accountant; Amanda, the creative director; and Josey, the circulation manager. She didn't meet the part-time help, which consisted of Katy, who handled the classified ads, and two young people who helped with Friday deliveries.

Zoë thought everyone was very pleasant, the whole office a-buzz. In return, she did her best to be personable and animated.

As they walked back to his office, Martin said, "We also make money printing legal notices because, well, they're legally required so the county pays us. And another thing—we have some freelance people that do regular features. As for you, I want you to tackle a piece of everything we do here, but I'll try to have you concentrate on writing news. I assume you'll want to deliver copies of all that you've done to Bud Wilhelm, so we'll try to make certain it's a considerable pile."

"Yes I do." As they sat down again, Zoë said, "They all seem very nice, Martin."

"They're also good at that they do. Back to where we were…my intent early on was to publish thought-provoking, intellectually stimulating editorials, even if nobody understood me. I had to learn a few things before I could do that, however. So I started to fill the paper with *all* the local news, which was a huge change since it had been really thin on content when I got here. We included human interest stories—some of them in-depth feature articles—obits with a lot more detail than they'd had before, the story about Johnny's Eagle Scout award, the schedule for just about everything happening around Demming for the next week, and sheriff's reports, which I turned into a humorous column since crimes around here are mostly silly minor offenses. We make every wedding, birth announcement and anniversary a big deal. The flashy local news item is rare, but sometimes, we'll give the lighter ones a dramatic push. I greatly expanded sports coverage.

"I avoided controversy until I could gain my readers' trust. A small market paper has to be sensitive to local attitudes, and I was an outsider. Here's a little side story. I met an old man when I first got here. I asked him, 'Are you from this area?' He said, 'No, I moved here in 1916.' The point? I'm still an outsider. Then I pulled in some free-lance writers that contributed short fiction—that's unique. In the end, we try to keep it all very low-key, casual, yet efficient and well written, and we try to have an end product that looks professional."

Zoë had some more questions, but he ignored her cues. Martin was on a roll.

"Now some details. We previously used Quark, but now use InDesign for all our work. Are you familiar with InDesign?"

"Yes, I'm fairly adept with it. It now dominates the newspaper publishing market since Quark stopped supporting their software."

"Good. We stopped printing locally some years ago, thank goodness, and we use a printer in Gillette, Wyoming. We have to transfer all our data by 1:00 P. M. on Thursday so they can print in time for their truck to be here by 5:30 A. M. It's a Friday-to-Friday paper, as you know. Have you looked at our website?"

"Yes, and I like the slide-show photography on it. I first saw it when I was in New York."

"Tom, the photo editor, does the bulk of that work. We're trying to be really good with website content and design so when the dead-tree business folds, we can make some money off the Web."

"Do people use the Web much here?"

"You'd be surprised. A lot of folks have broadband satellite connections and computer use has been growing rapidly. Think about it. If you live in some remote place, you can become connected not only to the community, but to the world in ways that haven't been possible before."

Zoë nodded her head although she also knew that these rapid changes could affect her career choice.

Zoë liked the speed with which Martin laid out everything and said, "This all sounds really good to me. I'm excited about getting to work. May I ask a question?"

"Certainly."

"You mentioned including short fiction. How does that work?"

"And poetry. When I bought the paper, the news stories were few and weak. So to give the paper some bulk and to fill space until I could get a proper news staff organized, I published cowboy poetry and stories using freelance Wyoming contributors. I didn't reduce my advertising prices, but gave more space for the same price back when newsprint wasn't as expensive as it is today. The community loved it. Now, I only include such things if we have a slow week. Adding pages is too costly. I would enjoy doing more of that, but I have to balance cost with desires."

"I asked because I've done a little creative writing, mostly short stories. Second question. You said something about 'intellectually stimulating editorials' and gaining trust. How did you gain the trust of the community?"

"Yes… editorial content. Early on, I wasn't sure about my audience. I didn't know who they were. I admit that I came here with some pre-conceived notions that led me to wonder if folks were going to understand me. While I was perfecting the style of the paper, and trying to get the business on its feet, I slowly developed the view that people in the area understood quite well what I was putting out there. And, if I listened to them, I might learn something.

"Hiring a good staff helped greatly. I listened to my people, although I sometimes wonder if they'd agree. I had to keep my ego in check. Ultimately, I never tried to impose my Columbia education or my background with the Times on the local citizenry. This was, and still is, clearly a culture of the West in support of cows, horses, the land, nature, civil society, and against government interference. It wasn't a case of me educating the ignorant masses. It was more accurately a function of me mellowing, understanding and learning the language and heart-beat of the people who lived here. I became part of them. I was telling them things they could easily understand because, through trial and error, I learned how. More importantly, I had changed, and I've never been happier."

Zoë looked at Martin intently, wondering what drives a man with his education and experience to end up here—and be happy—wearing a cowboy hat.

She then got settled at an old metal desk along the edge of the newspaper's office, secured supplies, got her computer set up, and became better acquainted with the staff, memorizing names with faces and with jobs performed. The conversations were all bright and cheery. She was inquisitive about them and responsive to their questions. Her desk was near Amanda's, and as Zoë was getting settled, Amanda said, "I'm really pleased to have you here. Aside from having extra help, I'm dying to know about your life traveling the world and living in New York City. I've never been to a big city except Boise."

In a cheerful mood, Zoë said, "I'll be happy to tell you about New York, but I didn't really travel the world. It was mostly in Europe."

"How exciting!"

Zoë noticed Amanda's pretty blonde hair and her striking blue eyes. She had a high level of energy, efficiently multitasking in her work space. Zoë liked her immediately and hoped that Amanda would add some spark to her short stay in Demming. Zoë asked her, "Do you live right here in town, Amanda?"

"Yes, I'm a single mom, and I live with my folks near the edge of town." Pointing to a picture on her desk, she added, "That's my son, Davie. He's four."

"Oh, he's a darling."

"I certainly think so. I'd be willing to show you around, if you like. Let's chat about it when I've got some free time."

"That would be great. I want to see everything I can while I'm here."

On Tuesday, Zoë was handed the task of writing an obituary, one of the first things rookie reporters learn to do correctly. Martin said, "I imagine you've done some of these in school?"

"Oh, yes. The first rule of obits: don't make any mistakes with the facts. The family can become really upset if you get it wrong, then you feel awful. If a lot of people knew the deceased well, you also might lose a few customers."

"Right. Here, we also try to include everything we can that's good about the person. We're not in the business of rating the quality of a person after they're gone. People know without us doing a pro and con analysis. If the piece is short, that tells people we had trouble finding much to say.

This one should be easy since Curtis Williams was well known, and there is a lot on file regarding his previous work on the town council and school board. He was also a renowned practical joker. Here are some names and numbers of people to interview. You take it from there. I'd like to proofread your first draft by 4:00, if you can find enough information by then."

"Okay." Zoë immediately started digging into the files after Amanda told her where to find them. Later, after two interviews—one on the phone and one face to face—she completed the obit. She took it to Martin's door, leaned in and said, "May I give this draft to you now?"

"Sure, how did it go?"

"Just fine, but it's still a draft." Casually, she left his office as he started to read the lengthy piece.

She was at her desk, pretending to work, when she heard Martin break out in laughter. Then he was at the door, saying so all could hear, "Listen to this everybody: 'Retired rancher and well-known contributor to the community, Curtis Williams, died Saturday night at 9:37 P.M. at his home on Hartzell Road. He was eighty-six years old. Ethyl, his wife of sixty-two years, was by his side during his last hours. The cause of death was from an acute case of restless legs syndrome.'"

Amidst the howls, Martin said, "Curtis would have loved it!" And Betsey said, "What did he do? Kick the bucket?"

As the laughter died down, Zoë looked at Martin, who was still smiling, and said, "I guess it needs a rewrite."

"Yes, I'm afraid it does; at least the first part. Someday I would love to print something like that."

As people got back to work, occasionally someone would chuckle and look over at Zoë. At the end of the work day, Connie went over to her and said, "You're going to fit in around here just great."

Chapter 6

On Friday about twelve-thirty, following a hectic early morning, Martin Coleman left for the day, instructing Amanda and Zoë to stick around until a Federal Express package arrived. After he left, Amanda asked, "So how did you enjoy getting up early to help deliver the papers?"

"Oh, it was fine. Josey is very nice, and those two boys did most of the heavy lifting. I'll admit, I do feel like I've put in a long day already."

"Did you know that the staff took a vote on whether you looked like Halle Berry?"

"Oh no! Dr. Wilhelm must have said something to Martin. Some guy brought that up in a class once, and people wouldn't let it go for a month."

"Before you got here, we were all looking at pictures of her on the Internet. We concluded that she had no *one* look. She looks like different people depending on the picture."

"I suppose good photographers can do that."

"Maybe it's the eyes or the mouth or your body, but the only thing we concluded was that you are very pretty." Laughing, she added, "And I hate you for it."

Zoë laughed with her as Amanda got a phone call.

When Amanda got through arguing with her boyfriend, she put down the phone and said to Zoë, "That was Cory on the phone, and he thinks he can earn a living riding bulls. So we're having a fight. I want a fellow who is more realistic about his talents and at least considers normal work that produces a steady paycheck. I've already been down that path of uncertainty, and I have no intention of being Cory's buckle bunny, traveling the circuit."

"'Buckle bunny?'"

"Yeah, a rodeo groupie…flaunts her stuff to the guys who win the buckles. Anyway, bull riders sure aren't the smartest people on the planet. Some are dumb as posts, and sometimes I think Cory has the personality of an elbow. Anyway, he's off to Laramie this weekend. I won't see him till next week, assuming his old truck makes the trip, and assuming he comes back in one piece."

Zoë said, "Gosh, I don't know anything about rodeos."

"Okay, you tell me about the tennis world, and I'll tell you about bull riders and their life of bullshit."

Zoë laughed. "Amanda, you said something about showing me around. What does one do on weekends? Reading the paper, I know there is some place called the Wagon Wheel nearby, featuring a band…? I don't remember their name."

Amanda said, "The Lost Litter."

"What?"

"The Lost Litter. That's the name of the band playing at the Wagon Wheel. They're locals, and they keep coming up with different names for themselves depending on who shows up to play. Sometimes, they go by the name, The Longneckers. Other times, they're The Longhorns, even though there haven't been any Texas Longhorns around here in about one hundred years. No wait, there's a small herd down by Dubois. Somebody's trying to sell them as healthier beef because they're leaner. Hell, it's just tougher meat, less marbling, that's all.

"Anyway, when the Bodecker twins join the group, they call themselves Three Guys and Two God-Fearing Women because the Boobsy twins— that's what I call them—are women all right, though I bet they fear sexually transmitted diseases more than they fear God. I know them all, and they're mostly older fat guys who drink too much, and occasionally, the twins with all four tits on display. They're quiet drunks though, the guys, that is. They just think they sound better than they do. Want to go?"

"Yes, I'm game for a little adventure…part of my Wyoming education."

"Okay, I'll double-check with Mom to make sure she'll watch Davie. My parents usually watch him Friday and Saturday nights and the occasional full weekend. They want me to have a social life so I'll get married again and move out." They both laughed and then Amanda explained the situation with her irresponsible ex-husband in more detail than Zoë would have expected someone would share with a new acquaintance.

Zoë felt sorry for single moms and their kids. At least Amanda had a safety net. Her mind back on track, Zoë asked, "How will we do this?"

"I have some evening chores to do at home. I'll have to shower and get Davie settled in bed, then I'll get you. I'll pick you up around nine o'clock at Mrs. Granger's house, if that's okay. The place where we're going is a road house with a bowling alley connected to it, nine miles out old Route 241, same as Sixth Street."

"Sounds fine. What do I wear?"

"That's easy—the tightest jeans and the smallest spaghetti strap top you can get away with…and mules if you don't have cowboy boots. A cowboy shirt would work, but I don't imagine you have one of those."

Just then, a tall, homely skinny kid, with the name "Kevin" on his blue Federal Express shirt arrived and moon-eyed Amanda, who ignored him completely. She accepted the package, signed for it, and said her thanks. He slowly exited and then Amanda and Zoë left, with Amanda handling the lockup.

Zoë said cheerfully, "I'll see you at nine."

"You bet." Amanda walked toward her unwashed, dented Subaru and waved goodbye. Zoë started down Superior Avenue to Shankton's Clothing Emporium. She already had tight jeans, and she was more a window shopper than a buyer, but she was going to look at a shirt.

Chapter 7

From San Clemente, Russ took the 5 north to the 241, to the 91, connecting with the 215 and the Pomona Freeway in Riverside, then Interstate 10 near Beaumont. He wanted to drive the back roads as best he could, so above Palm Springs he exited the I-10, connecting with Route 62, a fairly straight, but undulating, two-lane road across the Mojave Desert to Arizona. He passed north of Joshua Tree National Park, a place he and Sara had enjoyed hiking every May when the cactus flowers were in bloom. Once past Twentynine Palms, he saw only four vehicles all the way to the Arizona border. He worked his way up through Prescott, then through the old mining town, Jerome, a place where motorcyclists like to congregate, and then to Sedona, where he secured a relatively inexpensive motel room. He stretched his legs by walking around town watching the tourists. Russ stopped by an ice cream store on the main thoroughfare and had a chocolate soda, something he hadn't enjoyed in years, and decided that the treat would be dinner.

The next morning, Russ jogged up Route 89, turning around for the return to make it a five-mile run. Russ claimed he had a calibrated crotch—he knew his standard pace well enough to look at his watch and be able to calculate how much distance he had covered. After cleaning up, he ate the hotel's "free" continental breakfast, then drove through scenic Oak Creek Canyon into the outskirts of Flagstaff. As he stopped at a station to gas up and release his coffee—like beer, one only seemed to rent it—Russ saw a sign in the window advertising that a concert pianist was playing at a local community church at ten-thirty. It was Sunday, and he saw on his watch that it was ten o'clock.

He asked the attendant in the gas station's convenience store where the church was located. The young girl pointed down the street and said, "A quarter mile that way." Russ thanked her and proceeded to the church.

When the service began, the place was packed with all seats filled and people standing in the back. Russ listened to the announcements, learning that the service would be abbreviated so the guest pianist would have sufficient time to perform. After announcements, a prayer was offered, the offering plate was passed, and the congregation sang the Doxology. Then, the artist was introduced.

The pianist was a tall Jewish man in his mid-fifty's who had converted to Christianity while at Juilliard. He said he was raised in a family of devout Jews, and clearly, he was one of them in his commitment to Judaism. But after making friends with some Christians at school, he was convinced that he wanted to examine the New Testament. On his own, he did so and it was a shock to his system. He converted and his family disowned him.

Then, he proceeded to create the most beautiful music Russ had heard in a long time. And he played it on an old upright piano, the only piano the church had. Here was a man accustomed to expensive Steinway pianos on the world's concert stages, a man who had won international awards. But somehow, this little church had got him to play to its congregation with only a small upright as his instrument. He seemingly wasn't affected by the old piano as he played Beethoven, Mozart, Debussy, Scarlatti, and Chopin with intensity and depth of feeling. He was animated, like a hungry vulture, perched over the keys with head bobbing and hands vertical, pounding or delicately playing the keys as the music demanded. He stood and bowed in gratitude as the congregation clapped loudly after each song, with his final song receiving an uproarious standing ovation.

Russ was impressed with this remarkable talent. When the concert was over, Russ departed for his destination, his heart aroused, knowing why he had stopped, but wondering why this confluence happened on this day, this time, and place.

It was after noon, and Russ stopped at a restaurant busy from the Sunday church crowd, which he saw as a good sign. While he was in line to pay his bill, an attractive woman with slicked-back dark hair and a young boy, perhaps seven or eight, came into the restaurant and stood next to the sign that read, "Please Wait to be Seated." The line was getting longer at the register and more people were entering, so the server taking the money motioned to a teenage boy bussing a table nearby to help seat people. The teen dropped what he was doing and grabbed some menus, saying to the waiting lady, "Hello. Table for three?"

She said pleasantly enough, "No, there are only two of us." But with rapidly growing disgust, she added, "Now, why would you say that? Can't you see there are only two people standing here? Or did you just assume that the two of us wouldn't be here alone, that there just had to be a third person?" She hesitated for a moment, seemingly contemplating whether to carry her diatribe further, but concluded with, "No, I'll tell you what. Just forget it. We'll go someplace else." She then proceeded to take her son's hand and depart.

The busboy was red-faced and didn't appear to know what to say or do. Meanwhile, the waitress at the cash register threw him a glance of support as the teenager approached the next couple. As he asked them if they'd like to be seated, he seemed embarrassed and befuddled.

Russ was surprised by the woman's outburst, but revealed nothing by his bland expression as he looked back, catching the eye of a middle-aged man who stood behind him.

The man said to him, "That woman is a professional."

"A professional?"

"Yeah, she has perfected the art of being offended. It wouldn't surprise me at all if she goes through life looking for reasons to be ticked-off at people who have offended her sensibilities. She's the 'angry young woman.' The world isn't good enough for her, and righteous indignation is her instinctual response."

Russ wondered if the man was talking about "slick" or something broader, but said, "Well, you are what you think."

"Yeah, I suppose so."

Russ finished paying and left, reflecting on a conversation he'd had with his mother when he was about fourteen. They had been in the kitchen of their farmhouse in Indiana, and Russ had asked his mom, "What does Dad think about all day out there?"

"Why don't you ask him?"

"I did once."

"What did he say?"

"Something like, 'I used to worry a lot, but finally figured out that it didn't get me anywhere, so I just try to think pleasant thoughts.' I asked him, 'Like what?' And he said, 'How nice it's going to be when we get this baler fixed. Hand me that wrench over there by your foot, will ya?'"

"Well, your dad doesn't talk much."

"What do you think he thinks about, Mom?"

"For starters, I think…I hope…he thinks about what he's doing. Farm work and being around large animals and machinery can be dangerous. Beyond that, I think he does fill his mind with good thoughts. I know this because when he comes in all dirty and washes up, he'll pat me on the shoulder as he says hello, or gives a little hug. I never mind that he stinks like the barn when he does this. He wouldn't treat me like that if he were full of stress, or worried, or hateful, or angry at the world. Oh, he can get mad about some things, but it blows over quickly, and he isn't filled with it. Your father is a good man. Why are you asking?"

"Because my mind goes all over the place. I'm constantly thinking about stuff. And I imagine that even quiet people like Dad are full of thoughts, but they don't let them out."

"I expect that's true."

"What do you think about, Mom?"

"I think about how grateful I am to have Bill and you kids, and this life. I thank God every day for His gifts. And I hope and pray that Ruth and Grace and you can find happiness and that each of you can be as good a person as your father. It will actually be a little harder for Ruth and you to find your way. Grace is already there and will probably always be there. She is one of God's precious children. Remember this: what you think and feel and believe will determine who you are and what you become. So it's a good idea to try to go through this life grateful for whatever happens—and I know that can sometimes be hard—and fill your mind with the good things in life, not dwelling on the bad. You are what you think."

Russ offered no real response, but said "Thanks, Mom." Then he dashed outside to avoid the possibility of her asking him what he thought about. He didn't want to tell her that he'd been thinking a lot about Rebecca Walker, the blonde neighbor girl.

Actually, his mother was thinking, "I wonder what that was all about? That's the most that boy has talked in weeks."

Chapter 8

On Route 89, driving into Navajo country north of Flagstaff, Russ inserted a Norah Jones CD into the player and listened to her vocalize those haunting songs that Sara loved.

Russ welled up with emotion as he thought about his daughter, Grace, who had played beautiful piano music, and Sara, his shining star…both gone. Since it wasn't safe to drive when tears were clouding one's vision, Russ pulled over to the side of the road and parked, trying to regain his composure. He thought, "Oh, God. I miss you Sara."

He sat there for several minutes with his head down, then looked up and saw flashing lights from a police car parked behind him. An Arizona state trooper proceeded to walk up to his truck as Russ thought to himself, "Now what am I going to do?" Russ lowered the window as the trooper approached and looked into Russ's eyes while also scanning the interior of the truck.

The trooper asked Russ, "Are you okay, sir?"

"No sir. That's why I stopped. It's a personal matter. I wanted to collect myself before proceeding."

The trooper hesitated, further assessing the situation, then asked, "May I see your driver's license and registration, sir?"

As Russ retrieved the documents, the trooper asked, "What is your destination, sir?"

Russ handed both pieces of information to the trooper and said, "I'm heading to a cabin in Park County, Colorado. It's not near any town that one would recognize."

"Where is Park County?"

"South and east of the Continental Divide, across from the ski resorts at Breckenridge and Copper Mountain."

The trooper seemed to study the California documents for a long time, looked intently at Russ, and said, "I'll sit behind you until you are ready to go. Have a safe trip the rest of the way, Mr. Mack."

Russ was relieved. "Thank you, Officer. I'll be all right shortly." The trooper tipped his hat and returned to his car. Russ left five minutes later, under control and driving the speed limit. The trooper did not follow. He made a U-turn south toward Flagstaff.

Chapter 9

The front page story of the June 6th paper was headlined: "Jake Miller Injured in Riding Accident." The brief article stated:

Jake Miller, age seventy-nine, was found semi-conscious late Wednesday along Elk Ridge Trail, several miles up Blue Mountain near Cowman's Meadow, adjacent to his property off Bandy Road. Madge Wilson, who lives on Jake and Kay Miller's property, organized a search party after Jake didn't return from his two-hour morning ride. He was alone at the time of his departure. Joining her in the search were neighbors Martin and Sylvia Coleman. Also included in the party were three members of the Sheriff Department's Search & Rescue Team: Deputies Robert Barado and Gus Wittingham, plus Cody Nelson from the Forest Service. Not knowing which trail Jake took, the six searchers split into two groups, on horseback, and followed the two most likely trail options leading from Jake's property— Elk Ridge Trail and Cowman's Trail. A third trail, Mount Comfort Trail, had no visible fresh tracks since the heavy rain four days ago. Both groups were equipped with emergency medical kits.

Martin and Sylvia Coleman and Deputy Barado found Jake at 3:45 P.M., leaning against a tree, drifting in and out of consciousness. Fandango, his chestnut Quarab, stood near him. Sylvia said, "He wasn't completely lucid when he was awake, and he kept asking for water, then he'd drift off. I checked for broken bones. He looked like he had a concussion, and I was worried about moving him." Martin Coleman, using his cell phone, called the other party on Cowman's Trail, told them where to meet, and then called the ambulance to meet them at the trail head at the edge of Jake's ranch.

It took close to four hours to carry Mr. Miller down the mountain on Search and Rescue's two-piece packable litter, as he had gone farther than expected into some rough country, according to Madge Wilson. She also stated, "We don't know why he went way up into 'high lonesome,' or what actually happened, but I sure wish that old hombre wouldn't ride alone. I feel real bad I wasn't with him."

At the publication of this article, Jake Miller is at the Demming Medical Center. According to Dr. Cain, "He continues to be in guarded condition. Currently, there is nothing further to report. What he needs most, is rest. We're keeping a close watch on Mr. Miller." The Miller children and their families are reportedly on their way from Arizona to be with Kay and Jake during this uncertain time. A full investigation into the incident is underway."

Zoë had written the article on Thursday after interviewing Barado and Wittingham. The Wilson quotes were secondhand, but corroborated by Martin. She had inquired of Amanda, "What's a Quarab?"

"It's a registered breed, half-American Quarter Horse and half-Arabian. It's a nice horse. What the breeder is trying to do is get the best qualities of both types of horses—the spirit and stamina of the Arabian combined with the muscle and calm personality of the Quarter Horse. That's the theory, anyway."

"Like me," Zoë offered. "I'm half-Cuban and half-Jewish. Perhaps that would make me Jewban or Cuish. Do you know this gentleman who got hurt?"

"Oh yeah, but Martin and Sylvia know him a lot better because they're neighbors…not next door, but reasonably close. And Madge Wilson, who lives with the Millers, she's a real character…in her sixties and been through four husbands. The last one died a couple years ago. She said she's through, telling me once, 'It's one thing to throw 'em out 'cause they're no good, but when they start dyin' on ya', it's time to quit!'"

"Yes, she is a loveable old character," Martin added as he walked in, opening the door off the little mall perpendicular to Superior Street. Zoë thought he looked tired. He asked her to come into his office, told her to bring her coffee if she wanted. She said she would get some more and be right there, but Martin took her cup and said, "No, I'll get it. I'm headed that way to get a cup, myself."

A few minutes later, Martin entered his office. Zoë, already seated, thought about the protocol of standing in the presence of her elder and boss until he had seated himself. She quickly dismissed the idea. He wasn't batting an eye over the fact that she was sitting down.

Martin dropped to his chair, hard, put one foot on a lower drawer he had pulled out, and leaned back. "I know Sylvia has talked to you about coming out to the ranch this weekend. She told me she'd mentioned it when you two were visiting at the book store earlier this week. We feel kind of bad about not having you out yet. We're still going to have a Saturday afternoon barbecue, but the events of Wednesday have altered plans a bit."

"Amanda says you know Jake pretty well"

"Yes, I surely do. Here is what I'd suggest. Kay will be with family. We've argued for her to bring them all over, but she insists that it would be too much trouble. Sylvia is still working on her, but if she doesn't come with her brood, it will be you, Madge Wilson, Sylvia, and me, the minister and his family, a few of my staff, and several others from town. These events tend to grow in size so, in truth, I don't know how many will be there. Everybody brings food, so it's not a problem. The more the merrier. I'm still not sure if Amanda, Davie, and Cory are coming. You can take the van, so you'll have transportation over the weekend, and I'll give you directions."

Zoë didn't want to speak for Amanda, so she merely said, "That sounds great. What time?"

"There's more. I'd like you to mix a little business with pleasure. The barbecue will be, oh, around noon, but the time is a little flexible. I'd like you to go out to the Miller ranch sometime mid-morning and visit with Madge Wilson. Cody Nelson and Madge are the two key people you haven't interviewed yet. And hopefully, Jake gets on his feet so he can shed some light on the matter."

"I tried to reach Cody Nelson, but his office said he was out of town and wouldn't be back until Saturday sometime."

"He may be at our place Saturday afternoon. I don't know. Anyway, interview Madge. She's got a leaky mouth, and you'll learn a lot about what happened to Jake from her. We'll want to do a more in-depth, follow-up article." Seeing her reaction to the term, leaky mouth, Martin added, "I only mean she talks a lot. She'll give you a drink out of a fire hydrant. And she can sometimes be indiscreet, but it isn't harmful, usually."

"Oh."

Martin handed her a sheet of paper on which was drawn a simple map with a wide-tip, blue felt pen. The hand-printed words were large, maybe a twenty-four font, she thought. He said, "I draw all my maps that way for myself. That way, I don't have to get out my reading glasses while I'm driving. It's a habit."

"Is Mrs. Wilson expecting me?"

"Yes, but she doesn't know when. We weren't certain whether you had made some other plans. She's looking forward to meeting you, but we left it open."

"Shall I call her?"

"Yes, call her. The phone number is on the map."

"And Jake? What do you think…will he be okay?"

"That old coot? Yeah, he'll be fine. I hope."

Chapter 10

Zoë rose from her chair—directions in one hand and a cooling cup of coffee in the other—and left Martin's office. She went to the "space saver kitchen," where there was enough room on the counter for the coffee pot, a microwave, and a few coffee cups plus the sink. A full-size refrigerator, along with a small table and two chairs, filled out the room. Any more than two people in there felt claustrophobic. She reheated her coffee in the microwave for exactly thirty-three seconds, then went back to her desk. Martin was leaving for the day, perhaps going to see Mr. Miller or heading to one of his other sources of income—the Song And Story bookstore.

Zoë reasoned early on that Martin could not be making much of a living with the small weekly newspaper, given the implications of what he had said earlier, so the bookstore was a necessary part of his life. In addition, Martin earned some money from his ranch, but she understood that it was small. She'd find out more about that when she got there on Saturday. All she ever heard him talk about, when he spoke about ranch life, was how much work it was and in the same breath, how great it was to get up early in the morning and smell the fresh air. She questioned that, thinking that "bovine fecal matter," a phrase she'd overheard the day before while walking down Sixth Street, didn't exactly constitute fresh air.

Taken together, Zoë wondered if proceeds from the ranch, a newspaper that may be in trouble, and a book store, were enough to earn a living. She had visited the store earlier in the week. It was a small, crowded place on a side street full of tiny shops. Its main business was selling new and used books. The song part of the name, Song And Story, didn't come from selling CDs, but from selling small quantities of sheet music. They didn't have a great deal on hand anymore, but Sylvia had connections to get just about anything anybody wanted. She mainly used the Internet and 800 numbers, but she knew where to go when others didn't, and mostly the sheet music was Federal Expressed to them. The customers got exactly what they wanted, quickly, and all they had to do was have a pleasant conversation with Sylvia and pay.

The store had a bell that rang when opening the door; the checkout counter was on the right-hand side. Two aisles ran straight down the long, narrow shop. An alcove jutted off to the right, a back-room was used for storage, and a restroom for the help filled out the space. Zoë considered it a uniquely eclectic bookstore for Wyoming ranch country. Upon thinking this, she wondered if she wasn't being just a little bit snobbish.

Along with coffee table picture books of the Tetons, Yellowstone, cowboys, and cowgirls, the store sold books by the beat writers from the fifties and sixties. One section consisted of tomes on religion and philosophy with author names like Heschel, Cobb, Bertrand Russell, Wittgenstein, Slavoj Zizek, and many others familiar and unfamiliar to her. She also noted classic works of fiction, books on animal husbandry, fly fishing, and the latest from the various bestseller's lists. They also had books tagged as "Song And Story recommends." Each one had a little handwritten description on the tag, explaining why it was being recommended.

She had picked up a recommended book called *Monte Walsh* by Jack Warner Schaefer and scanned the attached note: "Possibly the best western ever written...enduring themes...friendship...loyalty to the brand. It's about Monte Walsh and Chet Rollins...live by a code...a man's word is his bond...don't talk; do. Chet adapts...changing world...Monte...out of step. In the end, Monte is a good man with a horse." Zoë had never heard of the book, but recognized the author since he wrote *Shane*, a book she had been forced to read in junior high. She asked herself, "Who are these people?"

Chapter 11

As he traveled down the endless stretch of highway, getting lulled into a numb awareness of only the road in front of him, Russ allowed his mind to wander.

He was raised on a southern Indiana farm, best described as a subsistence farm. It was a quarter section in size. Almost half of it was not tillable with hilly woods that nurtured hickory, walnut, and maple trees. It also consisted of an old orchard of little commercial value, two pastures rotated as necessary, and space for the house, barn, outbuildings, and corral, plus access roads to the fields and a long dirt driveway. In good years, the farm netted a small profit after taxes, but the good years from such a small operation were inconsistent.

Bill Mack had to work off the farm in order to make ends meet, and there were years when making ends meet was problematic. The farm did allow for the family to feed itself, however, and this was no small thing in the minds of Bill and Ginny Mack. Bill would occasionally say, "Everyone—especially those city kids—should learn how to feed themselves. Too many people think milk comes from a bottle."

Bill Mack figured he'd need three hundred to four hundred acres of good land in order to have a paying farm, whether that involved a dairy operation, a pig farm or any number of other choices, and that would require working it full time plus hiring additional help during planting and harvesting seasons. Since he didn't have the money to buy additional property, he tried to lease some, but all his neighbors within a considerable distance were maximizing their own lands, so none was available.

One year, before Russ was born, a hail storm ruined the corn and wheat, and since Bill and Ginny couldn't afford to buy feed for the winter, they had to sell off their few cows and pigs. They kept their chickens, one fat hog and one yearling steer to butcher, plus their two milk goats, Arrabella and Mehitabel. The latter was named for a Marjorie Main character in the nineteen-forty Wallace Beery movie, *Wyoming*. To add insult, their prized Jersey milk cow, Bossy, died that same year of unknown causes.

Also remaining on the farm were the dog—a smelly pointer named Rufus—and barn cats, their numbers in a general state of flux because of their propensity to produce new litters and then be eaten by a healthy, local population of hungry foxes. There was a small bounty on foxes back then, but Bill and a few close neighbors chose not to hunt them since they kept the rabbits under control, which helped protect their gardens. And as far as Bill was concerned, they kept the cat population in check, clearing out the old, slow ones and the younger, naive ones. These harsh facts of life were not discussed with the kids. Bill figured they would learn the details of reproduction and death in the country soon enough.

What did disturb Bill was the attachment of those well-fed foxes to his Rhode Island Reds. He had a coop and fenced-in chicken yard, which was pretty much impenetrable, but he liked to have the chickens roam the barnyard and lawn, so occasionally when they were out eating bugs, he'd lose one. Especially when he wasn't outside, a wily fox would intensify her schemes to secure an easy lunch as nature had taught her.

During the tough times, when the farm generated little or no cash, and Bill could not find steady employment, Ginny made and sold quilts and knitted blankets and sweaters, which helped fund the purchase of house supplies and needed clothing for their growing family. Bill and Ginny prided themselves on their ability to last several weeks without having to visit the nearest city, eighteen miles away, and without spending a dime. They could do this because, like many farms, they had their own on-site, elevated gasoline tank. As long as it had fuel, they didn't need to pay for having more delivered.

Most importantly, they had their own productive vegetable garden, one-hundred feet long and seventy-five feet wide. Bill and Ginny grew most of their own food and traded with neighbors for what they didn't grow… which was seldom necessary. Ginny canned large quantities of tomatoes, home-made relish, pickles, green beans, lima beans, peas, asparagus, sweet corn, plus applesauce and peaches from the orchard. She canned meat, which was sufficient for them and their regular, though infrequent, guests of extended family, neighbors, and church friends. Most of their family and friends were very busy looking after their own farms, so social affairs, while desired by most, were organized with prudence. Bill and Ginny also stored potatoes, apples, and apple cider in the root cellar, the cider eventually turning hard, which Bill particularly enjoyed. With an exaggerated tone, he would tell Ginny humorously, "It's for medicinal purposes, you know."

When Bill was working and things were going well, they would buy hog runts from a large pig farm, whose owner wished to cull them out rather than "waste money" feeding them. They bought them cheap and were amazed at how well they fattened up. The couple would eventually sell off several when they matured, and butcher one. They did the same with Hereford steers, buying feeder stock in the spring—calves or year-lings—and fattening them up in the pasture over the summer, then feeding them grain before they considered whether or not to sell them in the late fall. Their decision depended on the going price. If they had good quantities of feed, they might keep the animals for two years before selling them as fully matured prime beef at about eleven hundred pounds each. Bill and Ginny also kept a few Hereford cows, which were bred from Charlie Walker's bull, and formed the basis of their own small herd.

The beef cows, about forty chickens, a sow, the goats, a Shetland pony for Bill and Ginny's oldest daughter, Ruth, plus Rufus and the cats represented the menagerie that needed to be fed over the winter. If the harvest was bountiful, they would have enough, as well as additional grains to sell for cash. They never replaced the milk cow, and bartered their brown eggs with a neighbor for fresh milk. They made cheese from the goats' milk.

They went to church every week. Whether times were hard or not, gratitude for God's bounty was dominant in their minds. The small Presbyterian church was an old, white, frame building with a steeple for the bell, which was rung by a rope hanging in the narthex—a prized job for any youth arriving early enough to secure the position. It also became a good way for Pastor Mark to get several families to church early because their kids wanted to convince the pastor that they should ring the bell. He had to set up a system for choosing the child for the job, which involved memorizing Bible passages.

The town was three miles away from the Mack farm. Along with a collection of 1880 to 1930s-style frame houses, it consisted of the church, a general store, and a post office—formerly a one-room school house until Mrs. Jessup retired in 1947. At that time, the county built a new township grade school several miles away, which meant that the children had to contend with a long bus ride. The village was surrounded by farms. If one included everybody within a four-mile radius, one could count two hundred people living in the area.

Russ carried with him many memories of his childhood. Chief among them were the bounty of a good life on the farm, the pleasures of that little village, and the constant work involved in keeping the farm going. His mother once told him, "I hope that when you are old and you look back on this pastoral life that was part of your origins, you'll remember what it cost in time and effort. It wasn't always easy." He did know, and he learned from a young age not to shirk his duties.

What he didn't know until he went to the university—because there, people enjoyed pointing it out—was that he had grown up poor. On the first day of a sophomore economics class, the professor broke the ice with the question, "Have any of you ever attended a school where someone had no shoes?" Russ raised his hand. Not happy that this dull-looking young man had thrown a curve at his intended point, the professor asked, "So where are you from, West Virginia?" Embarrassed, Russ answered the question factually, saying that there was a shanty town near his township grade school, and occasionally, kids from transient families would come to school with no shoes. The school saw to it that they got shoes and that they were well fed at lunch since some had had no breakfast. There were a few mild snickers, more in deference to the professor's retort than in any mocking of Russ. The professor did not react to Russ's words. He simply moved on to make his point about how spoiled this present generation was compared to people who had endured hardship in the past, particularly during the Great Depression. Russ had only heard about the really tough times, which were mainly in the late 30s and during the 40s, before he was born.

Following WWII, Bill had a job working for Mr. Benjamin Felton, a Jewish entrepreneur with a small die casting company outside Evansville. Bill liked Felton, who mostly hired farmers because of their conscientiousness and work ethic. During the summers, the man would hire college students to allow the farmers time off for planting, cultivating and harvesting.

Growing up, Russ heard the story of Benjamin Felton many times. According to his father, Felton had made a mistake. He'd hired a man from Chicago who became an agitator, asking questions of his fellow workers about how much other people made. Nobody really concerned themselves with such things. Their attitude about their pay was much like the way Bill Mack felt about it: he took the job at what he felt was a fair wage and figured he provided his labor in a fair exchange with Felton. He worked hard and was always paid on time. The arrangement was all based on a handshake.

In time, the agitator became the in-house expert on seniority, everyone's approximate pay, and, what he saw, as the resulting inequities. "It's not fair" was his favorite line, and he succeeded in getting just enough votes to bring in a union.

Felton was incredulous, and at age seventy-three, he didn't understand what this union business was all about. He didn't comprehend what was coming, and he didn't know how to cope with it, even after he'd met with lawyers and experts for advice. His attitude and health were suffering. He concluded that he wasn't going to even try to deal with the situation.

Felton had good contacts in the industry, and after sufficient due diligence, he sold Felton Die Casting to his largest competitor in Cincinnati, Ohio, who was thrilled with the deal because of Felton's reputation for quality and service. Immediately after the sale, Felton and his wife, Goldie—the financial brains of the company—moved to Florida to be near their grandkids. Six months later, the new owners shut down the Evansville plant and consolidated operations in Cincinnati. Thirty-two men and women, including Bill, were out of work.

After that, Bill refused to work for a union shop or even one that looked like it might need one, which limited his options. He was aware that some businesses were exploitive, and as far as he was concerned, those that were, got what they deserved. Bill figured that he didn't need or want a group helping him negotiate with another group about the worth of his labor because that action seemed to "stack the deck" by creating an adversarial relationship between union and management. All that accomplished, in Bill's independent mind, was an advancement of those seeking power over other people. Their pastor might call them "the powers and principalities," but he wasn't sure. All he knew was that in such a setting, management gravitated toward looking at the employees as "bodies," while the union saw the workers as "victims" needing the union's help. Bill refused to accept either scenario. He wasn't a victim, a body, or a resource. He was a human being with value and integrity, at the very least, in the eyes of God and his family.

In the late 40s, while harboring this costly sense of self, Bill eventually found steady work at a large, nonferrous metals casting plant specializing in brass parts and fittings. He judged that the company seemed to agree with his views on employee relations, although he was not on any soapbox about them. He quickly endeared himself to the management with his ability to troubleshoot equipment problems and to fix anything. Besides, he was reliable. In short order, he was promoted to Maintenance Foreman for the expanding operation, then some years later, Superintendent. He lived up to the challenges presented him, and the Vice President of Operations never second-guessed the decision to advance him within the company. The greatest effect of this scenario in which Bill had a good job with a successful employer, was that the Mack family could now relax a bit and enjoy the farm more. A reliable steady income has a way of taking the edge off.

Russ loved these family stories that he'd been told and the one's he had experienced. He liked reflecting on his family, his upbringing and the things he learned during this phase of his life. They were safe memories, and it gave him a sense of peace to be alone with these thoughts. He knew it was an escape from the pain of recent years, but he did it anyway. He needed *something* to help him cope with the loss of the most important people in his life.

Chapter 12

On Friday, Amanda arrived for work in the newspaper office appearing to be anxious. She told Zoë that she wasn't real happy about the plans she had made for the weekend—a camping trip with Cory and Davie. Cory was being real sweet, just like he always was when he knew he was on thin ice, buttering her up, talking about how much she meant to him, blah, blah, blah. And she'd fallen for it, giving in to his camping trip idea. Davie would be along, and she knew he'd love it. But he'd also have a grand time with the other kids at Martin's picnic. And Amanda really didn't want to miss Martin's party, truth be told. Just because Cory didn't like parties all that much didn't mean that she should miss one. Maybe she could sweet-talk him, convince him not to miss the big event.

Later, when Zoë put the phone down after speaking with Madge Wilson, she said to Amanda, "That Madge Wilson is a character. She kept vacillating between concerns about Mr. Miller and delivering these funny little lines. I'm visiting her tomorrow, interviewing her about the incident."

"She'll talk your ear off, but she's fun, if you're in the mood for it. Sometimes it gets to be a bit much."

Zoë said, "I was thinking it would have been fun to go back out to the Wagon Wheel, but I'm not going alone…and you're leaving this evening. I don't know why I said that. I went out there last week with you and Cory, thinking, well this will be an interesting adventure, and it was." Laughing, she said, "While Cash what's-his name and the drunk on the dance floor didn't provide much entertainment value, I enjoyed being with you guys. It was nice that Cory cancelled his rodeo plans and joined us."

"I guess he felt bad. Also, he hadn't paid his entrance fee for the rodeo. As for Cash McCall, you sure set him straight after his 'fresh meat' remark. I loved it when he came at you with that smirk, looking around the floor under our table. Remember what he said? 'I seem to have lost my Congressional Medal of Honor somewhere around here. Can you help me look for it?' And without missing a beat, you said, "You need to be handsome and have big muscles to get anywhere with that line. You don't look like you have any of those things.'"

Zoë laughed. "I didn't set him too straight. It didn't stop him from sitting down and introducing himself. Then he started telling those jokes. He was a regular self-appointed comedy act. When he was doing his routine, I thought, 'Why is it that some guys try to become these great jokesters? They try to win you over with their comedic skills and alcohol. What happened to the strong, silent type who wins you over with alcohol and keeps his mouth shut?'"

"You noticed how bored Cory and I were." Amanda chuckled. "We've heard every one of Cash's jokes. We should have told him to stop!"

"And then he went into that long story about cowboy chariot racing. I had no idea."

The two women shared more stories about the previous Friday night, talking and laughing, enjoying their recollection of being out on the town. Zoë was happy she had found this friend from a different world.

Since Zoë had the old Dodge van available to her, she drove out to the Wagon Wheel, alone, on her second Friday night in the area and sat in the parking lot debating whether or not to go inside. She decided to leave. There weren't many cars in the lot, so the place probably wasn't very exciting at the moment. Maybe it was too early. She thought, "These

aren't really my people, anyway." She found herself gritting her teeth…
why, she wasn't certain. She drove farther out Sixth Street, right on Wolf
Pike and left on Bandy road until she reached the Miller ranch. She could
see lights on in the house and barn, and could just make out a big sign
at the ranch's entrance in the dark night.

Zoë turned around and drove back to town by way of the Wagon
Wheel. She stopped again, noticing there were more cars in the lot, now.
Feeling silly, she got out, locked the door of the van, and went in. She
ordered a Moose Drool, but was nervous about driving a borrowed
vehicle among people she didn't know all that well, so she promised
herself to only have one. She was just being prudent, and thought, "My
aren't you grown up…the responsible young lady on the loose. Well,
maybe not so young at that."

The group playing that night was the same group that had performed
the week before, The Lost Litter. They were playing the same music she
hadn't appreciated the first time she'd heard it.

Zoë felt uncomfortable, going to a cowboy bar alone. She didn't
know why since she had occasionally done the same thing in bars and
clubs around New York and Florida. She looked around her, but didn't
recognize anyone. After she'd finished her beer, she left, the country
music pounding in her head, and went back to her room. She was angry
at herself and she lay in bed for the longest time, wondering what the
hell she was doing with her life. She rehashed how her parents, after the
realization that tennis wasn't going to work out, suggested that she
should consider a career in television. Her father had said, "You have a
winning personality, your smart, and you're beautiful. Maybe you could
do that? I'm sure you could if you wanted to." And she thought, "they
never pushed me into anything, but they supported me in whatever
healthy thing I wanted to do in life—ballet, horseback riding lessons,
and tennis. God, the money they spent on me and my tennis! And I let
them down. Journalism was what? An afterthought? Something to help
me get into the big-time media world? And Darrel, the most manipula-
tive human being I've ever met." Tears came to her eyes but she withheld

an all-out cry. Zoe resisted pity parties. Her father had once told her, "Self pity is okay for a little while. Give it about thirty seconds, then move on." She eventually fell asleep listening to a Chicago jazz station on the radio. She questioned how she could get such good reception from Chicago all the way out in Wyoming.

Chapter 13

Zoë wanted to take something to the Martin ranch garden party since it was a potluck affair, so she asked Mrs. Granger for ideas. The woman told Zoë she could help her bake a couple raisin cream pies Saturday morning, so they'd be fresh for the event. Mrs. Granger was going, also, so the two pies would cover them both.

"Mrs. Granger, I have confession to make," said Zoë. "I don't know how to make pies."

"Well, for heaven's sake, honey. It's just a recipe we have to follow. I'll show you how. We'll do fine together. And I'd love to have somebody as sweet as you messing about my kitchen with me."

Early Saturday morning, prior to Zoë's departure to interview Madge Wilson, the women baked two raisin cream pies. Both were quite pleased with their accomplishment. These were the first pies Zoë had ever made, while Mrs. Granger had baked pies an untold amount of times. Regardless of the wide variance in their experience, both women took real pleasure from their accomplishment. Zoë cleaned up the kitchen, looking out over the panorama of mountains through the kitchen sink window, acknowledging its splendor and feeling good this fine morning.

After showering, fixing her hair, and dressing in her good jeans and a green shirt with a darker matching vest, Zoë retraced her steps of the night before, arriving at the Miller ranch a little before 10:30 A.M. for her appointment with Madge. Promptness was a habit she'd learned from her father, a doctor who always kept to a tight schedule.

When she pulled into the long driveway, she again saw the big wooden sign stretched across the entrance, positioned on two massive poles, high in the air. It said *Melody Ranch*, a name she was to learn later had nothing to do with the name of Gene Autry's radio show, and later, his own home. Rather, the place was named for Melody, the former owner's wife. It had been called Melody Ranch ever since.

A smaller, old, white metal sign was attached to a tree, which said:

Old Dog, New Dog
Several Stupid Dogs
Please Drive Carefully

In the morning daylight, off to the right, she could see the small, white, two-story frame ranch house with a detached, two-car garage. She had no idea how many square feet made up the house. Someday, she would probably learn to look at a house and figure out its size in this way. Her parents always talked about people's houses in terms of their square footage.

Two dogs were resting on the porch. A black one, which looked like a standard poodle without the poodle haircut, sat up at attention, watching the van. Another one looked to be medium-sized, and black and white, but it didn't move so Zoë couldn't tell what it was. There were no cars in the gravel driveway leading off of the main dirt entrance, and the garage door was closed. On the left, following wood fencing up the lane, was a large modern barn, while closer to the hills, was an older, wooden, two-story barn or stable with a big center door facing down the driveway. A pickup truck and a John Deer tractor were parked haphazardly in the area, and a weathered mobile home sat on the other side of the big barn, mostly out of sight.

To the right of the smaller barn was parked a horse trailer and a large, rusty stock trailer. There was a round metal corral to the left of the big barn, out in the pasture, in the distance. A woman with long, speckled hair, pulled back, was inside the corral along with a spotted horse, which was walking behind her. As Zoë parked and looked out the rolled-down window toward the corral, the woman saw her and hollered, "Just open that big door on the left of the barn, walk through, and you'll be here in no time." The horse was disturbed at the noise from the woman, tossing its head and moving its feet; the agitated movement visible to Zoë, even at her distance from the pair.

Zoë waved and nodded, saying nothing. She got out of the van, started to lock it, but didn't, and began the short trek through the barn. Then she saw two other dogs—Border collies. She was able to identify the breed because she liked to watch the *Westminster Dog Show* on television. Seeing these dogs made her think of the movie, *Babe*. The dogs came out of the barn door quickly, looking inquisitive and checking her out, but not barking, jumping, or sniffing at her crotch—she hated when dogs did that. These were quiet and well behaved animals, but alert to her every move. And they stayed that way, following her on her path to the back of the barn, darting in front, sitting, watching, then following behind before they darted in front again. Maybe they were trying to herd her someplace. She chuckled as she noted that she saw no pigs like Babe from that wonderful little kid's movie trying to herd sheep anywhere on the property. Zoë wondered about the white sign at the entrance. Border collies and poodles weren't considered stupid dogs.

After she entered the barn, she saw a room off to the right with the door closed and several stalls down the left side. In the center of the large barn was an arena, fairly good sized but not as big as the arenas she had seen as a child in Ocala, Florida. On the other side of the arena, there was another wide aisle and more stalls down that side. The door at the other end of the barn was open. She walked toward it, looking for horses in the stalls as she passed. There was only one stall with a horse in it, at the far end. The name *Fandango* was carved on a wooden plaque attached to the stall door. This was Jake Miller's horse.

She momentarily stopped. In the research she had gathered for the article on Jake's accident, she'd heard the elderly man's horse referred to as a chestnut. But she could never easily distinguish among the confusing variations in color within the horse world. This guy just looked brown in the dim light of the barn. He had a gorgeous main and tail. She knew he was a male, but she wasn't in a position to determine if he was gelded or if he had all his equipment. She went on, passed some hay storage while exiting the barn, and quickly found herself at the corral hearing a big "Howdy, you must be Zoë Valiente." It was a statement, not a question.

"Yes, I am. You must be Madge Wilson."

"Well, give me just a minute, and I'll be right with ya. I'm tryin' to train this horse to get used to bein' hobbled." With that, Madge Wilson picked up some thick white rope off to the side of the corral and while the horse stood naturally, she tied a figure eight pattern around the front feet of the horse, and then with another rope, the back feet. Then she just left the animal standing there and walked out of the corral.

She shook Zoë's hand heartily. "Real nice to meet ya! I've just been doin' some ground work with this youngster in the round-pen, the 'classroom' as Pony Boy calls it. Pony Boy's a famous Indian horse trainer. Let's go up to the tack room and get some coffee, set down and get acquainted a bit before we talk about ole Jake." Tilting her head sideways toward the horse, she said, "I want to just leave him there, stand alone for a while, anyway." Before moving on, she stood still for a few seconds, watching the horse to see if he was going to do anything.

Zoë noticed that the horse never moved except to watch Madge walk away. "What color is that horse, anyway? It's gorgeous! An Appaloosa, right? What's its name?"

"The color is called grullo. He's a real nice young stallion named Steely Dan. We picked him up not too long ago; he'd had a rough beginning, but he's coming around. Nobody's been on his back yet because he's too young. He'll be a pretty substantial horse when he's finished growin'—maybe sixteen hands. We're thinkin' he will be a great stud one day, make somebody some money. It's all about ground work for the time bein'."

As they walked to the front of the barn, the dogs following, Zoë commented that her mother listened to Steely Dan. She thought it funny to hear of a horse named after a '70s band. She asked, "By the way, is Fandango a gelding or a stallion? I couldn't tell."

"He's a gelding—a sensitive, but gentle, and damn smart horse who needs to be treated with respect. He's half-Arabian and half-Quarter Horse. That article referred to him as a Quarab. He is…and he isn't. I mean, the breedin' is right, but he ain't registered. Hell, I think Fandango was born before there ever was such a registry.

"Nobody yet can figure exactly what happened to Jake before he was found, 'cuz it ain't likely Fandango throwed him, not that Jake couldn't be throwed. It's just not likely that Fandango would do it. And, since Wednesday, Jake sure ain't talkin'."

As they reached the door to the tack room, off to the left at the front of the barn, Zoë stated, "Someday you'll have to help me understand horse colors. I've seen two horses up close today and can't figure out why Fandango is called a chestnut. And I don't know what a grullo is, at all."

"Fandango's a liver chestnut…got that nice, sleek, dark look. And he has a thick, flaxen mane and tail, makes him look fancy…at least fancier than most of the horses we have around here. Never been much for horses that were only good lookin', not that he is only that. Kinda wished I'da had the same philosophy about men when I was young—hah! There's various other shades of chestnut, too. And a grullo is a mousy gray or steely color. That's partly how he got the name Steely Dan. I just love the way his blanket of spots blends with the colorin' on the rest of him. But then, color doesn't ever make a good horse." Madge paused, walking over to the coffee maker. "I'll put on a fresh pot. This is two days old, what's left of it."

As Madge worked with the stained coffee maker, Zoë noticed that she was a stocky woman, but not fat or what you'd call a large woman… just big-boned, strong looking. She was about five feet, eight inches tall, and had a square, pleasant face with wrinkles from the sun. Zoë noticed that one of her rough-looking hands had half of both the little finger and ring finger missing. Madge's green eyes were large and almond-shaped. Her speckled gray/black hair was long, halfway down her back, pulled into a ponytail, and it looked unkempt. She'd probably rough combed it first thing in the morning, then hadn't thought about it again.

She wore faded jeans, tan laced boots—not cowboy boots—a plain, cranberry-colored, long-sleeved shirt with a small rip in the back, and a light tan, well-used, straw cowboy hat. She also wore sunglasses.

"I understand you're from New York?" she asked Zoë.

"I was born there, but my parents moved to Florida when I was two. I only go to school in New York, now. I have one more year to get my degree in journalism. I spent most of my life in Palm Beach, Florida. I took dressage lessons for a couple years when I was eight and nine, but then I began playing tennis. Not sure I'd know how to ride now. I had a good lesson horse, though. He was a black Hanoverian."

Standing by the gurgling coffeemaker, Madge drawled, "Well, we don't see many Warmbloods around here. Maybe while you're visitin' this summer, we can do somethin' about getting ya back on a horse, if you want. You probably forgot less than you think. Why'd your folks move to Florida?"

"The weather. My mother was from Brooklyn and vacationed in Florida when she was growing up, so she always wanted to live there. My father is from Cuba, but he and his family escaped to Florida. He went to medical school in New York, where he met my mother. He had an opportunity to join a good practice in Florida—he's a proctologist—and always said there were just as many assholes in Palm Beach as there were in Brooklyn."

"Hah! Never understood why a doctor would choose to be one of those."

"My dad always said it was because there were fewer doctors in it. Meant more opportunities for him than if he had specialized in ob/gyn or orthopedics."

"And your mother…what does she do?"

"She plays tennis and bridge with her friends at the country club."

Madge laughing loudly. "What's that? I never seen a country club before." She gave this hearty haw-haw-haw that Zoë wasn't used to hearing, but appreciated for its directness. As Madge poured the coffee, she asked, "How do you take it?

67

"Black, thanks. That's how I learned...never wanted to fuss with cream and sugar."

Madge poured two cups and to her own, added three teaspoons of sugar and milk from the ancient avocado refrigerator. She said, "I know what you mean, but I grew up with cowboy coffee. When I was a kid, I kinda had to doctor that bellywash in order to get it down. Now it's a habit. Know what cowboy coffee is?"

"Honestly, no."

"The old joke is that it's strong enough to float a horseshoe. You make it by takin' this old pot that's only used for coffee and never cleaned...'well seasoned,' as they say. Then you boil some water over a fire, throw in some fresh, loose grounds on top of the old ones, remove it from the high heat and let the grounds settle by sprinklin' in some cold water. Then you pour. You can also put an egg shell in to settle the grounds, but to tell ya the truth, there weren't never many eggs at hand if you were workin' somewhere away from the barn. Set yourself down."

The tack room was long and narrow, running across the front end of the arena. At both ends were racks for the saddles and places to hang bridles, halters, and various ropes. Some of the saddles were on racks with names on them while some weren't designated. In the center of the room were two old stuffed couches, a huge, dark wooden coffee table with several horse magazines on it, an old wood table, and four chairs. A small kitchenette and the refrigerator filled out the rest of the space, along with a bathroom at one end. The whole tack room was neat, but dusty, and smelled of horses and saddle soap. The rough knotty pine-lined walls were covered with old pictures. Zoë seated herself on one of the couches, sprawling comfortably while Madge sat on the other. "It's cozy in here, a nice place to hang out. Is it heated in the winter?"

"There's a furnace in the bathroom that manages to warm this room. It'd get mighty cold in here in winter if we didn't heat it. There's an old stall in the other barn, converted to a bunk house years ago, with a pot-bellied stove in it. It's now a little studio."

"Studio?"

"It's Kay's, Jake's wife. She used to paint landscapes, horses, and stuff before the arthritis got so bad she had to back off."

Pulling out a note pad and pen, Zoë wanted to be professional and start with the real purpose of the meeting— her assignment—although it would have been easy to just visit with this person. "Madge, if you don't mind, could you tell me exactly what happened during the incident with Jake? Go back to the beginning. Explain about Jake going on this ride, when you realized there was a problem, what you did."

"Well, Jake used to help with the chores every day, and we'd both go on a mornin' ride, three, four times a week. When my John was alive, the three of us would ride. Kay joined once in a while in the old days. In recent years, as Jake got older and my husband died, I moved out of the trailer and into the upstairs of the house. Jake and Kay moved downstairs. Anyway, it was just gettin' tougher for Jake to do mornin' chores, ride all those mornin's, come back to train horses all afternoon and then do feedin' and muckin' chores again in the evenin'. That's what he wanted to do, though. Like a lot of folks around here, he's indifferent to most human qualities other than endurance. Most days, by the time the sun gets around to settin, Jake's pretty pooped. He told me awhile back that he just had to cut back."

"Is that a picture of Jake on the wall—the one with the man standing by the horse?" Zoë noticed a small man next to a horse that looked like Fandango. But it must have been an older picture because if it was Jake, he didn't look to be in his late seventies. The man in the picture appeared to be short and maybe 140 to 150 pounds, and had a handsome, clean-shaven face. She had expected Jake to look different than that— a tall, square-jawed cowboy type with a mustache, like the man in the Marlboro ads.

"Yeah, that's Jake, maybe twenty years ago, with Fandango who was about three at the time. Anyway, back to your questions, he got up early on Thursday—to watch the dawn, he said—fed Fandango, and was saddlin' him when I got to the barn. I asked him where he was goin' so early, and he just said, 'Pretty day. Think I'll go for a ride.' I asked him if he wanted me to join him, and he said, 'Nope.' Kinda hurt my feelins', he was so abrupt. We've ridden out together many times, not botherin' each other with conversation, and I tried to join him most of the time because he's gettin' old. He shouldn't be doin' this kinda thing anymore. And I know his wife gets irked at him, too. Tryin' to stop him wouldn't do no good though…be like barkin' at a knot."

"When did he leave…what time? And did he say where he was going?"

"He left a little before seven, I guess. Don't have a watch, but I do have a sense of time. He never said where he was goin' and I didn't ask. He wouldn't have answered anyway. About two hours later, I started expectin' him back. By about midmorning, I started worryin' and after a while, I got on the phone and started askin' folks what we should do. Well, we all knew what we should do, so by about noon we were all gathered and off on the hunt."

"I don't suppose Jake had a cell phone?"

"You suppose right. He wouldn't touch the darn things. 'Never needed one before; don't need one now.' That's what he'd said when his daughter offered to buy him one. She thought it was a good idea. Her heart was in the right place, but he wouldn't have nothin' to do with it. Martin, Sylvia, and Deputy Barado found him and called us. I was with Cody Nelson and Gus Wittingham. They're some fine young men, although Gus has three kids, and his wife has one in the oven. Cody, though, now there's a catch. Maybe I'll introduce him to ya.

"Anyway, we was on the easier trail and actually went on up to Cowman's Meadow, then came down to where they were. We thought he probably took Elk Ridge Trail 'cus of the tracks, but we also thought we might get up higher quicker goin' the way we did. 'Course, we weren't sure how high he went, and the trail he took wasn't no trail for a seventy-nine-year-old guy to be ridin' by hisself.

"When I got there, Jake had just thrown up on Sylvia's boot. He'd asked for water. When she gave him some, he promptly got sick on her. He'd been half asleep when they found him, leanin' against a tree. Fandango was just standin' real stiff, off on a flat spot. They'd asked Jake what happened, but he was never quite alert enough to answer or just didn't want to. He can be a stubborn old waddy sometimes."

Zoë said nothing and was puzzled. "These people are hard to understand sometimes," she thought.

Madge didn't pick up Zoë's reaction to her words and carried on. "Cody, who's an EMT, went right to work, even started an I.V. Jake was dehydrated bad, so we got him loaded and carried him out on that folding litter those boys use. Wittingham and Barado carried him most of the way, but Cody and Martin jumped in when necessary. I took care of the horses mostly. Fandango wanted some attention—he needed water. We couldn't see anything out of the ordinary anywhere, or tell what happened. Still don't know. All we really know is that Jake has a concussion and is spendin' most of the time sleepin' at the Medical Center. And Fandango can't tell us."

"Why didn't Fandango run home, back to the barn?"

"Jake taught him not to… taught him to stay with his alpha no matter what. It was a habit Jake learned growin' up in West Texas."

"Oh, he's not from Wyoming? How did he get here…and his wife?"

"Well now, that's an interestin' story. Jake met Kay about forty years ago. He was in his late thirties and she was about thirty-four. She never did go past thirty-nine—hah! It was a case of him bein' a top hand on this big Texas spread, but she was the owner's daughter, who'd had a rough life with men, booze, and too much money. She came home from God knows where—the prodigal daughter—to dry out and get her life together. She tried to stay away from the cowboys workin' there; gettin' involved with them wouldn't do her any good and her father woulda been pissed if she had. She was a pretty little thing, then, from the pictures I've seen. A few weeks later, after bein' real good, she met handsome Jake. Well, they told me it was love at first sight. They've had many a good laugh over that time.

"Just as they were tryin' to figure out how they were goin' to spring the news on her old man without him havin' a hissy fit, he up and dies.

Her old lady was already dead, so the big question became what happens to the ranch. And it was big—about sixteen thousand acres. Not as big as some, mind ya, but big enough. Well, the old man had given up on Kay years before, and although he had begun to hold out some hope for her since her return, he hadn't fixed the will from when he'd cut her out. So the ranch went to her two older brothers, who treated her like white trash, mostly."

"That doesn't seem right."

"No, but she got some goin'-away money. Not big money, but enough for the two of them to sneak out of Texas with some good cow horses, come up here, take out a reasonable loan, and buy this place. Let me tell ya, five hundred acres are sure a lot less than sixteen thousand acres, though. The amazin' thing was, they didn't fuss and fight about it one bit. I always figured that was because of Jake's influence. Kay had a history of fightin' with family, but they both knew there was no love left in that family. So, Jake and Kay just took that little check from the lawyer and moved on without sayin' a word. She never went back to her old home, neither. Anyway, that's the story I heard from Kay many times.

A yellow cat appeared out of nowhere, jumped on the arm of the couch, then walked across the high back and eased itself down next to Zoë. It found a spot up against her leg and purring loudly, settled in, closing its eyes. "I guess somebody found a new friend," Zoë said as she began to scratch the cat gently behind its ears.

"There should be a gray cat around somewhere, too, and a bunch more around the property. Some are feral, doin' what they're supposed to do, I hope."

"Why here, Madge?" Zoë asked. "How come Jake and Kay settled here?"

"They were lookin' for a place with good grass and the right ground to raise foundation Quarter Horses. They wanted a place that had rough country…rocky, with gullies and hills…so the horses would grow up, learnin' early to be surefooted, have strong hooves, be athletic cow horses. Jake lets 'em get familiar with the hard winters too, like mustangs do. Wild mustangs get strong or die. Oh, there were other places in Texas, Kansas, Oklahoma, elsewhere, but they just wanted to get to some new country. They liked Montana, too, but this place had what they wanted, and they could afford it.

"This used to be quite a busy breedin' and trainin' spread at one time. We had a few cows, but it was mainly to keep us in meat and allow us to train ranch horses…cutters. It wasn't no real cattle spread. It's a horse ranch. Now, well, we're pretty much a rescue operation, only have about thirty-eight head right now. We take in horses nobody else wants, try to bring 'em back to normal if they've been abused, and find 'em good homes, or maybe just let 'em live out their lives in peace if they're old. Or we buy problem horses, horses that other people can't fix, or aren't willing to take the time to fix, and we retrain 'em and then try to sell 'em for a profit.

"Trainin' horses ain't rocket science. It just takes a little love, a lot of time, and great patience. You got to have respect for the horse's point of view. Jake's somethin'. He never gets angry at the horse. I'll bet he didn't learn that as a youngster, though. He learned the old ways—buck it out of 'em, break 'em. Not that the old ways are entirely wrong. On a real bucker, they sometimes would get 'em into a big tank, not the easiest thing to do. The horse would be up to his belly in water, and they'd work with him for a week if necessary, to get him settled. Usually, they'd come out of that and never buck again. And nobody had to beat the spirit out of 'em. The horse just found out it wasn't as scary as he thought.

"Or you look at that hobblin' I got that Steely Dan learnin'. 'Why hobble a horse?' you say. Well, two reasons. One, there's lots a places where you can't find anything at all to tie 'em to, and ground tying is a good thing to learn, but it ain't a sure thing. Second, it teaches the horse not to fight and fuss if he accidentally gets caught in some wire or somethin' so he don't hurt himself. Also, horses can move, graze, while hobbled, sometimes farther than you'd like. Hah! Reminds me, I think I should go check on him. Walk out there with me."

"Sure, I'd like to stretch my legs." As Zoë got up, she looked at her watch, saw that she had maybe forty-five minutes before she needed to leave and wondered what the heck she would be able to write about Jake Miller from the conversation so far. She followed Madge out the same door they had come in and strolled through the barn to the round pen. As they passed Fandango, he stuck his head over the bottom half of the closed Dutch door. Madge scratched his head and talked softly to him. Zoë remembered sliding doors in all the barns she had seen as a kid, but these were the old-fashioned doors. Zoë patted him and talked to him, also, and Fandango loved it.

Steely Dan had moved to a spot about ten feet from where Madge had left him, finding better grass by reaching his head through the other side of the portable corral. Madge entered the round pen, walked over to the horse, and carefully removed the hobbles. As Zoë watched the precision with which this simple procedure took place, she asked, "And what about you, Madge? How did you end up here?"

"Back in the late seventies, I'd already been through three lousy husbands. Talk about trailer trash! You know, I never liked that term 'cuz some hard workin' folks just can't afford much different, but I'm sure I fit the description of what people mean when they say it. Anyway, I met my John at a rodeo down in Fort Worth. I was barrel racin' back then, and waitressin'. He was a local farrier, workin' the rodeo—that's how we met. Well, we started goin' out, dancin' at those country joints that were popular back then, him bein' real shy, but a good dancer, and me bein' real cautious. I'd pretty much had my fill of abusive loudmouth cowboys.

"Well, we took it real slow. Several months went by, and I had this mare, my best barrel racer that I wanted bred. We'd read about this real good QH stallion named Poco Doc Holiday, that was standing stud up in Demming, Wyoming. So we decided to take a little vacation and haul my mare up there, see if we could work off the stud fee. It was Jake's stud, right here. Whiskey was about ready, and we thought it might be a fun time…no harm tryin'."

Zoë listened intently, never having heard such a story in her life. Madge didn't miss a beat.

"One thing led to another. Jake seen how good my big John was with horses. There were about one hundred-twenty head here at the time. Stayin' would have meant steady work without all the crap blacksmiths have to put up with most of the time. That's what you want—steady work, like at a race track, although that can be a problem, too. Or a good ranch where there's enough work, and they respect your abilities, where you can build a reputation. Jake and John hit it off, just naturally. They hardly ever spoke to each other, but they observed the quality of each other's work and just got along without any problem.

"John and I left Whiskey and the trailer, went back to Texas, got married, and hauled our stuff back up here a week later. We moved into the old barn. Eventually, we got that mobile home…looked good when it was new. I had to earn my keep, also, and I did. I worked as hard as any man around here. Jake wasn't too sure about me at first. Heck, most of the hands weren't too sure about me. But we established a peaceful way of workin' together over time. My John was shoein' a horse about two and a half years ago, and he just fell over. Jake saw it from a distance and thought he got kicked and knocked on his can. But no, he had a massive heart attack. John was about six feet, four inches and two hundred-eighty pounds…liked his meat and potatoes too much, I guess. The doc said he was dead before he hit the ground."

As Zoë left Madge, she passed a pick-up truck that was just turning into the ranch. She didn't pay much attention to the driver because she was deep in thought about Madge and the stories she told. Zoe decided that she liked Madge and wondered if it was because she was so different than anything she'd ever encountered before or because it was like she had just stepped out of a spaghetti western. In the end, Zoe decided it didn't matter. She didn't have anything substantial to add to her story about Jake's mysterious accident, but she had spent a delightful time. It made her think about her life in New York, where every minute had to be packed full of drama and movement. She wondered if big city reporters ever got to spend their mornings with someone like Madge.

Chapter 14

Russ had two older sisters, one thirteen years older and another eleven years older. When the younger girl was born, the doctor, the hospital staff, and Ginny knew immediately that something was wrong, but nobody was willing to say the words until the doctor actually spoke them. Ginny noticed the small rounded head, the round face with a short, broad, flat nose, the small eyes, the lethargic nature of the child. And before Bill was ever notified, she asked in her wavering voice, "What's wrong with her, Seth?"

Their family doctor, Dr. Seth Lawson, was old enough to be Bill's father, but he was the respected known entity in their part of the country, having birthed most of two townships. They attended the same church, and their families counted each other as good friends. As he squarely faced her, Dr. Lawson said softly and painfully, "Ginny, I don't know yet. I want to examine her more fully and then discuss my diagnosis with you when I am certain."

In her heart, Ginny knew what was wrong. As Dr. Lawson took the baby with noticeable gentleness and left the room, Ginny asked the nurse to get Bill. Then she broke down and cried.

It seemed to be hours later, although it wasn't, when Dr. Lawson arranged to meet with Ginny and Bill. When he entered the room where Ginny remained in bed with the yet-to-be-named nursing baby and Bill, who sat next to her holding her hand, he noticed her red eyes and the utter sadness on her face and Bill's. The couple looked distraught. He sat on a chair as near to them as he could and said gently, "I have completed my examination and have concluded that your daughter suffers from mongolism. I will explain what that means by telling you about the diagnosis, the etiology, the pathology, the prognosis, and how it will likely affect your lives."

Ginny and Bill did not react. They had already discussed the possibility while waiting for Dr. Lawson, and had gotten through their initial painful reaction and anguished questioning as to why. In both their minds, it was now time to listen and assess the facts of their future. The fact that they were angry at God was another matter best not dumped on their friend, Dr. Lawson.

Dr. Lawson continued, "This is not my field of expertise, but I have seen such children during my days in medical school." Then, he gave them a long explanation as to the possible causes, concluding, "I want to stress that the medical profession does not yet know the cause for this condition."

Bill spoke. "It doesn't matter what caused it. We need to know how we will take care of her and what kind of life she will have."

"I understand that, Bill. I just don't want you thinking that there is something either of you could have done to prevent it." Dr. Lawson went on to discuss the physical and mental characteristics of the condition, then said, "These details may be too much for you right now. I'd rather you read these things—I have some materials for you. Then come back to me with questions when we see how she is."

With a hurt voice, Ginny said, "Yes, please just cover the essentials now."

"I understand. I need to point out two very important things on the physical side. Number one is that mongols show an unusual susceptibility to disease of the respiratory organs. The most frequent cause of death in infancy is bronchitis or pneumonia. Those who survive the first two or three years of childhood generally succumb a few years later to some form of tuberculosis. Secondly, congenital cardiac anomalies are very common, and circulation is generally defective, which is why mongols are often cold. I have no insight as to how long your child will live, but her life will probably end as a result of one of these two conditions—a respiratory disease or heart failure."

"How long do they typically live?" Ginny asked.

"There have been rare cases of mongols living to adulthood, but most succumb in their early teens. My message to you, unless you are going to place her in an institution, is to take her home and love her for whatever time you have with her."

"We're not placing her in any institution," Bill said with a strained face.

Ginny added, "God has blessed us all our lives, and we're going to care for this little child, which is our responsibility to do, even though right now it doesn't seem like much of a blessing."

"Well, I fully expected you'd say that, knowing both of you as I do."

After a pause, with all three people thinking hard and not saying anything, Dr. Lawson spoke. "Interestingly, mongols love music, and they show a sense of rhythm, which may be a wonderful means of dealing with their wandering attention. They may listen to a piece of music and mark it in their own movements, finding pleasure.

"Another interesting characteristic is their tendency to imitate the actions of others about them. They can reproduce the movements they have observed, which means they can be trained through imitation to perform certain specific tasks, but they cannot adapt to any required changes in a situation."

Again there was a period of silence, with Bill showing his anxiety and Ginny alternating between stoic acceptance and shedding tears. Dr. Lawson spoke in a low, tender voice. "Now, the prognosis: you need to be aware that she could die here in our care. She is extremely susceptible to cold, and we don't know the extent of the congenital heart anomalies. On the other hand, she could struggle and hang on, but succumb after a couple years. Congenital defects coupled with low vitality does not auger well for resisting the invasion of disease. Adding to what I said earlier about life expectancy, the average age of death is about fourteen years, though some have lived into their thirties. As for therapy, little has been accomplished in the treatment of mongolism. But here are some things to do to make life better for the child and you.

"First, keep her warm with proper clothing and limited exposure to cold, which invites respiratory problems.

"Second, ensure that she acquires clean habits with regular bowel movements and relief of the bladder. Remember that she won't necessarily pay attention. For example, bedwetting is common, usually from *in*attention. But you can help by constant supervision. Keep a chart if necessary, monitor the activity, set a schedule for *you* to follow to get her to use the bathroom regularly. This is important because if neglected, digestive troubles may result.

"Third, if the health of the child is under control, and if her physical condition permits it, education and training should be considered. This needs to be about proper habits and developing an ability to be self-helpful more than trying to teach her to read or do math, which frankly would be of little or no benefit if the child is, in fact, classified as an imbecile. This will need to mostly be done in the home. The child will require considerably more attention than a normal child does, which will mean added work for you. Stimulate her with music, bright objects, and toys she can handle. You'll need to work with her as she learns to sit up and eventually, walk. With firmness, she can be taught to wash, dress, and feed herself, mainly through imitation.

"And one sad conclusion must be drawn. No treatment has brought about any appreciable improvement in any mongol child. These children are born with grave organic defects. We can hope and pray that she is in the upper ranges of intelligence and that her diminished physical capabilities can be managed, but, in the end, even with your patient love and diligence, your daughter will be what she will be. Have you decided on a name?"

Ginny said, "She looks so peaceful. We've decided to name her Grace."

Chapter 15

The Martin ranch was in a small beautiful valley off the main road. A Victorian house with a massive porch was accompanied by two barns, a corral, a chicken coop, and garden surrounded by a high fence. The mowed yard was huge, and the gorgeous views revealed peaks in the distance and rolling meadows. People were arriving for the party carrying food to the back yard, where long folding tables and chairs had been set up, loaned to Martin by their church.

As Zoë arrived, she saw Mrs. Granger's car, so assumed the pies were there, also. Martin and Sylvia came up to her and warned her that when most of the people were there, they were going to introduce her formally to everyone. Zoë said that would be fine, but she really didn't want any fuss, and proceeded to help carry and arrange food, paper plates, and utensils, meeting people along the way. As she worked, she noticed that in addition to the mountain of food, coolers filled with beer and soda had been set out, along with a large cooler of lemonade.

In a short time, Martin secured everyone's attention, except for the numerous children running around trying to sneak sweets from the dessert table. "Folks, I want to thank you all for coming to our little gathering today. We're planning to eat in an hour or so, after we're finished with all the barbecuing. Go ahead and get some refreshments and appetizers at the south end of the table, and enjoy yourselves. I have two other things to tell you. First, for those of you who don't already know, Jake woke up last night demanding to be fed and let out of that medical center prison."

There were some mumbled cheers and expressions of thankfulness as Martin added, "He might even show up here later today…but let's not count on it. Just know that he is doing fine. The doctor said he could leave today sometime, but he needed to rest…as if Jake is going to rest. The second thing is, I want to introduce our new intern, all the way here from Columbia University. Her name is Zoë Valiente, and I'll get this out of the way right now. Her mother is Jewish, and her father came over here from Cuba, thus a name we're not used to hearing. Anyway, please introduce yourselves to Zoë and welcome her to our community. Enjoy the day."

Zoë waved, saying *hello* as people said *hello* back. Some guests drifted to the beverages and food table, while several people went straight to her.

A young man spoke to her first. "Hi. I'm Joe Miller, Jake's grandson."

"Hello, Joe. I don't know your grandfather, but I hope to meet him."

"He's a great old guy. Everybody loves him. Tell me, what do you like about New York?"

"Well, it's an exciting place, not that I can afford to take advantage of all the excitement. I love to jog in Central Park and take long walks. My best friend, Lacy, and I…we'll wear tennis shoes, carry backpacks and go window shopping, check out the Dean & DeLuca store, walk up and down Eighth Avenue to Greenwich Village or SoHo, or walk around the Upper East Side, looking at all the brownstones. It's a great place to people watch, too." Zoë added jokingly, "Just don't make any eye contact with them."

Ken, the banker, a big older man with a boisterous voice, said, "I was there years ago, in the early seventies, during my investment banking days. I remember going to The Four Seasons and the 21 Club…pretty elegant spots. Also, there was this great old restaurant in Brooklyn with gas lights—Gage and Tollner. The waiters had hash marks on their uniforms for the number of years they'd worked there…old black guys who had been there thirty, thirty-five years."

"I've not been to any of those places. Remember, I'm a college student. I do work part-time in a fancy Italian restaurant, though—Antonio's.

There is this old bar where we like to go, down in the Bowery called McSorley's Ale House. It's neat. The suits—the stock brokers—eat lunch there. It used to be a men-only bar in the sixties, back when the feminists were burning their bras. The story goes that some women invaded it only to find out that there was one restroom, and it had a glass door."

Those listening chuckled, and Joe said, "I'd like to go there sometime. Is that where you want to live…New York City?"

"I'm a little conflicted. I prefer Florida, but then if I'm ever going to be a top journalist, New York is where the action is." Laughing, she added, "My dad thinks I could be another Katie Couric."

Ken said, "I heard about you in town. Martin said you used to play tennis. You could always follow the tennis tour, maybe write for the sports magazines."

"Unfortunately, that's become the domain of retired top players."

Joe said, "Yeah, I heard you played tennis and you look like you're in good shape. What do you do to stay that way?" Joe's wife, Susan, had noticed Zoë's good figure and heard her husband's impudent question. She looked at him with disgusted eyes, but her expression didn't seem to register with him.

"I run about twenty miles a week, and I work out when I can," said Zoë, answering Joe's question. "Here, I'll mostly just run and stretch. I used to do a lot of gym work coupled with the tennis. My sports endeavors even delayed college for me. That's my excuse, anyway."

Joe continued, "Don't know much about tennis. I do know who Andre Aggasi is, and John McEnroe. When you say 'a lot,' did you play seriously?"

"Yes, I went to a big-time tennis camp in Boca Raton, was on the high school team, won some local tournaments, and eventually played some minor tournaments in Europe for a couple of seasons. I didn't do too well. I had the theoretical knowledge of the game, and my skills were improving, but I kept getting injured. And I would have liked to have been a little taller."

"You're not short," Joe said, lightheartedly. "And I thought there were a lot of good, short tennis players."

Just then, a man joined the gathering…somebody Zoë hadn't seen before. She glanced at him as she went on. "Like in most sports, big, fast, and strong beats, small, fast, and strong. There was this South African— Amanda Coetzer. She was on the pro tour, the big show. She's short, and she ran her butt off…a good counterpuncher. She's fun to watch, a nice player, but just not good enough to beat the bigger girls who hit really hard."

"It works the other way in bronc or bull riding," said the newcomer to the group as he offered his hand to Zoë. "Hi, I'm Cody Nelson."

Zoë was struck by his presence, and found herself smiling at his good looks and gentle manner. She said, "Hello, I'm Zoë Valiente, and it's a pleasure to meet you." After she spoke, she thought she might have sounded a little too cheerful, too eager. In a more businesslike tone, she asked, "What do you mean, it works the other way?"

"Well, in most rodeo events, small, fast and strong works better than big, fast and strong, unless you're into steer wrestling or calf roping."

Joe jumped back in, "You ever see any celebrities at these tennis matches?"

"My family goes to Key Biscayne every year for the Lipton tournament, and my dad was a big Thomas Muster fan. Oh, that's another story. Muster was an inspiration for me, coming back from an injury the way he did. We also go to Amelia Island, and I've been to a couple U.S. Opens. A lot of the tennis stars are just walking around at the Open, going to and from practice courts, and nobody really bothers them except the kids looking for autographs. Years ago, I remember watching Steffi Graf practice. She was doing two-a-days, out there in her shorts and sweaty T-shirt…just drill after drill against practice partners—men. That's what it takes: talent and great discipline and not getting hurt. I loved watching her practice. Then she'd go play a match that evening or the next day. That lady was in shape…probably still is, even in retirement."

Joe continued. "Excuse me for asking, but isn't hitting a ball over and over just a little boring?"

"I wasn't good enough to ever get bored," she said, laughing more heartily than normal.

"Do you play anymore?"

"When I thought I was going to be great, I delayed even thinking about school so I could focus on my game. Now, I play socially, mainly when I'm home in Florida. Court time in New York is too expensive. I get invited to be a doubles partner for some of the older people at my dad's club." Especially the men, she thought. "I'm the ringer, and everybody knows it. I love the game. Maybe when I'm out of school, settled someplace, I'll become a teaching pro or a good local club player— a 5.5 or a 6.0—without having to work hard for it."

"A what?"

"Oh, it's just a rating system to help players match themselves with like players. A 2.5 or 3.0 is a beginner. Matching one with a 4.5 or 5.0? Well, it wouldn't be pretty."

During Joe's friendly inquisition, Zoë noticed that Cody had walked over to the coolers to get a drink. After she'd answered all of Joe's questions, she strolled around the lawn, watching some kids play catch and remembering a paper she had written in school about tennis. In it, she had borrowed heavily from Suzuki's *Zen Mind; Beginner's Mind*—how the novice at any sport sees everything at face value; everything is simple, straightforward. Then one moves into a phase where it's confusing, and one realizes that one knows nothing…the universe of knowledge yet to be learned is vast. Finally, one begins to understand the principles, and with time, the art of the thing one is doing. It's a circle. The master of a sport has a beginner's open mind. He's not encumbered by ego. He's let it go.

That's where Zoë had failed. She had gotten to the point of intellectually understanding the game better, but she could never get the connection of the mind and the body…to play in the present moment. She could never get the *feel* of the game, so it never became simple to her again. Rotator cuff problems, wrist and ankle injuries, hadn't helped, either. She had had to keep making adjustments to compensate for them, and had always seemed to strive so hard.

She remembered the opening phrase she had written for her essay: *The mind is like a parachute; it works best when it's open.* She had always liked that, but she didn't know if she had heard it somewhere or if it was an original thought.

Another group was gathering. Cody was there, and she caught herself looking at him. He had on jeans, Merrill shoes, and a yellow shirt. She liked his hair and his tanned athletic look. He had blue eyes and eyelashes that her girlfriend, Lacy, would kill for. She acknowledged the attraction she felt for him and hoped she could spend some time with him.

Meanwhile, elsewhere in the yard, Martin was offering his thoughts in a different conversation, saying, "Being a farrier is hard work. John told me about what it was like before he hooked up with Jake. They have to put up with a lot, mainly because too many horse owners don't train their horses properly and expect the farrier to deal with the mess they've helped create. Horses should be taught to have their feet handled, to stand still, and not lean on the person handling them. They need to be taught how to be cross-tied and become familiar with different people handling them. Some people just have no sense.

"John told stories, that's for sure. One time, a farrier was called out to a ranch at an arranged time. When he got there, he found a note that said, 'Sorry, had to go. Horse is in the pasture.' So, the farrier had to go catch the damn thing out in forty acres of pasture before he could even work on it, and it didn't want to be caught! He could have left, but then he'd have wasted his gas and his time for nothing. A lot of farriers charge extra for that kind of stuff, but it can still throw off a schedule. Or another time, some guy said he had three horses to do. The farrier got out there and oops, there weren't three, but six! So he did them, was late for his next appointment, and had to apologize all over the place for being late. These guys sometimes get stiffed, too. No wonder some of them get real grumpy. It's bad owners and untrained, or just plain mean horses, ready to kick their teeth out, that cause the good farriers be very particular about who they'll work for. Most of them are just trying to correctly shoe horses the easiest and most efficient way. It's not a job I'd ever want."

Madge said, "Yeah, Martin. John used to question his sanity for ever takin' it up. I remember once John had to shoe a horse that could kick a fly off his ear. Ha! That's a damn big kick, if you ask me."

Over by the grill, someone said, "Well now, with Kentucky-raised thoroughbreds, it's all in the water, so they say…and the limestone ground. There are over four hundred horse farms in Bluegrass country around Lexington."

Zoë drifted off.

And elsewhere, Madge was talking about Texas with a group of guests, responding to a question asked by one of them. After everyone finished describing places good and bad, they started exchanging jokes and rhymes. Madge hollered, "Hey, Martin, here's one for your newspaper:

> *There ain't no justice in this here land,*
> *The judge gave a divorce to my old man,*
> *But I shore laughed at his decision,*
> *'Cause he got the kids, and they ain't his'n!*

Zoë moved on to a spot in the yard where several guests she didn't know were talking. She heard one of them say, "Man, there are lots of opinions on saddles. The older Circle Y's are good, better than the new ones. You still have to be careful…fit is still the biggest headache."

Listening to all these conversations, Zoë thought it was like white noise—random signals with no meaning. But it wasn't because words were being spoken…things were being said that had significance to the people saying them. It was just so different from her life experiences in Florida, at the country club, in New York, and Europe. Zoë held the conflicting thought that these signals of life in Wyoming were both enlightening and something to resist.

Just then, Martin got everyone's attention by banging a pan. "Meat's ready, everyone. Let's start a line down each side of the food table and then we'll say a prayer."

As people organized themselves, including a good number of children having the time of their lives, Martin waited for the group to become quiet. "Lord, we thank you for the good news about Jake, and we thank you for bringing Zoë into our midst. We rejoice in this day you have made and for the fellowship of those here with us. We are mindful of those in need who cannot partake in this bounty. Bless this food for its intended use, in Jesus' name. Amen." He paused. "Okay everyone, enjoy."

Zoë sat next to Sylvia, who discussed the problems of running a bookstore and, in turn, asked Zoë questions about her career plans. Cody was across the table and several seats down from them. Twice he and Zoë looked at each other lingeringly.

The meal was fantastic. It reminded Zoë of family potlucks in Florida, which had always been great. The Cubans were all good cooks, and they would try to outdo each other with the most exotic dishes.

After everyone had eaten the main dishes, most wanted to wait for dessert. Many of them pitched in to clean up the tables and refrigerate those things that needed it. Zoë found herself in the kitchen washing empty casserole dishes and pans. Cody came into the kitchen and started to dry dishes. They talked amidst the chatter of several folks who were also in the kitchen assisting with the clean up.

Zoë told Cody about her parents, that she was an only child, and gave him more details about her tennis career and her studies in school. She also told him that one of the reasons she came to Demming was to take some time away from a failed relationship. She noticed that he seemed to pay special attention to that remark, but then, he was listening closely to everything she said. She liked that.

He told her about his family's ranch up near the Montana border where they raised wheat, hay, sugar beets, and a few horses and cows. He was a graduate of the University of Wyoming with a degree in forest management, had worked for the National Outdoor Leadership School for a time after college, and then joined the Forest Service. He was thinking about getting a masters degree in rangeland management, but wasn't sure. When Zoë asked him where he lived, he said, "I rent a rundown mobile home on the Miller ranch."

"I didn't know that. I saw it…from the outside. I was just there interviewing Madge before coming here. She never mentioned you were there. And Amanda said something about Madge living with the Millers, but never said anything about you being there, either."

Laughing, Cody said, "Maybe I'm not worth mentioning."

"Oh, I doubt that."

"Technically, Amanda is correct. Madge lives with them, and I'm in the mobile home. As for Madge, believe me, that was just an oversight on her part. I must have slipped in to clean up for this party after you'd left."

When the work was done and kitchen emptied, Zoë and Cody stood looking at each other. Cody started to say something, but Zoë beat him to it, excusing herself to find the bathroom. Cody told her where it was, and as she moved in that direction, she sensed that he was watching her…she could feel it…and it felt good. She thought, "Whoa girl. This isn't what you came here for." She was aware of her slightly elevated heart rate and remembered how, when playing tennis, she would sit quietly and breathe evenly during a changeover to calm her nerves before the next big service game. Perhaps she should do that now.

Chapter 16

Zoë got trapped in a conversation with Ken, the banker. Zoë couldn't remember how it happened, but something he said triggered her to say, "But we're raping the planet."

With great interest, Ken said, "How so?"

"We have a relatively small population in this country, compared to the billions who live in poverty elsewhere, and we consume the vast majority of the world's resources. And we're the major contributors to global warming."

Ken was ready to pounce, and he gave a long-winded speech about the phony global warming crisis as nothing but the latest excuse for a Marxist takeover of the economy, to spread the misery around…except for those in charge, that is. He then offered a solution, explaining, "Stop having children." Then he thanked the leftists for their great contributions, such as in Europe where they weren't replacing themselves. He said, "It might take a couple generations, but we have to take the long view. When us parasites are no longer here, or at least reduced to insignificance, the earth will do just fine. Al Gore is a piker. He emphasizes band-aid solutions, mostly in support of his investments…the hypocrite."

"I'd say that's rather cynical, Ken. We may not have the time to take the 'long view'."

"Then the savers of the earth should be happy because we are told that a lot of people will die. The population will be significantly reduced. But check back with me in ten years."

"You don't believe what the computer models tell us about tipping points?"

"No. I am amazed at how people can have so much faith in computer modeling. Like statistics, computer modeling can tell you whatever you want it to tell you—garbage in, garbage out. I'd suggest that it's virtually impossible to include all the variables necessary. They can't even put in known data from the past and predict the present!"

Zoe remained calm and detached, but she wondered if there were more like this loud assertive man in Demming. She said, "What if you are wrong?"

"Then the earth will eventually revert to its pristine nature without the masses of the raping Western culture to affect it. Perhaps on our way there, we'll be living like those cannibals in Cormac McCarthy's book, *The Road.*"

"Well, I think you're wrong."

Ken hesitated before speaking again: "Miss, do you know why people around here drive pickup trucks? Because they need to haul stuff. They need them to support their lives. They need them because you can't carry eight bales of hay, or a sick calf, or fence materials in a goddamn Prius!" Ken then tipped his cowboy hat and excused himself saying, "It's been a pleasure, ma'am." As he departed, she could hear him mumble, "Never trust anybody under thirty."

Chapter 17

Zoë drifted across the yard, finding shade, contemplating the conversation with Ken. She thought she was pretty firm in her beliefs about such things as global warming, but the pickup truck comment lingered. She had never thought to question her beliefs before. She'd been spending her time trying to define them into fixed positions. Her job was to stand staunchly and fight against all those didn't see things as she did—wasn't it? Seeing Cody in the distance, however, made her forget Ken completely.

She stood under a tree, paper cup in hand, the wind blowing her long black hair that reached the middle of her shoulder blades. Her eyes gravitated to Cody, then she shifted her gaze to the distant horizon. She could feel Cody's presence as he walked up to her.

"You look deep in thought," he said.

"I was just looking around at the surroundings…the mountains in the distance, the land, the horses grazing over there. They're such pretty animals." In a pensive mood, she said, "There surely is a lot of country out here."

"Do you like it?"

"When I first saw the Tetons from the air, then again driving through Jackson…well, they kind of take your breath away. Being a city girl, I don't know if I could adapt to this."

"The wilderness, this big country, the open plains can affect you. It tends to relax folks once they adjust to the distances, the lack of people.

There's something soulful about it, like good music." He paused, then added, "I saw Ken talking with you."

Taking in his words, smiling gently, Zoë said, "Yes, he was giving me his Mad Max view of the world."

"Oh, I've heard it. Ken can be quite blustery and opinionated at times. He lives a lot greener than he might sound. His favorite line is, 'I don't know anyone anywhere that doesn't want clean air, pure water, and unspoiled lands.'"

Zoë said, "I can be opinionated, too. And what do you think? Is Ken right? Or is Al Gore right?"

"I think Ken and Al Gore are both trying to make a point. I just don't think they have the answers. Say, would you like to see the Tetons up close? And you really ought to see Yellowstone before you leave. If you like, I could show you how it's coming back from the fire of eighty-eight, and you could see some buffalo."

Slow to respond, but pleased, she said, "Are you asking me for a date?"
"Yes, I am."

Playfully now, Zoë said, "That's awfully bold of you. We've just met. I thought men out here were supposed to be reticent with women."

"I generally am. But I saw you, and I heard you were only visiting until early July. I didn't want to waste time."

They eyed each other with intent, standing squarely, facing each other. "And how would this work? We're talking some distances to travel. We couldn't do it all in a day, so what are you suggesting?"

"We could break up the trip, or we could stay over one night, which could be handled without any loss of dignity."

Zoë asked, "Whose dignity?"

"First of all, mine…which I figure protects yours. I'm not going where I'm not wanted."

"And how could I be sure of that?"

"You couldn't. You'd have to trust me and trust your own instincts. You might also inquire about my reputation. I'm known around here."

She stared at him, trying to penetrate his mind, listening to the wind and the children in the distance, thinking her instincts about men were awful. Nevertheless, she decided to take a chance. "I think that would be real nice." Then she noticed her own growing tension and laughed to relieve it. "Goodness sake, I've been here only two weeks, and I'm picking up a drawl. Where did that slow 'real' come from?" Exaggerating it now, she said, "Ah think that would be reeaaal naace."

Smiling, not laughing, Cody said, "I think it would be real nice, too. Can I get you some more lemonade?"

"No, I think a beer is in order."

Chapter 18

A car pulled up with a driver Zoë didn't recognize. A man and woman sat in the back seat. Several people hollered, "It's Jake," or "He's here!" As he entered the backyard with Kay and Buck, the driver, Jake smiled as people started asking him how he was and what happened. "I'm fine everybody," he told them. " And I'm happy to tell ya what happened, but I want to do it settin' down." His expression grew grim and serious as he said, "Also, ya might want to send the women and children away. What I have to tell might be too much for 'em."

Sylvia said, "No way are we leaving. You just go right ahead, Jake. If we faint from all the excitement, there's a couple EMT's around here to take care of us."

"You're sure now? It could be a mighty strain on your psyches."

As Joe secured a lawn chair, someone said, "Jake, tell us what happened."

Jake said, "Okay, you asked for it. I was out ridin' old Fandango. Such a beautiful day it was. And we stopped just to look around the scenery. All of a sudden, a breeze kicked up, and the birds stopped flyin' and singin', and then we heard a cougar howl one of the loudest screeches I've ever heard. Well, Fandango gets real skittish, but me bein' such an expert horseman, I calmed him down right away. We both wondered what was goin' on. See, I can tell what Fandango's thinkin'. We're bein' real quiet when all of a sudden I smell this horrible stink in the wind. I turn in my saddle, and there it was. It just came out of nowhere! It was

94

huge. Oh, I almost can't say it…it was Bigfoot! No, wait. Don't laugh! There's more to tell."

Joe said, "Okay, Grandpa, tell us the rest."

"Well, he or she or it had a club in its hand. And it just tapped me on the head and knocked me out, so I fell off unconscious. I only had a glimpse of it. At least it didn't eat me. Fandango musta' chased it off… saved my life. What a good horse."

Paul, the minister said, "Jake, are you going to tell us the real story?"

Looking incredulous at the whole gathering, Jake said, "I just did tell you the real story. Don't ya'll believe me?"

Several said, "No!"

"Well, I'll be damned. Sorry ladies for the language. I just had a frightful experience with Bigfoot and my emotions are high. Nope, that's my story and I'm stickin' to it." He sat in his lawn chair with pursed lips, refusing to say anything more. Then he noticed Zoë standing by Cody and said, "I don't believe we've been properly introduced."

Standing on the other side of Zoë, Sylvia took her arm, walked over to him and said, "Jake, let me introduce you to Zoë Valiente. She's a college student, and she's here as an intern working for Martin at the newspaper for a few weeks."

While Jake stared at her, Zoë glanced at Cody and then back to Jake and said, "It's a great pleasure to meet you, Mr. Miller. A lot of people have been very worried about you."

"It's a pleasure to meet you, too, Miss Zoë."

Madge was standing near Cody and said, "Look at him, that twinkle in his eye. I'll bet he's up to somethin'."

As Sylvia withdrew, Zoë lowered herself so she could look directly into Jake's eyes and said quietly, "I've really wanted to meet you. I've heard all about you from Madge and others, and they love you dearly. I hope I can get to know you better during my short time here. Would you mind telling me what really happened, Mr. Miller?"

"Please call me Jake; and I'd love to tell you. But I sure aint' goin' to tell any of my *friends*." Then in a false whisper, trying to make it look like he was going to disclose a secret, Jake said. "I was on the ground leadin' Fandango a while. I was ready to mount, put my foot in the stirrup, and my right foot slipped on some loose ground. I fell and hit my head on a big rock. I'm a foolish old man, you know. Losin' my grip on life."

Zoë observed sadness in his eyes as he said the last of it. It was a quick transition from being ornery to a melancholic state but then he just as quickly toughened after he acknowledged his failing. She reached out to Jake and hugged him.

He hugged her back and started to whisper something, a real whisper, but stopped.

They held each other in the silence for a few moments more, Zoë wishing he would state his mind. As they slowly broke their embrace, she drifted into the background, noticing the absence of laughter in the crowd. She saw that tears welled up in Madge Wilson's eyes, and Kay's and Sylvia's.

Zoë returned to Cody's side, standing close to him. He squeezed her hand, then let go. She didn't want him to, and she leaned closer.

He looked at her intently. But she just looked straight ahead, close to him, watching people as Jake's friends came up to him to talk, glad he was back, glad he was with them…glad that he was Jake.

Chapter 19

Bill and Ginny didn't plan on having any more children after Grace, but as such things happen, in 1955, Russ was born. It was a concern to them because Ginny was forty years old at the time, and they were fearful of having another mongoloid child, even though, intellectually, they knew from Dr. Lawson and all they had read that this was highly improbable. As the hair on Bill's head was starting to gray, their prayers were answered. They got their healthy boy.

Grace especially loved Russ, tenderly holding the baby and talking to him in her own mumbled language. As he grew and came to understand that she was different from others, he became the child who could ease her concerns, make her laugh, and give some relief to Ginny by occupying the girl's attention. And she became the gift who taught Russ deep, abiding love.

Grace died at age thirty-one of heart failure brought on by spinal meningitis. She had lived a good life within the protective cocoon of her family and community, about as happy as anyone could be. She had become quite accomplished at knitting, using more and more complicated patterns as time went on. Much later, Ginny would comment, "You know when people say, 'don't stereotype' or 'you are just generalizing,' they are sometimes just wrong. There is a reason for the words. A stereotype exists because there is evidence to suggest that a pattern exists. It's the same with making a generalization. It doesn't mean that 'all' people are like what you might be describing, but enough of them are so that it's appropriate to make a generalization. Grace was the stereotypical mongoloid child…loving and happy in her affliction."

At the time of Grace's death, Russ was a freshman at Purdue University studying engineering. He had an aptitude for math, physics and, like his father, could build and fix anything. So engineering became his calling. Upon news of Grace's death, he rushed home to be with his family and, like them all, was devastated by her passing. Everyone in the whole community that was physically able attended the funeral.

The service began with a prayer by Pastor Mark, followed by the singing of "For The Beauty Of The Earth," Grace's favorite hymn, which brought tears to many eyes. Then Bobby Huggins told a childhood story about an incident when Grace attended school one year, and he convinced her to eat dirt in the playground. He said, "My father gave me the worst lickin' I ever had in my life." And then he talked about how he had become her protector-defender. Ruth Mack also told humorous stories about life with Grace, and then it was time for the sermon.

Pastor Mark read Psalm 103 and said, "Good people of this blessed church, let me ask you, how do Christians cope, as Ginny and Bill Mack have had to, with the terms retarded, disabled, abnormal, defective, or worse, 'imbecile,' to describe their child? Such a question may have occurred to all of us who have known this family so well over the years, but probably not with the personal impact that has confronted them. I know this because I've been with them. And it is a tough thing to think about theologically. I also know when our Ester was born several weeks after Grace's birth, my dominant thought was profound relief and gratitude for Ester's perfection. I am sorry to admit that it was one of those, 'thank God, it wasn't me' moments.

"The bigger question is why? Why mongolism? Or why multiple sclerosis? Or why any imperfection at all? Because of sin in the world? Because the world is broken? Because it is a fallen world? Because the cosmos is malfunctioning, and such things as flu epidemics, cancer, earthquakes, and tornadoes just happen and kill a lot of people? Is it just fate? Is it by design? We faithful Christians then say, 'But those terrible things are not of God because God is good.' Yes, He is good. But some abstract disaster somewhere else doesn't resonate the way something close to home does. So, what does 'His goodness' say about Grace and her life? Ponder that a while."

And he let them think about it for a full minute, a risky thing for a minister to do when one doesn't know what the flock might be thinking.

He went on. "Our logical minds draw us to questions like, how do we reconcile Grace with the concept of being created in the image of God? We are created equal in the eyes of God, but our practical sensibilities show us that we aren't. We look different from one another, have different skills and talents, and some are simply a lot smarter than others. Was Grace a part of His good creation, or was she a manifestation of something else?"

Again, he allowed silence to take hold. Russ was transfixed.

"Let me suggest this as a partial answer. We need to consider that we are all human, no matter if we've been stricken with affliction, physical, mental or otherwise, and more important, we're all redeemable, and I think those who are disabled in some way are maybe even more so.

"We are a people with limited capabilities and limited knowledge living in a finite world with Christ as our hope. Since the beginning, our sin has been what you have heard me say many times: 'overreach,' the exercise of our pride. We have wanted to be gods on our own. Nowhere biblically has it ever been suggested that being a vulnerable person lacking in abilities or of weak mind, that is 'the least of these,' means that such a person is less than human or of God's lesser concern. Treating people with this view is a human construct, and the horrible examples of it are legion. The Scripture says, 'For he knoweth our frame; he remembereth that we are dust.' I would offer that the 'image of God' includes Grace just as easily as it includes you and me.

"It is extremely difficult to see Grace and others with serious limitations as a gift. But I am here to tell you that she was a gift. Our awe of God, which is what 'fear of God' means, must include the idea that Grace was a part of the whole of humanity, and the only sin involved in her affliction was how people reacted negatively to her presence among us.

"You all are aware that Grace prayed. Her parents taught her, showed her how to pray. Now I cannot say one way or the other whether she ever had a sense of connection or fully understood what was happening during her prayers as her loved ones helped her along. But I do know this. God was surely pleased. And He was *with her.*

"The Catholics say, 'The souls of the just are in the hands of God.' Yes, I think we can say with assurance that Grace is with Christ this day.

"The doctors tell us that Grace died of a weak heart, a clinical reality. Engaging in a bit of hyperbole, I am here to say that that is not true. She didn't die of a weak heart or a broken heart or a heart with a defect. She died because she used it all up! This child of God, this possessor of great gifts, gave more unconditional love than ten people in her short life. And I mean ten Christian people!"

The congregation had never seen the always calm and kindhearted Pastor Mark become so animated, and his emotion was building.

"Do you have ears to hear, people? She gave this family and all of us in this little community who knew her, and know her parents, sister, and brother, lessons of true grace that will last them, and hopefully us, a lifetime." Becoming almost angry, he cried out, "You want to know and understand God's love? It was right before our eyes! By knowing Grace, you had the God-given providential opportunity to know *grace.* God bless this child. And God help us."

Pastor Mark left the pulpit, exiting through the back door to his office. The choir director led the congregation in singing, "There Is A Balm In Gilead" and then closed with a prayer and an announcement regarding the procession to the burial site followed by a reception in the church's fellowship hall.

Later, at the reception, Russ approached Pastor Mark, a man he knew well and greatly admired. As Pastor Mark gave him a big hug, Russ said, "You told me you were going to a place in your sermon you don't normally go. You certainly did."

"Maybe I went a little too far. But then, I'm often the most convicted by my sermons."

"Which Mother says speaks volumes about the nature of your kind soul."

"Well, that's awfully nice of her. Your mother is a rock. You know, Russ, Judas may have been the most important apostle of the whole motley crew because of his attitude, his impatience…'Do it my way. You're not doing it fast enough, Jesus. Use your power. Why are you holding back, Jesus?' That's my problem, too. The world is a mess and I'm angry at God, Jesus, and the Church because the kingdom hasn't been achieved. I want it done now. I'm no better than Judas."

"I don't believe that for a minute, Pastor. Yesterday, you said that we are to experience the Graces of the world as a witness to God's loving grace and accept His love. I believe my sister was a *gift*, just as you told us."

Then, Russ uncharacteristically hugged him back as Pastor Mark said, "Thank you, young man. You are a gift, also, and you do my heart good."

Chapter 20

People started to depart Martin's picnic around six o'clock…a process that took well over an hour given the lingering conversations among the guests. Cody and Zoë were near the last to leave. After the kitchen cleanup, they helped take down tables and chairs, and load them into Martin's truck so he could return them to the church the next day. They removed the trash and busied themselves returning the property to the condition it had been in before forty people had descended upon it. They stayed, of course, to spend more time together.

Finally, when there was nothing else to do at the ranch, they decided to go into town and have an ice cream cone. They both had vehicles, so they drove individually to Dickey's Ice Cream Shoppe. Cody had a mint chocolate chip cone; Zoë chose butter pecan.

Zoë loved the easy way in which Cody told her about his family and his job, and the respect he showed for the people in his life. She reciprocated with more details about her life. They lingered over coffee until ten o'clock, when Dickey's closed. As they parted for the evening, they agreed to go horseback riding on Sunday after having breakfast with Madge, Kay, and Jake. Cody would call her if that turned out to be a problem, but he knew it wouldn't be. He asked her to be at the ranch at eight o'clock. By that time, he would have been up for two hours, helping with chores and letting everyone at the ranch know that a guest was coming for breakfast.

Zoë went to bed thinking about the glorious day she'd had, knowing that she was smitten and liking it. The events of Sunday reinforced her emotions. The day began with fantastic sausage omelets, raw fried potatoes, home-baked sweet rolls, juice, and coffee for breakfast…and much laughter listening to the banter among Jake, Kay, and Madge. After breakfast, they all went to the barn, but Cody and Zoë were the only ones that went riding. Jake wanted her to take Fandango, and he openly voiced admiration on how good she looked sitting upon his fancy Quarab. Cody reinforced the point, and Zoë blushed, feeling warm inside. Cody rode his own horse, an eight-year-old, sure-footed, buckskin Mustang mare named Nunza. The pair rode off into the hills on the same trail Jake had taken when he'd fallen.

Cody said, "I'll lead. The trail gets tricky in about a mile when we start the real climb."

"It's hard to talk when we're riding single file like this. How far are we going?"

"It depends. There's a nice stream about three miles up, and at about four miles, there's a waterfall. Jake fell in a pretty spot a couple miles beyond that. How far do you want to go?"

"That depends on how my butt and legs hold up. I haven't ridden a horse since I was a kid."

"You'll have to let me know how far you want to go."

Feeling ornery, she said, "Is there some special way I should do that?"

He turned in his saddle to look at her. "Groan or something." And then, with a big grin, he turned back.

She smiled, then noticed how the trail was narrowing and starting to get steep.

They remained quiet as the horses efficiently managed the switch-backs. "So far so good," she thought. "Nothing hurts, yet."

They reached a flat, smooth section. Cody turned and said, "How are you doing back there?"

"Fine, so far."

"Good. We'll stop at the stream and take a break…drink some water."

She liked watching him. He sat straight in the saddle and handled Nunza like a pro.

When they arrived at the stream, they both dismounted and Zoë said, "I felt fine on the horse, but it also feels good to get off for a few minutes."

"Let's have some water while the horses drink. We can just let them go. They won't go anywhere." Cody grabbed her hand and continued, "Come over here on this rock. You can see a ways along the stream in both directions." He led her up to a big flat rock that jutted out into the stream. A squirrel followed them. They stood close to each other on the rock, and Zoë liked his presence. It felt good to have him near, and he smelled good. She wondered about the attractive powers of pheromones and what they might be doing to her. No matter. She liked it.

They took in the views, but then Cody just looked at her. She could feel his eyes on her. She turned to look at him, and he gently reached for her and kissed her. Zoë kissed back. It was a long kiss. Then they broke apart and just held each other, saying nothing. He gave her another soft kiss, and she eventually backed off saying, "Whew, let's go see the waterfall."

They smiled and hand in hand walked back to the horses to continue their ascent along the trail. Zoë, riding behind Cody, thought about the moment she had just shared with Cody. "Oh, that was nice. More would be even better."

At the waterfall, they again embraced and kissed...with a little more enthusiasm, this time. When she once again broke away, she shook like a wet dog might and said, "Oh, stop." Looking into his eyes, she added, "You are so tempting." She giggled and ran to Fandango.

He walked toward Nunza. "Do you want to go farther?"

She laughed. "Let's just ride to where Jake fell."

Cody smiled. "Well, that's what I meant."

Climbing on Fandango, she said, "Okay, let's go."

He chuckled. "Yes, ma'am."

They rode for quite a distance, not talking. Zoë's legs were beginning to feel fatigued, but she didn't care. They stopped and dismounted when they reached the area where Jake had fallen.

Cody said, "Gee, I hope we don't see Bigfoot." Zoë laughed. He went on, "You know, that was quite a scene at Martin's party. How do you do it? You just sweetly asked him a question, and he just lost all inclination to carry the joke further and spilled the beans."

"I don't know. Maybe I am learning how to become a good reporter."

"I think it's more than that. You cast spells over people."

She said coyly, "Do I?"

Smiling, he said, "Yes, I think you do." They drank some more water, shared an apple, and gave each horse one. Hand in hand, they walked around the meadow, looking at the peaks in the distance, feeling the cool breeze. They stopped, and he kissed her again. When they broke apart, Zoë said, "Why did you let go of my hand when we were standing in front of Jake yesterday?"

"I guess I didn't want to press my luck."

She just looked at him inquisitively, and this time, she initiated the kiss. They held each other for a long time, Zoë with her head on his chest as he stroked her hair. She said, "Oh, how I love my hair played with like that." Then she groaned. They both giggled, and she squeezed him hard and said softly, "We'd better go."

"I don't want to. But you're probably right."

After almost four hours, Kay said to Jake, "They've sure been gone a long time."

"Yeah, wonder what they're doin'?

"They kinda hit it off, didn't they?

"That'd be my assessment."

"Cody's a straight shooter, one of the finest young men she'll ever meet. And she seems like such a nice girl. I wonder if anything will happen between them."

Jake said, "You're not askin' me to form an opinion, are ya?"

"No, because I know what you'd say. You'd say, 'Well, let's just wait and see. It's none of my business anyway.'"

"Yep."

A while later, Cody and Zoë returned to the barn. They curried the horses and gave them water, then turned them out to the good pasture to graze. They spent the afternoon with each other, talking more, getting to know each other better. They liked each other's company. They also visited with Madge while Jake and Kay took an afternoon nap.

Kay had put a pot roast on and insisted they all stay for dinner. Zoë and Cody helped with the dishes and then visited a while longer. Eventually, Zoë went back to Mrs. Granger's when all the excuses for staying with Cody had been exhausted. She slipped into bed almost giddy with happiness, reliving the last day and a half, feeling like she was floating on clouds.

Chapter 21

On Monday, Zoë was sore from the ride and busy with another obituary and a feature article. Martin had told her to wait on the followup of Jake's story. He wanted to think about it and they had until Thursday before she needed to provide an update. She thanked Martin profusely for inviting her to the party, but said nothing to anyone about how she had spent the rest of her weekend. Her friend Lacy called her to talk about what was happening in New York, but they had to cut their conversation short because of Zoë's workload and deadlines.

Throughout the day, Amanda told funny stories about her weekend that had people in stitches. Zoë laughed, but she was so distracted, she couldn't remember the tales a minute after she'd heard them. She kept mixing warm thoughts of Cody with her efforts to concentrate on her writing. And she socialized with the staff in the manner she was accustomed to, as though nothing had changed in her life since they had all been together on Friday.

By the time she went to her room at Mrs. Granger's, one thought hit her like a bolt out of the sky: "I cannot do this. I cannot fall in love. And I will not just have a summer fling. I wouldn't like myself very much if I did that, and it wouldn't be fair to Cody." Then she wondered why she thought it wouldn't be fair to him and concluded that it was because his actions didn't indicate that he was interested in just a fling. "It would be easier if he were just some horny bastard wanting to hook up," she thought. "Then I could say no and walk away without any further thought. But that doesn't seem to be him. This could be a serious problem!"

She slept fitfully. On Tuesday morning, her legs, and her butt, and her head hurt. When she got to the office, Amanda said, "Anything wrong? You look a little out of sorts."

"No," she lied. Then she told part of the truth. "I didn't sleep well last night, and I have a headache."

"I have some aspirin in my desk."

"Thanks. I took a couple Tylenol this morning."

Unlike her usual effervescent self, Zoë slogged her way through the morning, taking care of the work as though digging a ditch. It was getting done, but it was drudgery. For lunch, she avoided the others by walking back to her room, washing her face, and slowly walking back to the office. She didn't eat.

Martin had his finger on the pulse of the office, and as he watched her, he figured that something wasn't right with Zoë. He let it go for most of the day to see if her attitude improved, but at three-thirty, he came to her and said, "Let's take a walk."

After they left, Connie said to Amanda, "Uh-oh. They're taking a walk."

Amanda just shrugged her shoulders, looking puzzled.

Martin and Zoë walked up Sixth Street, Martin saying hello to people as they passed, not saying anything to Zoë.

She was panicked, thinking, "I've got to do something. I cannot fall in love with some…." She started to tear up, but shook off her emotions.

As they walked, Martin said finally, "Let's sit down on this bench. You mind telling me what's wrong?"

Zoë proceeded to say things she didn't mean, lying about her own feelings. "I'm not sure what I'm doing here, Martin. I mean, everybody in the office is nice, but this is such a different world. Yesterday, doing some research, I read an article from an old paper about last year's local rodeo. I've never seen one, but at one level, it seems like animal abuse to me. What really got me, though, was the report about all the flag waving, topped off by a recording over the loud speaker of John Wayne reciting something called, 'America—Why I Love Her,' which the audience apparently revered.

"Then there's Mrs. Granger. She's a sweet old lady who putters in her garden, cleans the house, and reads her Bible every day. And I hear her praying out loud morning and night. She fixes a great breakfast and tells me pedantic stories of her past…sometimes the same stories every three days or so. As for Madge, she's delightful and funny, but doesn't care at all about the big issues facing the country. At your picnic, I was talking to her and mentioned something about the need to participate in politics. She says, 'Well, you go ahead, honey, but I've got to take care of a slew of horses every day.' Then I got to hear Ken's dumb theories on climate change. And Jake and Kay are wonderful characters but…well… people here have a whole different attitude about life."

Martin said nothing and Zoë couldn't interpret his non-response. "It seems people here live in this gorgeous flyover country and don't care about anything that matters in the world," Zoë continued. "To be blunt, I have very little in common with them, and I fail to see how my experience here is going to be anything but at odds with them. My world in New York is so different. And isn't this the state of that famous hate crime against that gay kid, Matthew Shepard? And aren't there wacko survivalists living out here? The other day, I saw a truck with two rough-looking guys drive slowly through town scowling at people. They had a Confederate flag bumper sticker…in Wyoming, for heaven's sake. I wondered, 'What? Are they the residue of John Birch or something?' I don't mean to be offensive, Martin, but…well, you get the point."

Calmly, Martin said, "Are you saying you want to go back to New York?"

Without bitterness, but with some tension in her voice, she said, "I'm not a quitter, but my world view just doesn't connect with anybody I've met." Then she gave an eloquent three-minute speech outlining her leftist political positions ending with the epithet, "George. Bush. Worst. President. Ever."

Martin still said nothing; his expression revealed even less.

Shifting her focus, she went on. "How is it that Dr. Wilhelm and you have this forty-year-plus relationship? It seems odd to me. He's fairly evasive about what he feels politically, particularly in class." She turned to stare at Martin. "And what about you? Your editorials never touch on the bigger issues, or if they do, they only touch the edges. If you have any controversy in the paper, it's over something like a zoning or land use issue, not anything meaningful in a global way. What was the expectation of what I might get out of being here? I just don't see any ultimate value in it."

Martin was silent as the two stared at each other. Zoë blinked first and said, "Aren't you going to say something?"

"You want me to fire you, don't you?"

She looked away and gave no answer.

He said emphatically, "Not going to happen. You can quit if you want to, and I'll be disappointed and take you to the airport. But you'd have to do a lot more than unload your leftist dogma and your dislike for the people around here for me to fire you. That's not a challenge, by the way. I'm not asking for you to cause trouble. I'm saying there is work here for you and knowledge to be obtained and skills to be developed, and I can fight through your sudden shift in attitude, your crankiness, for a few more weeks. But, you'll do the work. Or you can quit and go home."

She started to tear up, and Martin offered no sympathy, letting her compose herself on her own. "We're not far from Mrs. Granger's. Why don't you go there, think about what you want to do. It's your choice. Come back in the morning, and we'll talk again, sometime tomorrow."

"Okay. I'll see you tomorrow." Zoë trudged up Sixth Street feeling awful about what she had done. She knew she had just regurgitated some of Darrel's thoughts and wondered why she felt the need to. She'd left him, in part, because of his aggressiveness over politics and yet she'd just done the same thing with Martin. Why? She didn't know.

Chapter 22

Russ first met Sara when she appeared for a group bicycle ride in Huntington Beach, California. It was a casually formed group that some called a club. The group's leader, Buzz, insisted that it wasn't a club, or an organized group, and therefore he wasn't the leader of anything. He would say, "I'm going on a bike ride from this spot, south on PCH on Saturday morning at 7:00 A.M. If you wish to ride along, it's your choice." He wouldn't even say, "Please join me," fearful that somebody might think he was in charge of something. Buzz was a lawyer who had become paranoid about liability ever since a woman fell and broke her pelvis during a mountain bike ride, then sued him because he'd organized the activity. She lost the case, but he wasn't about to go through that again.

Russ noticed Sara immediately…this new person in the group of fifteen. She was shapely and had long blonde hair pulled into a pony tail. He kept his distance, but noticed her pretty face with sparkling eyes that looked right through you. Or maybe he was just self-conscious, thinking, "Why would she be looking through me?"

The group took off after everybody had greeted her. Russ wasn't certain who had brought her. He found himself riding easily behind her, watching—the view was pretty nice—until he realized that he was leering. He shook it off and reverted to his normal pattern of trying to keep up with the hardcore riders.

Sara was twenty-three at the time. She had been born and raised in Colorado, and was an English literature graduate from The University of Colorado. She was a preacher's kid, her father a Lutheran minister in Fort Collins. Sara loved Colorado from the skiing and healthy lifestyle to the diverse cultural settings. And she loved its people: the cowboys and farmers from the Eastern plains, the city people, the miners and oil men, the skiers and rock climbers, and even the artsy fartsy folks. Never sure what she wanted to do with her degree—she didn't want to teach— she and a girlfriend decided to move to California for a while to "see a different and exciting part of the country." Sara got a job as an assistant office manager at a high-class architectural firm in Newport Beach. She called the job, "glorified receptionist." Being personable and good-looking, she knew why she was hired. But it paid the rent. She planned to go back to Colorado eventually, but wasn't sure what she actually wanted to do there.

A year after the bike ride, Russ and Sara were married by her father in Fort Collins. After a skiing honeymoon at Vail—Sara the expert, Russ the novice—they quickly returned to California and moved into their recently purchased house in Irvine. Russ was a rising star within Dunstan Industries, so it looked like they were going to reside in Southern California for a while. Sara had changed jobs to work in a Borders store close to home.

Russ was sold on Colorado after his first trip there, and the pair already had plans for ski vacations and summer travel there. They liked California, too, but declared that it was just a pleasant stop along the way. Life was good.

When Sara became pregnant five years later, the sonogram indicated that it was a girl. So Sara started thinking of names. Should they call the baby, Samantha, after her father, Samuel? They could always shorten it to Sam. What about the name, Rebecca? Contemplating many names, settling on none, she asked Russ one day, "What would you think if we called our daughter, Grace?"

Cautiously, he said, "I think it would be wonderful, but would you really be comfortable doing that?"

"Yes. I know enough about Grace from you and your parents to be quite comfortable with it."

"And how do we explain it to her? That we named her after her deceased aunt who had Down Syndrome?"

"We explain it like you explained it to me. Your sister may have had limited mental capacity and physical deficiencies, but she was an extremely loving person who brought joy to your family's lives. We'll tell our daughter that whatever our iniquities—and we all have them—the lessons learned from Grace's presence in you and your family's lives were profound…that no matter what the circumstances, love can be found. We can tell our daughter that we named her in memory of a very remarkable human being."

"Do you think that will work?"

"Yes I do. We'll make it work."

Vacillating between joy at his wife's suggestion and concern for a little girl he did not know, he said, "I'd like to think on it a while."

She knew the routine. Russ liked to take his time with decisions… "sleep on it" if he could. He once claimed that it was because he was slow. He wasn't. Actually, it was a habit he learned at work, especially when employees would come to him with an urgent request claiming projects would be held up if they didn't get an affirmative answer immediately. Russ would say, "If you need an answer right now, the answer is no. If you're willing to more fully explain the scenario to me, lay out the pros and cons rather than give me this pressured sales pitch short on facts, the answer might be yes." Sometimes, he would give an immediate answer. But his employees learned to be well prepared when they came to him with a proposal. They made sure to describe the details of the situation in a setting where they had his undivided attention.

While deciding upon a name for their baby wasn't the same kind of scenario as Russ's work situation, Sara understood his pensiveness. She snuggled him and said softly, "Honey, I'm only three months pregnant. We don't have to decide until she's born. I just think it would be a very nice thing to do. Your parents would respect our decision, and I love the name Grace."

Chapter 23

Grace inherited her mother's brains, good looks, and bubbling personality. From an early age, she loved to play the piano, which Russ and Sara encouraged by providing lessons on a used upright. Eventually, they purchased a decent Yamaha baby grand. She'd practice for hours and gravitated toward jazz standards. She also developed a pretty good singing voice—the sultry kind. She was particularly fond of Dianna Krall, Norah Jones, and the old jazz singers, trying to emulate them. She went to Berkeley and majored in music.

Russ always admired those like his daughter who knew exactly what they wanted to do with their life, early in their life —the Olympic swimmer, the ballerina, or the boxer who started young and had a support system to nurture their endeavors. He not only loved his daughter, he admired her for having that commitment and gumption.

Russ had never had that focus. He loved engineering, but the interest evolved slowly from having skills in math and physics; plus an apprenticeship on the farm helped things along nicely. From the latter, he learned to solve problems, build barns, fix irrigation and plumbing systems, repair farm equipment, figure out internal combustion engines and electrical wiring. He learned these things not because he was a natural, but because he took things one step at a time, methodically, mastering small chunks of information, then putting them together logically. But it had never been a case of declaring at age five, "I want to be an engineer." He went to Purdue because an astute high school counselor suggested that it was a good career move based on his background and skills. Following graduation, he went to UCLA to get an MBA because his college counselor convinced him that he was "management material."

As for his daughter, Grace had, from an early age, showed helplessness when it came to the tools of living. Her parents thought this behavior was a matter of choice.

As a youngster, she once called, "Daddy, my bright light doesn't work."

"Is it plugged in? Did you turn it on?"

"Yes."

"Did you hit it with a hammer?"

"What?"

"Just kidding." Then he looked at it, found nothing wrong, but realized that she had plugged the cord into the electrical outlet that functioned from the wall switch.

"Daddy, you can fix anything."

Instead of pointing out the obvious—that he hadn't actually fixed anything—he lapped up her compliment. But this became her pattern, having no inclination to tinker with or think things through about all things mechanical, electrical or liquid.

Once when she had trouble with her first car, she called her dad and said, "Dad, the car's broken."

"What do you mean it's broken. What happened?"

"I don't know. It just quit. What should I do?"

"Did you run out of gas?"

"Daddy, I'm not some valley girl!"

While such occurrences were common in her youth, they happened less often when Grace reached her late teens. She became a self-reliant young adult, pushing herself hard with school, the piano, and her abundant social life.

In June of 2005, she borrowed her dad's Porsche and drove to Berkeley to participate in a small jazz concert, playing the piano and singing. It was a success and great fun. Afterward, she spent a long night there with friends. The next day, tired and taking the scenic route home for another gig, she went around a curve on the Pacific Coast Highway and slammed into an old Honda CRX driven by a single mother accompanied by her two young children. A five-ton refrigerated truck carrying frozen fish, following behind Grace's car, plowed into both vehicles, killing Grace, the young mother, and the two children. The trucker said Grace had crossed the double yellow line on the curve. He reported that her head had been down as she hit the Honda. There was no way he could have stopped in time to avoid the cars.

The police thought Grace had fallen asleep, and since there were no drugs or alcohol present in her body, that became the conclusion of the final accident report.

On that tragic day in June, torment and misery—a kind of living hell because there was no other way he could describe it—engulfed Russ and Sara Mack.

Chapter 24

After the great weekend with Zoë, Cody called her early Monday evening, but she didn't answer the phone so he left a brief message on her voicemail. He tried again around nine o'clock, got no answer and left no message. He didn't call on Tuesday.

Wednesday morning, Zoë arrived at work very subdued, but not looking as bad as she had the previous day. At one point, Amanda quietly asked her, "Is there anything I can do?"

"No, I'll be all right, Amanda. Thanks for asking."

The office was active with Amanda on the fly as usual. Zoë was busy working on a feature. Martin had meetings with advertisers, but by late morning, he came over to Zoë's desk and said cheerfully, "Let's go for a walk."

Connie and Amanda exchanged glances, and others could easily see what was happening as Martin and Zoë left. For her part, Zoë wasn't sure what was coming.

Outside, Martin said, "We're going to the park this time. It's a beautiful day. Let's get a coffee-to-go at Dickey's and find a place to sit and enjoy the scenery."

"Okay."

Zoë saw that Martin was in a good mood, speaking to people on the street and joking with the folks at Dickey's. He bought two lattes. At the park, they found a bench in the shade and sat. After a few moments, Martin said, "Are you feeling better today?"

"I'm feeling terribly guilty today, Martin. I want to apologize for the way I talked to you, yesterday. I am so sorry. I had no call to do that. I said things I shouldn't have. I don't really feel the way I sounded. You and everyone else here have been so good to me."

"Apology accepted. What are you going to do?"

"Well, I'm not quitting. I promised to stay here until July twelfth, so I'm staying."

"Good. But, what was behind your desire to push the conversation to the point that the subject of leaving here even came up? Why the attempted sabotage?" He paused and said, "You want to think about that a minute?"

"No. I've been thinking about that ever since I left you, yesterday." Wanting to be careful, she said, "I should never have made scapegoats out of you or anyone else I've met here, or this Wyoming culture, or used politics as an excuse, just because of a personal problem I may have. It was very unfair. I'm an adult—sometimes an emotional shit-head adult—but I need to learn how to take care of my own problems without lashing out at other people."

"That makes sense. But are you saying that your political stance isn't nearly as important as you made it out to be? Or are you just sorry that you said it?"

Zoë thought a minute and Martin let her. She quietly said, "Well, I do think the personal is political. *And* I am sorry I said what I did because it really isn't me."

"Zoë, everything one does in life isn't about *everything*."

"What do you mean?"

"Well, I'm not talking about the old militant feminism where 'the personal is political' came from. I mean everything one does in life doesn't have global significance. Oh, I know the drill. 'Don't eat that hamburger because you're affecting the food supply of starving Africans.' Most of them are starving because they live under the thumb of corrupt regimes looting their own countries. But my point is that it's pretty sanctimonious to want to view every move you make living your life

118

as having some tragic importance to the world. Do you really want to live sustaining that kind of self-righteousness? The world has an agenda—and by that I mean everybody is pulling at you or filling you with their vision of how everything is supposed to be—and the world wants you to become a part of that agenda. The pleas are relentless with 'don't you care?' or abject hatred if you don't buy in—if you don't *conform*. Whatever happened to independent thought? The world wants your fanatical commitment to its causes. The world wants your soul, Zoë. Be careful about how much of yourself—your integrity, your independence—you want to give up for other peoples' causes.

Zoe was speechless. What Martin said made sense—more so than she cared to admit—but she didn't quite know how to respond so she just shut up and let her boss talk some more.

"People around here resist that kind of thing because they see themselves as responsible to their families, their friends, their loved ones, and their work—and most importantly, themselves—the things they have some influence and control over. Spouting political rhetoric just doesn't do much for most of us here. People have too much work to do and they have lives that give them meaning. 'Know thyself,' Zoë.

"You said that what you said yesterday really isn't you. Do you know who you are, Zoë? Do you really want to be a journalist?"

She hesitated and said, "I wanted to be a journalist because my father put it into my head that I could be a television newscaster—it was just a suggestion; neither of my parents have ever told me what to do once I turned eighteen—and I bought it. Journalism seemed like a good education to pursue to get there. I didn't go to Columbia with a passion for the discipline, but I have enjoyed it, and I'm learning to love it. As for knowing who I am, I keep getting thrown curve balls, Martin, so I'd have to say I'm still working on it." She thought, "I've spent a good part of my life dealing with curve balls—failure at tennis and poor choices in men."

Martin calmly said, "Focus on that, Zoë. Think more about who you are and what is important in your life than on attaching yourself to worldly agendas, or even what your friends and family tell you—they are distractions. You have a good mind and you're full of life. Nurture what fills your life, your soul, and you'll do fine."

She thought that Martin had said all this in almost a fatherly way; he was trying to instruct her yet reassure her that she had integrity, that she was her own person. But her head was swimming and she wanted it to stop. She said, "You're in a pleasant mood today. I was worried that you'd be pretty unhappy with me after the things I said yesterday; yet you've treated me with kindness."

Smiling, he said, "I'm glad you see it that way. Most of the time I'm a glass-half-full guy, and there is no virtue for either of us turning this discussion into an ongoing fight. Also, I think I know why you were so grumpy yesterday."

"Why was that?"

"I think it's because you are afraid."

Puzzled, she asked, "Of what?"

"That you are beginning to like it here, and it goes against everything you thought you were before you got here—coming from the padded world of the university cocoon."

Zoë looked away for a moment as her eyes watered, then turned back to him. "I do like it here Martin, and it is becoming a problem."

Smiling, he said, "I understand."

She wasn't sure exactly what he understood but wished not to pursue it. She guessed that with the way Madge talks, perhaps word had gotten back to him about the previous weekend. But that didn't matter; she was going to have to figure out the Cody problem herself and keep politics out of it, especially since it had nothing to do with her 'Cody problem.'

He said, "Shall we go back?"

She gave a weak smile. "Yes, boss."

As they walked back to the office, Martin said, "I'd like to see some of your short stories."

"I'll e-mail a couple of my better ones, then you can decide if you want any more." She chuckled. "Dr. Wilhelm once said that 'the quality which makes someone want to write and be read is essentially a desire for self-exposure and is masochistic. Like one of those guys who has a compulsion to take his thing out and show it on the street.' James Jones apparently wrote those words, originally."

"I haven't heard that in ages. I suspect it's true. Author Steven Pressfield once said, 'Nobody wants to read your shit, not even your mother,' which was a way of saying that you need to avoid putting things into your work that only you are enamored with…stuff you love because you wrote it."

She nodded. "Have you decided how you want to handle the follow-up on the Jake Miller story? You said you wanted to think about it before turning me loose. Do you want it to be humorous, or a detailed, straight-up report, or do you want to downplay it?"

"As the man said in *The Man Who Shot Liberty Valance*, 'This is the West, sir. When the legend becomes fact, print the legend.' I want to bury Jake's story in a bland notice about his improved medical condition with little to explain what really happened. We'll put it on page seven. There was an accident. End of story. I should go riding with him while there's still time, not publish articles about his failings."

Speaking kindly, Zoë said, "So you're letting your personal friendship with Jake affect your willingness to provide an objective report of what actually happened?"

"You're damn right."

Zoë laughed; and as she locked her arm in his, she said, "Good." They continued back to the office saying nothing more.

Chapter 25

Seated behind his desk, Martin went through his mail, which included three letters to the editor. One handwritten letter particularly disturbed him. Of course, it wasn't signed. About half of the nasty, unprintable letters he received were unsigned and slipped under the door. The writers wanted to vent their rage but not spend any money on a stamp. This one was mailed locally. It simply said: "Your recent article on squatters living in the mountains was a piece of crap. Get rid of the Mexican kike who wrote it."

Martin set it aside, went through the rest of the mail, finding two other letters about Zoë's recent feature in which she analyzed the squatter problem. These praised her balanced approach, going on to say that some squatters lived that way because of hardship, or they were passing through and were careful to leave a small footprint, while others were making methamphetamine and poaching deer and elk.

Later, when he was with Zoë in the kitchen, Martin said, "I have something I need to show you." She followed him into his office where he asked her to sit down. Then, he handed her the letter criticizing her story.

Zoë scanned the lines, then looked up at Martin. "The writer thinks I'm part Mexican. How often do you get letters like this?"

"Infrequently, and I don't print any letter that isn't signed or is blatantly offensive."

"He apparently thought I was picking on him."

"It may have been a *her*. Squatters don't get delivery of the paper out there in the wilderness, and they generally don't have letter-writing materials and stamps, so whoever it was, happened to be in town for some reason. Either that or a friend of a squatter living around here was upset by your article. I want you to be aware of this kind of thing. I don't expect you to back off giving balanced reports on local issues that people may find controversial, but if this letter had indicated some kind of direct threat, I'd be calling the sheriff. I've had to do that before, and in all cases nothing has come of it. But I like the sheriff to be knowledgeable about such matters, and he wants to be, in case someone actually follows through on a threat."

"Perhaps I tweaked a sensitive matter involving illegal activities. Would the sheriff want to pursue some details?"

"I thought you referenced documented evidence from previous findings. Do you have information beyond that?"

"You're right. I don't really have any new details. I could try to get them, though."

"No. I don't want you exploring this squatter issue any further because you might compromise an ongoing investigation that I happen to know exists. We've done enough by raising general awareness. More importantly, it might put you in the middle of something involving some very dangerous characters. Your family and loved ones, not to mention Bud Wilhelm, would never forgive me if anything happened to you. And I wouldn't forgive myself."

"Thanks. I don't want anything to happen to me, either. But aren't investigative reporters supposed to stick their necks out?"

"Yes and no…if there was something to go on, then maybe we'd pursue it. As you know, Rick is a good investigative reporter…he has a good knowledge of the subject. Fortunately, what goes on in Wyoming isn't nearly as bad as what's happening in northern California. Also, I don't particularly want to send out people on fishing expeditions when law enforcement is trying to do its job. We don't want to further tweak any perpetrators of illegal drug activity just to sell papers.

"Besides, I want to give you another controversial topic to explore: the pros and cons of introducing wolves into Wyoming. We did a piece about a year ago, but there are new elements to examine given Washington's new approach. This subject has plenty of drama, and we both know somebody who knows a lot about it since he has a rancher's perspective and also works for the Forest Service."

"You mean Cody Nelson."

"Yes, I mean Cody Nelson. You need to conduct an in-depth interview with him. The Forest Service doesn't have official jurisdiction—Fish and Wildlife manages endangered species—but Cody has a balanced view and can direct you to some people that you can quote officially."

"I can do that."

Chapter 26

Cody tried to reach Zoë again on Wednesday evening.

This time, Zoë looked at her caller ID and answered her phone. "Hi Cody."

"Hello. I've tried to reach you a couple times since Sunday." He didn't wait for an explanation, and none was forthcoming. "I was wondering if you'd like to go to a movie, Thursday night. It's the one night a month our theater in town shows art movies, foreign films, or old classics…the same as you find on Turner Classic Movies, but it's fun to see them on the big screen. The other nights, it shows first-run movies after they've played someplace else. Anyway, tomorrow is an old Bogart film called, *To Have and Have Not*. I've never seen it."

Zoë thought it might be a good way to ease into ending the relationship, spend some time letting her mind zone out on a boring old movie, but still have a chance to broach the subject and focus on her original plans. Also, she could interview him about wolves. She said, "Sure. I read the book. It's one of Hemingway's stinkers, but I read somewhere that the movie is better. What time?"

"The movie starts at seven-thirty. How about I pick you up at seven-ten?"

"Okay. See you then."

"Zoë, are you okay?"

"I'm fine. I'm just tired from working hard. I do need to see you about your perspective on wolves. Martin wants me to do an article. But I need to get a shower now. I'll see you tomorrow. Bye."

Cody picked her up on the appointed day and time. Zoë was cordial and pleasant, talking about Mrs. Granger, Amanda, and little mundane events at work, using chatter to fill any possible voids. She could sense that Cody was a little uncomfortable, no doubt because she'd avoided him for three days.

After the movie, Cody said, "I'd like a cup of coffee. Does that sound good to you?"

She said that it did and locked her arm in his, close, as a strong wind blew down the street. She lowered her head into his shoulder to block it. They proceeded to walk to the Demming Café.

Over coffee, Cody said, "Tell me about the Hemingway book—you said you'd read it—and the differences between it and the movie."

"It's about Depression-era life in Key West and Cuba during my grandparents' time. As I remember, I had difficulty actually caring about any of the characters. They were all flawed, broken people. Like in the movie, the main character is a charter fishing boat captain who gets ripped off by his client. In the book, he resorts to smuggling to support his wife and three daughters. He doesn't even like his girls. He just feels an obligation. The adventures mount, and I forget how, but he kills a bunch of bank robbers with a Thompson sub-machine gun and is mortally wounded in the process, leaving his wife wondering what the hell she is going to do. At the end, life goes on in a depressing way. It's a dark book."

"And the movie? What did you think?"

"It's an entirely different story. Did you notice in the opening credits that William Faulkner worked on the screenplay? That, alone, helped me appreciate it more. But, on balance, it was a dated and corny film. It's a man's movie. My father or older men familiar with the nineteen-forties would enjoy it more."

"A man's movie?"

"Yeah…gorgeous young babe falls in love with homely older man who saves her from the bad guys…every old guy's fantasy. I did think it interesting how they worked in such sexy scenes back when censorship didn't allow the kind of thing we see in films today."

"Yeah, like when Slim says, 'You don't have to act with me, Steve. You don't have to say anything and you don't have to do anything.' She said something else but I can't remember the exact lines, then 'Maybe just whistle. You know how to whistle don't you Steve? You just put your lips together and blow.' I also liked the line when Slim says, 'I'm hard to get, Steve. All you have to do is ask me.'"

Zoë didn't say anything, but that last quote had registered with her during the movie and again when Cody repeated it.

Cody went on, "I read a couple Hemingway books. My favorite was *The Sun Also Rises*. Once, I was with a girl in the library at school discussing the main character, Jake Barnes. I said I liked the part where Jake says his sexual inabilities from the war injury only bothered him at night. Those weren't the exact words, but that was the point. And this girl tells me I'm a romantic. I wasn't sure whether that was a good thing or a bad thing."

Zoë only displayed a soft smile as she said, "Could we talk about wolves—the pros and cons of the recovery program under the Endangered Species Act? And what about this talk of hunting them again?"

"Sure. I'll tell you what I know."

Cody talked as Zoë took notes. Twenty minutes later, Cash McCall entered the café with a gum-chewing girl in spiked heels. She had frizzy blonde hair, too much makeup, and wore a velvety, fake leopard blouse over tight black pants covered with blond dog hair. Cash noticed Cody and Zoë, but only gave a weak nod in their direction as he tried to direct the girl to a booth far away. Frizzy noticed them and hollered, "Hey there, Cody! I haven't seen you in ages, darlin'." She began dragging Cash over to their booth.

Cody said, "Zoë, meet Penny Haines. Penny, meet Zoë Valiente. Cash, I think you and Zoë have already met."

Penny smacked her gums and glared at Cash, saying, "You have?"

Zoë said, "Yes, I was on a manhunt at the Wagon Wheel almost two weeks ago, and Cash taught me all about chariot racing."

Cody just watched the fun as Penny now appeared to want to get as far away from the pair as she could. She pulled Cash across the cafe, saying, "You never told me about that, darlin'. What were you doin' at the Wagon Wheel with that *girl*? Who is she, anyway?"

Cody and Zoë could hear Cash on the other side of the restaurant say, "Shut up and sit down, Penny."

Grinning, Zoë leaned over the table toward Cody and said, quietly, "I guess that voice is a prime example of shrill?"

"Yes, I'd say so."

Sitting back, she added, "What's their story?"

"Cash is a bricklayer and stone mason by trade and has been known to drink a little. Penny is a grocery clerk by day and a floozy by night. She calls everybody 'darlin'.' She had an abortion a couple years ago and talks openly about it."

"And how does that go down with people living here?"

"Most of them are pro-life, but they also know who Penny is and know she'll have to live with it."

"And what are you—pro-life or pro-choice?"

"I am pro-choice. Just this morning I chose grapefruit juice instead of orange juice at breakfast, and I chose to ask you to a movie tonight."

"You know what I mean."

"Oh, that. Well, I am pro-choice…but reluctantly so."

"What do you mean?"

"I mean that I have empathy for the autonomy of a woman—having control over her own body, so it is her choice—but I also think it can be a rather disgusting choice."

"What about women's health?"

"This whole topic was bantered about when Penny got her abortion, so I've heard the health argument. But I would bet that of the—what is it?—almost forty-five million abortions since 1973? I'd bet a relatively small percentage has anything to do with women's health unless it's been completely dumbed down. In other words, poor health requiring surgical intervention now means, 'I'll be really upset if I have this baby. It will mess up my plans.'"

"So you think it's a casual decision for women?"

"No. I do not doubt that it is a gut-wrenching decision for a great number of women. One they live with for a long time. But I also think some women look at it as just another birth control option, which is what Penny appeared to do."

"And now she's hated for it?"

Looking puzzled, Cody said, "No, most people feel sorry for her. And they feel sorry for the little girl that got snuffed. What? Is this a test?"

"No!" But she looked down at her coffee knowing she was lying. She knew what she was doing. She was going to dig until she found something to give her an excuse to stop the relationship from progressing further. Then she could say to herself, "I really liked him, but I couldn't handle his views on…whatever." Then, she could remain unchanged. She'd be safe. She could stay until July, do her job, and avoid becoming entangled with Cody...something she needed to do because becoming involved with him had no future.

A short time later, at the door of Mrs. Granger's house, she was nervous and quiet, feeling the tension between them, but not showing it. Cody just looked at her with a mildly disappointed face. They stood close and he reached for her hand; she let him take it but offered no encouragement. He said, "I don't know what's happened but I feel like I'm getting very mixed signals from last weekend compared to tonight."

With some defiance, she said, "Are you telling me I'm being pissy?"

"Would you prefer that I avoid being honest—act as though nothing's changed when I can see that it has?"

She said, "no," and offered no further comment. But she was frustrated. She didn't really want to be mean to him, so she looked down avoiding direct eye contact.

Finally, after what seemed to Zoë like two full minutes, he said, "Zoë, please don't let this just end. You know as well as I do that there is something here for us." After a pause, he let go her hand and departed.

She watched him go, turned and entered the house. She went up to her room and sat down on her bed. Her shoulders were slumped and she stared at the floor thinking what a bitch she had been—and he didn't deserve that at all. After a long time—long enough for her to feel her poor posture causing tension in her neck—she slowly got ready for bed. When she crawled in, she turned out the light, curled around her pillow and cried, "What am I doing? I really like him. What am I going to do?"

Chapter 27

Russ had found the furnished cabin to rent on the Internet. He'd arranged with Mrs. Robinson, the half-owner, to lease it for the summer. Mrs. Robinson's husband had suffered a stroke, and the family would not need their summer place for the foreseeable future. Russ had given her an estimate of his arrival after departing California, but also called her during his travels to arrange a specific time to meet her at the cabin. He wanted a walkthrough, and he needed to obtain a key. He had seen pictures of the inside and outside since she had emailed them to him before he agreed to the three-month lease. The place looked quite nice.

He arrived before she did and was impressed with the cabin's appearance and location. It sat on ten acres of wooded land on a ridge, but with enough cleared trees to have a view south. It was off a quiet dirt road and had a fairly long dirt driveway when one considered the necessity of snow removal. He thus understood one good reason why this was a summer place.

The cabin was thirty years old, built in a very rustic style, and was about fourteen hundred square feet in size. It had a large front porch with the main door in the center, plus a large wood-burning fireplace at one end of the house. He'd been informed electric heat would warm the place during cool summer evenings, but he guessed the fireplace would be a less-expensive way to provide heat. There was a huge stack of wood available outside, located at the back of the house.

The original advertisement had indicated a living-dining-kitchen area plus one bedroom, a bath, and small laundry closet on the main floor. The second floor consisted of another bedroom, bath, and a small loft. There was a separate two-car garage on the property.

He was peeking in the window when a red Cadillac Escalade quickly pulled into the driveway, its driver slamming on the brakes so that the car narrowly missed the U-haul parked by the cabin.

Mrs. Robinson got out, looking like a best-dressed model for geriatrics. She wore a stunning outfit. She had big hair, dyed black. Her taut skin told Russ that she'd had more than a couple plastic surgeries to remove wrinkles from her face. He imagined that she wore the turtleneck to cover a wrinkly neck. "California has reached Colorado," Russ thought.

She jovially introduced herself and said, "May I call you Russ?"

"Yes, by all means."

"Good. You can call me Mrs. Robinson, Russ. You aren't into plastics by any chance, are you?"

"I was. Exotic metals, Kevlar and carbon fibers, and high tech plastic materials."

"You don't get the joke, do you? Mrs. Robinson…'hey, hey, hey'… plastics. The movie, T*he Graduate*?"

Smiling, he said, "I do, now."

"Such a serious young man."

"I'm not so young. I'm fifty-three."

"Well, let's just say I'm a little older than that, therefore you're young. Let's walk through the house, and I'll show you where everything is. We haven't been here for so long that I had some people come in a few days ago and give it a good spring cleaning and wash the windows."

"That was very nice of you."

"You're darn right it was."

As they proceeded, Russ asked, "How is your husband doing?"

"Not too well. We're talking about selling this place, although we hate to…thinking about just staying in Cherry Creek. Would you like to rent it for more than the summer, maybe for a year? I can cut you a deal."

"I don't know. I can imagine that snow removal could be a problem during the winters."

"Not really. The road is actually a school route, even though there aren't that many people up here, so the county does a good job keeping it plowed. And there are two neighbors who have tractors with plows that look after most of the folks living here year 'round. We used to come up during the winters in years past and never had a problem with the roads or the driveway. We did occasionally have to scrape ice off the car windows if we left the car out, though. Regardless, sometimes we just stayed in, read books, and watched the fire."

"I just don't know where I'm going to land, or what I'm going to do. Let me get settled first and…"

"It's not like it's a booming real estate market, so enjoy the area and think about it a while. If you want to stay, give me a call."

She showed him around, told him how everything worked, pointing out the décor and where everything was purchased. He noted the expensive furnishings—the log bedroom sets, the quality leather couches, the log dining table and chairs, the rustic furnishings out of *Architectural Digest*, including the kitchen ware. Though small, it was a rich couple's retreat. He considered that most people would probably furnish such a place with things they no longer wanted in their main house. It was very nice, and he quickly assumed that he was going to like the place.

It had a 42-inch LCD HDTV with a satellite available if he wanted to get it connected, but she told him, "Other than that, entertainment within the cabin will have to be generated by you and whomever you bring in with you. You replace the wood burned—there's a lot of deadfall on the property—and no smokers please. Anything broken, you replace."

These last things were part of the lease, but apparently she wanted to solidify it verbally. Russ said simply, "Got it."

"Also, since we haven't been here for several months due to my husband's condition, I cleaned out all the food so the mice wouldn't have anything to keep them here. There isn't even any salt and pepper. I did leave some paper products and cleaning supplies. There's a Safeway and a King Soopers a few miles east on the main highway. Either store will have what you'll need to stock up."

He asked her about the neighbors. She told him there were a couple with horses—they were the ones with tractors—and there were other younger families nearby with school-aged kids. Older working couples, a few retired folks, and others who kept to themselves rounded out the residents living in the area. There were no single women in the neighborhood, so he needed to watch out for angry husbands if he were so inclined to show interest in the area's pretty females. Some of the men had guns. Further, as far as she knew, there were no murderers or crazy cultists living in the region. He'd find out soon enough who the Republicans were and who were the Democrats. She said she suspected that most of the neighbors would know fairly quickly that a single young man was living in the Robinson house. Somebody might even invite him to a party. They had a block party at least once every summer, sometimes more often.

Russ said, "You don't get the sense that many people actually live up here. It's so quiet, and you cannot see many of the houses."

"At night, you'll look over to that hill over there, and you'll see lots of lights from houses you can't see during the day. That's what they see when they look over here. I have one restaurant recommendation for you."

"What is it?"

"Hank's Diner. It's a breakfast and lunch place with really good food, three miles down the road. Try their grilled raisin bread. It's located at Hank's Junction. They call it that, but there really is no such place officially. It's just a crossroad. Be careful, though. You could get fat eating there too often."

Russ watched her depart, driving way too fast, and then began unloading the trailer. His tools, bicycles, and the boxes of books and engineering drawings went into the garage. As he worked, he spied one of the most beautiful red foxes he'd ever seen lope across the driveway. It stopped and looked at him, then proceeded without any interest in the strange human and his activities.

Then he unloaded the truck, moving everything into the house to where he thought it might end up. He didn't want to unpack any of it yet since he was hungry.

Now that Mrs. Robinson was gone, he thoroughly inspected the whole house, working out a list of needs. He washed, locked the cabin, and drove out to the main route to Denver, passing Hank's because it was closed. Then he came to a small town where he saw a Safeway store off to the right. He stopped, loaded up on food and necessities from his list. He asked the girl at the checkout counter where the nearest Costco was, and she told him how to get there. It was about thirty minutes away. "Down the hill," she said. He wanted to make a Costco run for some of the items that made sense to buy in bulk.

Within two days, he was settled with food in the pantry, the refrigerator and freezer reasonably stocked, some laundry done, and clothes in the closets and drawers. He'd returned the U-haul and opened a local bank account in Gilson, the town with the Safeway store. He'd met two of the neighbors—one mother and her twelve-year-old daughter who brought him banana bread. Settling in had been easy. This was indeed a nice place.

After cleaning up after an easy dinner of grilled chicken, wild rice, and green beans, and with nothing further that needed to be done, Russ sat on the big, comfy leather chair with his mind blank. Then the thought that always entered the void when he didn't want it to, rushed in: "God, it's so lonely without you, Sara. What am I going to do?" He broke down and cried.

After Grace's auto accident three years ago, Russ had buried himself in work as his way of escaping the pain of her death. Sara grew deeply depressed and stopped paying attention to her health. She hadn't been to the doctor in years. so the breast cancer she didn't know she had, metastasized into the lungs, bones, and elsewhere. When they found it, it was too late. Russ felt guilty for not being alert to her needs, for not getting her to a doctor earlier. If he had, maybe the cancer would have been caught in time. As it was, she was gone—seven months now. This is what always drove him to despair, this recurring feeling he was having.

Chapter 28

Cody didn't call Zoë after their date Thursday evening. Saturday, he went fly fishing with his father and brother on the Lewis River. The Lewis River flows south from Shoshone Lake, through Lewis Lake, and then goes over a series of falls and through a gorge, merging with the Snake River near the south boundary of Yellowstone National Park. Sunday, the day after his fishing trip, Cody helped out on the family farm after church.

Cody hadn't said anything to her, but Zoë had heard on Friday what he was doing. Small towns have a way of letting information flow, even when it isn't solicited. On Monday, Zoë was still troubled, feeling crappy about her situation and missing Cody. But she was afraid of making any kind of commitment. Also, a new thought entered her mind. Perhaps she didn't trust her ability to discern what a good man was, or what love really was. She said to herself, "You don't exactly have a decent track record here, Zoë." She didn't know what to do other than busy herself with work.

This same day, a large note card arrived for her. It was from Cody. And everybody knew it since Josey announced it as she sorted the mail. Upon opening it, Zoë saw that the cover had a picture of the Tetons. She read the note, wanting to appear detached from its content in front of her colleagues. It said:

> Dear Zoë,
> I don't know the rules anymore. I'm old-fashioned. I ask a girl
> out, pick her up on time, open the truck door, and I'm considerate.

I walk her to the door afterward. If it goes well, I ask her out again. Those things don't mean people fall in love, but it is how you treat people with respect.

I've never met anybody like you. You scare me, but I can't stop. I'm taking a risk. I fell in love with you that first day we met. I knew I loved you when you spoke to Jake when he was sitting in that lawn chair. Standing there with you, after you hugged Jake, I let your hand go, but then I said to myself, 'I want her. I don't know how it's going to work, but I want her.' But I won't go where I'm not wanted, or where I'm being evaluated against some standard I don't even understand. Please call me, and let's take a chance together.

Love,
Cody

With everybody watching, Zoë stuffed the note into her canvas brief case and said, "Amanda, we have to talk." Josey and Connie and others said, "Hey, we want to hear." But Amanda just laughed, and Zoë said nothing.

Later, over lunch, Zoë said to Amanda, "You promise to keep this a secret?"

"Wild horses couldn't drag it out of me."

"When was the last time you had lunch with a wild horse? I need to know that I can trust you."

Zoë thought Amanda seemed a little hurt by her words, but she was only seeking help and assurances. Before she could say anything, Amanda looked directly into Zoë's eyes and said, "I can keep your secret for as long as you want me to."

Zoë breathed easily, squeezed Amanda's hand, and handed her the note.

Amanda read it a couple times and then said, "It's corny, but kind of cute."

"That's what I thought. I liked the phrase, 'open the truck door.' Most people would say, 'open the car door,' but he doesn't have a car."

"Is that what struck you most?"

"No. I'm just easing into this conversation. What struck me most was his bold admission that he loves me."

"Yeah, after one afternoon picnic. It doesn't seem like Cody. He's not that rash."

"Oh, there was more than one afternoon picnic involved!"

"Really? Okay Zoë, we've got to talk."

"That's what I said."

They talked…or rather, Zoë talked and Amanda listened. Finally, Amanda was on the spot to say something. "Okay, let me feed this back to make sure I've got it straight. You've had lots of boyfriends over the years, and except for early teen hormonal puppy love, there were three times when you felt like a relationship might get serious enough to involve marriage. The first time was with a stud tennis player from Argentina. Then, somewhere along the line, he got a crush on Hanna Kichnakova, which went nowhere, but he'd already dropped you when he thought he'd struck gold with her. After that, there was a long string of 'just dates,' and you've never been interested in just hooking up for a night, like waking up in the morning next to some guy saying, 'What's your name again?'

"You don't have any sexually transmitted diseases, and you do want to find the right guy and get married and have kids, eventually. The last two boyfriends—which you thought, at various times, might bring you real love—you eventually dropped because they were jerks. So you don't trust yourself enough to know how to pick the right guy, or know when love is true love. Got it so far?"

"Yes, that's about right."

"Okay, so now you've launched your new career—not a bad thing really—but you meet this cool guy and had a grand time with him over one weekend. And you're afraid that he's going to screw your life up if you let things happen with him and then you'll never get Katie Couric's job. And you might regret it when you find out that he just wants you to keep him supplied with beer—like Goldie Hawn living with Kurt Russell in that crazy old movie *Overboard*—while he belches and farts his way through college football games on TV."

"I didn't say that!"

"I know. I was thinking about my Cory. Sorry. Where were we? Oh, yeah, so now you're into your career, and you're hyper about politics, and you meet this guy from a whole different culture who is going to screw it all up. Oh, wait! I already said that. Anyway, you're scared. Right this time?"

"I wouldn't say 'hyper.'"

"From what you said about your conversation with Martin, I would! How about over-stimulated. Would that work?"

"It means the same thing."

"I know, and I'm not giving it up. Look, I'll just say it straight up. The most important things in life have to do with loving relationships— something that I failed at once but am still going after—and family, and good friends, and one's faith…and hopefully one can love their work."

"Faith?"

"Yes. I'm not defining faith, here. *Everybody* has faith in something. They just won't admit it. I happen to believe in the Christian God and Jesus Christ. I happen to believe there is a spiritual realm to the universe that is filled with mystery beyond our material reality. Others believe in stoning young girls to death if they've been raped, or they believe in their horoscope, or crystals, or a witch doctor, or their government, or money, or themselves, or that they'll have another beer. Some even believe that when they die, they're no different than a mangled deer alongside the road, so why not live it up?"

"We haven't talked about any of this."

"Okay, but don't you personally struggle with the big life questions?

"Amanda, I'm struggling with one right now—Cody has become a big life question."

"Yeah, that's why we're talking, isn't it? Look, I've always wanted to know, 'Why is there something rather than nothing? Why am I here?' Anyway, I don't know if this is fair, and I hate psychobabble, but you seem to have attached yourself to your 'different' life and politics as an escape. I'm talking about your diatribe with Martin here. It doesn't matter what kind of politics we're talking about, either. Golly, you could find places all around the country with overstimulated right-wingers doing the same thing—wallowing in their beliefs like they know what the hell they're talking about, like they have all the answers to every issue out there.

"People do that, you know, with a lot of stuff. They can't figure out their own meaningless lives so they fret and worry themselves to death about things they can't control. Or, they simply attach themselves to some cause because it's the only thing that makes them feel like they have worth. They get all drippy about it. It's where they find their identity.

"From what you said, you love your family back in Florida, but your own love life has sucked, your friendships have been mostly superficial, you have no BFFs, and you couldn't make it in the tennis world, which really frustrated you. And your faith? I don't know what your faith is. Maybe it's faith in Democrats. My question is, are you going to give up this guy just so you can work for the frigging DNC for a few weeks? That's going to make you happy? That's going to make you flourish? No, don't answer that right now. Think about it. I'll tell you this. There isn't anything you don't already know about Cody Nelson that is bad. It sounds like he's made up his mind, rather quickly, that he wants you. Now it's up to you. It's your choice. Love is a choice."

"Yeah…it is?"

"Yes! Good things are sometimes given to us, but they have to be chosen. They have to be accepted to be experienced."

Zoë just sat there saying nothing, staring at her salad plate.

Amanda asked, "So what are you going to do?"

"I thought you just said I should think about it."

"I did, but I really want to know what you're going to do."

Zoë smiled and said, "I don't know, Amanda. What I want to do right now is jump his bones."

"It's probably a good thing he's not here. The town has never seen anything like that in public, and you'd get arrested."

That made Zoë laugh outright but, sobering quickly, she said, "But in a couple hours, I'll probably revert back to thinking I need to find a way to gracefully stop this. I had other plans. I don't want to hurt him but...I don't know."

"You don't want to hurt him. Is that out of a general kind of kindness or guilt or because he matters to you?"

The women fell silent, then Amanda went on, "He's gotten to you, hasn't he?"

Zoë looked away, but could feel Amanda staring at her. Then she turned to her new friend and said softly, "I have a question that I don't have an answer to, and I don't expect that you do either: why did Cody and I meet? I didn't come here looking for this. Why did this happen?"

"You're right. I don't have an answer...except...sometimes good things happen to good people."

Chapter 29

As the day progressed, the deadlines of work allowed Zoë to avoid daydreaming about Cody and their relationship. In her free time, she wanted to call him, but resisted, and thoughts of him weighed heavily on her. She wondered about the complications that would arise if she gave her heart to this guy she hardly knew.

That night, she slept fitfully, sometimes angry with herself for allowing her relationship with Cody to get as far as it had, and so quickly, too. But mostly, she just clutched her pillow. She was beginning to resign herself to the fact that she was in love, a gripping kind of love…and there wasn't anything she could do about it. She had already given her heart to him, and for her to change that course would bring on a pain she didn't want to bear…and for what?

It took her a while to figure out how to approach Cody. It was early afternoon on Tuesday when she called the Miller ranch. Madge answered the phone on the first ring. "Madge, oh, I'm glad I got you. This is Zoë."

Speaking softly, Madge said, "Yeah, I can tell. I'm sitting by the phone 'cuz Jake and Kay are nappin'. What can I do for ya?"

"I have a big favor to ask. When you see Cody come home from work, please call me. If you don't call, I'll assume he didn't get home before you went to bed."

As she gave Madge her number, Zoë added, "And please don't tell him I called, but also don't let him leave. I have to see him."

"Well, I don't know if I can stop him from leavin' if he wants to. Shall I shoot out his tires if he tries to go? I'm a pretty good shot."

"Madge…"

"Okay, I'll handle it, dear. You're going to surprise him, huh?"

"I'm not sure."

Zoë got the call from Madge at six-fifteen that evening. She had already showered, and since the day was hot, she had put on comfortable yellow shorts, a white sleeveless blouse, and sandals. But she took some tennis shoes and socks with her when she left the house, in case she might end up walking in the barn, as well as a jacket for when the sun went down. Trying not to be anxious, she drove the van only ten miles an hour over the speed limit, parked upon arriving at the ranch, and seeing no one outside, walked directly to Cody's ugly rented mobile home.

Zoë knocked and Cody hollered, "Come in." Zoë entered and found him slicing green onions on a cutting board. She closed the door and stood there, saying nothing. Cody turned and looked at her, a paring knife in one hand and onions in the other. She noticed he was wearing tan shorts, a loose, olive-green T-shirt, and no shoes or socks.

He didn't smile. His expression was one of mild wonderment as he said, "I should probably put this knife down."

"You probably should. I wouldn't want to get hurt. You can put the onions down, too."

"I was just fixing a tostado. But I think I'll wait now."

"That would be a good idea."

He dropped the knife and the onions, quickly wiped his wet hands on a towel, walked over to where Zoë was standing and kissed her. Lovingly, she kissed him back. Cody kissed her more, pulling her close as he nuzzled her neck, ears, and eyes. She was getting weak in the knees. After some time, she finally said, "Wait. I need you to know some things. I need you to know that I'm frightened. I need you to know why I'm here."

"You want us to calm down."

"No, I don't." Zoë pushed him to the couch, where they fell. They kissed, and he fondled her gently but held back from any real sexual advance. After a time, and much passionate kissing, Cody said, "Zoë, we'd better slow down."

They relaxed, but he still kissed her face gently. She melted into a state of pure calm, and they stopped rubbing each other. They lay together on the couch, simply holding each other, Zoë sensing the slowing down of their breathing.

Cody said, "I want you to see the sunset tonight from that little ridge up there." He pointed out the back window. "I'll see if we can get some better shoes for you. It's just a short hike."

"I brought tennis shoes. I didn't know if we might be walking in the barn."

"How did you know I was even here?"

"I have spies."

"Madge?"

"Uh-uh."

"I love that woman. Are you hungry or thirsty?"

"I'm thirsty. I don't think I can eat right now."

"Me, neither. I have water, diet Coke, Moose Drool, Stone IPA, and red wine."

"I'd like some water and a glass of red wine, please…a big glass. I look a little disheveled, don't I?"

"You look great!" And he kissed her passionately once more.

Zoë tucked in her wrinkled blouse, fluffed her hair with her hands since her comb was in her purse in the van, and they went outside. Cody carried his IPA; Zoë grasped a glass of merlot. They strolled across the yard, holding hands and watching horses graze in a distant pasture. Near the barn, they could see Jake in the round pen leading an animated Steely Dan in circles, working to calm him down. They waved, but he didn't see them.

At the house, Madge and Kay peeked out at them from a window. They didn't notice.

Cody said, "I know we have things we need to say, but can we just let this happen naturally? Everything will come out in time."

Zoë squeezed his hand and leaned toward him, saying, "I like that idea. I don't want to have a meeting. I just want to be with you."

144

Chapter 30

Russ soon created a simple routine in his new Colorado surroundings. One day, as he fixed his normal oatmeal breakfast, he thought, "Now the hard part." He needed to go see Sam and Elsie in Fort Collins. Sara's parents were wonderful people, but this was a difficult time for them. In particular, life hadn't been easy on Sam lately.

Russ hadn't seen them since Sara's funeral, although he'd talked to Sam many times. One Sunday in June, he met them at their church. After the service, they had lunch at the couple's house.

After the meal, while enjoying hot tea, Russ said, "Sam, I see now what you've been telling me about Elsie…how much she has deteriorated with her Alzheimer's. I guess that's why you wanted to have lunch here. Speaking of which, you make a very good vegetable soup, Sam."

"Thanks, Russ. Soups are my specialty. As for Elise, she's been in a fairly rapid decline ever since Sara's death. What about you? How are you handling things, Russ? I'm glad to see you've moved to Colorado, even if it's temporary. California is a fine place to live if you're a grape or an orange."

"Well, I found this neat little cabin to live in, very well appointed, but I'm too new here to have involved myself in any activities, yet, or meet many people."

"You don't want to just do nothing. It's very hard to do…you never know when you're finished."

Russ laughed. "Okay, where did you get that one?"

"It's a Leslie Nielson quote, or something close to it. As a minister, I was a closet comedian, and I stole all my lines. Do you think God will forgive me?"

"I certainly hope so! And I do know that it's not healthy to just mope around. I know that I need to find some things to do to work my body and my mind. Sara wouldn't want me to wither away, and I don't want to, either. I also need to make some friends."

"Well, you need to look to your future because that's where you're going to spend the rest of your life. I assume you are okay financially."

"Yes, I have everything I need. I don't want much."

"Well, you can't have everything. Where would you put it?" Sam paused and asked gently, "Are you still angry with Sara for dying?"

"No, Sam. I'm angry with me for not noticing her pain, for being so wrapped up in my work as my own way of dealing with Grace's death that I didn't focus enough on her. Sara was my shining star—strong, beautiful, my best friend. She knew me like a book. God, I miss her. It really hurts. Every day I wake up she's not there, and I miss her."

Sam said, "You remember that famous Woody Allen line, 'I tended to place my wife under a pedestal'?"

Russ nodded, wondering why Sam would mention it.

"Well, at least you never did that with Sara. You never put her under a pedestal. Look, Russ, there was no way for you to have known that she had cancer. You couldn't have known."

"I know, Sam. Somehow it doesn't help."

"You both have suffered a lot. And I can tell you, it's tough on us old folks losing a daughter. You're not supposed to outlive your children. It's a law. It's in the Bible."

"No, it isn't, Sam."

"I know, but it should be. My own way of dealing with losing a daughter and a granddaughter, dealing with Elsie's declining state, and just getting old, is to crack jokes. It's Elsie's nap time. Let me get her settled. Then, what do you say that we put on the Rockies game and play some chess?"

"You'll beat me again."

"That's why I want to play. I'm not doing it with an expectation of losing."

"Okay, I'll clean up the dishes while you take care of Elsie. Then I want to tell you about the cabin where I'm living and the owner, Mrs. Robinson. I'll try to distract you, so you make a mistake."

Chapter 31

On a Thursday in mid-June, Zoë and Amanda went to lunch together. Having exhausted herself trying to pump Zoë for information about her Tuesday and Wednesday evenings with Cody, Amanda was having fun sparring with her friend. This time, she tried a different subject. "Okay Zoë, you've been here a little while. What have you noticed about the staff?"

"Let's see…off the top of my head, I see that you and Betsy are the most energetic. I like that about you, Amanda. You get an assignment, and you charge right into it. If there is a gap in the work, you go looking for some. You're like a hummingbird in heat."

They both howled and then realized they were making too much noise and quieted down. Amanda said, "You are the same way. And I know you impress Martin with your focus on your work."

"I'm not so sure that I impressed him a while ago when I unloaded… telling him that he wasn't doing enough with his editorials."

"You need to stop beating yourself up over that. We've been through that. He's resilient when he's criticized, and he likes your work. What else have you noticed?"

"I notice that Rick seems awfully placid around the office, and he never looks at me. When I went out with him one day on assignment, he was all business. He sounded like a cop interviewing certain people and then with others, he sounded like a priest. He was very good at getting the information, but he pretty much treated me as the intern I am. He thinks the world of Martin…very loyal."

"Okay, here is some office gossip," said Amanda. "Martin lost a good reporter about seven years ago to alcohol, so he advertised and found Rick. The guy had been an English professor at CU in Boulder, CO and was accused of sexual harassment by a student, then placed on administrative leave. Rick's wife left him, which was in the works prior to the whole mess, but it lent support to the harassment charge, at least among the gossipers.

"Martin knew all about this during the hiring process. Anyway, outside the office, Rick is personable with the public and professional. Inside, he is aloof, only conversing with women in a detached manner and only when other people are around. The women in the office would be much more open with him, but he keeps us at arm's length. Nobody likes it, but it probably should be expected."

"No doubt he's afraid to get too close or to be seen as getting too close."

"He does have a girlfriend, Stephanie, but she's not a topic of discussion because for Rick, nothing personal is a topic of discussion around here."

Zoë said, "All the other guys seem very relaxed, easy to get along with. I sometimes think Tom lurks around me a bit too much. He's always under foot."

Amanda laughed. "Zoë, he's gay!"

Laughing with her, Zoë said, "Oh, I didn't know that."

"He keeps it well hidden. Who else can we talk about?"

"Well, Betsy hustles and bustles, and the other ladies are diligent workers, but not as driven. The men, however—Phil, Tom and Rick— they all seem so much more laid back."

Amanda was animated and said, "Yes, but it doesn't seem to affect the quality of their work. They just approach things without the aggressiveness that people think men should have…the cultural view of the driven man climbing the ladder of success. I think men, in general, have decided that if women want to rule the world, then, well, it's like a lot of them agree. They never went to a convention or took a vote about it, or anything like that. But still, they seem to say, 'Go ahead. For the last fifty years, you've been bitching about the lousy job we've been doing, so have at it. It's your turn. Good luck.' It's subtle, and perhaps it's just anecdotal evidence based on my observations of the office here, but not one guy even tries to compete with any woman here…for anything…*anything*. It's as if their mothers said to them, 'I am woman, hear me roar,' and each of them responded, 'Roar at each other. I'm going fishing.'"

"You think this is the way men have reacted to feminism?"

"I said it was possibly based on anecdotal evidence here in the office. I can't speak for what it may be like elsewhere or everywhere."

"Okay. Even with that, Amanda, Martin certainly acts like the boss 'here in the office.'"

"He *is* the boss. He owns the place, though he's not arrogant about it. But what I just said is even true with him. If one of us really wanted to do something, take over a responsibility, he'd agree…unless it compromised the integrity or the solvency of the business. He's never turned me down when I've asked to take on some new responsibility. Not once. As a consequence, I've had to learn to be careful what I ask for."

Zoë said, "Most of my experience with this has been in the tennis world and at school. In competitive tennis, I think both men and women are *really* driven to succeed. It's all about beating the person across the net. You want to annihilate your opponent. In school, there certainly are more women getting degrees than men, all over the country. School life can be very competitive. Oh, I forgot the restaurant business—my family—the Cuban side; that's still dominated by the men. And you have to consider that not all men are alike any more than all women are alike. We all have different personality types."

Amanda said, "Look, I may be all wet, but just watch and see if you find this undercurrent, this changing trend in attitudes."

"If it were true, I suppose another question to ask would be, is it a good thing or a bad thing?"

Amanda said, "Well I see it as a good thing, except that we'll probably be the overstressed ones getting ulcers and dying off early from heart attacks, and the men will be filling the nursing homes."

A thought hit Zoë quickly, and she said, "Not for people like Jake. What a special old gentleman he is. I see him wanting to leave this life out somewhere in the hills on a horse."

Amanda said, "Yeah…on Fandango."

"What are you saying?"

"I am not saying he went out to die—to commit suicide—but I am saying he will not stop trying to be what he is inside. And someday it might kill him. He's always been what he wanted to be. For Jake, dying on the trail would probably be a blessing."

Zoë said, "Deacon Blues."

"Huh?"

"Oh, my mother was a big Steely Dan fan, and I know most of the songs. There's this line from "Deacon Blues" that says something being free and being what one wants to be."

Amanda just nodded, while Zoë thought about people deciding for themselves how they were going to live out their lives.

Amanda said, "Here's another thing to think about. While I may have depicted a view of modern men in the changing West, I can also tell you about an extremely chauvinistic culture right here in good old Wyoming ranch country. In some cases, involving domestic abuse."

"Really?"

"Yes. There is a lifestyle among some cowboys and farmers that limits a woman's role to cooking, cleaning, looking after all domestic matters, breeding on demand, raising the children, and otherwise keeping their mouths shut…especially when the men are talking and making decisions. It's very old-fashioned and provincial, and it's what I ran into with my husband after we got married. He was pretty good at hiding it before-hand. Either that or I was just foolishly in love and didn't see it."

Zoë thought about Cody while listening to Amanda. She showed her concern when she asked, "Is it anything I need to worry about?"

"I don't know if it's anything you have to worry about. You've told me very little about what you and Cody have been doing, although I can pretty much guess, given your happy state."

"We've spent the last two evenings together, and I hope to spend much more time with him."

"What did you do?"

"Tuesday, we just visited and 'found' each other, and took a walk in the hills to see the sunset."

"Found each other?"

Zoë smiled. "Yes…you know what I mean. Then Wednesday evening, we had dinner with Madge, Jake, and Kay. Then I worked with Steely Dan in the round pen under Jake's supervision. That was fun. We ended the evening on the front porch of Jake's house with hot tea and home-made chocolate chip cookies and talked until eleven-thirty."

"And 'found' each other some more?"

Laughing, Zoë said, "Yeah, there was a bit of that."

"Cool. I'm glad to see it. You don't have to worry about Cody. When you meet his parents, you'll understand. His family is great. They've been down here a couple times."

"He hasn't said anything about me meeting his parents. Amanda, did you ever have an interest in Cody? You talk so positively about him."

"Maybe once or twice the thought crossed my mind. The reality is, we're more like sister and brother, or just friends, than anything else. I admire his qualities so I'm not shy about speaking about them. He's mostly kept his distance with me, but then, I was married when I first met him. He's always friendly, and he likes to tease, but there's never been any magnetism between us.

"And he's friends with Cory. Cory is more my type, although he can frustrate me at times. Cory was there when my marriage was falling apart, and he helped me get over the pain of my divorce. He's very caring, and he's really good with Davie. As a mother, that's really important to me."

"I can imagine that. Can you name any of Cody's faults? I haven't seen any, which bothers me because it says more about me than it does about him."

"Hmmm… Sometimes his mind wanders because he's deep in thought somewhere else, so you'll have to whomp him upside the head with a two-by-four to get his attention. He's just like Cory in that regard. I'm beginning to think it's a cultivated trait of most men when they don't want to listen. They just tune out. Another thing about him…perhaps if he thought you weren't interested, or if you strayed somewhere else after he thought you were committed to him, he wouldn't fight for you. He'd call it fate—your decision—and he'd live in quiet misery. In other words, he can be stubborn."

"How do you know this?"

"I don't for sure. I don't see him that often. I'm just guessing from what I've heard him say about things for the five years he's been around here. He kind of rolls with the punches, accepting things as they are. Crap happens, and he adjusts. He doesn't go all crazy about it. His little note to you even suggested it—he won't go where he perceives he isn't wanted. The good news is that you are open with your feelings, although you've clammed up with me a couple times."

"I don't like to talk about my problems until I get my head around them. Once I've done that—thought it through a little—then I'm a ratchet mouth with the people I trust. I've certainly told you a lot."

"Where did you pick up that 'ratchet mouth' phrase?"

"Madge."

"Yeah, sounds just like Madge. You're settling in, huh? You have told me a lot, and I love the fact that we're becoming good friends. And I do understand not wanting to speak up while you're thinking something through. I tend to think things through out loud…gets me in trouble sometimes. My point is, you don't play games. Cody shouldn't have any trouble knowing exactly what you want or where you stand."

Zoë said, "I hope he can handle it."

Chapter 32

Hank's Diner was an L-shaped clapboard building with a double entrance to avoid the cold winds or snow blowing through the main door as people moved in and out. As one entered, there was a long counter with a dozen stools on the left facing the big grill. This was where the short-order cook, Jimmy, was planted, dazzling the patrons with his skill in managing multiple breakfast orders of eggs in various forms, pancakes, home fries, bacon, ham, and sausage, and the house specialty—homemade raisin bread slathered on both sides with real butter and grilled. The excellent coffee was also produced in the grill area, and the other accessory foods like oatmeal, juice, and milk were supplied from there, as well.

Behind the grill area—visible from a pass-through window—was a fairly large kitchen where employees baked all the homemade breads, prepared most of the limited lunch menu, and stored supplies. Straight in from the front door was the main dining area with booths running down both sides and tables jammed in the middle. It was an old building, but maintained well, appropriately decorated to fit the mountains. The place offered a warm, friendly atmosphere.

It was Saturday, Russ's first time there. He sat at the counter, mesmerized by watching Jimmy, thinking, "I couldn't do that." Jimmy's every movement was efficient, nothing was wasted. He worked off verbal orders from the counter and written food orders delivered by the hustling waitresses.

The counter was half full at seven o'clock in the morning. Two fly-fishermen came in and sat next to Russ as his breakfast was being delivered. In raspy tones that reminded Russ of Paul Newman's voice in his later years, the one closest to him said, "Haven't seen you here before. Passing through?"

"No, I just moved here. I'm renting a cabin in the hills three miles west of here. Are you a local?"

"Yes, sort of. I've lived here for twenty-five years. Where'd you move from?"

"California."

"The Ford in the parking lot with the California plates—that yours?"

"Yes, it is."

The man with the Newman voice had a full head of white hair and a striking presence. He said humorously, "I'd get those plates changed as soon as possible, if I were you. Don't get me wrong. We love people up here. But we don't like it when people leave California because of all the problems there and then move here and try to turn Colorado into another California. What do you do for work?"

"I'm a retired aerospace engineer, kind of. I'm between jobs at the moment. I lost my daughter three year's ago in an auto accident and wife several months ago. I came to the mountains to live differently, to get my life back on track." Russ couldn't believe he'd said that. He'd come right out with his private thoughts—and to a stranger.

Gently, the man said, "I'm very sorry to hear that. My name is Pete, and my young bearded friend next to me is Willie. I'm a retired Methodist minister. Willie is a civil engineer working on environmental projects."

Russ introduced himself and as the three men shook hands, he said, "My wife and I were Methodists; my father-in-law is a retired Lutheran minister. He and my mother-in-law live in Fort Collins."

"What's his name? I may know him."

"Sam McClure. He retired long ago."

"I think I may have met him at an interfaith conference, long ago. Have you found a church here?"

"I'm sorry to say, I haven't even thought about it, yet."

"When you do, there's a nice Methodist church in Gilson where we attend. It's a mountain church."

Jimmy came over to Pete and Willie, taking their orders. He looked at Russ and asked if everything was okay. Russ said, "It's fantastic! You'll be seeing me more around here."

"Glad to hear it. We try hard."

Jimmy went back to his multiple tasks, and Russ said to the men next to him, "I'll give your church some consideration. What's the story on this restaurant, by the way? It's out here, a little distance from any town, yet it's filling up quickly. It apparently has a good reputation. And who is Hank?"

Pete said, "Hank is Henrietta, the lady sitting on the stool at the cash register."

Russ glanced at the slightly overweight older woman at the register.

Pete continued quietly, "She's very sharp…been running the place ever since her husband ran off with one of the waitresses. It was called Wayne and Hank's Diner back then. The next day, after it happened, she's up on a ladder painting over Wayne's name on the sign. He left her with five kids, all in high school and grade school at the time. Out of necessity, this became a family operation. When the locals heard about her plight, the business improved, but it was still tough going. She worked her butt off, raising those kids and running a restaurant. Back then it was open for all three meals from 7:00 A.M. to 9:00 P.M. She lives in the frame house up the hill behind the diner. Jimmy is her eldest, and he lives about a quarter mile away. He's now got a wife who works as a real estate agent and has three kids."

Pete stopped talking as Jimmy delivered their food.

The men fell silent as they worked on their meals. After a time, Willie leaned forward and said, "This is a cash-only business, but it leaves the family vulnerable. A few years ago, some punks passing through robbed the place. They were caught in New Mexico and went to jail, but they'd burned through a couple thousand pretty fast. The locals stepped up then also, supporting the business. It doesn't hurt that the food and the service is excellent. These waitresses are the best. You'll notice that when you pay. There are no receipts involved unless you ask for one. Is this your first time here, Russ?"

Chewing, Russ nodded his head.

Willie went on, "Sit where you can watch the waitresses next time you're in here. They write nothing down. They pay close attention to what you've ordered, then they put these little hieroglyphics on a small pad of white paper as they walk over to the grill, and stick the sheet of paper in the rack up there so Jimmy knows what to make. There is no bill. You just go up to the register and tell Hank, or whoever is there, what you had. Hank mostly adds it up in her head, tells you what the cost is, and you pay. It's remarkable."

Russ nursed more coffee as the two men finished their breakfasts. He asked, "Where are you going fishing?"

"The Tomahawk," said Willie. "It's a nice meandering stream through some open ranch country southeast of Fairplay. We just hope it isn't crowded, which it could be on a Saturday."

Russ thought fly-fishing was something he might like to try. He certainly hadn't had much opportunity in Southern California.

The three men were ready to leave. Hank wasn't at the register, but a blonde waitress was. They individually paid while Pete and Willie chatted with the attractive, shapely waitress with the pleasant smile. Russ learned that her name was Karen.

Chapter 33

The second time Russ went to Hank's was after an early twenty-two-mile bicycle ride. He sat in a booth and was waited on by Marion, who followed the pattern as Willie had described. Karen was there, as well, along with a third, younger waitress named Elaine. All three seemed to know everybody. This time, he tried the oatmeal and the grilled raisin bread—something healthy and something to negate the health benefits.

The third time, he showed up about 9:30 A.M. with his newspaper and relaxed over oatmeal, fresh fruit, and coffee. As he was finishing, enjoying another cup of coffee, Hank sat down across from him and said, "This is the third time you've been in here over the last few days, so I thought I'd better meet you. I like to know my customers." Sticking out her hand, she said, "Hello, I'm Hank, and I own this place."

Russ shook hands and introduced himself. As conversation unfolded between the two, Russ told Hank about his daughter, Grace, and his wife, Sara. He also described the circumstances surrounding his decision to sell his company and move to Colorado. For a man normally reticent about his personal life, he told her a lot about himself.

Hank proceeded to be open, as well, telling him the story of her husband, Wayne, leaving her, and how she held the business together with the help of her kids. "Jimmy is the rock of the restaurant. Wade owns the gas station and convenience store across the road. They're the only two businesses at Hanks Junction. Both boys and their families live a quarter mile down the road. Henry is a Marine stationed in Germany, and Elaine"—she pointed to a young waitress—"is right there. She's

158

twenty-nine…a really good kid. She lives in Gilson with her family. My fourth boy is Bobby, and he is at Florence."

"Florence?"

"That's the maximum security prison about two and a half hours from here."

Wanting to know the details, but not about to ask, Russ said, "I'm really sorry for you. That must be very difficult."

"Well, four out of five isn't bad. The rest of the family is really on firm ground, and I've got ten beautiful grandchildren. I'd better go. There are some people wanting to pay their bills. It was very nice to meet you, Russ. Please do come back."

"I will, Hank."

Chapter 34

It was on Saturday, June twenty-first, that Zoë's cell phone rang. She could see that the call was from Lacy, her roommate friend in New York. "Lacy, hello! You'll never guess where I am!"

Giggling, glad to be talking with her, Lacy said, "Is that why you tried to reach me yesterday—to ask me to guess where you are?"

"No, I called to tell you that I'm staying here for the summer. I'll be back in time for school."

"What! Oh, there's got to be something juicy there. What about your job and volunteering for the Dems?"

"Well, I need to tell Antonio that I am quitting, just for the summer, if he'll let me. The DNC will just have to get along without me stuffing envelopes or making phone calls or whatever. But, I also realize that I've created a problem with the apartment."

"So I can tell by your voice…did you fall in love? Does he look like Tom Selleck?"

"His name is Cody Nelson, and no, he doesn't look like Tom Selleck."

"Cody? I don't think I ever met anyone named Cody. Send me a photo."

Zoë turned to Cody—the two were sitting on a bench at the time—and held up her cell phone, saying to him, "Smile." *Click.*

To Lacy, Zoë said, "The picture will be there in a minute." She paused, then added, "Lacy, with you leaving in September, I expect that the girls will want to decide now on the fourth roommate to fill the gap and cover rent for the rest of the summer. How hard do you think it will be to find someone?"

160

"I don't know."

"I'm really sorry I've put you in this position. I haven't said anything to Midge and Pidge because I wanted to let you know first. I'll need to talk to them. How are they?"

Lacy choked with laughter. "Midge and Pidge. Now you've got me calling them that...and they kind of like it."

"Well, Toni is short, and Judy is pigeon-toed, so the names fit them."

Cody turned and looked at her, about to laugh, and got up to leave so Zoë could finish her conversation in private. Zoë grabbed his arm and rapidly said to him, "Please-don't-go." She locked her arm into his, leaning into him, trying to be one person.

Lacy said, "Toni and Judy are the same. Well, one thing is different. Pidge, as you call her, has added a few body piercings since you left— Hey, nice picture. Handsome dude. What's he do?"

"He works for the Forest Service...has a degree in forest management from the University of Wyoming."

"So what's in the background? Where are you?"

"We're in Yellowstone National Park, at Old Faithful. We're waiting for it to let loose."

"Cool. So are you going to get married?"

"I don't know. We're taking it one day at a time." As she snuggled him, squeezing Cody's hand, she said to Lacy, "My returning to New York at the end of the summer presents a little problem we have to work out."

"Have you told your mom and dad?"

"Not yet. I'm trying to figure out how. There is a lot to be sorted, and I don't have the answers yet. The other thing is, Mom and Dad are leaving for a tour of Israel in a week or so and get back about the same time I was scheduled to return to New York. I have a prepaid ticket, so I was thinking one option might be to change the routing to Palm Beach and discuss the whole thing in person, then fly back here."

"With your Cody along, or alone?"

"Haven't worked that out yet. You're asking questions we haven't completely thought through."

"Okay, I'll stop bugging you. Will I get to see you again?"

"I expect so. School starts before you were planning to leave, so I think I will, unless you've changed plans."

"I haven't. What are you going to do out there besides enjoy your hunk?"

"My boss here has agreed to keep me on. I can cover for staff on vacation through the summer. That's what I've been doing. It makes it easier for everyone to actually take a vacation if they know their work is covered. They really like me here, and I'm not expensive. Check out the *Demming Gazette* on line. I've written a lot of stuff."

"Will do, kid. Hey, what's that noise?"

"It just blew…Old Faithful. Wow! I'll send a picture." *Click.*

"It's hard to hear you. Please call again when you have a chance… and good luck with your new guy. I'll spread the word. I won't say anything about the apartment until you talk to Midge and Pidge. Let's be sure to talk again soon."

"I'll see you. Love you, Lacy. 'Bye."

Cody said, "She sounds like a good friend."

"She is…but I've grown cautious in making claims about good friends."

"Why?"

"Well, I don't know if this happens with guys, but girls can be ruthless with each other, particularly when they're young, junior high age and sometimes high school. Little clicks form, and one day someone that was in, is out because she talked to somebody else's boyfriend or said something nasty about someone. That pattern lessens in time. In high school, I had some great friends. With a couple of them, I thought we'd stay connected forever. They went on to college. I was playing tennis and training, going in a different direction, and we just drifted apart. Same with my tennis buddies. After I left the game, we just lost contact. I could probably renew some of those friendships, but the phone works both ways. People just get busy with their own lives. Take Lacy. When we're together, we have a great time. But she's moving to Boston in September, planning to marry Robert, and with my unsettled plans, I don't know how we can keep the friendship going, I mean, a truly connected, long-term friendship."

Cody said, "What about Facebook, e-mails, and text-messaging?"

"I see some virtue in those things, but I also see them as poor substitutes for face-to-face contact. I'll give another example. I really like Amanda. She's a hoot, and we've gotten to the point of being very comfortable telling things to each other." Cody raised his eyebrows slightly, and Zoë said, "No, I'm not going to tell you what things! Anyway, my guess is we'll continue to build a great friendship over the summer, but then what?"

Cody, asked, "So why do you think it's like that?"

"I think it has to do with the mobility of people. If good friends live in the same town or the same neighborhood forever, then it's easier. But when people move all over the place, and contact is limited to the annual Christmas card sent to someone you haven't seen in ages, is that what makes a strong friendship? I don't know. I suppose it can, but it's just harder that way." Chuckling, she added, "Do you send Christmas cards to old friends?

"Ah…no."

Playfully she said, "Do you know what I'm talking about?"

Cody laughed and said, "Yes, I know what you're talking about." He paused then added, "I remember spending time with a family of a friend during school. At the time, they lived in Laramie. But, they'd moved around the country a lot, and they had this very same conversation we're having.

"My friend ended up in California, and I haven't had any contact with him since college. Maybe I'll see him at a reunion some day. I don't think you can worry too much about what it will be like if you move a thousand miles away. In your case, with your gregarious nature, my guess is you don't have any trouble adapting. Doesn't Martin maintain a close, long-distance relationship with your Dr. Wilhelm?"

"Yes. I'll admit I haven't quite figured out their friendship yet."

"Maybe the simplest explanation is the most accurate," said Cody. "They were good friends a long time ago, and they've worked to maintain it."

"Yes, a variation of Occam's razor, 'All other things being equal, the simplest solution is the best.'"

"We may want to keep that in mind as we figure out our future plans."

"I have a short-term future plan," Zoë said. "I want to see a bear while I'm here at Yellowstone."

Chapter 35

On Thursday, June twenty-sixth, Cody was hiking in the Wind River Range, an area of the Shoshone National Forest on the southeastern side of Yellowstone National Park. He was traveling with his Forest Service colleagues, Terry and Dick, to conduct a formal timber-stand exam. They departed the Wapiti Ranger Station—the first ranger station built in the United States—before sunrise, in order to get to the trailhead.

On a steep section, several miles into the hike, a tall, broken, rocky wall with scrub trees growing in the cracks rose to their right. A thick aspen grove was on the downhill side of the trail past an open space. Breathing and not talking was their default position for this particular stretch of the trail. Their mistake was that they were too quiet.

With Cody in the lead, they reached the crest and turned a sweeping corner on the flat. About one hundred feet away from them was a fully grown female grizzly and her two cubs. Cody guessed the mama weighed nearly eight hundred pounds. They were too close to the animals for them to be safe. A separation of one hundred-fifty yards would have given them a more secure margin.

They thought the bears were standing over a kill site, probably a small elk, but the men couldn't tell for sure. Mama bear was curious about them at first, just standing and looking at the men. But as the cubs started making noises, she began growling. She had a clear path to them.

They knew what to do: get out the bear mace, split up, move slowly, and watch her every move without making eye contact with her. The bottom line was for them not to act like they were a threat to her and her cubs. If she felt threatened, she'd only pick one person to attack, in theory. By splitting up, each man had a better chance to survive.

The two cubs were scrambling about, looking for trees to climb. There were none around them. Mamma bear stood tall and assessed the threat.

Grizzlies can run thirty miles per hour for short distances. They run better uphill than down because of the structure of their legs. Mama bear started a slow jog down the slight incline toward the men—perhaps the beginning of a false charge—making noises as she built up speed. The men moved back slowly.

Terry was well behind the other two, so Dick called to him in a voice loud enough to be heard, but not so loud as to alarm the bears, telling him to head back down the trail, over the crest, and out of sight. He could then work his way into the nearby aspen grove from the back. The other two might need him to save their butts. They wanted him to be out of harm's way.

Cody and Dick angled off in different directions toward the grove. They moved slowly downhill as trained. If they could reach the trees before the bear charged them, and could get deep enough into the midst of them, the bear would have trouble getting past the closely packed trees and might give up her pursuit, especially if they were quiet and waited her out.

It was steep ground and maybe seventy-five feet to the grove. The bear picked Cody as her target, apparently deciding she was going to respond to the threat he represented with grizzly vigor. She picked up speed.

Cody had to make a quick judgment. He could run, and if he made it far enough into the trees, he might be okay. But he risked further riling a bear already agitated by presenting her with the sport of a chase. While he could defend himself with the pepper spray, a bear in full charge might not give a damn if he blasted her. Or, if he had no chance to make the trees, he could lie down in the proper position, with spray can in hand, and see if what he'd been told in training actually worked.

Dick cried, "Cody, get down! You won't make it!"

The bear was gaining ground fast. At the last moment, Cody curled into fetal position, burying his head into his knees, wrapping his arms around his legs. The ground wasn't flat enough to try the other technique— lying flat on one's stomach and locking hands behind the neck. Dick hollered and made noise, trying to divert the bear's attention. The animal was now running at full speed toward the edge of the trees.

Dick yelled, "Terry, where are you? She's going after Cody!"

With difficulty, Terry was weaving through the aspens from the back end of the grove and yelled, "I'm coming!"

Cody lay on the ground, scared shitless, as the bear slowed to a stop and started sniffing and pawing at his pack. The pack offered him protection, but it also contained lunch. The bear continued sniffing and began nudging him. Cody was afraid he'd lose his position and become a movable feast, rolling down the hill if the bear pushed too hard. The bear got more aggressive. Her claws dug into his shoulder and the back of his head, drawing blood.

Terry caught up with Dick and said, "Quick! We've got to spray her. Cody, hang on!"

Cody couldn't hang on. The bear started ripping into the pack and chomped down on an edge of it, firmly catching his shoulder. She partially raised him off the ground like a rag doll as he screamed in pain and sprayed her in the eyes, closing his own in the process. Terry and Dick were there in an instant, and as the bear dropped Cody onto the scree, they both sprayed her. The bear wheeled in anger, becoming disoriented, but she didn't leave.

Terry and Dick dragged Cody into the grove. It would be harder to treat Cody's wounds in there, but they had to get away from the bear. Hopefully, she'd decide to go back to her cubs, soon. Quickly, the men got out their first-aid kits. Cody's bleeding from the scraping claws was relatively minor, except for one spot where his scalp had been ripped open. That was a bloody mess. But the real damage was to the shoulder, the result of two deep puncture wounds and some tearing.

The men worked fast, trying to stop the bleeding after pouring hydrogen peroxide over Cody's wounds. He went into shock. They removed his pack to retrieve his first-aid supplies since they would need the items in all three kits. They looked around them, quickly assessing their situation. The bear had left. They could see her in the distance, pawing at her face. The cubs didn't know what to do. A couple minutes later, as the men finished bandaging Cody, they could no longer see the bears. But while the animals were gone, the men were still near what they thought was a kill site. Eventually, the bears would be back. The men just didn't know when that would happen.

Dick said, "We've got to get him to a hospital."

"Yeah, I know. But we're eight miles into the woods."

"He's in shock, now, but my guess is he'll be alert and hurting bad in a little bit. We've got morphine, and we can give him a little if we have to, but we can't drug him too much. We have to walk him out."

Terry said, "It will be slow going, but he should be able to do it. I don't think we can do the fireman's carry down the trail with that shoulder of his."

Dick tried using his VHF radio to alert a medical team. After a few minutes, he told Terry, "Nothing. Maybe when we get out of this pocket we'll get reception, farther down the trail."

"I wish we had one of those GPS signaling devices that Aron Ralston is advertising."

"You mean the guy who had to cut off his own arm somewhere near Moab?"

"Yeah. The device he's pushing broadcasts coordinates, giving search-and-rescue crews fairly exact latitude and longitude," said Terry.

"It's a cool device, but no helicopter is going to land here. We'd have to get Cody out ourselves, regardless. We just need an ambulance waiting at the trailhead."

Cody was coming around, groaning in pain. He looked up at his pals and groaned. "Man, my shoulder hurts bad." He was kicking one heel into the ground, writhing slightly, his facial expressions showing his pain.

Terry said, "Cody, you're going to have to walk out, so I don't want to give you any morphine."

"Shit!"

"Just stay where you are for a moment," Dick said. "You tell us when we can get going. But you can't wait too long, buddy."

Chapter 36

Willie, Pete, and George met for breakfast at Hank's at 6:30 A.M. every Wednesday morning. They referred to these encounters as their therapy sessions, and their friendship grew along with their sanity. On this Wednesday, Russ entered the restaurant shortly after the three friends were seated in their preferred booth, and Pete motioned him over, saying, "It was nice seeing you at church, Sunday. Care to join us? George, this is Russ. He's new to the area."

Russ greeted George, and they all shook hands. Then Russ said, "Sure, I'm happy to join, but I don't want to intrude."

"You won't be intruding," said Willie. "You might bring some fresh thinking to our conversation."

Russ sat as Karen came over, looking at Willie, Pete, and George individually. She said to the trio, "Coffee, coffee, and tea." She turned to Russ. "And what about you?"

"Coffee please—black." Russ looked at her smiling face.

Pete introduced Russ to Karen.

"I hope you realize, Russ, that you've just entered the inner sanctum of a very exclusive club," said Karen. "I know these are church folks, and they tell me they're 'inclusive,' but these three gentlemen have been coming here every Wednesday for over two years and seldom has anybody ever joined them, not that anybody would want to. You must be very special."

"No, I'm afraid not. I just happened to arrive about the same time they did, and they took pity on me."

"Well, you don't look pitiful to me. I'll be back with your coffee and tea shortly."

Pete said, "Russ, this exclusivity notion is Karen's little joke. She was more correct in suggesting that nobody wants to be with us."

Russ saw that each of the three men were smiling. "So, you guys have breakfast here every Wednesday."

George said, "Sometimes we'll miss one—travel, family obligations. But this is our little touchy-feely encounter group. We used to try to solve the world's problems."

"How many have you solved?"

Smiling, George said, "Ouch. We concluded that after two years, when it appeared that nobody even knew we existed, any problems we thought we'd solved, really weren't solved at all. Except maybe in our own minds."

Willie said, "Which really means we weren't accomplishing anything except honing our bullshitting skills."

They all laughed as Russ said, "Sounds confusing."

George offered, "Confusion is our normal state. And we usually have something to say about everything—under informed and over opinionated."

"Russ, tell us a little about yourself," Pete said.

Karen arrived, saying, "After I take your order, please. The usual for you three?"

They acknowledged "the usual," and she looked at Russ.

"Grapefruit juice, oatmeal with brown sugar, raisins, and skim milk. And coffee, please."

"Coming right up."

Russ noticed that Karen wrote nothing down and watched her walk away. Then he turned to the three men and offered them a succinct, five-minute explanation of his personal history leading to the major downsizing of his life and the journey to Colorado.

George said, "You've gone John Galt."

"Well, not by design. After the deaths of my daughter and my wife, being a productive citizen, striving for excellence, and making money

171

just seemed kind of pointless. I'm taking a needed rest, that's all. I'm living lean and figuring out what I want to do. I don't think this is Galt's Gulch, is it?"

Willie asked, "Who is John Galt?"

George chuckled, saying, "That's exactly the question posed in *Atlas Shrugged*. John Galt leads a strike of the world's producers—the inventors and capitalists—to bring about the collapse of the looting collectivists, the non-producers in charge. The premise is that parasites don't do well without a host."

Willie rolled his eyes. "Oh, Ayn Rand."

Russ said, "Okay, so what about you guys? Tell me your stories."

This took longer than Russ's speech because of the banter among the three friends. Also, the meal came and the pleasure of eating interrupted the flow of conversation. In the end, Russ took in their core information.

Willie, a native of Colorado, had attended the Colorado School of Mines, then MIT for his PhD in physics. He explained that he worked for an environmental concern. He had a wife called, "Mousey," who was an elementary school teacher, and they had no children. Russ thought that Willie was in his late forties, although the beard made the man's age difficult to ascertain. Nobody offered an explanation of why his wife was named "Mousey," and Russ didn't ask.

Pete went to the University of Wyoming and then got his advanced degrees at Perkins School of Theology at SMU. Married to Helen, he had three grown, married daughters—a family physician in Virginia, a school principle in Ohio, and a missionary in Haiti. Pete and Helen didn't see them often because of the distances separating them from their parents. Now retired, Pete's main activities revolved around books, study, writing, volunteer work, and fly-fishing.

Originally from Chagrin Falls, Ohio, George said he was a long-suffering Cleveland Browns fan, a condition 'not unlike being an abused spouse,' he had declared. Russ thought he was about five-feet, ten-inches tall. He learned that George skied with Willie on Saturdays, but wasn't as accomplished as his friend, and that he worked as an IT Manager for a large medical supply company, "down the hill." He loved the job. George added, "I love my wife and kids more, however."

Feeling a twinge of guilt over a past in which Russ had loved his family, but too often had appeared to love his work more, he said, "How old are your kids?"

"Eight and five. I have a couple pictures."

Russ smiled, looking at them and noticing their darker skin.

George explained, "Tara, my wife, is biracial—half-black and half-Thai. Here's her picture."

Russ said, "You have a beautiful family, George. You are a fortunate man."

They all departed at eight o'clock since Willie and George needed to go to work, and Pete had errands to run. Nothing was said regarding Russ's future participation in the Wednesday Breakfast Club, but he would likely see them all at the Gilson church since they were regulars.

Russ got into his truck and sat there. He wanted to go on a long bike ride and get back before the expected afternoon rain, but he was feeling depressed. He just wanted to sit a minute by himself and think. Seeing the pictures of George's family made him feel, what? envious? jealous? Is this the way it was going to be? He engaged in self-talk: "These are nice friendly men. Is any developing friendship going to be tainted by your inability to face the fact that others have happy lives? This is crazy. Why can't you just be grateful for them? Why would anyone in their right mind take it personally? George has a beautiful family. You no longer do. And you're going to somehow make George pay for that? There is no model in your entire life that would suggest envy of someone else's good fortune was a worthy thought or emotion. You've got to get over this."

He drove to his new home, angry about his own misguided thoughts, and proceeded to exhaust himself climbing hills for twenty miles on his bike.

Chapter 37

Zoë got the call from Dr. Havers at West Park Hospital in Cody, Wyoming at nine o'clock, Thursday evening. She was already in her pajamas, lying in bed reading, when her cell phone rang. She didn't recognize the number, but answered her phone anyway. Dr. Havers told her that he was caring for Mr. Cody Nelson following an incident with a grizzly bear that morning, and that he was fine.

Zoë was shocked at the news, but Dr. Havers told her the nature of Cody's injuries, and was light, cheery, and reassuring on the phone. It was obvious he was trying not to worry this unknown woman. He went on to tell her that Mr. Nelson wanted to talk to her before they gave him something to help him sleep.

She said, "Oh, please, put him on."

"Hi."

"Cody! What happened? The doctor said you are fine. Are you really okay?"

"Yes, I'm just groggy right now. But I'm the most lucid I've been in a while given the drugs they keep dripping into my veins. And they want me to sleep tonight, so they're ready to give me a bigger dose."

"What happened? I want to come up there right now."

"No, don't. I won't be awake, and I'm coming home tomorrow. They told me I won't check out until late morning, and it will take a few hours to get back to Demming. Terry will drive me in my truck, and Dick will follow to bring Terry back up here. Please stay there to greet me with kisses, and be my nurse a little while when you're not at work. I'll tell you what happened when I get back."

"What time will that be tomorrow?"

"I don't know. I'll call you when I get out of here and give you an ETA."

Zoë heard a nurse say, "I think you need to rest now, Mr. Nelson."

He said, "I've got to go now. There's a policewoman-nurse here, limiting my access to the outside world. Actually, I think she's just busy and needs to be done with me. I'll see you tomorrow."

"I love you, Cody. Please come back to me safe and sound."

"I will. And I love you, too."

It was the first time they had said those words to each other.

Sitting on the edge of her bed, Zoë cried, first out of fear, then out of gratitude that Cody seemed to be okay. She knew her emotions represented a release of nervous energy. Then she got herself together and called Martin, telling him the little she knew. Next she called Amanda, but not Madge since she realized that household would be asleep. Both Martin and Amanda were surprised by the news, but seemed to readily accept that such things happen in the wilderness.

Later, Zoë thought, "The man I have just fallen in love with is out in the woods getting attacked by grizzly bears? This isn't normal. Normal people don't get attacked by grizzly bears. They have other kinds of accidents—like car wrecks, or they fall on the ice and break something, or they get mugged, or they get hurt playing sports. Life is full of accidents. But they don't get attacked by any damned grizzlies! Except, my guy does."

Chapter 38

Cody didn't get home until 7:00 P.M. the next day. Zoë was there to greet him. Immediately, she noticed how tired he looked. She fussed over him and stayed close while Dick and Terry told the story of what happened to the whole Miller-ranch gang. Cody only talked when a question was specifically directed his way. He wasn't feeling all that great. Jake, Kay, and Madge were all asking questions along with Zoë. In a short while, Cody wanted to go to bed, and Dick and Terry wanted to head north, so the group dispersed.

As Zoë and Cody walked back to Cody's mobile home, she said to him, "Do you want me to stay with you tonight? I could help you if you needed anything."

"Yes, but I'd prefer if you were spending the night under different circumstances. All I'm going to do is plop into bed."

Feeling helpless, she inspected Cody's bandages and said, "Does anything hurt right now? Are you taking something for the pain?"

"Yes to both questions. That's why I need to get to bed. I'm exhausted, and they've given me lots of pain pills. Why don't you go back to Mrs. Granger's, get a good sleep, and come early in the morning."

"Are you sure?"

"Darling, I'm sure. But before you go, please help me get this sling and shirt off. And then I need to get the sling back on."

Zoë thought he looked awful. They kissed goodbye, and he was flat on the bed before she left the bedroom. She said softly, "Goodnight, my love. I'll be back in the morning and pamper you the whole weekend."

The next morning, Zoë got up early, showered, and put on running shorts, T-shirt, an old blue tennis warm-up outfit and tennis shoes. She drove to the Miller ranch to fix Cody breakfast and play nurse the rest of the day. When she got there, he was partially dressed in shorts. He was shaving, and after greetings and kisses, he said, "I'm surely glad you were here to meet me yesterday. It brightened my day, although I was pretty dopey."

She laughed and said, "Yes, you were. There was no way that I was going to miss being here when you arrived." Inspecting him, she said, "You look a little better this morning."

After he had finished shaving and she had helped him remove his sling, she wanted to inspect the bandage…and him. She acted clinical, but enjoyed seeing and touching his taut upper body. Washing his chest and back, she was careful to avoid the bandage. She could sense her own growing warmth as she worked, and began kissing his bare chest. Cody stroked her hair, holding her to him with one hand.

Zoë stepped away and said, "Oh, goodness. You're distracting me from my work. How many stitches did you get?"

"Twenty."

She looked closely at the back of his head where the medical team had shaved away a portion of his longish dark auburn hair and bandaged a strip about four inches long. "The other scratches don't appear to be too bad, but until your hair grows back, you're going to look a little funny."

"Oh, well."

She helped him put on a big, comfortable, flannel shirt, slowly buttoned it up—being cute, acting like she didn't want him to have his shirt on—then assisted him with the sling. Back to business, she said, "What would you like for breakfast?"

"Bacon, two eggs, toast, OJ, and coffee. I'm starved."

"Coming right up."

Cody could hear cupboard doors and drawers opening and closing while he straightened his bed covers. "You need to know where something is?"

"No, I'm finding everything I need. This kitchen isn't that big, and there are only so many places to put things." As she found the frying the pan, she said, "You should see the sardine can I call home in New York. The kitchen is a little smaller than this. How do you like your eggs? I've never fixed you a meal before."

"Over easy."

"Okay." Zoë started the bacon and checked out the surroundings. The place was old, worn, and dusty-dirty. Men evidently don't dust, she thought. Cody's torn pack and duffle bag from his trip were piled in a corner, right where Terry had put them the night before. Fishing gear and waders were on the floor in another corner. She thought that, in general, Cody's place wasn't the disaster that her apartment in New York was, but then, she lived in her place with three other girls. She peeked into his hall closet as Cody said, "Looking for something?"

Coyly, she responded, "No, just snooping. Are you a minimalist of some sort? You don't have much here."

"Kind of. I have more at my folks, like my winter gear, but there's also stuff here in the bedroom."

Cody joined her in the kitchen, and as she cooked the eggs, he moved aside her long black hair and held her from behind with his one free arm, kissing her neck. She said, "Ooooh, don't stop." As the toast popped up, she said, "Okay, stop."

After breakfast, Cody said, "I think I will lie down a while. This is ridiculous. I haven't done anything! Yet I'm tired, and I have a headache."

"You've been through a lot and your body is telling you so, even if your mind says its 'ridiculous.' I'll help you and then clean up." Several minutes later, she went back to him. He was on his back, asleep. She got her book and quietly lay next to him, propping her head on a big feather pillow to read. An hour later, Cody stirred, awakening slowly. She then heard him say, "Hi."

She put down the book and snuggled him gently, rubbing his arm. She moved closer and kissed him, then nestled into him. He said, "What are you reading?"

"*The Road*, by Cormac McCarthy. I'm familiar with the author. I read *The Border Trilogy*, but I've never read this one. It's the book Ken mentioned when he gave me his Mad Max theory at Martin's party. I borrowed Sylvia's copy."

"What do you think of it?"

"Well, I haven't finished it yet. So far, it's terrifying. But ultimately, I think it's a love story, the way a father looks after his son."

"That's what I got out of it, that no matter what happens, no matter how despicable life can be, somehow, love abides."

Zoë thought, "That doesn't sound like some tough guy, to say that 'love abides.' Where would my cowboy-forest ranger pick up a phrase like that?"

They stayed as they were on the bed, and Cody drifted back into sleep. Zoë slowly resumed her former position and continued reading.

Eventually, Cody woke and turned to her. He stared at her a long time as she read. Then, he said, "How do you think this is going to play out between us?"

She turned, propped up on her elbow, and said brightly, "Let's see...I think we'll have a wonderful summer together, then I'll go back to Columbia while you pine here for me, but we'll talk a lot and perhaps visit each other when we can afford it. Then I'll graduate and get a fantastic job at the *New York Times*, and we'll go see all the great musicals on Broadway...."

"I love musicals...except for all the singing and dancing."

Zoë laughed. "Oh, that's cute. Or maybe I'll get a job at the *Boston Globe* or the *Washington Post*. Wherever I am, I'll get a beautiful apartment, and you'll come live with me as my houseboy and take care of my new watch dogs—two toy poodles named Rolex and Timex. How's that sound?"

He chuckled, but it hurt doing so. She began caressing him. He relaxed and said, "I was thinking of something a little different."

"Okay, what's your version?"

"I was thinking that we'll have a wonderful summer, and you'll go back to Columbia but you won't be able to stand it without me, so you'll come out here and get your degree in Laramie. Then you'll get a real job with Martin, after we get married."

Zoë wondered if this was a proposal but she didn't ask. She just looked at him longingly, feeling a happiness she'd never experienced before. Finally, she said, "After all that, where will we live?"

"Right here, of course."

She laughed, and he said, "What? You don't like this place?"

"I'm enjoying it immensely at this moment. I just don't picture it as my long-term residence."

After a brief pause, Cody said, "Next weekend is the Fourth of July holiday. I want to take you up to my folks' place. I want you to meet each other, and I want to show you some things."

"What kind of things?"

"I don't want to say. I want to show. Trust me."

As she snuggled into him, she said, "I do trust you. And you make me so happy. I don't think I've ever felt like this before."

Chapter 39

Willie, Pete, and George decided to ask Russ to join them for their Wednesday breakfasts. They thought they needed the stimulation of a new person in the mix, and they figured it might help him get connected with people. Fortunately, Russ showed up at church that Sunday so they could invite him. They wouldn't have known how to reach him otherwise.

Russ was pleased.

At the next Wednesday breakfast, Russ asked Pete, "How is it that you became a Methodist minister?"

"The short answer is that I felt the call, partly a result of having been raised in a healthy Christian environment surrounded by Methodists. As it turned out, I didn't really understand John Wesley until seminary, where I learned the depth of his approach to the faith. And I studied a wonderful scholar, Albert Outler, who reinforced my appreciation for Wesley's theology. Wesley said, 'In essentials, unity. In non-essentials, liberty. In all things, charity.' And Methodism never asked anyone to leave their minds outside the door of the church." Pete paused. "So, why are you a Methodist, Russ?"

"I was raised a Presbyterian. Sara was raised a Lutheran. Mine was a small country church with no money and hers was a large thriving church. When we got married, we found a local Methodist church we liked. It was our facile compromise. We were fairly regular participants, but Sara would occasionally accuse me of being a nominal Christian. I was always too busy with work."

181

Pete replied, "I'll apologize in advance if I sound like I'm making false assumptions, or if I'm being preachy. But, it might be a good time for you to start understanding faith development, in other words, understanding the significant difference between opinions and convictions. One shouldn't die wondering what his convictions are."

Chapter 40

Zoë and Cody were lying in bed. It was Sunday, Cody's second day of recuperation in his ugly, rented mobile home. Zoë had arrived in time to fix his breakfast, bringing with her some homemade cinnamon rolls that she and Mrs. Granger had baked early that morning. She had also taken some to Jake, Kay, and Madge, which they appreciated greatly. They wanted to talk, but Zoë excused herself, saying she would catch up with them later.

While fixing Cody's breakfast, Zoë asked him what could be done about making things safer in the woods so getting attacked by a dangerous animal was less likely. She knew it was a dumb question as soon as she asked it, but there it was, out there for Cody's response.

He said, "There are some absurd things that could be done, like killing or capturing all the carnivores. But that would create overpopulation of other species for the available habitat. In the end, you can't make it safe so that nobody ever slips off a steep slope, or no dead tree falls on your tent. If society tried to create a purely safe environment, then we wouldn't have any wilderness. I've always said, the best thing we can do for the wilderness is not go there. But that isn't realistic. Ultimately, you cannot keep people out."

After cleaning the breakfast dishes, they took a short walk, visited with Madge a bit, and returned to his domicile so he could rest. He was lying quietly, eyes closed, but not sleeping. Zoë finished her book, set it aside, and said, "You're twenty-nine, smart, good-looking, and personable. How come you're not already married? I want to hear about your past loves."

He opened his eyes, turned to her and said, "I notice you waited until I took another Vicodin to ask me that. And you know, this goes both ways. I tell; you tell."

"Well then, never mind."

"Okay by me."

They continued to lie there, saying nothing for a couple minutes until finally Zoë said, "Okay. You go first."

"Are you tricking me?"

"*Moi?*"

"Yes, you."

"I promise to tell you as much as you are willing to tell me. How's that?"

"Fair enough."

A long silence ensued. Finally, Zoë said, "Well? Aren't you going to say something?"

Laughing, Cody said, "Oh, you mean right now?"

She leaned over and kissed his cheek. "Yes, I mean right now."

"All right…now. First of all, there were only two serious relationships. The first was in college with a cute blonde named Lisa. At the time, I thought she was the perfect girl. I was head-over-heals for her. The problem started because I graduated before she did, and I couldn't keep the relationship together long distance. Apparently, I had found the perfect girl, but I wasn't the perfect guy. We just drifted apart, and there was nothing practical that I could do about it."

"What do you mean, 'practical'?"

"I mean that short of dropping everything I was doing—that's when I was working for NOLS, which didn't exactly reflect a stable career path—and going to her in a fit of passion, like in the movies, proving to her that I was the one, and then riding off into a life of bliss, there was no way I could save the relationship. I had no solid plans, no way to define what a life of bliss would even look like. In fairness, I don't know that she was looking for an upgrade in a man compared to me. But she did find one. And I wasn't exactly presenting myself as a sensible alternative."

He fell into a reflective silence.

Zoë asked, "And the other one?"

"That was Shellie. I spent a year working just north of Ketchum, Idaho, near Sun Valley, a very ritzy place."

"Isn't Ketchum where Hemingway lived…and killed himself?"

"Yes, and there are places to visit there that celebrate his life. There's a memorial—he's buried in the Ketchum cemetery—and I think he finalized *For Whom the Bell Tolls* while staying at the Sun Valley Lodge in the nineteen-thirties. Anyway, I met Shellie in a bar, and, no, she wasn't some barfly. She was a very bright, engaging girl."

"What color was her hair?"

"She was a brunette. Why does that matter?"

Zoë was having fun, snuggling and caressing him. "Well, Lisa is a blonde, Shellie is a brunette, and I have black hair. What? Are you making your rounds? Going for a redhead next?"

"Hey, that's an idea!"

She gave him a love punch and said, "Okay, go on with your story. I'll try not to interrupt."

"Shellie has a teaching degree, but when I met her, she was just hanging out, skiing a lot, living in her parents' ski chalet. On our first couple dates, we'd meet up at parties. After that, we decided to go out to dinner. I picked her up at the chalet. It was a ten-thousand-square-foot log home, one of three her parents owned. The others were in Seattle and Maui. Her dad had retired early from Microsoft after clearly making a lot of money. Anyway, Shellie and I dated quite a while, and things went well. But she was worried about what people would think—her with her wealthy upbringing and me, a rancher's son, working for the Forest Service.

"Did she say that?"

"No, but I could tell. She was comparing me, with my lackadaisical attitude about success, with her father who was a real go-getter. I wasn't measuring up. She wanted me, so she kept pushing for me to expand my horizons—like there was this list of things I had to become before I would be acceptable. We ended up in a big fight and she called me a slacker. I said I wasn't going to piss on my life to become something I'm not. It was simply a clash of cultures between us. Our relationship had taken ten months to grow; it died a lot faster than that. Then I got transferred and moved here."

Zoë just looked at him a moment. "That wasn't very subtle."

"What do you mean?"

"I mean about the difficulty maintaining a long-distance relationship with Lisa and the clash of cultures with Shellie—two things you and I face. Although I'm not personally rich, I do come from a very different world."

"Yes?"

"Well, you told your story in a way that made the points you wanted to make. Pretty slick."

"I just told the truth and nothing but the truth."

"But not the whole truth."

"I guess that's right. I told what I was willing to tell. Now it's your turn."

"I'm sleepy. I think I'll nap."

"No, you don't get way with that."

Chapter 41

Cody grabbed Zoë's hand and started kissing it, then her wrist. She moved toward him and got close. She let him kiss her neck, and she wanted to do things to him—she could feel the urge deep inside her. But she knew his shoulder hurt when he moved.

They stayed in an embrace for a long time. Finally, she spoke. "My first real love was an Argentinean tennis player named Carlos Montanya. He spoke very good English, but then, I speak Spanish, so we could communicate either way. He made it to the big show, but you probably never heard of him because he didn't advance very far in any of the major tournaments. He was a handsome, smooth-talking Latin. Since I've seen a couple of those within my own family, I knew what I was up against."

"What do you mean?"

"Roving eyes. Some of them like to play at being Latin lovers."

"Oh."

"It's tough competing in tournaments on different circuits and still working on relationships, but we tried it for a couple years. I was certain I loved him, and he loved me, but then he fell for Hanna Kitchnakova before anybody outside the tennis world knew who she was."

"I've seen pictures of her."

"Most men have. She toyed with him. They lasted about a month. The truth is, Hanna wasn't the first one with whom he had drifted. He tried to come back, but I said, 'Not this time.' Nonetheless, it hurt."

Cody said, "Well, you've only had one other relationship, and it was years ago. You were young and impressionable. No problem."

"Sorry, friend. Then there was Vic in Florida. It was in the summer between my freshman and sophomore years at Columbia. I'd had rotator cuff surgery so I was rehabbing by the club pool and met this tall blond. He was the son of a well-connected real estate investor. He was a college junior, home for the summer from Florida State. We started dating, and we had a nice time, going out to dinner and spending time at the beach. His senior year, I'd see him when we'd both come home from school for holidays.

"Things became difficult between us the following summer, after he graduated. He was a pretty boy, always sucking up to people, always trying to network and find the angles for landing the big job when he graduated. He was practicing how to be the super-salesman in the investment world. We started fighting about his blatant greed. He was into money and doing whatever was necessary to get it. I was into my 'equality' phase. I just couldn't see things his way. His great desire was a red Ferrari. He apparently wanted it more than he wanted me. I knew he was upset with me—I might say something inappropriate at a cocktail party that would damage his prospects. And I was disappointed in him. The relationship just ended. And he started working for Bear Sterns."

"'Equality phase?' Do you know Wyoming is 'the equality state'?"

"I do. It was the first state that allowed women to vote."

"And hold public office and serve on juries. Wyoming voters elected the first woman governor in the 1920s. But, back to you…explain your equality phase."

"I'll cover it when I tell you about Darrel."

"There were more men in your life?"

"Yes."

"Oh."

"I dated Darrel last year, before I came here. He works full time at Antonio's, where I work. He's thirty-six and has a master's degree in labor economics. He wrote his thesis on the decline of the labor movement, incorporating strategies to reverse the trend. It was a fairly radical paper. He's a political activist who earns money working in a restaurant. He likes the free time the restaurant affords in order to do his political work. He's also schizophrenic, not clinically, though. He's more like a mild Dr. Jekyll and Mr. Hyde. In his case, he swings between great excitability—sometimes manifesting itself in anger—and his predominant pleasant side. He can be Mr. Sensitive, showing his feminine qualities, which is the side I've mostly seen—at least, it was the side I mostly saw early in our relationship."

"Feminine qualities?

"Yes. You have them also, you know. You are very aware of my needs, and you're nurturing."

"If you say so. What did you mean by 'mostly'?"

"I'd see his feminine side at work, on dates, most of the time. But he can get worked up when discussing some hot issue, and it lingers. He won't let it go. He has a short fuse, gets mad at a talking-head on television, and then yells at the TV. I only experienced the full extent of his Mr. Hyde side once, when we went to watch an anti-war rally. We were with a bunch of other people, on the fringes, listening to a speech. He got angry, pushed his way through the crowd, jumped onto the makeshift stage, grabbed the microphone from the speaker, and started hollering that the speech was bullshit. He felt the speaker hadn't been strong enough in denouncing George Bush and his evil administration. He swore and screamed at people. He really went off the deep end when the police came and arrested him. They had to work to subdue him—he'd been a wrestler in college and stays in shape. Still, they didn't keep him overnight. They didn't have room."

"What did you do?"

"Went home. When I talked to him the next day, I asked him, 'What is this? Are you trying to be a twenty-first century Abbie Hoffman? You think that theatrics like that accomplish something? Maybe you would be more effective if you calmed down. The anger thing gets in the way of accomplishing things.' Then he got angry at me…became defensive about what he'd done, which just made everything worse. At least I didn't need to tell him the anger thing was hurting our chances of a serious relationship because it was around that time that he started dating Gerty."

"Gerty? What an awful name."

"Yes, it is. Her parents named her after her grandmother, who was named after Gertrude Stein. She just appeared one day, hanging out with Darrel's group of friends. She's a free spirit...has a cute round face, big boobs, and dark hair. I'd guess she's in her late twenties. One time, she told me that as a kid, she was a gymnast, and at age thirteen she became infatuated with her instructor. She had this big crush on him and started to show it publicly. He sensed that he was going to be in trouble, so he fled the country. He went back to somewhere in Eastern Europe before the ugly story about what he'd done was ever revealed. He was *molesting* her. She dropped gymnastics and spent the rest of her high school years going through a series of psychiatrists.

"Then she went kind of wild. In her early twenties, she had a Harley and was riding alone to Sturgis, South Dakota when she hit some loose gravel going too fast on a sharp turn. Gerty slid off the edge of a hill. She fell a hundred feet down. Somehow, she avoided being crushed by the motorcycle or smashing her head, which was a miracle considering that she wasn't wearing a helmet.

"Gerty lay on her back, awake in the hot sun for hours, thirsty. And she had to pee. Her pelvis was cracked, so even though every movement hurt, she skooched down her pants as best she could and relieved herself. Her pants got wet anyway, and she couldn't pull them up because it hurt so badly. So she just lay there like that. A while later, a nineteen-year-old cowboy stopped his truck along the road to pee—a lot of urinating going on in this story—and he saw her down the hill. He ran down to help her, and he put his ten-gallon hat over her hoo-hoo before he called 911. Stop laughing! She was hurting, but it really is funny when she tells it."

"It's really funny when you tell it."

"Anyway, he went with her to the hospital and hung around the whole time she was there. He kept calling her 'Miss Gerty.' She had cuts, bruises, and broken bones, and the guy visited her every day. She moved into his shack with him for a few weeks after she healed, then she just got bored and left. When she tells the whole story about the quirky cowboy and their sexual exploits, she has everyone in stitches. She could be a stand-up comedienne."

"I've never seen a gymnast with big boobs."

"Is that where your head is?"

Smiling, Cody said, "What does she do for work?"

"Nothing, really. Occasionally she'll waitress—she's good at it—and she teaches Pilates infrequently. I've always thought that she's a trust-funder, living off her parents. It's just a hunch. She's pretty secretive about how she pays for things, but then she's not extravagant in any way. She watches her spending. Everything she owns fits into her Gregory backpack and a duffle bag. Anyway, Darrel apparently liked her, in part, because she agreed with him more than I did. Darrel considered me too soft, not aggressive enough in my thinking. I needed to get into peoples' faces, according to Darrel. When he started seeing Gerty, our political discussions turned into arguments because he wouldn't listen to any alternative or nuanced view. He has this notion that it's morally out-rageous to have political views in opposition to his. It's his way, or you are stupid."

Zoë stopped a moment, then said, "that speech I told you about, the one I gave to Martin the day I unloaded on him at work—that was like Darrel talking except that I cut it short. Darrel wouldn't have stopped like I did. One of his heroes is Saul Alinsky."

"Who is that?"

"A guy who wrote a book called, *Rules for Radicals*. It was written in 1971 and is out of print, but Darrel loves his ratty old copy. The one Alinsky quote I remember goes something like, 'Pick the target, freeze it, personalize it, and polarize it.' He promoted the use of ridicule, fairly ruthless stuff, all for the 'revolution.'"

"Out here, people are a little more civil."

"Darrel wasn't interested in civility; he was more interested in dominance, in marginalizing and ridiculing any idea not consistent with his. Anyway, when I challenged him about Gerty, he tried to downplay the fact that there was any romantic interest between them. She was just his political soul mate, he said, implying that I was failing him. I didn't believe him, and he started to admit that he was attracted to her, but didn't want to lose me. He gave me some crap like, 'we have such a special, you know, meaningful relationship.' I said, 'I've had it with guys who wander off looking for other girls to be sweet to. Been there; done that. Call me selfish if you want, but we're together or we're not. You can't have everything you want just because you want it.' And he said in that dreamy voice through his Brad Pitt lips, 'All that is gold does not glitter; not all those that wander are lost.' It was at that moment when I realized he was pathetic. I said, 'Yeah, I know—Tolkien,' and I walked out.

"You know what Darrel's favorite movie is? It's *Wild at Heart*, a weird, erotic David Lynch film with the creepiest characters I've ever seen in one film. It starred Laura Dern, Nicolas Cage, and a great supporting cast, plus all this symbolism from *The Wizard of Oz*. A bunch of us sat through it one night, watching it on IFC. At one point, the Dern character, Lulu, says to her boyfriend, Sailor, 'You got me hotter than Georgia asphalt.' I thought the line was camp, an excess of bad taste. Later, Darrel asked me if I'd ever say that to him. 'In your dreams,' I told him, then I added another line from the movie: 'The way your head works is God's own private mystery.'"

"So what about this equality thing?"

"When I first met him, we would have coffee or a drink after work. Or, when work was slow, we would talk in the restaurant's kitchen. Our conversations always gravitated toward politics because he sent them there. We didn't talk about each other much. He was educating me, or trying to, and our relationship developed with that as its beginning.

"My father is anti-Castro, anti-communist. My mother had something of a socialist mindset at one time. She told me she had wanted to live in a Kibbutz before I was born, but she stopped thinking about such things when she started living the good life in Florida. There was a time when

I thought she'd sold out—dropped her principles for a big house. I no longer have that view of her. Anyway, when I started at Columbia, I carried with me a sense of my mother's history. I was in an environment of mostly progressives, I was learning, and during my sophomore year, I'd been through the hassles with Vic's 'greed is good' thinking. He used to say that greed provides moral clarity. Darrel provided a coun-terbalance to that perspective. He offered a kind of comfort because, at some level, I shared more of his views of the world than I had with Vic."

"Didn't you tell me your parents get along?"

"Wait. I've only told you about three guys. There are seven more!"

"Oh, really? Busy girl, huh?"

"No." She snuggled with him a moment. "As for my parents, they do get along great, and they are nothing alike. I've always admired them for it. They established a truce of some sort, probably influenced by the fact that their political and religious differences simply evolved to political and religious indifference. And they've had other things to do."

Slow to respond, Cody said, "Do you think we will have to establish a truce?"

"I don't know. You've not told me your thoughts on political matters. The same for religion, We haven't talked about it."

Cody just lay there, finally saying, "First of all, I'm as mistrustful of politicians as I am of used-car salesmen. I see them all as skillful bamboozlers full of happy talk. Politics just doesn't fill my life with anything constructive or meaningful. I don't even watch or read the daily news. And religion? I'm fairly weak in that regard. My upbringing gave me some grounding, but I'm not much of an authority on the subject. More apropos to us, I've never enjoyed the sound of my own voice. I prefer hearing you talk, the way you explain things, the way you justify yourself but then come back with such complete honesty. You think things through, and you analyze what other people say, and you're not afraid to say what you think about it. And you change your mind when a new insight comes into your thinking. I admire your process, and I'm fascinated by your thinking. I'm not sure I can measure up."

Zoe thought about what Martin and Amanda had said, about being responsible to your own life, about how she had unloaded Darrel's philosophy on Martin, like it was her own and how stupid that was, and yet how nice he was about it. Again she thought about being careful not to tie your life to the world's agendas. She quietly said, "Cody, let me be clear. I'm very much trying not to measure you by your opinions regarding politics and religion. Amanda told me I was hyper about politics—this was in our discussion about my diatribe with Martin. I never saw myself that way, but maybe she was right. In truth, I don't want to be like that, like some shrill woman judging other people, looking for little signals to get PO'd about. Much of my dissatisfaction with Darrel was that I didn't like what he was doing to me and I didn't like what I was becoming. I promise you that I will do my best not to make political opinions some kind of a litmus test between us. I do want to know what you think, but I'm more interested in getting to know you better, bouncing things off of you and having a conversation, not keeping score. I'm beginning to get it. It's really about me understanding who I am and allowing you to be who your are."

"And me allowing you to be who you are."

"You do that already."

"That's because I like who you are. I see us getting to those differences of opinion in due course. I have my views, although they won't be as articulate as yours. I just don't want them to affect what we're feeling for each other."

"They don't have to. Does the fact that we come from completely different backgrounds worry you?"

"A little. But what worries me more is that on Labor Day, you're going back to New York for your senior year, a place where two ex-boyfriends live."

"There's nothing to worry about in that regard, Cody. I could never live in Vic's world, as arm candy keeping my mouth shut while he glad-hands his way around Wall Street. Darrel is simply unbalanced. And he expected complete loyalty to his philosophy. In their own way, each man wanted me to be a Stepford wife."

"Stepford wife?"

"You know the movie, *Stepford Wives*? In it, the men turn their wives into robots—beautiful, compliant, never crossing the will of their husbands. My mother rented the movie and suggested I watch it after Vic and I broke up. I can really pick'em, can't I?"

"Does that worry you? Are you concerned about 'picking' me?

"Only in that I know that I have a poor track record with men. I've worried about whether I'm capable of recognizing the right guy, if I can trust my own feelings. All three ex-boyfriends—Carlos, Vic and Darrel—represented relationships that took time to develop. You'd think that time would have some bearing on actually understanding what you've gotten yourself into."

"It does, and it did."

"Yes, okay, but then there is the fact that you and I have had no real time together. You hit me like a ton of bricks. I melt when I'm with you. When you kiss me, my temperature rises. It's really pleasant, but I don't understand why this is happening."

Cody rolled toward her, wincing slightly. He held her close, caressing her, kissing her. As she relaxed into him, she said, "You're showing your feminine side." They both laughed and then they fell asleep.

Chapter 42

At the weekly breakfast of Russ and his new friends, Willie wasn't paying attention to the conversation. George was telling Russ all about the medical supply industry, a story that had been told a dozen times.

As the meal and George were winding down, Willie finally spoke up. "I have an announcement to make."

The men looked at him, wondering where this was going. Pete said, "Okay."

"Mousey left me."

The three friends were shocked, and Russ didn't know what to think. Pete asked, "What happened?"

"Monday after work, I got home and discovered that most of Trudy's stuff was gone. I found a note from her, saying that she was unhappy, and she had found someone else. She said she was sorry, but her happiness was at stake, and she was going to take a chance. She didn't say, but I think she's taken up with a guy at her school. He's the janitor, six years younger than she is."

George said, "The janitor? This is crazy!"

Willie said, "Trudy is a female Caspar Milquetoast. Walking out on me—making any kind of change—is way out of character for her. She has the nickname of 'Mousey' for a reason. She's docile, meek, sits around reading tabloids like the *National Enquirer*. She hardly speaks at home, except occasionally she'll say something like, 'There's an article in here about a newborn baby in India that looks like an alien. They even have a picture.' Then she'll show it to me, and the picture will look like a doctored photo of *ET*.

"She's indecisive and afraid of her own shadow. I never dominated her by design, but it worked out that way because of her submissive nature. If I'd waited on her to make a move in life, we'd still be waiting. How she got a teaching degree, I'll never know. I always protected her. But the truth is that our relationship was built on physical attraction. She has those big, brown cow eyes and, well, she exhausts me. But then, she's twenty years younger than I am. Everybody thinks she's this spiritless dud, easily led, because she, well…."

Pete broke in. "I'm really sorry to hear this, Willie. How did the janitor enter the picture?"

"I don't know, and I have no idea how long their relationship has been going on. But a week ago, she came home and wanted to tell me a story about this friend of hers at school who was having all kinds of issues because of job stress. I figured she was referring to some teacher with problem kids, or someone having difficulty with the staff. She said, no, it was Todd, the janitor. So I asked what the problem was.

"She told me that part of his job was to clean all the tables and chairs in the cafeteria dining hall, then remove them so he could mop and wax the floor. Then he has to put them all back into place. She didn't say any more. So I asked her what that had to do with stress? And she got angry, saying that he only had so much time to get it all done and it had to be done correctly, so, yeah, that was stressful! I said, 'You've got to be kidding,' and she got more upset and stormed off to the bedroom. I've had the cold shoulder from her ever since. Then on Monday night I got the note. I called her yesterday at her school, and she told me she'd moved in with Todd. And she wants a divorce. Nuttiest thing she's ever done in her life."

The three recipients of this information were dumbfounded. George said, "I feel bad for you, Willie. What are you going to do?"

"Get a lawyer and cancel a bunch of magazine subscriptions."

Chapter 43

Cody and Zoë left Demming at 6:00 A.M., Friday morning, on the Fourth of July for the drive to his parent's ranch. They wanted to take a leisurely drive on a circuitous route because Cody planned to show her some sights. They'd packed a lunch and expected to make it to the Nelson ranch easily by suppertime. For the first part of the trip, they left the main thoroughfare to take a back road, which was slow going. Near the Continental Divide, they arrived at an area called Alkali Creek. Immediately, Zoë saw why Cody wanted to take her there—wild horses.

"I got Nunza out of this herd during a BLM horse sale," explained Cody. "The Bureau of Land Management office in Lander had a big sale six years ago, and I was home for vacation, helping out on the farm. I drove down there and bought this buckskin two-year-old, then took her home for my dad to start training. He was real busy and couldn't do much with her. I couldn't take her to Idaho because there was no place to leave her that I trusted. I brought her down for Jake to train when I moved to the Miller ranch five years ago. Jake worked with her, and with me, and we got her to be the great horse she is now."

Zoë said, "Oh, how wonderful! Look at them run. They are so beautiful—and free!"

"It's a tough life for them, and up close, some of them are pretty scruffy looking. They graze about fifteen miles a day, always on the move, and the winters can be brutal, killing off the weak. The bigger problem is that there isn't enough habitat to handle the growing herd—they're sharing the land with elk and deer—so they have to be managed…

culled. Nobody is making glue out of them anymore, but they do get rounded up occasionally. Some of them get sold to people like me. The BLM is very careful not to sell them to agents for the Canadian slaughter houses. There aren't any official ones in the U. S. anymore."

"The meat mostly goes to France, doesn't it?"

"Yes, that's one place, but how did you know that?"

"Well, I work for the *Demming Gazette*, not the *New York Times*. I picked that information up at the office. Oh, I could sit and watch them for hours."

"Let's get out and walk a bit, get some different views."

They found a rock to sit on, which afforded them a good view of the herd. The great stallion in charge was a buckskin, perhaps Nunza's sire, Cody speculated. After some time spent just absorbing the scene, they went back to the truck. There, they began to kiss passionately, pressing against the truck's warm metal as their own emotions heated up. After a time, they pulled apart, and Zoë got into the truck on the driver's side. Cody's shoulder was improving, but it needed a little time in the sling and not at the wheel.

As she drove, Zoë asked Cody, "You told me about Lisa and Shellie, but you moved to Demming five years ago. Did you date anybody after Shellie, or were you just waiting for me?"

"I was waiting for you, of course."

"Uh-uh. You must have dated. I can't imagine that the girls would have left you alone, unless you went into hibernation."

"Yes, I dated. But I told you about the serious girls, the ones I thought I might end up marrying. After Shellie, I dated a few others, but none of them ultimately meant anything serious. They were nice girls, but nothing clicked."

"Was Penny one of them?"

"Definitely not my style. I did date Susie off and on for about a year. She was a lot of fun, but we both knew it wasn't going anywhere."

"What was she like?"

"Another brunette, a cheerleader type, perky and a good time."

"A good time?"

"Yeah, she liked to party and dance so the two of us did that for a while. Then she moved in with some cabinetmaker near Jackson. When we were traveling about, she used to sing Shania Twain songs.., like *Forever and For Always*. It was our little joke, we both knew the words weren't serious for us."

"Was she a friend with benefits?"

Cody smiled, looked at Zoë and said, "yes, 'a friend with benefits.'"

After a while, both of them being quiet, Zoë was thinking about Carlos, her first real love. She bluntly said, "You've never told me that I'm beautiful."

Cody did a double-take and said, "I never thought you needed to be reminded of it."

She laughed and said, "I've always disliked it. The only person who could get away with it was my father. Carlos was the worst. He used to say with that Argentinian accent, "I love to see you bounce around the tennis court." Vic often brought up my looks but not having a Latin lover-boy personality, he wasn't quite as bad as Carlos. Darrel never said it much. He wanted me to let the hair grow under my arms and be his radical hippy chick, so beauty wasn't that high on his agenda. On the other hand, I never saw him spending time with girls who weren't good looking. I like it that you don't judge me—at least, I don't think you do—only on my looks."

"Well, there is certainly a physical attraction. I can't deny that. It's not like I didn't notice you at Martin's picnic and want to meet you. And it's not that I don't want to see more of you. As a matter of fact, I'm quite physically attracted to you right now."

Brightly, she said, "Feeing better, huh? Would you like me to pull off the road so I can attack you?"

"I'd love you to, but let's wait."

"Can I drive faster?"

"It's going to get curvy up ahead so maybe it's best if you don't."

Chapter 44

After a series of curves, Zoë turned a corner and saw a beautiful ranch house and barn ahead of her. She said, "Wow! Look at that place. Who lives there?"

"Caroline Kent. She purchased it in the early eighties."

"*The* Caroline Kent? The famous singer from the sixties and seventies?"

"Yes, she bought it about twenty years ago, moved in, and hired armed guards."

"Armed guards? Why?"

"To keep the locals from taking a shortcut across her property to fishing and hunting sites on BLM land as they'd done for three generations. A guy I know in the Forest Service called her a 'snobbish, Eastern spoiled brat.'"

"But it is her land?"

"Of course, and around here property rights are pretty sacrosanct. But the point is that she wasn't interested in the established culture or customs. And she didn't make friends with the locals. In this part of the country, it's important to be neighborly because you need your neighbors, they're your only real security when you live around here."

"Does she still live on the ranch?"

"Yes, but I recently learned that the property is for sale—for about twenty million dollars."

"Darn! That's just a little beyond what we can afford."

"Looks like an ugly mobile home for us."

Zoë groaned as Cody said, "Let's pull over when you see a good spot and have our lunch. We'll be driving through pretty country for a while, so we ought to be able to find a nice, quiet place."

As she found a turnout with a view, Zoë parked the truck. The couple enjoyed the chance to stretch. Cody took off his sling and moved his arm around to exercise the muscles. They got out Cody's cooler, which contained sandwiches, water, and sodas. They had also brought a bag of vinegar-and-salt potato chips. They chose to remain standing while they ate, enjoying the scenery. Very few cars passed by.

Zoë said, "I need to go to the bathroom."

Cody rummaged through a bag behind the seats and pulled out a roll of toilet paper. Handing it to Zoë, he said, "I won't watch."

Zoë looked around and couldn't see a good place to hide her bare butt. "This is not something us city girls are used to doing, but here goes." She trotted off into the trees.

When she returned, she said, "You men surely do have it easier."

"Can't help it. Now it's my turn." When he came back, he said, "I'd like to drive. My arm is feeling better. But, before we get started, it would help if you could rub right below and above the wound. It's starting to itch."

The pair stood beside the truck as Zoë began working on his shoulder, at first gently, then increasing her pressure. Both were stimulated by the activity and began to kiss passionately. Breathing heavily, Cody said, "I can't keep my hands off you."

"I've noticed. I'm enjoying that you can't keep your hands off me."

"I'm glad."

Zoë said, "We should probably go. Standing here, doing this to each other, isn't helping either of us."

"True. But it sure is nice."

Chapter 45

Cody drove for a good hour and a half through more ranch country before they stopped for some expensive gas in a small community. Back on the road, they followed another curvy route that led them to an open plateau. On their left were mountains; side canyons were on the right. Cody said, "We're not far, now. The farm is out there"—he pointed in the distance—"but we're going to turn into this canyon."

"It's very pretty here."

Cody drove onto a seldom-used dirt road with two tire tracks and a strip of grass running down the middle. They traveled a few feet and came to a locked gate with a sign that said "Private Property." Cody got out, unlocked it, edged the truck through the opening, then closed the gate. He drove along a creek and into a canyon with walls that seemed to shrink down upon them.

Zoë said, "It's really narrow going through here. I'd hate to be caught in this place during a forest fire."

"With a wind, it would simply run up this canyon, taking out everything in its path. Wait until you see what it leads to, though."

In a short while, the narrow canyon opened onto a large meadow surrounded by mountains that grew taller as the native grass meadow widened. The stream snaked its way through the meadow from its origins in the hills. In the distance, Zoë could see a modern log cabin near the stream. Perhaps eighty feet from it crouched a small, low log cabin that looked quite old. There was no barn, corral, or fencing, nor any other building.

The path-like road on which they'd been driving led to the modern cabin, and they followed it. Zoë said, "Oh Cody, this is beautiful. It's like a picture in an art gallery. Where are we? Who owns this place?"

"J.W. Nelson Farms, Inc. This is part of our ranch, but it's not contiguous to it. We simply call this area the 'Meadow.'"

Zoë was completely taken in by the beauty of the great meadow surrounded by mountains, and she was full of questions. "Does anybody stay here regularly? What about the winter? How do you heat the place? Does it have indoor plumbing? Is there electricity?"

"First of all, this was an old ranch from the late eighteen hundreds," Cody responded. "That little old cabin back there was built by the second generation of owners, originally constructed in 1919. There was once a main house here, but it burned down fifty years ago. We reconstructed the old small cabin, soundproofed it to keep the noise down, and installed an insulated steel door. Inside is a gas-fired generator, powered by a propane tank, and we ran the muffled exhaust through a hole we cut in the backside of the building. Electricity is run underground for lighting, cooking, and to power the well pump and hot water heater for the new cabin. We can heat it with electricity, but we hardly ever do so. We mainly use a wood pellet stove, which is very efficient, or the fireplace when we want ambiance. And yes, it does have a bathroom and shower."

They parked. Zoë was excited to get out and see everything. "Did you think about using wind or solar power?"

"Wind is probably the best choice up here because we have plenty of it. But when we looked at it, we discovered that the costs were prohibitive, as was the price of connecting to the grid if we wanted to go that way. Also, we already owned the generator as a backup for the ranch. A lot of people off the grid in the old days used wind generators, and it's a good option that we may still consider. The technology keeps improving. We wanted to wait for a breakthrough in battery technology. When the time comes, conversion shouldn't be difficult. It will just take some money, hopefully there will be tax credits."

"And you helped build this place?"

"We built it when I was in high school—my dad, brother, sister, mother, and me. We used pros to do things like put in the septic, dig the well, do the major plumbing and electrical. And we hired hands to help lift and place the bigger logs. My family and I did everything else. I learned a lot being involved in the whole affair."

"It's fantastic." Zoë ran over to the stream, saying, "I love that sound. You could sit on the porch and hear it. It's so peaceful." She ran back and hugged Cody. "Let me see inside."

Cody pulled a key from his pocket and opened the door at the center of a long front porch facing the creek. They stepped inside the modern cabin. Zoë saw a massive fireplace at one end with a living area organized around the fireplace as the focal point. The furnishings were rustic, and the couch and chairs were dark brown leather of good quality. Straight ahead of her was a hallway where she could see one bedroom. In her ear, Cody said, "There's a second bedroom to the right of the room you can see from here. The bathroom is on the left."

Zoë's attention returned to the spacious main room, noticing a good-sized kitchen area off to the right. A dining table and six chairs rounded out the furnishings in the large room. There was no second floor.

Zoë needed to use the bathroom, but Cody said, "Let me turn on the power first. Go ahead and inspect the place while I do that. I know the water was turned on in June, but we won't have hot water for a while since the generator hasn't been running."

Later, after a more complete inspection of the cabin, Zoë said, "This place is amazing. Who uses it?"

"Well, a lot of people. My mother is the official scheduler. My folks come up here every so often—even during the winter—just to feel like they are on a vacation, and they don't have to drive but ten minutes. In the winter, they snowmobile in. My brother brings up his family. My sister and brother-in-law used it for part of their honeymoon, but they don't come much anymore. We let a family we know live here for several months after their house burned down. Mom and Dad didn't charge them rent, and the family bought that set of leather furniture for us. It was a very nice way for them to say thanks. We let neighbors fish the creek for trout, but that doesn't happen too often, and they call for permission. I stayed here for a few weeks one winter with some friends from NOLS. We did a lot of backcountry skiing and practiced avalanche rescue."

"Avalanche rescue? First I learn about encounters with bears, and now I hear about avalanche rescues?"

"I guess I better not tell you about my jumping in quicksand pools in southern Utah."

"No. Let's just take these things where you could kill yourself one at a time. I need to get used to them slowly. Can we go outside, again? I want to walk around, get different views, and see the creek one more time."

They ambled about the property with Cody enjoying the fact that Zoë was so excited about the surroundings. She was like a kid, happy with life in the present, taken in by its beauty. They saw some mule deer way out in the meadow, which pleased her. He said, "I love it that you love it here."

"Oh, I do. It's like a private Shangri-la! Do you have to worry about vandalism?"

"Never had to yet. Fortunately, it's not a well-known location, and we don't go around bragging about it in public. Most people turning into the road would think they're in a narrow canyon that ends as a small box canyon. It's a box canyon all right, but you'd never expect it to open up like it does."

"There is no other access road out?"

"No. The only path out is the road we used. There's also a horse trail, but it's near the road, not at the other end. Someone could hike in or out, but it's rugged wilderness with no designated trails, and it would be rough going."

"Do you ever bring horses up to ride?"

"Sometimes we'll bring them up for a ride, and then while we're in the cabin, we'll keep them in a portable corral we've trucked in. Occasionally, we spread manure up here to help the meadow's growth. The deer and the elk love it that we keep this so nice for them. There are even a few moose around."

"It's so pristine. It's your own little secret heaven."

They walked back to the cabin, entered the front door, and Zoë kissed him lovingly, saying, "Tell me again. When are your folks expecting us?"

"About five-thirty or six. Supper is planned for six-thirty."

As she melted into him, she asked, "What time is it?"

Cody had already looked at his watch as he followed her through the door. He said, "Four o'clock."

Chapter 46

Cody and Zoë pulled into the long driveway of the Nelson farm at five-thirty-three. Cody's dad, John, saw them and announced their arrival to Becky, Cody's mother, who was working in the kitchen. Cody removed the luggage from the truck, then he and Zoë walked up the steps of the expansive porch surrounding the large farm house. As a mere courtesy, Cody knocked, then immediately walked into the house, seeing his parents approaching, glad to see them.

Almost immediately after the introductions, Cody's dad said, "Well now, young lady. This is truly a special occasion considering Cody hasn't brought any woman here to meet us in over five years. All I can say is that this is a major event in the Nelson household."

Becky Nelson said, "Oh, John!"

Chastised, but with humorous exaggeration, John said, "Well, gosh! All I did was tell the truth. You're making it sound like I was being mean. Gee!"

Zoë smiled, and Cody said to her, "I should have warned you. It's already started. This weekend is going to involve relentless teasing. It will even be worse when my brother and sister get here. They'll fall in love with you, talk about my faults, and if anything goes wrong, I'll get the blame. Such is my plight."

Cody's mom said, "Oh, you poor boy. You have it so rough around here. Zoë, would you like something…some tea or a glass of wine?"

"I'd just like some cold water right now, thanks. For some reason, I'm very thirsty."

As she got Zoë some water, Becky said to Cody, "I want to take a close look at the back of your head, and I want to check out your shoulder. Sometimes you scare me to death."

Cody said, "You're not helping, Mom. I hear about it from Zoë."

"Well, the two of us are just going to worry about you together, then."

"Where are you putting us? I'll haul up the luggage."

"You get your old room, and Zoë gets Margaret's room."

Zoë smiled inwardly, thinking, "Well, of course they'd put us in separate rooms like that. They don't know me, after all."

Cody carried one bag upstairs with his good arm and then retrieved the other one as Zoë visited with his parents. She asked if she could help Becky with dinner but was assured that there was nothing to do. The table was already set, the lasagna was about done, and all Becky had to do was finish the salad and toast the garlic bread in the oven.

Dinner turned into a two-hour affair, mainly because of all the conversation. Cody had to give his parents full details of his bear attack. Then he sat and listened to Zoë—enamored with her every word—as she answered questions about her tennis career, Columbia University, and how she came to Wyoming.

Becky said, "Tell me more about how you two met. Cody gave us one of his one-sentence explanations: 'I met her at Martin Coleman's picnic.'"

Zoë covered pertinent details of that weekend, some of her apprehensions, and then laughing, said, "I came to Wyoming with other life plans in mind."

John said, "Well now, God has a great sense of humor about our plans. He has a way of surprising us sometimes. When was the picnic, again?"

Zoë said, "Saturday, June seventh."

John said, "So, almost a month has passed. Becky and I knew where we were headed in about two weeks, and that was forty-two years ago."

Becky said, "Now don't be presumptuous, John."

He said, "Just look at them. Have you ever seen two people so smitten with each other?"

Cody just smiled and shook his head side to side while Zoë's eyes sparkled.

Becky said, "Yes I have—you and me forty-two years ago. Why don't you and Cody give Zoë a quick tour of the farm before it gets dark, then in the morning, you can tell Zoë more about how this place works. I'll clean up the dishes."

John said, "No, we can all clean up the dishes. It will be quicker and then you won't miss anything by being in here alone while we're out talking. You can also keep an eye on me so I won't say anything embarrassing."

"A lot of good having me around does with that. But you're right, I don't want to miss anything."

After the kitchen was clean, Zoë, Cody, and his parents walked around the barns and outbuildings. The main barn had a large paddock inside, and Zoë asked about it.

John explained, "I don't keep many cattle like my parents and grandparents did because I saw what happens in the winter with large herds that get caught outside trying to fight the blizzards. The old-timers would call me sentimental today, but I've had to deal with dead cows bunched up in the coulees covered with snow. Or worse, the ones that lived but were never the same with their frozen ears that fell off and frozen noses. They lived in agony for a while and most died anyway.

"The losses can be devastating to the ranch business, but it also hurts because you care about the animals. You may think that's strange considering the steers are going to be butchered anyway. But it isn't. I don't trust any man who feeds his own fat face in the morning before he takes care of feeding his stock. Anyway, when it looks like we're in for a three-day blizzard at twenty-five below and eighty-mile-an-hour winds, I bring my fifty head inside. No more frozen cattle for me. If I keep this up, I'm likely to be accused of being an 'all hat and no cows' cowboy."

It cooled off considerably after the sun went down, so the foursome returned to the house. John and Becky went to bed at nine-thirty, while Zoë and Cody moved to the porch, cuddling under a blanket on a patio love-seat.

"They told me that they really like you," Cody told her. "They're pleased that we found each other."

"That's good. They are very nice people, and I like them. I thought your dad's story about the cows was interesting. I've never heard anybody say something like that."

"It's an ethic that a lot of people have. Unfortunately, some don't. For instance, I've never liked feed lots, where cattle are concentrated in one place. The stench just never goes away. But that's just me."

"Cody, this has been an absolutely glorious day. Thank you." Zoë held him close. "I want you to meet my parents. They're nice people, too, although my extended family can be a little intimidating." She placed her head on his chest. "I can hear your heartbeat."

He squeezed her gently and kissed the top of her head. "I love you, Zoë."

"I love you, too…with all my heart." They held each other close for a long time and then went upstairs.

Standing outside their bedrooms, holding each other, Cody said, "My parents' room is right underneath us, unfortunately."

Zoë giggled softly and said, "It looks like we'll just have to suffer through the night in separate beds."

She kissed him passionately, and he held her close. After a time, Cody said, "I don't want to let go."

She pulled back slightly, looked into his eyes, and said, "Don't then. Don't ever let me go."

Chapter 47

At breakfast the next morning, Zoë asked Cody's parents, "What's the difference between a ranch and a farm?"

Becky said, "There's no rule that anybody has to follow. I suppose if you're raising more crops than livestock, it's technically a farm. This place was originally a cattle ranch, though."

"It probably does sound confusing," added John. "We just don't think about it much. We use the words interchangeably."

"When did the Meadow become part of the ranch?"

"My dad bought it from the Harrington's when their house burned down back in 1958. He wanted to keep the Meadow natural with Wyoming short grass and have a summer pasture for his cattle and horses. When my parents died and I took over the ranch, we just followed the tradition. But I always wanted to have a nice cabin up by that creek, so the boys and I built one."

"It's such a beautiful place. How many acres is the Meadow?"

"About thirty-five hundred. We own half a section—three hundred twenty acres—closest to the road. The rest is Forest Service land, which we leased for a long time when we were grazing up there. But when I reduced the herd, I let the leases run out. What we have up there isn't enough to turn into a moneymaker all by itself. You need lots of land in the west, compared to eastern farms, because of the lack of water."

Cody added, "The main farm is just shy of eight sections—approximately five thousand acres—and it can support Mom and Dad, plus my older brother and his family, but it's a lot of hard work. Some years, getting by is about all anyone can expect to do. Everybody eats well, but if it's been a tough year, there isn't much money for luxuries. The taxes are a killer, especially if something happens like a hail storm ruining the crop. But my family has been able to hang on to the Meadow."

Looking at Cody, Zoë said, "Your sister and her family live about twenty-five miles away?"

"Yes. They have about thirty-seven hundred acres. Theirs is more of a cattle operation, so if you want to play cowboy, that's the place to go. Bruce is a fourth-generation owner."

Following breakfast, Zoë was treated to a more in-depth tour of the farm. She viewed a wide array of farm equipment, barns, corrals, storage facilities, and irrigation pipes. Then, John Jr. and Gail arrived with their two girls and one boy. The three children were received with excited fanfare by their proud grandparents. It didn't take long for the five-year-old David to develop a crush on Zoë, and the ten-year-old Bethany to completely attach herself to the lovely new person. The middle child, eight-year-old Kimberly, was too shy to make any gesture toward Zoë, instead seeking refuge with her uncle Cody and showing a little jealousy when he paid attention to Zoë.

John was older than Cody at thirty-seven years of age. Taller and stockier than his younger brother, he was six foot three, with similar features, although he wasn't as handsome as Cody. He had big hands, and his mannerisms were more animated than those of Cody.

Gail was a cute blonde, about five foot nine and slender. Zoë felt that this woman would be someone she would like once they got to know each other.

Later in the day, the younger John, Gail, Cody, and Zoë went riding, following a trail from the main farm, across the stream at the low end of the Meadow and toward the cabin. As they rode, they talked and teased one another, winsomely welcoming Zoë into the fold of the Nelson family. They stopped by the cabin, and after hobbling the horses and removing bridles so the horses could graze, the foursome gravitated to the front porch, arranging the furniture so they could converse easily.

At one point, John turned to Cody and said, "Okay, little brother, when are you going to marry this girl and move up here and help with the farm?"

Chapter 48

Zoë said nothing but was very interested in how this conversation was going to go. Gail smiled at her and Zoë raised her highbrows at Gail.

Cody said, "I have to make sure she'll have me first. And we decided a long time ago that the place probably couldn't support three families."

"Depends on how much you eat, and whether you can make your own clothes. And it assumes you don't ever go anywhere, you just stay on the farm and work."

"That's why I chose to go do something else."

"The problem is that Mom and Dad are slowing down. They're both getting tired and forgetful."

Stone-faced and with a slight edge in his voice, Cody said, "You're not concerned about Alzheimer's, are you?"

"No, this country just ages you, that's all. Like Granddad and Grandmother, they're working themselves to death. And hell, I'm getting forgetful."

Gail said, "You can say that again."

"What am I supposed to say again?"

They all laughed as John went on, "The other thing is, I'm concerned that Dad's going to get hurt. He climbed the tall ladder and was up on the barn roof doing some minor repairs before I got here the other day. It was only seven o'clock in the morning!"

"We can't let him do that kind of stuff." Cody shook his head.

"How is anybody going to stop him?"

"I don't know. I do know by just watching Jake Miller that people can be productive well into their old age. Jake's seventy-nine. In all fairness, he doesn't have the heavy workload that Dad does. Over time, he's consciously reduced it to a level he can handle, and he focuses on what he does best—training horses. Madge does most of the feeding and mucking stalls, and I pitch in when I can. He's got it so he can take a nap almost every afternoon."

John said, "Given the ridiculously low rent he charges you for that dump of yours, you ought to be mucking the stalls all the time." Cody rolled his eyes as John continued. "Dad's always been the standard bearer. I've never seen such a hard worker. Now, the work goes so much slower than it used to, and the amount never diminishes because, unlike your friend, Jake, he simply won't let some things go."

"He reduced the herd a few years ago."

"Yeah, but that was more about income and government leases that needed to be renewed. The work, itself, hasn't diminished, it's just changed. He wants to do what he has always done to keep this place shipshape and earning its max potential. I understand that, but we put in long days. Sometimes he falls asleep while Mom's making supper. He eats and then falls asleep over the paper. Then they both go to bed at eight-thirty or nine. Of course, by that time of night Gail and I are home at the other end of the ranch dealing with three very busy children. And heck, I'm tired, which means Gail gets saddled with too much mommy work all the time. We need help."

"It's only going to get worse, isn't it?"

"I'm afraid so. Someday, we're going to have to take care of them… like they took care of us."

There was a long period of silence as minds were busy wrestling with the aging parent problem. Zoë didn't know what to think. Her own parents eventually planned to go into a retirement center, as there were some good places near them in Palm Beach. But she had always thought that time was a long way off. And they didn't act like it was high on their list of things to worry about. Her dad was still doctoring, and Mom was active in her social circles. Right now, she was curious as to what Cody would say about his own family situation.

Cody asked, "Have you discussed this with Margaret?"

"We talked about it recently. But she has a very tough life on their cattle ranch, so she just doesn't have much time to think about this stuff. Besides, I think you need to be a part of the discussion."

"And how much help have I been so far?"

With sarcasm, John said, "Zilch."

"Let me think about it a while, John. Let's talk with Margaret and Bruce when they get here. I doubt that we'll come up with a brilliant plan, but...."

"We've done that before, and we never resolve anything. And, believe me, Bruce won't be any friggin' help."

"No, we probably won't solve anything. Because in the past, it has always comes down to the fact that you want me to move back and help work the place, and I suggest that we get Dad to hire some additional help, which he could easily do. But he won't do that because he wants me to come back, just like you do. So, we end up at an impasse."

John said, "Yep. It's entirely your fault."

Cody's smile was more a grimace. He looked at Zoë, who had remained expressionless—she was trying to be impartial during the conversation, to be quiet and listen.

John went on, "Speaking of doing stupid things—like climbing up on a steep barn roof when you're in your seventies—tell Gail and me about your run-in with the grizzly."

"Why don't we wait until Margaret and her family get here? Then I only have to tell the story once."

"Okay. By the way, I was thinking that we should plan a weekend of fly fishing on the North Fork of the Shoshone in late July or August, once the water has settled down. This ought to be a good year to get some sixteen or twenty-inch rainbows. You could introduce Zoë to some quality fishing, if she's interested."

Cody said to Zoë, "You should be aware that the East Yellowstone Valley is prime bear habitat. We've fished it many times without running into one. You just check with Humble Fly or North Fork Anglers—local fly shops—for any recent bear activity. If no animals have been around, we go. But we carry bear mace just in case. Also, the Shoshone can be deep, fast, and it has a lot of slippery rocks. Why my brother thinks this would be a good place to take you, I'll never know."

John said, "Well, I just thought that since you're so interested in dancing with bears, you might as well get a little fishing in, and Zoë could watch the fun."

Gail said, "Oh, John!"

"You sound like my mother."

"I was trying to sound like your mother."

Zoë said, "I've never done any fly fishing, but if I do, could you guys introduce it to me without the added drama of being in an area where bears hang out?"

Cody said, "I think I can find a more suitable place for a beginner. The stream we're sitting by would be a nice place to start."

Chapter 49

After the group rode back to the farm, Margaret arrived with her children—nine-year-old Bobby, seven-year-old Katie, three-year-old Kirsten, and the baby, Doug, who was ten months of age. Margaret told them that Bruce couldn't make it because he'd been in Sheridan the day before and had to get some things done. She said, "He sends his apologies."

Becky said, "Oh, that's too bad." John Sr. added, "He seems to go to Sheridan every week." Zoë was the only one who noticed John Jr. and Gail glance at each other with frowns at these words.

Zoë saw that Cody's older sister, the middle child, was attractive, but very much a farm girl in her mannerisms and expressions. Margaret had beautiful long eyelashes like Cody. She looked very tired, worn out, and older than her thirty-four years. From a picture she had seen, Zoë knew that Bruce was a stereotypical cowboy in appearance—tall and lean, with a big droopy mustache. He had had that stern cowboy look in the photo. Zoë suspected he had been hamming it up for the picture.

Even though Bruce was missing, Zoë was sure that John Sr. and Becky loved that the rest of the family was together. Everyone started talking, catching up on news. Zoë was their center of attention, whether she wanted to be or not.

At one point in the conversation, Cody noticed that John Jr. was quieter than normal. By inclination, he was the motor mouth and Cody was the quiet one. Then Cody's attention shifted as everyone asked him to tell them all about the bear incident. After he finished, Zoë was asked about herself. She gave what was becoming her standard speech about her recent life history, how she had come to Wyoming, and how she had met Cody. Everyone relished hearing these stories, tales that could end up becoming family folklore.

Saturday evening dinner was a big affair, with prime rib, Yorkshire pudding, garlic mashed potatoes, green beans, a salad, and homemade pecan pie. And it was a raucous affair with seven noisy, active children requiring much attention. The cleanup was handled efficiently, with everyone participating except the youngest children.

Zoë was troubled with the thought that John Jr. might be exaggerating his immediate concerns about Cody's parents. John Sr. and Becky seemed energetic and involved in the activities of the weekend. Yes, they were aging, but their situation didn't seem as serious as John Jr. made out. Indeed, John Sr. talked about the farm and future projects with enthusiasm.

As the evening wore on, Zoë realized that Bruce was never discussed. On another front, John Jr. tried to get together with Margaret and Cody to have a discussion about their parents. Margaret was resistant; Cody was apathetic. Thus the matter of what to do about their aging parents and the farm workload was never addressed. Margaret left at eight o'clock to get her kids home and to bed. John Jr., Gail, and their children left shortly after. Zoë noticed that John Jr. appeared to be frustrated with Cody when the brothers said goodbye to each other. She planned to ask Cody about the whole thing after his folks went to bed.

John Sr. and Becky wanted to visit for a time with Zoë and Cody, but they didn't last long as John started yawning within minutes. By nine-fifteen, the older couple decided to go to bed. Zoë gave each of them a hug, thanking them for their gracious hospitality.

On the front porch, huddled under a blanket with Cody, Zoë said, "Tell me…" she paused awkwardly. "Do you think your brother is exaggerating about your parents, and about your need to come back?"

"I really don't know. It seems like it, but I don't know why he would do that."

"Your dad or mom never mentioned the need for you to come back. Is it possible that there is something else going on?"

"Mom and Dad wouldn't say anything. What do you mean, something else going on?"

"I don't have any insight, but I am observant." Trying to be delicate, she said, "I was just wondering if your brother was reaching out to you in some way, needing you here, because of another problem he doesn't know how to tell you about. Did you notice that he seemed a bit irked with you when he left?"

"Yes, but I didn't think much about it."

"I'm just speculating here, but what if your brother is ill or something?"

Cody looked squarely at Zoë, and she noticed his concerned face. He said, "Do you usually come up with such happy thoughts when you can't figure something out? If he were seriously ill, *that* would be a problem for the whole family."

"It's not what I think—because I don't know anything—but I do believe there is something going on with your brother that's about more than his concern for your parents."

"The easy thing to do is for me to just ask him. If there is something wrong, he won't keep it hidden from me. We know how to talk to each other. We'll see him at church tomorrow, and I'll catch him afterward. Or maybe it would be better if we swing by his place on our way south, after church. Speaking of which, I forgot to tell you that there'll be communion at church, tomorrow. They have it the first Sunday of the month. You don't have to take it if you don't feel right about it."

"What will your family think if I don't?"

"They'll think it's because of your Jewish-Catholic upbringing, and it won't concern them a bit." Smiling, he added, "Either that or they'll think you're a heathen."

"Oh, thanks. You know, I've never been inside a Protestant church."

"This one is very small. Everybody knows everybody, and it's casual and old-fashioned. Actually, traditional would be a better description. No holy roller stuff, no fire and brimstone, no snakes."

"Hey! No snakes. That's good." She paused, then added, "You still feel a part of this church, don't you?"

"I grew up in it. We went every Sunday, unless the weather was impossible or someone was sick. I got away from it when I went to college, and it was easy to stay away. I never quite connected with anything in Demming, but I suppose that's just laziness."

Chapter 50

Zoë and Cody visited John Jr. and Gail after church. Cody and John Jr. went out to the barn with no excuse given for leaving the girls. They sat on a bale of straw, and Cody said, "You want to tell me what's wrong, John? Why is it so important for me to come back to the farm? There's something you're not saying. Are you ill or something?"

John looked at him quizzically and said softly, "No, I'm not sick. I don't have cancer or anything. But I am concerned about the family."

"Why?"

"Because after I shoot that son-of-a-bitch Bruce dead, and I go to jail for the rest of my life, who is going to take care of this place…and Mom and Dad, and Gail and the kids, and Margaret and her kids? There are seven children involved, here."

"John, you're not going to shoot anybody."

"No, I'm not. But I don't know what to do. I'm trying to keep things from Mom and Dad. It doesn't help that Margaret won't talk to me anymore."

Cody demanded, "What's going on?"

"Remember when Margaret fell off her horse two years ago and broke her arm? And last August when she got hit in the face with a softball? Well, she didn't fall off any horse, and she didn't get hit with any damned softball. Bruce did that to her. Margaret is scared to death. She told me about those events two weeks ago because I went out there one day and found her crying. Bruce wasn't around. She said he'd just left after screaming at her. He told her what a lousy wife she was, called her stupid and useless, and made her feel like dirt. He didn't hit her that day, she said, but after she told me all this, she got really frightened and wouldn't say any more.

"Hell, who knows how long the abuse has been going on? I never saw anything before that would suggest it. I just thought Margaret was tired and listless all the time, and Bruce has always been aloof. It's happened before, out on these remote ranches. The husband is a complete jerk, he can't make a decent living at something he was supposed to be able to do, something that his whole family succeeded at for two or three generations before him, and he takes out his frustrations on his wife. Yeah, he's a real man, all right. He can beat up his wife." John Jr. paused, anger written all over his face. "When was the last time you've been out to their place?"

"Maybe three years. I always see them at Mom and Dad's."

"You wouldn't recognize it. He's let it go. The cattle aren't in good shape at all, the manure pile by the feed lot is huge. He's got rotting hay outside and junk all over the place. But he has his new fancy Dodge Hemi. Larry Hensley told me he's seen Bruce in Sheridan with a girlfriend. He apparently goes there once a week 'on business,' and sometimes doesn't come home until the next day."

"That's awful."

"We've got to get Margaret out."

Cody said, "John, I don't want you to misunderstand me. Margaret and the kids are the priority, but what would my coming back do to help the situation?"

"It's just that I don't know what to do, and I want my brother around to help me. Together, maybe we can convince Margaret to turn Bruce in, press charges and send him to jail. And then we can help her get that ranch in shape. Or maybe we have to call the sheriff ourselves, get a court order, and go out there to confront the bastard, then get her and the kids away. And I'm trying to keep this from Mom and Dad."

"Why? They're not fragile. They're two of the most mentally tough people I know."

"I don't know…I just don't want them to be hurt, I guess. I've been trying to figure it out on my own."

"Does Gail know?"

"Yes. She wants to take an old pair of clipping shears and cut Bruce's balls off."

"Bruce usually goes to Sheridan on Fridays?"

"I think so."

"Okay, I'll come up next Friday, whether he's around or not, and we'll find a way to talk to Margaret and get something done. I'm not sure keeping it from Mom and Dad is the best thing, though. They may have some advice that's worth listening to. This is a family thing and we all have to be involved. We have to take care of it because nobody else is going to. You know you can always call me about things like this, John. You don't have come at me from a different angle. Just tell me!"

"I hate talking on the phone, and I didn't want to say anything about Margaret in front of Zoë. I didn't want our first gathering with her around to be about spousal abuse within the family. It might scare her off, and you need all the help you can get. Can you get the day off?"

"You should be aware that Zoë already thought that something was amiss with all this talk of me moving back here, but to answer your question, I'll make it happen. Whenever I ask for a day, my boss just says, 'You owe me, Cody Nelson.'"

"About scaring Zoë off, maybe I should scare her off. How are you going to handle a trophy wife, Cody? I mean, you are a rancher's son working in the woods for heaven's sake. And she's a sophisticated lady from a ritzy area in Florida. She's seen a lot of the world, hob-knobbed with tennis celebrities, and goes to Columbia working to get a big job. How are the two of you going to work out the differences in your backgrounds?"

"I don't know."

"You don't know? Could this end up like those other two serious relationships of yours? Both women came from money, a different life… and you said you didn't measure up to their expectations. So, aren't you a little concerned about this one, or are you just hot for her and nothing else?

"There is that…yeah, I'm hot for her. But this is different. With Zoë, I'm comfortable being able to live in my own skin, and I don't have to become someone else, someone I don't want to be. She seems to accept me as I am, and I give her the same consideration. Will that work in the long run, or will it change? I don't know. I want it to work, but I'm no fortune teller. All I can do is the best I can and let the chips fall where they may."

Chapter 51

Zoë and Gail were in the house. Gail said, "So why did you guys stop by? I mean, you're certainly welcome, but I get the impression that Cody has something on his mind…needing to talk with John."

"Cody's trying to find out what's on John's mind, so he's going to ask him."

"Between us girls, I'll tell you what's going on, although John wouldn't want me to. Bruce is abusing Margaret, both physically and mentally. He broke her arm a couple years ago, and smashed her face about a year ago, and he's cheating on her. We don't know how long it's been going on or what else he's done to her. Sometimes they bail out on a planned visit, and we suspect it's because Margaret doesn't dare show her bruises. John only found out about it a couple weeks ago. They've had their marital problems, but we never expected this. We both want to kill the prick. Nice thing for me to say after church, huh?"

Zoë was shocked. "Oh, God. Oh, I feel so sorry for her. I've never known anybody who did such things."

"It happens. I imagine it happens in a lot of communities. I mean, I don't think it's unique to northern Wyoming."

"My friend, Amanda, down in Demming, told me about this sort of thing. She said that there is a part of the culture that's very patriarchal, and sometimes things get out of hand…maybe because of the remoteness," Zoe offered.

"I don't know. Some families breed kindness; some breed hate. And sometimes, things just go bad. It's pretty remote right here where I am, but John is my best friend, and he's one of the most caring people you'd ever want to meet. He's very worried about his sister."

"What are you going to do? No, that's the wrong question. What can the family do? What can we do?"

"That's what John is trying to figure out. He wants Cody's help, and he wants to have it solved before his Dad and Mom find out. I think he should tell his parents, but he doesn't want to. He's churning inside. Margaret may be the biggest problem in finding an answer because she's scared to death and is paralyzed in her mind, basically," Gail continued. Zoë could tell she was pissed as hell about the situation.

"Oh, this is really going to bother Cody. He loves you all so much," Zoë finally decided to say. She wasn't sure how to react to such personal information but she liked the fact that Gail was including her. Being open about such a horrible situation meant that she was being accepted.

Hearing what sounded like a herd of animals running through the house, Gail said, "We'd better change subjects. Your fan club is arriving. I'll just say that I get mad when I think about what's happening to Margaret, and I want to castrate the son-of-a-bitch." She fell silent as the three children entered the room.

Bethany and David pounced on Zoë. Kimberly sidled up to her mother. Gail said, "Okay, lunch time. Go wash up, and I'll serve up one of your favorites—liver."

All three turned up their noses and in unison said, "Eeew, No!"

"Okay. No liver, then. We'll have macaroni and cheese."

"Yea!"

"See Zoë? It's easy to be a hero with kids."

As the children clamored into the washroom off the kitchen, Zoë asked Gail, "How did you and John meet?"

"I met him at Laramie. He was in Ag school, and I was in a women's studies program, learning about feminism. I don't know what anybody does with a degree in women's studies except teach it, or work for some enlightened corporate personnel department and make sure the men are behaving. I have a minor in English…thought I might be able to peddle that if I had to. Anyway, there I was and there he was, and we just fell in love. We graduated, got married, and I became a farmer's wife. I guess I completely failed at feminism. I enjoyed learning about it, but I was more passionate about John than feminist rhetoric suggested I should be—you know, 'marriage is rape' and 'men are pigs'—the worst of that stuff.

"Another thing, what happens when you become something other than what other people thought you were going to be—when you change and you don't live up to their expectations? You lose friends, that's what. You find out who your real friends are. People don't like it when you exercise your independence and do what you think is right and good and say goodbye to what they had in mind for you. I'm not talking about teenage rebellion here. I'm referring to an adult thinking like an adult." Gail spread her arms, looked around her house and said, "So here is what I chose. Sure didn't expect this, but it's been a good life, and our kids are a blessing."

Zoë was fascinated by this very open woman and she said, "I had a couple boyfriends that wanted to mold me into something I'm not. Thank goodness, that's in the past."

I'd love to hear about that sometime, 'between us girls.'"

Zoë said, "I'll tell you some day when we have more time. Where are you from?"

"Laramie. My father is an emergency room doctor, and my mother is a judge, accomplished people. The good news is that they enjoy coming up here and seeing how happy I am. They've stayed at the Meadow a couple times and love it, and they think the world of John and the kids. So what are you and Cody going to do?"

"I know it's a cliché but we're taking it one day at a time, and the days have been pretty spectacular. The whole thing has been a shock to my system. I told Cody's dad that I had other life plans when I came to Wyoming, and he said that God has a way of surprising us, disrupting our plans. I always thought stuff just happens, and I've never been sure what God has to do with it. Is He even out there?"

"I think that sometimes He or She does have something to do with the way things work out, but there's no telling when or how. You and Cody are so different…your backgrounds, your personalities. You're so personable; Cody's kind of quiet, even boring; but I think there's an interesting principle at work here and he's a good example."

"What?"

"Sometimes, people that are happy—that know who they are and what they want—are boring. They go about living their non-dysfunctional lives in a state of grace—they're solid, well-grounded people. That's not necessarily exciting to the rest of the world. Criminals and Hollywood personalities are exciting. Normal people aren't."

Zoë chuckled and said, "I can see that, but Cody is pretty exciting to me right now, not boring at all; and he's done some pretty crazy things out there in the wilderness. I'm more worried about what new adventurous things are to come."

Gail laughed and said," His biggest adventure may be you."

Zoë laughed with her as Gail added, "You'll be able to make it if you want to. Just for the record, I really hope you do."

Brightly, Zoë said, "Thanks."

Just then, John and Cody entered the house and went into the living room. The kids were eating in the kitchen. Zoë and Gail joined the men. With mild defiance, Gail said to John, "I told her."

John looked at Gail, sighed, then said, "Well, that's not really any surprise."

Gail gave him a peck on the cheek, looked at Zoë, and grinning, said, "We women can handle it."

John smiled as he shook his head and said quietly, "Cody's coming up next weekend. We're going to organize an intervention, like we know what we're doing."

Knowing the kids were not far away, Cody said, "We'd better get going. I'll tell Zoë our thoughts, and you kick it around with Gail. I'll call you tonight from Demming. We'll get this sorted out."

There were kisses and hugs all around, including the kids, with Zoë getting special attention. As she and Cody pulled out of the driveway, with John and his family on their porch waving goodbye, Zoë said, "I'm so sorry Cody…for Margaret and what it puts you all through."

"I feel sorry for her, too. She doesn't deserve this." Cody then gave Zoë a complete rehash of his conversation with John, adding, "John's going to talk to the pastor and the sheriff. Maybe by next week we'll have something legal figured out. We're in the dark about this kind of thing."

"Do you want me to come with you? Give you some support?"

"Yes, if you can get Friday off. I need you with me."

Zoë observed that no other man had ever said that to her: *I need you with me.* But then, she had never said it to any man, either.

Chapter 52

It was Sunday, July sixth, and the breakfast boys were socializing after church, having coffee and cookies in the Fellowship Hall. Willie was quiet mostly, not participating much in the conversation, a pattern familiar to his friends ever since Mousey had left him. When they asked how things were going, he responded, "No change. I haven't talked to her."

Pete said, "Do you guys realize the significance of tomorrow—July seventh?"

George said, "It's the first day of the running of the bulls in Pamplona, Spain."

"I didn't know that. But no, that's not what I'm referring to."

"It's not your birthday."

"No, I don't have those anymore. It will be the three-year anniversary of the London bombings. Fifty-six people died, including the suicide bombers, and seven hundred people were injured."

Willie commented, "Oh, a cheerful Sunday thought."

George said, "Yeah, why do the Muslims do that? There are, what? A billion or more of them in the world? Call it only a billion. And if ten percent of them hate the West, that's one hundred million people. If ten percent of those are potential suicidal fanatics, that's ten million people! That's a lot of nuts to worry about. And they're all out to kill the infidels for the right to enjoy seventy-two 'Virginians' in heaven. Did any of you ever read the Koran?"

They laughed at the 'Virginian' remark as Pete said, "I read it years ago, and I can't honestly bring myself to study it again."

"Why?"

"I've spent my whole life working out my own faith, and I'm running out of time," Pete replied. "Before this conversation goes any further, Russ, you should know that Willie is the progressive of this little group, George is the more conservative, and I'm the ecumenical balancing act. I'm supposed to be the wise and calm influence. Sometimes I am."

Smiling, Russ said, "I always thought it was smart of liberals to adopt the term 'progressive' as their self-description since the word 'liberal' has taken on an illiberal meaning. And the opposite of progressive suggests that one is an intransigent, moss-backed fogy. Nobody wants to be an intransigent, moss-backed fogy."

Willie asked, "What is your political affiliation, Russ?"

"I'm an Independent."

"Which means what?"

"It means I try to avoid the subject."

Pete said, "That will make our breakfasts an easy adaptation for you. We decided a couple months ago to avoid any further discussion of politics. We wanted to see if we could actually communicate with each other without reference to what politicians say."

Russ said, "Good. I have the same attitude about politicians as pigeons do…as in, their treatment of statues."

They laughed. Then George's wife, Tara, arrived with her two children. Pete and Willie said hello, and George introduced her to Russ. She said, "It's a pleasure to meet you, Russ. I haven't been here for a few Sundays because I've been on call. Being in the medical profession means I'm not here a lot. Let me introduce you to Naomi and Obe."

Russ squatted down to their level, introduced himself, and asked, "How are you kids today?"

In unison they said, "Fine."

Naomi, eight, and Obe, five, asked to be able to get some cookies and upon affirmation from Tara and George, they disappeared.

George said to Tara, "I saw you were cornered over there by Nancy."

"Yes, and I had to cut short our conversation again, not fulfilling her desires, *again*. Maybe someday she'll give up…. Sorry gentleman, Obe's got a whole handful of cookies. I'll be right back."

Russ said, "You have a lovely family, George." This time he offered the compliment with the focus on George and didn't twist it in his mind toward self-pity or envy.

"Thanks. That little conversation Tara mentioned having with Nancy refers to the fact that Tara's a target of everybody in this church with a progressive cause. Nancy's into supporting a number of them and because Tara is biracial, Nancy hits her up for contributions. Tara says, 'When they gang up on me, it's like being nibbled to death by ducks.' We give money in support of this church and its missions and elsewhere, but…."

Tara returned, overhearing the last part of George's comment. She said, "Some folks around here believe in the one drop rule. Since I have at least one drop of African-American blood, they assume that I simply *must* think like Maxine Waters. Little do they know that I get a perverse pleasure by not telling them my more conservative biases. Is that bearing false witness, Pete?"

Smiling, he said, "You could say that."

"Hmmm…do you think they'd appreciate it if I told them what I really think of their moral preening?"

"No, they wouldn't. But whatever you do, remember to do it in love."

Russ liked Pete's comment. But he wasn't thinking of Tara's church issue. He was thinking about what he needed to do to get his mind right.

Chapter 53

In 2008, Hamas and Palestinian militants located in the Gaza Strip launched approximately three thousand Qassam rocket, Grad rocket, and mortar attacks on Israel. Until the ceasefire of June 19, 2008, 2378 rockets and mortars were launched, which were 739 more than had occurred in all the attacks throughout 2007. In July 2008, there were only four rockets and eight mortars launched by Hamas and Palestinian militants into Israel, and on July seventh, a mortar shell was fired into Israel from Gaza landing near the Karni crossing.

But it was not militant activity, nor rocket and mortar attacks, that killed Hector and Ellie Valiente on July 7, 2008 as they traveled in Tel Aviv. It was a speeding taxi whose driver ran a red light on his way home that T-boned the taxi in which they were riding. The message did not reach Zoë until July eighth via a phone call from her uncle in Florida.

Zoë was at work when her cell phone rang. She saw that it was her Uncle Joe's number, answered it cheerfully, and heard him crying. She immediately panicked.

He said, "Zoë, there's been an accident in Israel…" And then the next words came: "I am so sorry to have to tell you this, Zoë, but both your mom and dad…are no longer with us…."

Zoë broke into tears, and everybody in the office saw it. Amanda went to her as Zoë screamed into the phone, "Oh, no. It can't be! They can't be gone!"

Her uncle talked, giving details, but she only heard scattered words: "Taxi…T-boned…DOA…flying the bodies home…funeral…need you here…arrangements…so sorry….” The phone call ended with both of them crying, and Uncle Joe trying to give her comfort. She was in a daze and went to the bathroom because she felt sick. Amanda went with her.

Martin and all the others were waiting for her to come out of the bathroom, many in tears, touching her, saying how sorry they were. Martin, taking charge, said with affection, “Come into my office, and let me help you sort out your travel plans.”

White-faced, Zoë said, “I need to call Cody, first. Can I do it in there, please?”

“I’ll give you some privacy.”

She reached Cody. He was one hundred miles away, heading back into town. Obviously upset, she told him the essentials. He tried to say all the right things, telling her that he would call her when he was three miles out of town and come to her, wherever she was.

Later, the couple sat on the couch in Mrs. Granger’s living room. The elderly lady had left, giving them some time alone. Besides, she had errands to run, she had told them.

They hashed through the terror of the news. Then Zoë knew it was time to talk about schedules. She said, “I’m flying to Florida, Thursday morning. I have a very early flight out of Jackson, so I need to stay there tomorrow night. Martin got me a hotel room and offered to take me. But, I’d rather have you drive me. Can you?”

“Yes, I can. I’ll stay with you. Do you want me to come to Florida with you?”

“While I was waiting for you, I thought about that.” She laughed nervously. “I desperately want you with me. But, I’m trying to be adult about all of this, and I know that asking you to come with me isn’t fair to you. You don’t know anybody in my family, and it’s a large crowd. But the big thing is, you’ve got a commitment to keep for your sister, and I don’t think you would be happy with yourself if you weren’t there for her.”

“Zoë, I will break that commitment to be with you.”

“I know. That’s why I’m not going to let you do that. Your family needs you, and I'll be back as soon as I can." She leaned over his lap, softly weeping.

Cody stroked her hair. Nothing was said for a long time. He just played with her hair and patted her.

Chapter 54

Early Wednesday morning, Cody called John Jr. to tell him about the death of Zoë's parents. John and Gail were both on the line. When Cody got through the part about Zoë's rationale for him to stay in Wyoming, Gail said, "That's quite a smart girl you have there, Cody. Hang on to that one."

Solemnly, he said, "I intend to. I'm taking her to Jackson this afternoon, and I'll stay with her there. She gets on a plane early Thursday and then I'll drive straight from there to your place. What's the plan so far for Friday?"

John said, "I understand that Mom and Dad called you. So you know that they know about Margaret."

"Yes, they called yesterday. They reacted with obvious great concern, but also with resolve to get the situation fixed, now."

"Oh, yeah. Dad and I were at the sheriff's office and the courthouse yesterday. Dad knows Judge Vickers pretty well, so the legal stuff is getting pushed through. Tomorrow, the sheriff will pick up the papers for the restraining order."

"Dad told me."

"Both Mom and Dad visited with the minister," John went on. "That was a long meeting because the minister is concerned about Margaret's ability to cope and adjust and relieve her fears…to become whole again. I just don't know anything about spousal abuse and what it does to people. I don't understand it."

Cody said, "I don't either. We're not made that way, brother."

"So the plan is that we're going to Margaret's place Friday morning at nine. If Bruce is there, the sheriff will temporarily remove him to the patrol car while we get Margaret to sign the restraining order."

"Are they going to arrest him?"

"Probably, once he's located."

"Who's all going besides you and me?"

"Gail, Mom, Dad, the minister, and the sheriff, Big John Dawcettt. You don't know him, Cody. He's new, and he's nobody to mess with. Gail has a neighbor watching our kids, and she's going to keep Margaret's kids occupied."

"It's not going to be pleasant…"

"I'm afraid not. And then what? There could be a long tail to this…."

Chapter 55

Cody drove Zoë to Jackson, to stay the night and take her to the airport the next morning. Both were subdued, Cody not wanting to intrude on her grief, and Zoë not wanting to talk any more about her parent's death. They spent their time in small talk, discussion of schedules, being quiet and affectionate. Zoë sat in the middle with her hand on Cody's leg, just being close. At one point, after a long spell of saying nothing, Zoe told Cody of her conversation with Gail, about Gail's rejection of feminism as a career and what she said about Cody being boring but full of grace. At another time, this would have been a conversation filled with humor, but not now. Zoë was matter-of-fact, relaying pure information, perhaps reinforcing in her own mind that Cody had deeper qualities than she had already recognized, qualities that went beyond the strong physical attraction. Cody was a good listener and reassuring to her.

They had a light dinner and stayed in one of the motels in Jackson with cabins, the one Martin had found. It was clean and had a fireplace although they would make their own fire on this summer night. They made love for the second time in their short relationship, the first being at the Meadow. Zoë initiated it as Cody was cautious. And as she passionately took him, she completely engulfed him, crying softly and absorbing him wholly, filled with the terror of loss and the desire for new life with Cody. Afterward, they were spent, and wrapped in each others arms with tears and words of love, they eventually fell asleep. Little did Zoë know that it would be a month before she would experience anything close to this with her lover again.

After taking her to the airport, and the two of them saying their goodbyes, Cody drove five hours to his brother's house for a nervous evening of anticipation.

On Friday, the Nelson family, their minister, and the sheriff caravanned to Margaret's house and walked inside as a group. Bruce's truck wasn't there, so they assumed—correctly as it turned out—that he wasn't there.

Margaret had seen them coming. She started crying, glaring at John Jr. and screaming, "Why did you do this? You told, didn't you? You bastard! Now what am I going to do? How am I going to take care of the kids?" She paused, scanning the group, then continued glaring at her brother. "How am I going to live? You son-of-a-bitch! I hate you!"

John Sr. and Becky immediately went to her side and held her. Becky said, "No…no, Margaret. Please don't say that. You can't let this go on, honey. You just can't. We're all here to help you. Your brother did the right thing. He loves you."

Margaret just looked at her mother with terror on her face as Becky and John Sr. helped her to the couch. The others left them alone and went into the kitchen. John Jr. looked like he'd seen a ghost. Gail went to him in tears and held him. She said to nobody in particular, "Where are the kids?"

Cody said, "I hear the TV downstairs. I'll check." He followed the sound of a blaring television. Three of the children were watching cartoons; little Doug was settled in a Pack 'n Play. They saw him, and Bobby said, "Uncle Cody, what are you doing here?"

"Well, there is a problem…and your grandma and grandpa are here to talk to your mother. Uncle John and Aunt Gail are also here, along with the sheriff."

Katie said, "Oh, he's scary."

"What kind of problem?" Bobby asked.

Cody said, "Well, your daddy has done some things that aren't real nice to your mom, and we're trying to work something out so it won't happen any more."

Bobby and Katie started crying. Young Kirsten and baby Doug watched their older siblings, then they started crying, too.

"Hey, come here, guys. It's going to be okay. We're all here to help you."

Just then, Gail and John Jr. came down the steps. Gail said, "Need some help?"

Cody nodded and repeated what he had told the children as he turned off the TV.

Gail said, "It sounds like they've seen it. They know what's been happening."

Cody said, "Oh, what an impression to leave on young kids. Has she signed anything yet?"

"No, but Becky will be the one to make sure she does," answered Gail. "They're having an intense conversation right now. It's that mother-daughter thing. The minister is going to join them in a few minutes."

Bobby, Katie, and Kirsten were listening to the adults talk, and the decibels from their crying were reducing. The three hung on to Cody and Gail.

John Jr. hadn't said a word. He picked up Doug and hugged him close. Then he walked over to the others.

Cody said to him, "Are you all right, brother?"

"No…this was the right thing to do, wasn't it? I had to do it, didn't I?"

Chapter 56

Sheriff John Dawcett was six feet, six inches tall and two-hundred-eighty pounds. He had a pocked face and wore a four-hundred-dollar, custom-made cowboy hat with a Montana crease. He was a kind and reasonable man, but his presence scared little children and anyone in trouble with the law.

On Saturday morning, Big John was in his patrol car on a side road, waiting. He was reading reports and doing menial paper work, but became alert whenever a vehicle approached. He was looking for a specific truck to pass by on the road from Sheridan.

It came. Big John started his car and pulled out in pursuit of the Dodge Hemi, turning on his siren and flashing his lights. He pulled over the truck and walked to the driver's side.

Bruce said, "Hello, John. What the hell is this all about? Was I speeding or something?"

"You were going a little fast."

"So? There's nobody out here but you and me. Did you have the radar on me?"

"Let me see your license and registration."

Bruce dug out the documents and handed them over, unhappy but saying nothing.

Big John studied the papers and returned them, along with an official-looking document saying, "I have this for you."

"What the fuck is this?"

"It's an arrest warrant."

"An arrest warrant? What the fuck for?"

"Spousal abuse."

"What? That bitch—I'll kill her!"

Big John got close to Bruce's face and with all the meanness he could muster, he said, "You shouldn't have said that, Bruce. Once you make bail, assuming you do, anything happens to that girl or those kids, or any part of her family, and I'll hunt you down and see to it that you suffer to the full extent of the law…and maybe then some. And by the way, I also have a court order that says you're not allowed within a quarter mile of your property or any Nelson property, which means you'd better stay off Blue Creek Road."

"But that's my ranch! It's been in my family for over a hundred years!"

"Tough shit. Turn that engine off, get out of the truck, and go sit on that bank of the ditch over there while I call for someone to drive your truck to the impound lot. I'll haul you in. It'll be a pleasure to listen to you bitch and whine about your mistreatment."

Chapter 57

When Zoë arrived in Florida, a favorite cousin, Laline—Uncle Joe's daughter—picked her up at the Palm Beach Airport and drove her to Uncle Joe's house, where Zoë would stay.

It was a hot, sticky day—ninety-five degrees and ninety-five percent humidity. Zoë didn't miss such weather at all. It only made her feel worse as she thought about the funeral with dread. She also hated the thought of going into her mom and dad's house to go through their things. The only thing that helped Zoë were the phone calls with Cody. She talked to him every day, checking on Margaret's situation. In turn, he listened to her tell him about her day.

The funeral was Monday, a closed casket affair with one hundred-fifty people in attendance. Zoë had hated making decisions about caskets, flowers, the form of the service, and even the dress she wore to the funeral. She'd turned over the job of deciding where to have the funeral to her Uncle Joe.

A Catholic priest presided. The service was long, crowded, and hot. It was exhausting for Zoë. Just being with all the people, many of whom she hadn't seen in years, many of whom she didn't know, wore her out. She was glad to see her uncle from New York, though. A rabbi, he was a kind man. She had always liked him.

The first time she went into her parents' house was the day after the funeral. Uncle Joe and Laline were with her. The air-conditioning hadn't been on, so it was hot and sticky inside. But it still smelled like their house. She walked into the kitchen and saw two crystal cocktail glasses on the counter, the two that she had bought them for Christmas, along with a fifth of their favorite Scotch whiskey, Laphroaig. They must have had a drink before they left. She picked up one of the glasses, clutched it to her chest, and slid to the floor, crying.

When Zoë returned to her uncle's house and regained her composure, he said to her, "I know that was tough…to go in there. Go back again only when you're ready. But Zoë, there are some things you need to do. We can get a dozen or two family members to help clear out the house, but you'll have to tell us what you want done with your parents' things, the house itself, and the cars."

"Let's just sell the house and the cars, and give the stuff to family and Goodwill."

"That can be done, but you don't want anything? What about all your possessions? No photographs? No special keepsakes? Nothing that keeps the memory of your parents in your heart? Are you sure?"

"I don't want to think about all that. I want my parents back."

"Zoë…."

"I know…I don't know what to do."

"There is another thing. As you know, your dad was a silent partner in the restaurant chain. Because of his passing, ownership may have to be reorganized and some legal documents will have to be signed. But first, you'll need to decide if you want to retain partial ownership as the sole beneficiary of the estate, assuming you are sole beneficiary, of course. So, you need to reach your dad's attorney to determine the contents of the trust documents and the will before anything can be done about restructuring the business or disposing of any assets. It affects both your Uncle Julio and me, so we need to know what you want to do."

Zoë's head was swimming. She hadn't bargained on this. "Attorneys? Restructuring the business? The estate? I don't know anything about that. What am I supposed to do?"

"Well, like I said, I think you need to call your dad's attorney. He's also my attorney, and I could call him, but I don't want to be seen as meddling in your estate. You need to find out what the will says. Then we can proceed from there. Nothing can be done until then."

"I'll call him tomorrow."

"Here's his card."

———————————

The next day, Zoë summoned the courage—a sheer act of will—and drove her mother's Boxster to her folks' house, alone. The air-conditioning had been turned on the day before, so the place was cool, but it still felt eerie. First, she went to her own room. She opened the door of her large walk-in closet and thought, "What am I going to do with all *my* stuff, let alone my parents' belongings?" She stared at her tons of clothes, a dozen rackets in a big duffle bag on the floor, boxes piled high with old keepsakes, tennis trophies on a shelf. She shut the door and looked at her dresser, which was full of even more stuff.

Then, she went to her parents' room and looked in their two large walk-ins. Both were filled to the brim with quality clothes—Tommy Bahama for her dad and St. John and Coldwater Creek for her mom. And shoes…boxes of shoes. Zoë had never seen anybody with as many shoes as her mother.

She looked around the rest of the house, noticing the gourmet kitchen with Sub-Zero and Viking equipment, even though her mother hardly ever cooked, the paintings, the expensive furniture, and the large dining set.

Zoë heard a noise and looked out a window into the backyard. A pool man was cleaning the pool. She went to the couch and plopped down, not wanting to deal with any of it. Eventually, her logical mind overtook her depressed state and she thought, "Maybe I should just move in here for a few days and force myself to dig in, decide what to do with stuff, put it in piles. It'll be like when I forced myself to get up at five-thirty to practice tennis for three hours. I may not have felt like it, but I did it anyway. Or, I could set some ground rules for the family, like telling them only to take what they'll keep, not sell, and let them come in and pick out what they want. Then I could give the rest to charity."

She returned to her room, opened the closet door, and pulled out a large box from the back. She opened it and found old things from her teenage years and before—scrapbooks, an old Halloween outfit, games, year books, a box of pictures, and souvenirs from Europe. She spent almost two hours on the floor looking through the scrapbooks, recalling memories of her privileged youth.

As she came back from her reverie, Zoë realized that she had gotten sidetracked, like watching the match on the next court instead of playing your own, and began to organize things in two categories: keep and dispose. With vigor, she dug into her closet and made decisions. After hours of this activity, she saw that the "keep" pile was about as large as the "dispose" pile. Ruthlessly, she attacked the "keep" pile again, reducing it to the bare minimum. There wasn't a trophy in it. The fact that she was able to let go of them pleased her.

By the time she'd had enough, she realized she was hungry. Also, she hadn't called the lawyer, and it was too late to do so. She plopped on the bed and fell asleep.

Later that evening at Uncle Joe's, Zoë told him what she had done and that she had forgotten to call the lawyer. He was disturbed, but forgiving. She said that she would proceed with her work in her parents' home for the next few days just as she had this day, then let in the family.

He said, "You'll be exhausted, and you may not get it all done. I mean, you'll probably get to the point that you will have satisfied yourself about the more important things and just say 'to hell' with the rest."

"That could be. That's okay, isn't it? I just want time alone with Mom and Dad's things"—her eyes welled up with tears—"to touch them and get my mind around letting them go."

"I understand, honey. It's probably a good way for you to do it."

Going for a tissue, she said, "There's one thing. When we have the family come to look things over, I don't want Aunt Adele anywhere near the house."

"Oh Zoë, she's your Uncle Julio's wife. How are you going to stop that?"

"I don't know. I just cannot handle her being there. She's like a vulture, ready to pick the carcass for anything that's worth anything."

He merely shook his head and said, "Please call the lawyer. Nothing can be done until you do."

Chapter 58

Zoë returned to Demming in early August, emotionally exhausted and desperate to see Cody. He picked her up at the Jackson airport, and she sat close to him with her hand on his leg as he drove. He held her hand tightly until she was ready to talk. After sitting there for a while, she said, "I'm so glad to be back."

"I'm really glad you're back. I've missed you."

"Some of my time in Florida was awful. I'd meet with a lawyer, and he'd say he needed some time to check into things, and I wouldn't hear from him for three days. But then, you and I talked about that on the phone. Anyway, it's done." She shifted in her seat to look at Cody. "Fill me in on how things are going with Margaret. How is she doing? In our phone calls, we've talked mostly about me and my trials. You know, I am really tired of talking about me and my trials." She started to cry.

Cody pulled off the road and stopped. "Oh, Zoë, I'm here. I'll be your rock to lean on."

"I know, I know, and I thank God you're here. I'm just really feeling sorry for myself right now. I miss my mom and dad. I wasn't expecting this, and I miss them."

"We'll work through this, Zoë. I'm here for you."

They sat there a while and when the time was right Cody told her that Margaret was merely okay and the kids were actually doing better. The problem was going to be money and disposition of assets, but it was too complicated to get into now. She asked him how John Jr. was doing, wondering if things had smoothed over with Margaret, and Cody said they were closer than ever.

She was going to be staying at Mrs. Granger's. Although there was a long list of people who wouldn't have cared at all if they moved into together, they had agreed not to break community convention for the short time she would be in Demming. They would have plenty of opportunity to be alone with each other without actually living together in the ugly mobile home. But this first night back she would stay with him. She wanted and needed him and told him so. She wanted to repeat those wonderful moments the last time they were together; but this time without the tears.

A couple weeks later, they were cuddling on Jake's porch when out of the blue, Zoë said, "I recall that conversation I had with Amanda where she said that everybody believes in something."

"Yes…."

"Well, I'm just trying to figure out life. It's like the rug has been pulled out from under me over the last two and a half months…coming here, getting to know all these people, and *you*. Falling in love with you has changed everything. Then the death of my parents…I cannot reconcile it all."

"Do you mean why good things happen, and why bad things happen?"

"Yes. I mean, is it just fate?"

"I don't know, Zoë. I've never understood what was just fate or luck or what might be providential. I have a hard time thinking that the bad things that happen to people have anything to do with God. Something brought us together. What, I don't know.

"But how is it that some man driving along a lonely mountain road at the same time there is a rockslide, and a big boulder just happens to land on his car at the exact moment necessary to kill him. A couple seconds might have saved him, but instead, he's dead. Is it just the randomness of the world? Fate? I don't know enough to offer an explanation. I just look at the good as blessings—things to be grateful for, like you—and the bad as something to deal with, fix if you can, accept if you can't. It's kind of a coping strategy. Look at the situation with Margaret. The family jumped in because who else was going to? We're dealing with it and Margaret is learning to cope. Hopefully, the good outweighs the bad. Mom always said, 'It's a good life if you don't weaken.' Is that too simple of an explanation?"

"No, I don't think so. It's just hard, that's all. What's evolved is that you are my life. I've lost everything else that's important. Oh, I have relatives—some I hardly know—and some friends and there's school work, but it's you that means everything to me."

"That's okay isn't it?"

"It is and it isn't. I need to add some balance to my life. You're balanced. You have a wonderful family that you're close to, a job you like, a community you're a part of. I'm not in the same place. I'm all wrapped up in you—and what if I lost you?"

"Don't think about that Zoë; don't think about losing me. I'm not going anywhere. I'm yours for as long as you want me."

Zoe was uneasy. Cody didn't want her to go back to Columbia for her senior year. He wanted her to transfer to Wyoming. They'd even had a spat about it a few days earlier. She eventually told him that she'd feel guilty for not following through with her parent's wishes after all they had done to support her. Her father, particularly, was thrilled when she got into Columbia because it was his alma mater and she just couldn't sacrifice that trust, especially now that they were gone. The argument hit its apex and ended at the same time when she said to Cody, "I've made up my mind. I have my own mind, you know. You tell me you like my independence. You like it when I think for myself. Well, I'm thinking for myself."

Cody simply agreed. She knew he was capitulating, that he didn't like it, but she'd stated her position and both of them were going to have to deal with it.

Chapter 59

At Wednesday's breakfast, the guys talked about the Colorado Rockies' latest game, the recent fly fishing adventure the men had had on the Frying Pan in western Colorado, and they picked apart Pastor Stephens' sermon from the Sunday before. The topic had been mysticism and coming full circle, the men concluded that Stephens had made his point skillfully.

George asked Pete, "What's a mystic, anyway?"

"It's a prayerful person, one who exercises great devotion, who believes in the possibility of attaining insight into spiritual mysteries transcending ordinary human knowledge beyond our capacity to reason. I enjoy reading the mystics, but I've always had a difficult time relating to them. I'm too much of a realistic old pastor, I guess."

"Isn't every Christian supposed to believe in the possibility of attaining insight into spiritual mysteries beyond human knowledge?"

"Yes, Wesley's essentials suggest it. And you know that thing we recite in church every Sunday, the Apostle's Creed? It suggests it. What separates the mystics from the rest is that the mystics are very devoted to it as a constant in their prayerful life."

Willie said, "You wouldn't make a good monk, would you, Pete?"

"There is this story of a monastery where the monks were allowed to speak four words once a year. So this monk had his chance and told the head monk, 'Bed is too hard.' A year later, he had another chance and said, 'The food is terrible.' The head monk threw him out of the monastery. The head monk's secretary asked why he had done that. He replied, 'Complain, complain. That's all that guy ever did was complain.'"

Karen came by with a coffee pot, and they declined more as she collected the dirty dishes from the table. They were all quiet, inwardly smiling at Pete's joke.

Russ liked Karen's warm voice and noticed, as he had many times before, her smooth skin and her attractive figure. He couldn't figure out her age. The small hint of crow's-feet around her eyes and the fact that she had an eighteen-year-old daughter starting at CSU suggested Karen was in her early to mid-forties. Her tanned, unblemished skin and figure suggested younger. He'd heard that she was divorced and living in a nice area in Gilson. She had gotten the house in the divorce settlement; her ex had gotten the bimbo. Russ started feeling guilty for thinking about her in that way, so he stopped, suddenly missing Sara terribly.

A few minutes later, Willie and George left the café. As Russ started to get up, Pete said, "Sit with me a minute, Russ."

"Sure."

"I know Karen very well because I counseled her as she was going through her divorce. I also counseled her daughter, who is a smart, well-balanced kid. You would do well to keep an open mind about Karen, even if you are not ready to consider another woman in your life."

"Thanks, Pete. I'm not ready."

Pete said nothing, hoping Russ would talk, let out some of his feelings. He did. Russ spoke eloquently about his courtship with Sara, their maturing relationship, the things they enjoyed doing as a couple, Grace...their deep love. Russ said, "I miss her terribly, and I am lonely. Sara was my sweetest friend. This developing friendship with Willie, George, and you is helping me adjust to my new life but..."

"It isn't enough, is it?"

"No."

Pete remained silent, knowing that sometimes words were not needed. After a minute, Russ stirred to leave. He didn't look at Karen as he departed, but she watched him.

Part 2

Chapter 60

It was November 2008, shortly after the presidential election. Zoë had voted out of a sense of duty, but her heart wasn't in it. She'd voted for Obama—it seemed a practical solution to her. She wasn't willing to switch sides, but unlike most of the people she knew at school, she'd become skeptical of his so-called messianic qualities. Besides, with her new outlook on life, politics was less important, and she chose to spend less time with those people preoccupied with the subject.

Lacy and her new husband, Robert, had embarked on the first part of their honeymoon. It had been a small, quick wedding with only seven family members in attendance. Now, they had come to spend time with Lacy's best friend, Zoë, and enjoy the sights of New York City before they left for Rome.

Robert and Lacy spent one night at the Waldorf, enjoyed the helicopter flight around the city, went to the Statue of Liberty, Ground Zero, and generally savored everything they could on the pleasant autumn day. They had a late night flight from Kennedy airport and were having an early dinner with Zoë at Antonio's. Zoë wasn't working at the restaurant that evening. She knew the place well, and was certain that the three of them would be exquisitely attended to by Antonio, with help from his youngest daughter, Angelina, destined to be a great chef, herself.

The three appetizers to share arrived—prosciutto-wrapped asparagus, smoked salmon and goat cheese crostinti, and baked brie with pecan sauce. With the Cloudy Bay Sauvignon Blanc, the trio were embarking on a memorable dining experience. They chatted about Midge and Pidge being in St. Bart's for two weeks, and Lacy further discussed the events of her big day in New York with Robert.

Eventually, Lacy said to Zoë, "I know that you're having a tough time this year, with your parents gone and your guy in Wyoming. How are you?"

"I'm going to sound like a real whiner if I tell you, and that's normally not me."

"Go ahead, kid. I can take it, and Robert knows how to handle a pity party."

He said, "I do?"

"Yes. You listen, occasionally offering a little sympathy. You know just to be there. And you're not like some damn psychiatrist: 'So, you're feeling a little depressed right now,' after I've just said I'm feeling a little depressed right now."

Zoë smiled and said, "School is going really well. It's a place where I can dig in and keep my mind off my miserable present life, or keep me from thinking ahead, dreaming about when things will be better. I've buried myself in my schoolwork and I'm beginning to think that I could be a darn good journalist. And Dr. Wilhelm loves me. Work has been fine. I am making good tip money here. Antonio has been great, accommodating my schedule, considering all the changes I've put him through over the last few months. And best of all, I only have to work with Darrel one night a week.

Lacy asked, "How's that going?"

The meals arrived at the table, with Antonia and Angelina adding flare to the presentation of the salt-encrusted, Chilean sea bass with mango sauce on the side, a parmesan cheese risotto, and sautéed spinach with enough garlic to be exuding from ones' pores for the next two days. All three diners had the same thing since the sea bass was large, and it was Antonio's special creation for them.

As they started to consume their main course, moaning softly with delight, Zoë said, "You'll never guess what I did a couple weeks ago."

"Okay, I give up, but you eventually have to answer my question about Darrel."

"I went to church."

"Really? In this hotbed of secular culture?" Laughing, Lacy added, "My, my, Zoë, what are we going to do with you?"

Giggling, Zoë said, "Okay, enough. I went to the Fifth Avenue Presbyterian Church. What really impressed me was its Gothic style. Did you know that there are no right angles inside the structure? Every pew seat has a view of the pulpit, and every person can be seen from the pulpit. The stained glass was beautiful, and the massive amount of woodwork remains as it did in the late nineteenth century."

"So you went there to inspect Gothic architecture?"

"No, I went there to see if I could learn anything."

"And what did you learn?"

"After I sat down, there was this nice, old man—had to be in his eighties—who came up to me, knowing I was a stranger, in a church with thirty-five hundred members. Anyway, he told me all about the building and their program helping the homeless and then he simply welcomed me. He wasn't pushy at all. I had the preconceived notion that I might be approached by someone wanting to save me, or I would be ignored.

"Anyway, then there was a sermon about the will of God. The pastor quoted some guy and said that the phrase, 'It's the will of God,' is used too loosely, often after some tragedy. He said that we shouldn't look at the will of God as something for which a man would go to jail… and we need to come to terms with the idea that the intentional will can be defeated by human will for the time being…and if this weren't true, then we would have no real freedom at all. The ultimate will cannot be defeated, whatever that is."

Lacy said, "Oh, the problem of free will."

"Yes, and the jihadists behead infidels and Fred Phelps pickets soldiers' funerals because of their view of the will of God. The preacher said, 'Figuring out the will of God is one thing. Doing it is quite another.' And he spoke of trust in spite of contrary evidence."

Robert said, "Yes… okay…but it only matters if you believe in God."

Chapter 61

As they ate, Lacy said, "So, how is it working here with Darrel?"

"It's okay. We do our jobs and ignore each other. He and Gerty are still dating, and they seem to be going hot and heavy, fortunately not in our apartment. Now that Gerty is my new roommate, I was concerned about that, at first. Anyway, he and I are civil, but he's never asked me about what I'm doing. We've written each other off."

"How is Gerty as a roommate?"

"Well, when you told me she had moved in over this summer, I couldn't believe it. I mean, I had no say in it since I wasn't around, and I'd dumped the roommate problem on Midge, Pidge, and you. Like, I was a little preoccupied?"

Lacy said, "But I was leaving, so it was really Midge and Pidge who had to find your replacement."

"At least filling the slot was easy. But, boy was I surprised that my new roommate was going to be Darrel's girlfriend."

"She wasn't bad to live with, for me, anyway. I mean, she did her share of the work and didn't cause trouble. Considering that the four of us were living there like confined rats, that was important. She paid her portion of the rent on time, and she's funny."

Robert said, "The money you were paying was way too much for what you were getting in that place."

Zoë said, "It's what's available near campus. The worst part is that the air conditioning doesn't work in the summer, and it's too hot in the winter. Other parts of the building can hardly get any heat, but we're right near the furnace, so we get blasted."

Lacy said, "Yes, and Gerty seems to milk the 'it's too hot' thing for all its worth." Looking at Robert, she added, "She's an exhibitionist… likes to walk around the apartment with hardly anything on, complaining about the heat."

Zoë nodded. "Midge and Pidge just think it's funny. Midge once said to me, 'What is she trying to do? Entice Pidge to drop me and have a relationship with her?' Maybe she's just flaunting her wares in front of me since Darrel and I once dated."

Lacy said, "Could be. Sort of like, 'Take a look at this. Darrel does.' She does have a haughty streak."

Robert held up his hands simulating claws, and he made a growling cat sound.

Zoë laughed. "Her exhibitionism notwithstanding, we all get along, and she is funny. But I'm not enjoying living there, which says a lot about where my head is. It's like getting along with classmates because you are all just there in the same room. Or you're with people in the dentist's office, and the hygienist is nice, the doctor is nice, the people at the front desk are nice, but it's not like you're going to bare your soul to any of them. At the apartment, we function without any stress, but I'd rather be with other people. I've missed you, Lacy. And I'm glad you look so happy. I miss Amanda, and several others out in Wyoming, too, but I really miss Cody. Being separated from him is a lot harder than I thought it would be."

"It's probably pretty hard for him, too. You talk every day?"

"Yes, sometimes more than once a day, when we can. Occasionally, he's out in the wilderness, out of cell phone range, and gets back too late to call. I'm glad that you and I have talked often since I got back. It's helped."

"Are you going to get together around Thanksgiving or Christmas?"

"Christmas. I have three weeks off. I'm going out there. If he came here, there'd be no place for him to stay. Besides, he doesn't like big cities.

He quotes Steve McQueen: 'I'd rather wake up in the middle of nowhere than in any city on earth.'"

"But you like cities."

"Yes, but I'm learning to appreciate that there are other attractive lifestyles that do not involve living in a confined area with millions of other people."

Antonio came by the table to ask how they liked the meal. All three complimented him profusely, Robert saying, "It's the best meal I've ever had in my life." Antonio beamed and departed.

Lacy leaned over to Zoë and said, "He says that about every good meal. The most recent meal is always the best meal he's ever had in his life."

Robert smiled and added nothing. This was their little joke about fine dining. He had been consuming his sea bass faster than the girls were eating theirs, so he slowed down, looked at Lacy, and said, "Lacy don't get me wrong." Then turning to Zoë, he said, "I kind of envy Cody and you, and I don't even know him." He grabbed Lacy's hand and continued, "I couldn't be happier than I am right now. But I also see myself finishing my doctorate and ending up at some major university, grubbing for government grants to support my research, tearing my hair out to make a breakthrough, striving to publish and be heard, and generally playing the game in academia for the next thirty-some years."

Lacy said, "But you love academia."

"Yes, that's true. And I'll do just what I said. But there's this lingering thought in the back of my head that says, 'Maybe there is something more to life than striving for these things that I've decided are so important. I'd really like to find a balance—do what I love to do in my field of work, but also learn how to live. You help me with that, more than you know, Lacy."

Zoë said, "I have to admit that I got some lessons on the matter from a few people in Demming, things I remember Mom and Dad saying, but I wasn't paying much attention…about segregating the important from the unimportant. Sometimes it means taking care of the little things where you actually have some influence and not worrying about those things where you don't."

The horror of Uncle Joe's phone call last July and the painful aftermath shot into her head. "Losing Mom and Dad was a real blow. I still cannot accept that they're gone. It hurts…and here, right now, I just feel so lonely. My man is in Wyoming, and you guys, living in Cambridge and on your honeymoon, and I'm turning this conversation into the most depressing, self-involved, bunch of…let's talk about something else before I cry and make a complete fool of myself and ruin your evening."

Lacy reached over and touched her arm. "Zoë, wait. You're not ruining anything, and you're my best friend. Why don't you just finish school at the University of Wyoming? I know you promised your parents to complete your education here because they were so impressed with the idea of a Columbia education. But don't you think they'd understand if you switched schools? Speaking of what's important, Columbia just isn't that important."

"Believe me, I've wrestled with that idea. Cody and I once had a fight about my coming back here and I won, like it was something to win. I often wish I had listened to him so I may just do it. I may go out there for Christmas and not come back. I could meet with Dr. Wilhelm and talk to him about it. He wouldn't like it, but he'd help me work out a transfer. I simply must get my degree. If I didn't, I'd feel like I'd really failed my parents who worked so hard with me through my adventures in tennis, then helped me with school. I'd also feel like I'd failed myself if I didn't finish."

"Do it, kid. Do what's necessary to be happy." Lacy paused. "Why don't you come up to Boston for Thanksgiving? Our wonderful old brownstone has plenty of room, and we'd love to have you. We'll do some touristy things around town. We can go to the Locke-Ober Café in Beacon Hill, and maybe Cody could fly in and join us. We'd love to get to know him. I know it's coming up fast, and it's a long trip for a four-day weekend, but, hey, see what you can do!"

"Oh, that would be so nice. Thank you! I'll work on Cody."

Angelina stopped by the table and asked if they would like to have her father's special cheese cake made from Stilton cheese. Though Robert thought it sounded odd, the women assured him it was fantastic. They ordered one piece and three forks, plus coffee, and moaned their way through the dessert.

Robert paid the bill and wouldn't accept Zoë's plea when she insisted that he let her contribute some money. Before Lacy and Robert took a cab to JFK, they wanted to walk Zoë to her apartment. It wasn't far from the restaurant, they still had time, and she accepted.

Chapter 62

As they walked along West 116th, they saw Darrel, Gerty, and another man come around a corner. Zoë and Lacy didn't know the man. The three had obviously been having a good time, given the loud conversation, but were sober enough to walk straight and converse semi-intelligently. Still, Zoë knew they had been drinking because Darrel said, "Zoë, you look fuckin' hot tonight!" She ignored him.

There were introductions all around for Robert and Gary Cleese, an old, long-haired friend of Darrel's visiting from Oregon. Zoë recalled the name from the past. She thought he was one of Darrel's *Earth First* friends. They were walking Gerty back to the apartment and insisted on escorting Zoë, explaining that the best place for Robert and Lacy to secure a cab was back at Antonio's.

Zoë saw that Robert was ready to depart the party, and she was fine with that. So Zoë, Lacy, and Robert said their thanks for everything and their goodbyes with much well-wishing, and confirmed Thanksgiving plans. Then Zoë walked with Gerty several paces behind Darrel and Gary, toward the apartment.

As they walked, Gerty told Zoë that Gary worked at Powell's Books in Portland, in the political section. She said he once got in trouble for hiding a pile of Ann Coulter books from sale, but they forgave him, figuring the incident was one more example of his quirky sense of humor. Gerty explained that he could talk his way out of anything.

Zoë told Gerty about Robert and the nice time she had had over dinner with the newlyweds. In turn, Gerty described the Pisco Sours the three of them had drunk at Dinghy's.

The women were walking about twenty paces behind the men when they heard Darrel yelling at somebody in front of him. They couldn't tell what was being said, but a young man was hollering back. The man turned to continue on his path as Darrel charged forward and approached him angrily. The man ignored Darrel. Words were exchanged, but Zoë couldn't make them out. Suddenly, a fight ensued. It ended quickly when Darrel threw the man over a railing onto a set of stairs descending to a basement apartment. The man appeared to fall head first. Darrel spun around the railing, flying down the steps, then reemerged and ran back toward Gary.

From behind the men, Zoë hollered, "Darrel, you stupid idiot!" Darrel said something to Gary and they ran toward Zoë and Gerty. Darrel grabbed both girls' arms, pulled at them, and all four started running. Zoë was resisting so Darrel concentrated on making her move. They turned a corner and Zoë saw a man in a dark-hooded sweatshirt with "Number One" printed in white on the back running on the other side of the street. They turned another corner and Zoë stopped, pulling away from Darrel. She yelled at him, "We have to go help that guy you threw down the steps."

"No fuckin' way! He's okay. He was getting up. I checked on him. Didn't you see?"

All were breathing heavily, more from excitement than exertion.

Zoë was adamant, "I saw you disappear down that stairway. I didn't see that he was okay! We need to go back. If he's okay, why are we running away?"

"Because I don't want any complications, that's why."

"You went berserk and hurt that guy! Why? Did he say something political, something you didn't like?"

"I know that guy, and he's an ass. And it doesn't matter what was said. It was just a little tussle. It's not like I meant for him to fall over that railing."

"What do you mean, 'fall'? You threw him over! You might have killed him!" Zoë shook her head. "We need to call 911. Another stupid overreaction on your part, huh, Darrel?"

"No! Nobody's going to call anybody. He's okay. I'll double-check on him later. And I don't need any crap from you, Zoë. Just shut the fuck up."

They were nearing the apartment, Zoë stomping her way there and breathing heavily. Gerty pulled her aside and said, "Look, you're just upsetting him. Why don't you go upstairs? I'll go back to Darrel's place with them and try to talk some sense into him."

Zoë didn't like Gerty's plan. "Are you going to stay with Darrel all night? Because if you are, I'll bolt the door and see you in the morning. If he hasn't done anything on his own by then, I'm going to the police. You can tell him that. I am going to the police!"

Gerty said, "Okay, I'll be back by 10:00 A.M. Give us until then. I want to find out what that altercation was all about as much as you do."

Zoë entered her building, shut her apartment door, slid two deadbolts into place, and hooked the chain. Then, she sat and tried to calm herself before calling Cody. She knew she wouldn't reach him so she left a message: "Cody, first of all, I love you and miss you terribly. I want to see you so bad! Anyway, I had a wonderful time with Lacy and Robert. They want us to join them in Boston for the four days of the long Thanksgiving weekend. So, I want to talk to you about that. Also, I need to tell you about an incident tonight involving Darrel. He didn't do anything to me, so don't worry. But he did blow up and hurt somebody. I'll give you the details when we talk. I'm going to the police in the morning if he hasn't done so, himself, by then. Bye, honey. Let's talk when you get back tomorrow night."

Chapter 63

The next morning, wearing shorts and a sports bra under an old pair of sweats, Zoë went for a jog in Central Park. It helped clear her head of the bad ending to what had been a good time the day before. She returned at nine-thirty to shower and wait for Gerty to arrive. After walking into her apartment, she shut the door and saw that Darrel was in the bedroom stuffing Gerty's clothes into her backpack.

Zoë was ticked. "How did you get in here?"

"You've got to be kidding."

"What are you doing in my bedroom?"

"What does it look like?"

"And what happened to that guy? He's dead, isn't he? You killed him didn't you?" Darrel looked at her angrily, saying nothing. "Darrel, get out right now!"

Without a word, he walked over to where she was standing in the living room and grabbed her throat with his left hand. She clutched at his hand and tried to scream, but he tightened his grip. She could only make strained guttural sounds. He was hurting her. She let go of his hand and tried to scratch at his eyes. Darrel fought her off. Then his right hand reared back, and he smashed it into her left eye, stunning her. It caught her nose as well, which started bleeding. He hit her again in the same place.

By this time, the only thing keeping Zoë on her feet was Darrel's hand at her throat.

He ripped at her sweat pants, pulling them down, then her shorts. After tripping her legs out from under her with his leg, he knocked her to the floor. She tried to rise, grabbing at him. In response, he hit her jaw before he proceeded to pull off her shoes and pants, then he ripped off her sweatshirt and sports bra.

Zoë flailed and fought, scratching at him, but he was too strong for her. She felt his fists, elbows, and knees controlling her. She tried to scream again, and he grabbed her throat, squeezing hard enough to shut her up. With his right hand, he pulled down his pants, and with hand and knees, forced apart her legs.

The rape didn't take long. As he smothered her and began to abuse her violently, she had a fleeting vision of a grizzly bear attacking Cody. She stopped fighting. It was getting her nowhere. Zoë fell into a state of complete resignation, like a deer in the final throws of death after an attack by a mountain lion, realizing there was nothing to do but die. She didn't try to scream, she surrendered to a kind of death of her soul.

Darrel got off her, stood, then slumped on the couch. She slowly rolled away from him, curling into a fetal position.

A long silence fell upon the room. She could hear only her breathing. Vaguely, she was aware that she lay there naked except for her running socks. The room was hot, and she had been sweating from the fight, but now she noticed that she was starting to cool. Aside from the pains all over her body—she couldn't concentrate enough to count them—she felt blood dripping from her nose and realized its flow was slowing. Her head lay in a small pool of more blood. Her eye was beginning to swell shut, and it hurt like hell as it throbbed.

After what seemed like forever, Darrel got up. She could hear him pull on his pants and close his zipper. He approached and stood over her. Even though she couldn't see him, she knew he just stood there, looking at her. She could feel it.

Zoë didn't move. She had no intention of moving. She thought that this just might be her final resting place.

She heard Darrel return to the bedroom. "He's probably packing clothes again," she thought. He made a phone call, and she heard him say, "Hey. There's been a change in plans. Meet me at Nellie's Deli with my stuff. Get out of there right now, and I'll meet you at Nellie's when I can…maybe in an hour or two. I've got a couple things to do. I'll explain when I get there." Then she heard him stomp on something, breaking whatever it was.

He came out of the bedroom and stood over her once again. He said, "Look at me." She slowly moved out of her fetal position and stared up at him. She saw the Gregory backpack next to him. He held Gerty's laptop computer in his hand. She saw his face with the Brad Pitt lips looking like nothing had happened.

When he was sure that she was paying attention, he said, "I don't know why I ever got involved with a slut like you. You only care about yourself, and you got what you deserved. You're just a selfish bitch with no value whatsoever except as a receptacle."

Her tears streamed again, and in a burst of adrenalin she tried to scream at him. But her words came out choked, more as a muffled cry: "Get out!"

He kicked her hard in the ribs and as she writhed in pain, he leaned down, pressing his face against hers. He whispered, "If you report anything about last night or today, I'll find you and cut your fuckin' face beyond recognition. And don't bother running. You'll only die tired." Slowly, he rose and left, gently shutting the door behind him as though to say, "I'm not angry. You're the one out of control."

She grimaced and curled into a fetal position once again. When she heard the building's outer door shut, she tried to get up. Everything hurt, especially her ribs, left eye, and throat. She ended up crawling to the door on hands and knees, pulled herself up, and bolted and chained it. She staggered to the bathroom and got down on her knees in front of the toilet, vomiting until there was nothing left in her stomach. Her ribs hurt every minute that she retched. Now, the only things leaving her body were a flood of tears and Darrel's ejaculate running down her leg.

She fell into a dream state thinking about tennis, about her life in the past….anything to escape the nightmare of her current situation.

I prepare early. I split step and get my racquet back, watching the ball all the way from my opponent's racquet to mine, keeping my head still. I move my feet often, small steps within a small circle. This helps me maintain good balance. I work to make contact in my power zone, breathing out at the impact of the stroke. I say "back" on the back-swing and "pow" on the stroke, to help stay relaxed. I follow through completely, hitting through the ball, finishing the stroke. On low balls, I exaggerate the follow-through with bent knees. I take high balls on the rise and farther in front of my normal contact zone. I finish in a balanced position. I am relaxed. I pay attention to my breathing. While I have a single-minded focus on the ball, I also have relaxed muscles so I can swing rhythmically for optimum power and control. I let the racquet do the work. I think about soft hands and racquet head speed. I relax the grip, like I would if I were holding a small bird in my hand. I can feel the difference between a swing with a relaxed grip and one where I've tightened up. When things aren't going well, I improve my footwork and complete the proper stroke. I am patient. I stay in the present moment.

Chapter 64

It was several minutes before Zoë was able to wipe the blood from her face. She wanted to shower or at least wash her legs—she felt so dirty—but she was scared, thinking she might end up blind in her left eye. The more she thought about her eye, the more it throbbed.

She dressed in a warm-up outfit and put on running shoes over the socks she still had on. She saw her cell phone smashed on the bedroom floor. There was no land line in the apartment. She needed medical attention, and she feared pregnancy, but she didn't want to go to the hospital. She just wanted to curl up on her bed, or crawl into a hole. Actually, a grave would have been fitting.

Reluctantly, Zoë left the apartment, locking the door behind her, and walked several blocks to the Columbia University Emergency Medical Center. It was slow going, and she held her ribs as she walked. People saw her swollen eye and her pained look, but said nothing as she trudged toward the hospital.

Zoë walked into the emergency room and saw the main desk. In the waiting room, she noticed an old man holding his head. A mother sat with her three children, one of whom had a broken arm. A man on a gurney rolled by with his wife saying, "He's had a stroke. Oh, my God, he's had stroke!"

At the desk, a young woman whose name tag read, "Julie," looked up from her computer as Zoë said, "I need help. I've been raped."

Julie said, "Can you wait right where you are while I find Trish?"

Zoë nodded.

Immediately, Julie left her post to look for Trish. Within a minute, a middle-aged, African-American woman hustled toward her and said, "My name is Trish. Please come with me. We're going to take good care of you."

Zoë almost stumbled as Trish put her arm around her. Zoë started to sob.

"There, there, I know, I know. I'll be with you the whole time. You just lean on me, and I'll help you. Dr. Sanders will be with us in a bit. She's the best."

They entered an empty examination room. Trish pulled the curtain as a nurse named Sandy entered. The two women helped Zoë remove her clothes and put on a hospital gown. Then they assisted her onto the examination table, covering her with a sheet and blanket. She had no purse, valuables, jewelry, money, nor identification…just her apartment key, which Sandy secured. Trish leaned close, held Zoë's hand, and said, "Our first priority is your general health. We're going to check out that nasty looking eye and anything else that's hurting. Then we're going to do a rape exam, paying close attention to the chain of evidence. First, I need you to sign a consent form. Because of the privacy rules under HIPAA, we need your consent to be able to inform the police."

"I'll sign it. I have a crime to report."

"Yes, the rape."

"No, another crime and the rape."

"Okay. This precinct will probably send either Sherry or Christine. Both are good people. Lastly, we'll provide treatment and recommend that you seek counseling."

Sandy left to get the proper form as Trish said, "Now, before we start, can you tell me your name so we can talk a little easier?"

Zoë froze, and her tears flowed. She just stared at this black woman with the kind eyes, having lost any sense of what she should do. She knew her name and could recall her life, but she didn't want to recall it. She felt dead inside. And she had already said she'd sign a form. She wanted Darrel punished, but she didn't want to be Zoë. She thought, "I'm not thinking right." And, with a deer-in-the-headlights look, she said, "My name is Jane Dorn."

Doubt obvious in her voice, Trish said, "Okay…when did this happen?"

Slowly and deliberately, Zoë replied, "About nine-thirty this morning."

Trish looked at her watch. It was ten-forty. "Okay, aside from that eye, where do you hurt?"

"My ribs where Darrel kicked me, and my throat where he choked me. He also hit me on the jaw, but my eye and ribs really hurt."

"So you know the assailant?"

"He's an ex-boyfriend."

Sandy had returned with a clipboard, handed it to Zoë who signed, "Jane Dorn" to all the forms. Trish and Sandy exchanged glances, then Trish looked closely at Zoë's eye and said that she wanted Dr. Sanders to examine it. She moved on to Zoë's ribs, applying pressure and getting clear signals where Zoë hurt and where she didn't. As Trish looked at Zoë's throat, she said, "You're going to have some bruising here. It's already starting to show color. Does it hurt to talk?"

"A little."

"Then we'll try to keep talking to a minimum."

Dr. Sanders walked in and introduced herself. Trish filled her in on Zoë's status. The doctor carefully examined her eye, asking Zoë to shift her focus in all four directions. Then, she said, "I'm concerned about a blowout fracture and a tripod fracture, so we're going to schedule an orbital CT." She quickly confirmed what Trish had told her about the ribs and said, "We'll also want x-rays of those ribs. They won't tell us much, but they may be needed in court." She checked out Zoë's jaw, which was bruising. Zoë told her that she didn't think any of her teeth were broken or loose, but she felt general pain in her mouth.

Dr. Sanders said, "We'll start the rape exam when the police get here. Sandy, get me some ice packs, then see when we can schedule the CT and x-rays." Dr. Sanders and Trish pulled back the sheet. Protecting Zoë's dignity, they checked for badly bruised areas or scratches on her body.

"Did you shower?"

"I wanted to. I just wiped off the blood from my nose and cleaned my legs. I feel filthy, but I was scared. And I knew I needed medical attention."

Dr. Sanders said, "We'll try to clean you up after the exam. I see you had rotator cuff surgery."

"Yes."

"From a tennis injury?"

"How did you know?"

"Your right arm is slightly more muscular than your left."

"The surgery was from years of accumulated injuries."

"Did it go well?"

"Yes, my right shoulder is probably stronger than my left now."

"Do you know if any muscles were wrenched or ligaments torn during the rape?" The doctor moved her arms and legs in multiple directions… bending, pushing and pulling. Then she asked Zoë to tell them what hurt as they checked her out from head to toe.

When Dr. Sanders completed this part of the exam, she said, "You're going to have a few bad bruises and sore muscles for a while."

A woman in a police uniform entered the room and introduced herself as Christine. Dr. Sanders left, asking Trish to start the rape exam.

Trish explained, "We have a very specific protocol that involves a blood test to determine if you were pregnant prior to the rape and…"

"I'm not. I had my period a week ago, but I haven't been diligent in taking my birth control pills. I'd like the morning-after pill…just to be sure…" Zoë's voice trailed off.

"Of course. But first, we'll still do the blood test and conduct a pelvic exam to look for any trauma. After we swab the cervix, we'll make a slide and examine it under a microscope looking for motile sperm. Three additional swabs from the cervix and three from the vaginal vault will enable us to check for any foreign materials, like pubic hair. We'll also take samples of your pubic hair and scalp, and samples from under your finger nails. Finally, we'll take cultures for diseases, look for lesions, check for herpes, etc. All of these specimens will be checked, sealed and put in a special envelope, and used later for the trial. Did you notice any lesions on the assailant's penis?"

With some disgust, Zoë said, "I wasn't in a position to look at it."

Trish said, "You know the person, though. Do you have reason to suspect any venereal diseases present?"

"No."

"We'll check closely, anyway."

Trish nodded at Christine, as though to say, "Your turn."

Christine said, "I need you to tell me everything that happened, and I'll take notes. But I also have a recorder, if you'll allow me to use it. I first need your name and address."

Zoë just stared for a moment and then gave Christine the fake name and a phony address, saying, "Turn on the recorder. I'll tell you what happened."

Zoë started by telling the police officer about meeting Darrel, Gary, and Gerty on the walk back to her apartment the night before, then described everything that happened after that, finally stopping after she'd provided every awful detail of the rape, as well as the aftermath and Darrel's threats. She cried uncontrollably when she told of him saying that all she was good for was as a receptacle. But mostly, she told her story with detachment, as though it was about somebody else. She made sure that Christine had Darrel's full name and address, knew where he worked, who some of his friends were, and his politics—that he was a leftist activist but didn't belong to any organization. She unloaded everything she could about Darrel, anything that might help the police find him. She speculated that something bad had happened to the man that Darrel had thrown over the railing and that Darrel was probably on the run with Gerty along for the ride. Zoë didn't mention Cody, or her message to him, or anything about the dinner the night before.

Christine made no comment except to say that she wasn't aware of an incident like Darrel's attack of the man the night before. But she told Zoë she'd check it out when she called in to the station.

The telling took a while. Trish took all the swabs and the blood test as Zoë spoke, managing the evidence as required. Zoë occasionally had to drink cold water or suck on ice chips because her throat hurt, but she got through her story.

Christine wanted to know more about what Zoë had been doing before walking back to her apartment, but Zoë was hurting and said she was done talking.

Then, Sandy proceeded to take Zoë for her CT and x-rays.

Trish said to Christine, "Now that was a fairly complete story, wasn't it? What's your take on the threat?"

Christine said, "I don't know. I did notice that during the attack, Darrel choked her enough to shut her up, but not enough to kill her. She's damn lucky there. I figure he's on the run. And I've heard that line, 'don't bother running; you'll only die tired' before, but I don't know where. I'll check it out with some tough guys I know at the precinct. He may have just said it to give him some time, scare her, intimidate and humiliate her a little more for some reason. He sounds like a sociopath… another bastard completely indifferent to what he's done. In his mind, she deserved it because she pissed him off. I'm going to go make a phone call and then head back to the station."

As Christine turned to leave, Trish said, "She sure is a pretty thing. She looks a little like Halle Berry."

Chapter 65

When Sandy brought Zoë back to her room after the CT scan, she stayed while Trish held Zoë's hand, telling the girl that it wasn't her fault, that Trish knew the guilt and the feelings of being unclean and unworthy of love could be overwhelming. She advised Zoë to seek help…not to tell the world, but to talk to somebody she trusted—a minister, her primary physician, a rape counselor, or a psychologist—so she could get on with her life and be with her loved ones.

Trish also told Zoë that she didn't believe the name she had given them in the report, but that it was okay. She understood…it was about self-loathing, which was why Zoë needed to get help. She assured Zoë that she would get through this, and happiness was still possible, then asked Zoë if she had somebody they could call for her, and if she had a safe place to go.

Zoë had been a zombie throughout most of Trish's attempts to comfort her. Now, she roused herself to say that she would have to go back to her apartment because she didn't have any other choice.

Trish said, "That could be quite traumatic. It's likely that you will face things there that will trigger pain from your awful experience."

"I don't have a choice. What triggers are you talking about?"

"Like looking at the floor where the rape occurred. Or envisioning him in your bedroom again, walking toward you, indifferent to your wishes. You could hear a song that might have been playing in the back-ground when it happened, or see a program on television about rape. Outside of the apartment, triggers exist, too. For example, the sound of a zipper opening or closing could be upsetting to you. Or maybe you run into somebody named Darrel who may be the nicest guy in the world, but hearing the name will trigger an emotional response in you. Someone yelling in anger at somebody else could upset you. You'll possibly react strongly to anger or coercion by any male. And while you'll try not to think about what happened, something like these things will trigger you to do exactly what you don't want to do. That's why we suggest you seek help from a counselor or support group."

Trish gave her two phone numbers for rape crisis centers where she could seek counseling and maybe get help to find a safe place to stay. Trish hugged her, patting her back gently.

Zoë barely felt Trish's hand. She felt dead inside.

As Zoë left, Trish said, "I'll be praying for you…whoever you are." Zoë just kept walking away. When she was out of sight, Trish's eyes welled up with tears as she said to Sandy, "I must be a terrible nurse, getting attached to these kids every time. God help her."

Sandy said, "No, you're one of the best."

"I don't know. That poor girl is devastated. She's not thinking right, and there's nothing we can do about it."

Zoë walked back to her apartment with prescription pills in her pocket and a bill for $2437.62 in her hand. She had taken two Lo-Ovral pills—the "morning-after drug"—with instructions to take two more in eight to twelve hours. She'd been given the antibacterial drug, amoxicillin, for any potential gonorrhea or syphilis infection, and one gram of Valtrex for herpes. Rounding out Zoë's supply of drugs was a thirty-day supply, with two refills, of Ibuprofen—800 milligrams each—to reduce inflammation and for pain. If she needed something stronger, she was told to call Dr. Sanders and ask for it.

Dr. Sanders had told her that they'd taken a blood test for possible HIV/AIDS infection and to call in four weeks for the results. The doctor had given her instructions on caring for her eye and had also told her that time, alone, would heal her throat, ribs, and bruises. Zoë's jaw seemed okay. Finally, she'd been advised to see an optometrist if she had any difficulties with vision.

Chapter 66

Detective Kowalski was a twenty-four-year veteran of the New York City Police Department, having spent his entire career assigned to the Twenty-fifth Precinct near Columbia University—they called it the "two-five." He was entering the smallest of the three interrogation rooms with Freddy Polk. Freddy was a short, stocky man with scraggly hair and a cauliflower ear. He was about forty-five. He looked sixty. He had on grubby, oversized pants, well-worn athletic shoes, and a dark blue hooded sweatshirt that had "Number One" printed on the back in large but filthy white letters.

Detective Kowalski said, "Have a seat Freddy. How's it going?"

"Well, I'm not a slave to anybody. I don't have any debts."

"That's a good thing. It's nice to see you again."

"Yeah, I'm here so often, people will begin to think we like each other."

"I do like you, Freddy. You talk to me. Most of your friends out on the street just grunt or babble about missing their mommies. How'd you break your nose? That looks new."

"Jimmy the Snitch hit me across the face with half a bottle of vodka a couple weeks ago…gave me a new look."

"It's quite becoming. Makes you look tough, like some washed-out boxer."

"I am a washed-out boxer. What do you want from me?"

"Where were you last night, between nine and ten?"

"Hanging around the corner of 116th Street and Broadway, where I always am."

"See anything unusual?"

"Yeah."

Silence descended on the room. Finally, the detective asked, "Do I have to ask every question you know is coming, or are you going to be good and tell me what you saw?"

Freddy hesitated only a few seconds, then said, "I saw two young guys with two broads walking several paces behind. I didn't recognize any of them, but one of the broads was sharp—in a short blue dress and heels, and a nice jacket. The other one was cute, too, but she had on jeans, a jacket, and running shoes. I couldn't see the details. I was paying attention to the one in the blue dress. I couldn't see the guys too well, but one of them had long hair in a ponytail. Can I have some coffee?"

"The usual?"

Detective Kowalski left momentarily, returning with a cup of coffee with cream and sugar, which he handed to Freddy.

"A glass cup?"

"Yeah, we stopped using Styrofoam to save the planet. Now we wash out real cups with NYPD printed on them."

"Cups are nice, but the coffee's the same."

"Continue Freddy. I haven't got all night."

"So, I hear one of the guys yell something to somebody way up ahead of them. And that guy—he was alone—yells some shit back."

"What was being said?"

"I couldn't tell. I don't hear too good anymore. They were just yelling at each other. Then the guy up ahead just walks on, never turning back. The guy without the ponytail yells some more, and runs up to the other guy. Pretty soon, a fight starts. The guy without the ponytail flings the other guy over a railing, down into the entrance of a basement apartment. Then the two guys started running back toward the girls, grabbed them, and made them run, too. The girl in the heels couldn't run too good, and she was arguing with the guy who threw the guy over the railing. They were coming right toward me, so I started running down 116th as they turned down the same street. They were on the other side. So they're running down one side, and I'm running down the other, and I finally just stopped. Didn't see much point in running anymore. Those guys weren't chasing me. They were trying to get away."

"You like the word 'guy,' don't you?"

Freddy looked puzzled and said, "Yeah, so what? Everybody's just broads and guys to me."

"Did you hear anything that was being said?"

"Naw. The broad in the heels swore at the one guy and said something about helping the guy who got tossed, but I don't remember the words."

"Anything else?"

"I don't recall."

"Where'd you pick up the legal jargon, Freddy? Never mind. One more question. With winter coming, why don't you go down south where it's warm…maybe Key West? Why do you want to stay here?"

"That's two questions."

"Just tell me, Freddy."

"I tried that once. Got as far as North Carolina, where the cops picked me up for vagrancy. They asked me which direction I wanted to go because they were going to put me on a bus out of state. But it couldn't be south because the sheriff's brother-in-law was a lawman in South Carolina and they didn't want to send any problems his way. I wondered why they bothered to ask, but I said, 'Send me north.' I really didn't mind having to come back to New York—all my friends are here."

"Like who?"

"Like Jimmy the Snitch and Janet. Janet gives me comfort whenever I need it."

"For Christ's sake Freddy, Janet will give you AIDS."

"Yeah, I know. But she's nice about it."

Chapter 67

The next day, Detective Kowalski informed Christine that his conversation with Freddy corroborated the story that "Jane Dorn" had given her at the hospital the day before. He said, "Why do you think she gave you a fake name? It wasn't even original. Jane Dorn was really lame, showed a lack of imagination."

"Yeah, and both Trish and I saw through it. Rape victims sometimes want to deny who they are, and she seemed pretty traumatized. Maybe she wanted to skip the bill. People do that all the time: walk into the emergency room with no ID, give a phony name, and walk out on the bill. She may end up doing that, but I don't think that was going through her head when she gave that name. The address was false too, huh?"

"Yeah, it was a convenience store owned by some rag heads."

"You bigot."

"Somebody's got to counter all this political correctness bullshit."

Christine dropped the subject. "Did you find anything at this Darrel guy's place?"

"No. He left quickly. It was a tiny loft apartment. No roommate. And we couldn't find this Gertrude Castlethwait, either. But then, we didn't have an address for her. She left with him, apparently."

"The guy died?"

"Yeah, blunt force trauma. He landed on his head. Real unlucky, for both him and this Darrel Holt. It's manslaughter at the minimum."

"Who was the guy?"

"Somebody named Harold Friedkin. His last steady job was working as a window washer, got fired about nine months ago. He'd been bouncing around with part-time work ever since. He also worked for some organization registering people to vote."

"So he's not a DA's son, or some prodigy violinist where the world will weep."

"No, just a schlep who got into an argument over something and got his head broken. There won't be any publicity driving us to find this Darrel Holt."

Christine said, "Something will turn up. The Jane Doe—aka Jane Dorn—had to have friends. Maybe she's with her friends, getting her confused head straightened out, and she'll come forward with more information. Or, if she's in hiding or skipped town, her friends will be looking for her and then maybe we'll learn more about Holt after we find her. The way she talked about him at the hospital, he seems like some kind of sociopath."

"Is that a diagnosis? You into psychology now?"

"No, I'm just stating an opinion. I said, 'He seems like some kind of sociopath.'"

"You know, I figured out where that line he used during the rape came from, the one where he said, 'Don't bother running; you'll only die tired.' It's something professionally trained snipers say, for Christ's sake. And this Holt is no sniper. He's a fuckin' piss-ant. We have some limited information on him. He's an activist, some kind of anarchist, not affiliated with any organization that we know of. He has delusions of grandeur, and he probably raped her for—hell, I don't know why he raped her. But I don't see him as a threat, somebody who will chase her down. At least, I hope not."

"She may believe he'll chase her down, though. What he said to her was chilling."

"Yeah. Could be.

"Christine, let me tell you about a real sociopath. Last week, I was listening to this eleven-year-old kid talk to this psychologist and someone from Juvenile. It seems the kid was walking down 112th smoking, and some eighty-four-year-old man sitting on the steps in front of his building says, 'Hey kid, you're a little young to be smoking those things.' The kid walks over to the old man and jams the burning end of the cigarette into the old man's cheek, then grabs the back of the old man's head and smashes it into his upraised knee. After a lot of preliminary talk, the psychologist finally asks the big question, kind of slips it in: 'Why did you do that?' And the kid says, 'He deserved it. He pissed me off.' The kid never batted an eye, just said it like he was asking for a peanut butter and jelly sandwich. 'He deserved it. He pissed me off.' That kid is going to be in prison, or dead, before he's out of his teens. I sometimes wonder what we're breeding out there."

Chapter 68

Cody had called and called the New York City Police Department about a missing person and got the runaround each time because they'd never heard of Zoë Valiente. He sent them a photo of Zoë and a copy of the transcript of her last phone call, and he'd sent a priority letter to Midge and Pidge, telling them to please contact him when they got back from St. Bart's. When they called and told him about the blood on the floor and that Zoë was missing and they'd been to the cops, Cody became frantic, immediately thinking the worst. He called Martin, who organized the trip—the flights, the hotel, the calls to the roommates and Bud Wilhelm. He even tracked down Zoë's rabbi uncle.

They all gathered at Martin and Cody's hotel and walked into the Twenty-Fifth Precinct together. Martin handed the desk clerk a picture of Zoë and said, "We want to see the person who is investigating this woman's disappearance."

"What's her name?"

"Zoë Valiente."

The clerk started to check her computer when Martin said, "You probably won't find her in there. But my friend, here, sent a copy of this same picture to this precinct a few days ago. We want to talk to the person who has it. We'll start there."

The clerk secured details of each person's identity and said, "This could take a while. Have a seat over there."

An hour later, in the bowels of the police department, a relatively

287

new police officer found Detective Kowalski in a hallway and said, "I've been sent to find you."

"So you found me."

"Remember those two lesbians that were here a couple days ago? They're back, and they have with them a Columbia University professor of journalism, an owner of a newspaper who used to work for the *New York Times*, a rabbi, and some guy who works for the feds. They want to see you."

"Jesus Christ, what now! Is the big room open?"

"Yes, I think so."

"Put them in there and tell them I'll be with them shortly. What about Christine? Is she around?" The rookie nodded. "Then ask her to join the party."

Kowalski and Christine entered the room full of anxious people, asked for introductions and after getting them, Kowalski said to Cody, "So you're the boyfriend, the guy from the feds. You the one called the Forest Service the feds? A damn Smoky the Bear is now a 'fed'?"

Cody said, "No. I simply said to the woman up front that I worked for the Forest Service. She wanted to know if I sprayed trees, 'like a lawn and tree service.' I said, 'No, it's an agency of the federal government.' I can't help it if your people don't know anything about the Forest Service."

"Shit, the way it came to me, I thought it might be the FBI or something." Looking at Martin Coleman, he said, "And you, you own some newspaper in Podunk, Wyoming. When did you work for the *Times*?"

"Thirty-five years ago."

Kowalski looked at Martin and said, "Okay, I get the rabbi relative and her local college professor and the distraught boyfriend and the roommates who brought us the information on this Zoë, what's her last name again?"

Several said, "Valiente."

"Yeah, and it took us a while to make the connection with Jane Dorn but, why are you here, Mr. Coleman?"

Martin said, "I came because Cody asked me to."

"What does Jane Dorn have to do with this?" asked Cody.

"You don't know shit about what's going on here, do you?" asked Kowalski. "That's why you're all here. I guess we'd better tell you."

Everyone sat in silence, waiting for one of the police officers to start talking.

Kowalski said, "Christine, you want to do this, or shall I?"

"I'd better. I was there when she gave her statement." Christine took a deep breath, aware that all eyes were on her. "On the morning of November eighth, the department was called by the Columbia University Medical Center to come to the hospital. A crime had been committed, and I was the only one on duty who handles these situations, so I went there immediately."

Cody said, "What situations?"

"I'll get to that."

Cody just looked at her, noticeably frightened, and waited. She went on, "I met with Trish, the hospital specialist in these cases, and Dr. Sanders, and this young woman calling herself Jane Dorn who had been beaten—and raped by a man she called Darrel Holt."

Cody began to tear up. He slumped in his chair, then started squirming in anger. Martin, sitting next to him, grabbed his arm and said, "Hold on Cody. I'm with you, pal." Bud Wilhelm was ashen-faced, and Midge broke into tears while Pidge's thin lips grew taught as anger consumed her. Zoë's rabbi uncle was noticeably shaken.

Martin asked, "This was Zoë, right? Is she okay?"

"Yes, it was Zoë," Christine replied. "She was physically okay when she left the hospital several hours after her examination and treatment. She had some damage done to her eye, a couple cracked ribs, and a sore throat from being choked, but that will all heal in time. The rape is another matter, not physically, but psychologically. And Mr. Nelson, when you find her, don't ever ask her about the details. Don't ever ask her what Darrel said to her, or did to her, like, 'You can tell me because I love you.' That doesn't work. She'll tell you what she wants when she's good and ready, and it may take years. The gory details shouldn't be your major concern, anyway. And I'm not giving you any details of what this guy did or said to Zoë. The other thing, I don't want to give you false hope. If she doesn't want to be found, you may not find her."

There was a long pause as people just sat there, dazed. Cody was in no position to talk, but Martin asked the obvious question: "What if something terrible has happened to her? What if she didn't just run away, but this Darrel did something to her?"

Kowalski said. "We really don't think that happened. Maybe you'll understand that when Christine gives more details."

Within the boundaries she had set, Christine told them the whole story as she knew it, starting the night of November seventh—the fight and the death of Harold Friedkin, the corroboration of Freddy Polk, the aftermath of trying to find Darrel Holt, Gertrude Castlethwait, and Zoë, aka Jane Dorn. She told them about how the department had eventually made the connection between Zoë and Jane Dorn. It had happened when Christine had walked by a clerk's desk and saw Zoë's picture. She had immediately gotten it to Kowalski.

Christine said, "The reason we don't think that this Darrel Holt killed Zoë is that we have information he left town while she was still in the hospital."

Kowalski jumped in, "We'd learned from the two of you who room with Zoë, that Nellie's Deli was a favorite hangout of Darrel and Gertrude Castlethwait, who is also missing. So we went out there and talked to the owner. He knew the pair. He told us that he had overheard conversations among Darrel, a pony-tailed guy, and Gertrude. It was pretty well established that Darrel Holt had a plane ticket in his hand, and that he left in a cab for the airport at 1:30 P.M. He had luggage with him."

Christine added, "And Zoë didn't leave the hospital until 2:55 P.M."

With a shaking voice, Cody said, "How do you know for sure that he got on a plane?"

Kowalski said, "We don't know for sure. But we do know the Yellow cab that picked up the 1:30 fare at Nellie's took a man to LaGuardia and dropped him off at the United Airlines ticketing area."

"Do you know where he went?"

"No. We think he has a fake ID. That's another thing we're looking into."

There was a period of silence and then Kowalski added, "Just so you don't think up some conspiratorial movie version of this, like, 'he could have doubled back,' we don't think he's that smart…or dumb, depending on your perspective. We know this guy from previous run-ins with the law—he's an anarchist—and, according to the deli owner, he was scared. He wanted to leave New York fast. So we're treating this as a murder case—of Harold Friedkin—and, separately, the rape and beating of Zoë Valiente. We don't believe two people have been murdered, here. Our priority is to find Darrel Holt because of the murder and rape."

Martin said, "Are you telling us that you're not trying to find Zoë?"

"We'd love to find her because it supports the case against Holt. But our priority is finding him. It's a matter of where it's most efficient to devote our resources."

Martin said, "What I sense is that as time goes on, your interest in finding Zoë will diminish."

"It's reality," said Kowalsky.

Christine added, "We're hoping she'll get her head straightened out and contact us."

"She had been out to dinner with her friend, Lacy, and Lacy's new husband that night," Cody said quietly. "The couple are still on their honeymoon in Italy. Lacy's maiden name was Oishi. I didn't know Robert's last name until I talked with Midge. In Zoë's message, she wanted me to fly to Boston and meet Lacy and Robert, and be with her for Thanksgiving. She was coming to Demming for Christmas. I was going to give her an engagement ring then."

Kowalski said, "That fit's with her phone message to you."

Cody said, "She lost her parents in an automobile accident in Israel in July and it was devastating. Now this? She didn't deserve this."

Christine had a pained look and said, "She lost her parents? I'm not a psychologist, but I've been around. This is very likely a woman who will not be thinking logically."

"Why would she use the fake name?" asked Cody.

"Because of unbelievable guilt," replied Christine. "The shock of being brutalized. She didn't want to be Zoë Valiente. I assume she's still suffering because she's not around anywhere so that we can talk to her. We don't know what she's thinking. My guess is that it will take time for her to heal emotionally. She shouldn't try to deal with the aftermath of her trauma alone. She needs to connect with someone who will help her, so she can face you again and not feel dirty and unworthy."

Cody said, "Unworthy? Why would I think that?"

"This isn't about you." Christine shook her head. "I don't know you, Mr. Nelson, but my recommendation is for you to get some counseling on the whys and wherefores of rape victims, and how to deal with them appropriately. And you need to examine what you are feeling about what happened to Zoë. Get your thoughts very clear in your head. That would help you and her, if and when, she is found."

Chapter 69

After leaving the hospital, Zoë arrived at her apartment, too frightened to enter. She stood outside, listening for several minutes. Finally, disgusted, she barged in, checked out the whole place, saw that nobody was there, and locked herself in. She lived there quietly, with no television or music, in hiding. The most noise anyone would hear from the apartment, should someone be listening, was the sound of running water or a flushing toilet.

She nursed herself, placing cold compresses on her eye at first, later replacing them with warm wash rags. She napped a lot, sometimes with her head elevated to help her eye heal, but mostly lying in a tight fetal position. The naps took her in and out of dream states, where she recalled her childhood, or she'd wake up feeling Darrel's violent penetration, or feel him kick her. She ate what was in the apartment: canned soup, eggs and toast, ramen noodles, and salads. She bathed often, and washed her hair every day. Bathing soothed her muscles and gave her the illusion of being clean. She occasionally had bouts of uncontrollable sobbing, jumping from one thought to another: "Why did I yell at him to leave? I feel so empty. I don't know how I can ever be happy again. I cannot tell anybody." The worst was when she realized how she had mentally criticized Cody for putting himself in a situation to get attacked by a grizzly bear; and yet, she walked into her apartment and confronted Darrel when she could have just left—then none of this would have happened.

She had moments of terror, feeling as she had when she had first entered the apartment and had seen her dried blood on the floor. She moved the rug out from under the coffee table to cover the place where Darrel had raped her. Occasionally, she would just sit and stare into space. There would be lapses of time—sometimes hours—when she couldn't recall how she had just spent them. But she knew she never left the apartment, regularly checking the double-bolted and chained door.

She spoke to no one, and no one came to her. She thought she heard someone knock on her door once when she was sleeping. Afterward, she didn't know whether it had actually happened or it had been a dream. Another time, she was near the door when someone knocked loudly. The sound sent chills up her spine. But she concluded that if it was Darrel at the door, he would have tried the key—Gerty's key. The dead-bolts would have blocked his entry. Still, if it was him, then he would know she was in there. She had looked through the peep hole and had seen Scott, Dr. Wilhelm's indentured servant PhD candidate. Apparently, at least Dr. Wilhelm was looking for her.

She thought about Cody and felt like damaged goods. She asked herself, "How could he ever love me now? He deserves somebody better than me, somebody not scarred, unclean, filthy. It was my fault. I should have left! I shouldn't have yelled at Darrel. I knew he had a temper, and I yelled at him. How could Cody ever understand that I caused it, that I didn't stop it, that I didn't leave when I had the chance? I should have been able to keep this from happening." On this particular occasion, as an act of self-mutilation, she took a pair of scissors and cut her beautiful long hair off at the neck. Then she showered, dropping to her hands and knees on the tub floor and letting the warm water run over her, washing her tears down the drain, wishing she could go there also. She had hit a depth of self-loathing she had never thought possible.

She did not emerge from her apartment for three days. On the fourth day, a pleasant, warm fall day, Zoë took stock of herself. Her eye was terribly black and blue, but at least she could see, and the pain was subsiding. She dressed in jeans and a Columbia University sweatshirt, and after a breakfast of the last of her eggs, she walked to her bank and closed her account, withdrawing several thousand dollars. She requested that the bank give her the sum in one-hundred-dollar bills, and change. She asked the teller to place twenty-five hundred dollars in a plain, manila envelope and the balance in another envelope. The bank teller thought her request was irregular, but said nothing. After carefully checking Zoë's identification with their records on file, the teller counted out the cash as requested and watched her depart.

Zoë walked to the hospital where she had been treated after the rape. She went to the billing office, presented the invoice she had in her possession, and gave the billing clerk the manila envelope with twenty-five hundred dollars in cash. She secured a receipt and her change of $62.38, which she shoved into the front pocket of her jeans, and left. The girl at the billing office thought the transaction was odd, since cash payments were extremely rare, but said nothing.

Zoë stopped at a small travel agency and asked to see Greyhound bus schedules. The agent asked her where she wanted to go; she told them she didn't know.

Zoë stopped by a small grocery store where they knew her, and the woman at the checkout said, "What happened to you?"

Zoë said, "I got hit by a tennis ball."

The cashier was too busy to pursue Zoë's curious response. But she couldn't help but think that if Zoë had been hit by a tennis ball to cause that injury, it must have been made of cement.

Months before, Darrel had told Zoë about a Russian woman who knew a man who could get her "anything" she needed. She stopped at the small newsstand/ convenience store where the woman worked, and waited until the place was empty. Then Zoë said to the Russian, "I understand that you know people in low places."

In a thick accent, the woman responded, "Who sent you?"

"Darrel Holt."

She raised her eyebrows, acknowledging the name, and possibly something else that Zoë didn't understand. She went on, "Yeah, I know people in low places. You'll need to cover up that eye with makeup so I can take your picture. Do it now and give me two hundred dollars. You

295

can pick up your identification card here, at three o'clock tomorrow. I'm a little backed up."

Walking back to her apartment with her groceries and caked-on makeup covering the dark eye, Zoë began noticing her surroundings. The sky was grey and whatever scraggly foliage that barely survived a New York summer had long fallen to the ground. She saw a small group of middle-aged couples stop abruptly in front of her as one of the men said, "I'm trying to picture the scene that put that there!" He pointed to something on the sidewalk. One of the women in the group giggled. "Oh, stop that." As they walked on, Zoë looked down at the sidewalk, searching for the object to which the man had gestured. It was a black thong. She found no humor in it.

Then, she noticed a twenty-something standing near her. His jacket was open showing a "Buck Fush" T-shirt underneath. Elsewhere around her, she saw the normal array of iPod people, folks speaking other languages, an older woman with huge collagen lips—a regular Frankenstein Barbie—and a Lolita with no bra wearing a T-shirt that said, "I'm Ready When You Are." Upon turning a corner, Zoë saw "Bambi" in her white cowboy boots, short shorts, and halter top, and "Thumper" in her CFM shoes, mini skirt, and see-through blouse. The women wore long, flowing rabbit fur coats, hanging open. They entered a rundown apartment building. Zoë thought that they were probably going home to sleep through the day after a long night's work.

Suddenly, she realized that, except for the couples on a lark who had encountered the black thong, no one she had seen had smiled. But then, Zoë hadn't smiled at anyone, either.

Zoë spent the rest of the day curled on the bed, or methodically packing her roller-board suitcase, her small duffle bag, and her day pack with the possessions she wanted to keep. She didn't have much to pack because of the apartment's space limitations. Those things she didn't want to take with her, she left. She trashed one specific outfit: a pair of shorts, a sports bra, an old pair of sweats, a pair of socks, and her old running shoes.

Zoë thought about writing letters of apology to Dr. Wilhelm and Antonio, as well as Midge and Pidge, for what she was about to do. But decided against it. She didn't want to tell anybody she knew what was going on. She didn't even want to see or talk to anybody she knew, for any reason. She snacked on smoked turkey, yogurt, and diet Squirt. At nine-thirty, Zoë took a Tylenol PM and went to bed. She slept for eleven hours. Sleep was her refuge.

At 1:00 P.M. the next day, dressed comfortably and with an improved appearance, Zoë left the apartment. She hauled her luggage down to the street and took a cab to Carnegie Deli on 7th Avenue and 55th Street… a place known for "dispensing delectable deli daily from dawn (6:30 A.M.) to distraction (4:00 A.M.) and delighted to deliver." She took her place in a long line that stretched outside, standing behind a woman that looked and acted like Leona Helmsley back from the dead. Apparently, "Leona" shouldn't have to wait in line with the little people. After all, Bill Clinton didn't wait in line when he ate there.

Zoë noticed a homeless man standing near the curb. He held a cup saying, "Please help me." She asked the man behind her to save her place and walked over to the homeless man. She asked him, "Are you hungry?"

"Yes."

She noticed his pleading face. "Okay, it's going to take me a while to get in there, but I'll bring you a pastrami sandwich and a Coke."

"That would be great."

When she got a table, she ordered the sandwich, a side of coleslaw and a diet Coke with a regular Coke to go.

In close quarters next to her, a woman said to her male companion, "I'm surely glad that's over."

He said, "Me, too. It's all going to work out okay."

They looked at the pretty girl next to them with the butchered hairdo and damaged eye. In turn, she acknowledged their presence with a glance. They introduced themselves as Bob and Maxine. Zoë responded, and Maxine started telling her story.

Bob and Maxine had just spent four hours at the passport office on Hudson Street because Maxine's passport was in her purse when it was stolen while dining in a Park Avenue restaurant. Even though there had been ten people at their table in the restaurant, no one had seen someone slip her purse off the back of her chair. The thief, or thieves, spent twenty-three hundred dollars using her credit cards before she ever knew the purse was gone. Bob called all the credit card companies. He told Zoë it was a laborious exercise trying to find an actual human being to cancel the cards. Since she had no passport, they missed their flight to Heathrow for their European tour.

Maxine said, "The passport office was a zoo. Before we even got in, some official hollered, 'All those with seven-thirty appointments line up along the wall. All those with eight o'clock appointments line up after them. Back up now. Against the wall! All those with no appointments get in line in the back.' We were being herded like sheep. Then during the security check, some guy said, 'No need to hurry folks. Nothing moves fast in this building.' We did have a very helpful woman pull the information together. But then we had to wait and wait for the finished passport, and that lady was frustrating. She'd get a pile of passports delivered to her, but she would shuffle papers or talk on the phone behind this glass partition for several minutes while seventy-five people were anxiously waiting. Then, as though a great favor was being bestowed, she would finally look at the documents that had been given to her several minutes before, and read eight or ten names of those with passports available." Maxine added sarcastically, "Those receiving their passports were oh, so appreciative."

"It's the tyranny of the clerks," Bob added. "It's not the leaders of the world that run things, it's the bureaucrats. They exercise power in these passive aggressive ways. You get the sense that they derive great pleasure from controlling other peoples' lives."

While sympathetic to their plight, Zoë did not encourage the conversation. She couldn't help wondering what the couple would say if she told them, "Oh, that's nothing. I just saw my ex-boyfriend kill somebody and then he beat and raped me." She guessed it might be a real conversation stopper.

Zoë had made four sandwiches out of the one delivered with the five-inch pile of pastrami, using the extra rye bread provided by the deli. She added mustard, ate two of the smaller ones, and wrapped the other two in napkins along with dill pickles. With the Coke to go, she worked her way through the crowd.

With kindness, Bob helped her with her luggage as she moved through the line to pay for her food—the deli only took cash—and then outside. She delivered the food to the homeless man, who took it appreciatively and said, "You're an angel."

Zoë said, "No, I'm not, but thanks, anyway." She also slipped him a twenty-dollar bill.

As Zoë retrieved her luggage from Bob, Maxine said, "What happened to your eye?"

Zoë smiled and said, "I fell and hit it on the corner of a chair. Glad you were able to rebook your flights. Have a good trip."

"You, too. Where are you going?"

"I don't know."

She caught a cab to the newsstand near Columbia University, got there early, and had to wait until three o'clock to pick up her fake ID. She paid an additional one hundred dollars for information regarding Darrel's purchase. Then she took a cab to the Port Authority Bus Terminal, bought a ticket, and got on an all-night bus departing at 6:14 P.M.

She didn't know where she would end up, or what she was going to do. She couldn't face Cody. In fact, anything to do with Cody tore at her heart. All she knew was that she had to find a way to get her life back.

Part 3

Chapter 70

Zoë's Uncle Joe had teamed up with Cody to develop a regular schedule to discuss Zoë's whereabouts and the possibility of any new leads. It didn't accomplish much other than it helped both of them feel like they were doing something to find her. Joe claimed he was watching all of Florida for any sign of her. Spring was in full force. It had been months since she'd disappeared.

Cody called Joe at his new home—the house his brother and sister-in-law had owned before their deaths. Zoë had signed papers transferring the mortgage over to him in late October, but Joe had waited to move until after the holidays. The house was worth a little less than the mortgage, but Joe figured that he would be there long enough for the real estate market to turn around. It was a grand house compared to where Joe and his family had lived. Now, Joe's eldest son and his new wife lived in Joe's old house. Zoë had said it was like musical chairs within the Valiente clan.

Joe answered Cody's call, saying, "Cody, there is nothing new to tell you. I've traced Zoë's old tennis pals, checked with the USTA, met with her old school friends, alerted police departments, and we've heard nothing. We've put out flyers. I swear, if she's in Florida, someone is going to know it."

"I appreciate what you are doing, Joe, but at this point, I don't believe she's in Florida. I thought at first that she might want to connect with family, to help her through this, or hibernate a while, but that doesn't seem to be the case."

"I should tell you, Cody, that she hasn't tapped any of her funds here. You know about the money she inherited?"

"No."

"Her folks were silent partners in our restaurant business, and the corporation deposited funds into their account every month. They spent money pretty rapidly, so it's not like we're talking about big money, here. But ever since last July, when they died, the money has been accumulating, and Zoë hasn't touched it. She knows about it because she had to sign papers."

"That's a little frightening, Joe. Maybe she can't access it."

"I don't know. I'm just saying that she hasn't made any move to get money in order to exist, and I don't know what that means. Any leads at your end?"

"None. I check in regularly with Dr. Wilhelm, and Midge and Pidge in New York. I also stay in touch with Lacy in Boston. They have their networks watching and waiting, but nothing has turned up. Everybody around here is on the alert. I also talk to Detective Kowalski at the Twenty-Fifth Precinct and he's just as frustrated—no sign of Darrell Holt or Zoë at his end. My guess is that the police have new priorities, and this case may be starting to collect dust."

"Where do you think she is, Cody? What do you think she's doing?"

"I don't know. I keeping hoping she will show up on my doorstep one day. Or maybe I'll get a phone call and I'll hear her say, 'Please come and get me.' I think she's hurting, and I hope and pray that she gets help. I don't want to lose her."

"Cody, what are you doing to help yourself? This has got to be driving you nuts."

"Sometimes I just want to holler, 'Come to me. Now! Why are you not here? I'll help you!' But I am just venting. I'm really worried about her, wondering what she's thinking and what she's going through."

A few days later, Martin and Cody met for lunch. They'd discussed Zoë's disappearance often, neither of them knowing what to think or do.

Martin asked gently, "How are you doing, Cody?"

"About the same. Once, after I got attacked by the bear, Zoë asked me if I had been afraid. I told her, 'hell yes,' and she wondered if I had ever been afraid before that. I told her a story of when my dad took my brother and me on a hiking trip in the Wind River Range. I was thirteen at the time. We were on this remote trail and thought we might be lost. We ran into some guys camped nearby in these big canvas tents, and we decided to ask them if we were on the right trail. There were six of them. They had horses and pack mules in this makeshift corral in a high meadow, and they had hunting rifles. Some had long beards, and they were really rough-looking fellows.

"Dad tried to show them our map and ask for advice. Nobody spoke. They ignored him. Dad asked again, and one old guy grumbled, 'Can't help ya mister.' Dad said his thanks and told them that we'd be moving along. John Jr. and I were scared because of the way they looked at us, and Dad hustled us out of there. When we were far away, he told us that they were probably poachers, possibly a money-making operation and not just for their own food consumption. They could have killed us. Had they done that, nobody would have ever found us.

"But neither of those situations were as scary as what I'm feeling right now. I'm afraid I've lost Zoë. Once, she told me, 'Never let me go.'" Cody's eyes grew watery. "I mean, how am I going to do that? What can I possibly do?"

"I don't know, Cody. Something will turn up. She's bound to show up."

"I told her once that I'd always be here for her but I'm thinking I need to move on. It hurts to even say that. But I might take a sabbatical from the Forest Service, maybe go to the University of Wyoming or CSU for a master's degree. They'd let me do that, though it's probably the only reason they'd let anybody take a sabbatical. I've also thought about going to Alaska, make some money fishing, maybe go live in the bush, but I don't dare leave unless, and until, I'm convinced that she's never coming back. I'll hang on a while longer, at least through the summer. I'm keeping busy with my job, and I seem to be spending every weekend at my folks helping out with Margaret's mess."

"What's the latest there?"

"Bruce hasn't done anything illegal since he went to jail and got out. Somehow, he came up with bail, but there's been no real trial yet, only preliminary court hearings. And he's honoring the restraining order. In the meantime, he sure has been obstinate. It took way too long to get those poor cattle sold. Bruce and Margaret split the money, but her half will last only so long. We got the place cleaned up as much as we could before winter set in, but there's more to do. She's still living there, and Mom and Dad are helping her out with the kids, mostly. Margaret is trying to find a job, and no one knows if Bruce is working. He's living in Sheridan, apparently. Also, nothing has been resolved regarding the ranch. Bruce doesn't want to sell it because it's family land, but then he doesn't want to split it, either. Margaret doesn't want to stay there. She wants to move on with her life—move into town, get the kids into a better situation—but she thinks that remaining planted keeps the pressure on to get this whole affair resolved faster. I don't know what the courts will say. It sure is dragging on."

"It sounds like the best answer is to sell the place and the two of them split the proceeds."

"My guess is a judge would have to decree that. I don't know how that works."

"Is it good land?"

"It *was* very good land, but Bruce hasn't taken care of it. The house is nice, and Margaret keeps it that way. If the ranch were mine, I'd tear down some decrepit outbuildings, get rid of some of the corrals and that stinking feed lot. I'd turn it into an operation like Dad's—light on the cattle, with more emphasis on the farm. It might take a while to make a go of it."

"How many acres?"

"It's just a couple sections. Bruce had some leases, but he got into trouble for overgrazing on the leased land, and he lost his leasing rights. Why are you asking, Martin?"

"Just thinking. I often explore things and never follow through. And I'm quite happy living at my own little place in my own community. Would your dad ever consider buying it?"

"He doesn't want to, and I don't blame him. He has more than enough to keep John Jr. and him busy, and the land he has supports them. They don't need to take on a third property."

"Maybe you could buy it?"

"With what?"

Chapter 71

At a Wednesday breakfast in March, Russ said, "I have something I want to share."

Willie said, "You're dating Mousey?"

They all laughed.

"I thought she was with the janitor." Russ smiled at his friends. "No, I went skiing at Keystone on Monday with a lady."

This tweaked everybody's interest, but it was Pete who asked, "Karen?"

Willie said, "Our Karen? Oh no, this won't be good. You'll get special treatment, and she won't pay any attention to the rest of us."

"Yes it was 'our Karen.' We had a nice lunch on the mountain."

"Alpenglow Stube?"

"Yes."

"Oooo…very fancy."

"What did you do afterward?"

"I took her home."

George said, "Could this be the start of something?"

"I don't know. It could be. I'm moving very slowly."

Willie joked, "Implying that she *isn't* moving slowly?"

Russ laughed. "No, I get the sense that she's being cautious, also. She's probably wondering about me. Here I am, extending my lease to stay another year, basically taking a very early retirement. I'm certainly not revealing any intention to be a productive member of society living like I do."

Pete said, "But you are busy. You've gotten yourself in good physical condition from all the biking and skiing. You've gotten Mrs. Robinson's property in good shape, too. You're reading a lot, educating yourself, and you've committed to some voluntary work."

"Yes, my days seem to be quite full pursuing my life of leisure."

"At least they're healthy leisure activities. From my perspective, you are doing exactly what is good for you as you cope with the loss of your family. And life will improve for you as a result. It all depends on how you measure productiveness."

George asked, "So when is your next date?"

"Saturday night. I'm taking her out to dinner."

"Fill us in at church on Sunday."

"I don't think so."

Chapter 72

Karen was born in Traverse City, Michigan, but left as a young child. Her father flew C-130's for the Air Force, so she spent most of her young life living near bases in houses decorated "early MAC," which stood for "Military Airlift Command." This decorating style consisted of inexpensive furniture the officers had a habit of buying in Thailand, India, Japan—almost anywhere they could—and hauling home.

Karen's father retired from the Air Force and then became a United Airlines pilot. That didn't end too well, given United's financial problems, so he retired from that position, too. Her mother was a teacher. They lived in northern Michigan on a small lake.

Karen went to the University of Michigan, where she met her former husband, Shawn. He played football as a second-string wide receiver, and he was in pre-law. She met him in a British Empire history class, and they dated for two years. They married after graduation and she taught high school history while he went to law school on a big loan. After law school, he got a job with a large firm in Denver.

Shawn became enamored with the life of being a hot-shot lawyer. He looked the part, worked long hours, and made good money. Meanwhile, Karen taught her history classes and raised their daughter, Rebecca, pretty much on her own. The marriage ended because Karen needed to be wanted, and Shawn needed to screw every young thing he could get his hands on. Being good-looking and having money meant that his desires were easily fulfilled. He settled into a condo in Denver's "LoDo" neighborhood with his girlfriend; Karen got the house in Gilson.

Alpenglow Stube is the highest restaurant in the United States. Located at an elevation of 11,444 feet above sea level, on North Peak at Keystone Resorts, it's near the Arapahoe Basin and Breckenridge ski areas in Colorado. The restaurant is considered to offer a high-class dining experience. On their recent date, Karen and Russ had entered the restaurant after six ski runs, put on the fuzzy Austrian slippers provided by the restaurant, freshened up, and sat down for lunch.

Russ noticed Karen's cheeks, rosy from the sun and wind, and her pleasant smile. She had combed her hair, and her eyes sparkled. They engaged in happy small talk as they ordered and ate their lunch.

In between bites of his Rueben sandwich, Russ asked her, "What's Rebecca's major?"

"She's not sure and hasn't declared. She wanted to be a ski racer, but tore her knee up really bad in a grand slalom race when she was sixteen. So she's feeling her way right now."

"And how is it that you're working at Hank's?"

"I've waitressed in the summers ever since my university days. Mostly, I worked down the hill. Anyway, I knew Hank from church. We both went to the Presbyterian church. I don't go there anymore, but that is another story. I would eat at Hank's now and then, and she knew I had experience waitressing—she only hires people with experience—so last year, she gave me a job for the summer. I continued on after the summer was over, and I've never gone back to teaching."

"Really? Why?"

"I taught one AP class where I loved the students because they wanted to learn. But I had three other classes and each required separate prep work. That began to frustrate me immensely. After a few years of dealing with students who didn't care, and with the general lack of discipline at school along with all the administrative stuff and the politics involved, I got tired of it. Also, I love working at Hank's. I'm a social animal, and I enjoy talking with the clientele. The folks who work there have become friends, especially Hank. She's a dear."

"I'm glad you are there."

With a smile she said, "I'm glad, too." With a slight hesitation, she added, "You know, you seem awfully young to be retired."

He laughed. "Well, I haven't actually retired. I just haven't decided whether or not I want to go back to work. Whatever it is that I am doing, I'm taking the Outward Bound approach to experiential education: just do it, with energy and commitment, and reflect on it later. Living as I do, I could carry on this way for a while. I'm not certain that doing so would be good for me, though."

"I know about Outward Bound. It's a great organization. How did your friends and colleagues feel about your exiting the business world at such a young age?"

"Are you trying to find out how old I am?"

"I already know. You're fifty-three. Pete told me."

"Oh…. Well, many expressed a certain amount of envy. However, just as I left my job, I went to this trade show to say goodbye to customers and schmooze with industry people. I ran into a couple associates that were clearly of retirement age, but each of them suggested that they'd be bored to death if they didn't work. I dismissed such talk about being bored or having the fear of being bored. I looked at them and wondered— was standing in a trade-show booth the only constructive thing they could do with their life?"

"Well, you seem to be doing some constructive things. I don't know much about business, though."

"Sometimes I think I don't know much about it, either. And it took the deaths of the two most important people in my life to realize that my work—engineering projects and the business—was not where true abundance is found."

"And where *is* 'true abundance' found?"

Russ looked at her, seeing that she was being serious, but reflecting care, even grace. "It took losing it to realize where it's to be found."

Slow to respond, since he really didn't answer her question, she said, "So what are you doing to find it again?"

"I don't know how to answer that, Karen. Live one day at a time? Searching…trying to make a new life?"

The waitress arrived at their table to ask if they wanted dessert, which broke the intensity of the moment.

Later, over coffee, Karen said, "Do you want to try some moguls?"

"No, this is the most skiing I've ever done in any single season. I may be improving, but I'm quite happy to stick to the groomed slopes."

"We could try some bimps?"

"What are those?"

"Bumps for wimps."

Laughing, Russ said, "Okay, let's do some 'bumps for wimps.'" He liked that she could be serious one moment, then become a smart ass when the conversation's mood lightened.

Chapter 73

Hank awoke to the sound of a running car motor outside her window. It was 4:50 A.M. From the window, she saw an old white van illumined in the all-night light that shone on the dirt parking lot. Someone was sitting inside the vehicle. Hank assumed that the engine was running to keep the van's occupant warm. There was snow on the ground, and it was about twenty degrees outside.

While it was earlier than Hank liked to get up, she was awake. So she followed her normal routine. She marched down her path to the back entrance of the diner, turned on the lights in the café, and got the coffee going. It was only 5:30. The van was still there with the engine running.

Boldly, Hank walked out the front door and saw Oregon plates on the van. She walked up to the driver's side. A woman sat up with a start and lowered the window. Hank said, "May I help you? We don't open until 6:30."

The woman said, "I know, but I didn't know how long it would take me to get here, and I wanted to be here before you opened. I came in response to your advertisement for the job as a waitress."

Hank had advertised the job opening on Craigslist. Marion was pregnant, and early on, she had started bleeding. The doctor had prescribed total bed rest for her. "My advertisement said to please respond by e-mail or call to set up an appointment."

"I know. I'm sorry, but I wanted to come in person right away…to maybe…I'm sorry."

Hank looked at her. She was just a girl…maybe in her mid-twenties.

Hank recognized how someone might see the advantage of just showing up to interview for a job. She decided to take a chance on this girl, and said, "Come on in and have some coffee. Convince me why I should hire you. By the way, I'm Hank. What's your name?"

"Brett Ashley, and I have a lot of experience as a waitress."

Hank sized her up as they walked. Brett was very attractive, had short black hair, a good build, and walked with purpose. Under a winter coat that looked like it had come from Goodwill, Hank saw black pants and a white blouse. Brett wore comfortable black shoes and didn't carry a purse. Hank asked her, "Where are you from?"

"New York City."

Hank didn't detect a New York accent. "Where do you live?"

"Right now, at the Big Chief Motel on Colfax. I bought a week. It's all I can afford at the moment." She saw Hank's reaction and realized she'd have to explain why she was living at a motel an hour away from this spot once they sat down over some coffee. She really wanted coffee.

Hank had been down this path before—the desperate woman needing work, willing to do anything, but with baggage, whether it was a drug or alcohol problem, a big debt, mental instability, or a criminal record. She'd had a habit of taking in strays in the past. One of them had even run off with her husband. But then again, Marion had come to her in questionable circumstances, and she worked out fine. She was a gracious lady and a hard worker.

Hank got two cups of coffee, and the women sat at a table. Hank said, "Tell me your story."

Hank's cell phone rang. It was her daughter, Elaine. She had the flu and couldn't keep anything down. Hank told her to stay in bed, get better, and not to worry about coming in to work. Hank would check on her after closing. Hank looked at the girl.

Brett said, "As you can probably tell, I'm alone and broke, and I'm trying to get settled. I don't have any kids I've dumped somewhere, I'm not a criminal, and I don't do drugs. I do know how to waitress. I've worked in busy, high-class restaurants with fussy clientele, as well as fast-moving family restaurants. I can work a point-of-sale software system, and I can do manual. I'm smart and personable with the customers. I can learn the menu quickly, and I really need a job. I'll work hard. You won't be disappointed."

Hank questioned her, seeking details. Brett was quick with her responses, naming restaurants in New York, offering anecdotes on how she managed things while working at each establishment, outlining various duties beyond waitressing for which she had experience.

Hank said, "We're too small to have a POS system, but we expect our waitresses to memorize what's been ordered, repeating it back if necessary, but not write it down on an order pad at the table. Then our waitresses jot down the order on a slip of paper for our cook, Jimmy, using a shorthand system. This way, Jimmy knows what he has to make without the customer watching. It's quirky, but it impresses the customers, especially when mistakes aren't made. Meanwhile, Jimmy is taking care of the counter with verbal orders, so he hasn't got time to interpret indecipherable scratches on the order."

"I can do that."

Hank hesitated, not revealing anything with her face. Brett just sat there, looking at her with anticipation. Finally, Hank said, "I'll tell you what. I'll give you a menu and the code sheet. The system isn't that complicated. For example, two eggs over easy are written as 2OE. Grilled raisin bread is GRB. Go in the back and study it. When you're ready, come and tell me, and I'll put you to work *provisionally*. We'll see how it goes."

"Am I dressed okay?"

"You look fine. We'll not ask you to handle the cash register. I'll take care of that." Hank told Brett what pay to expect for the job, slightly higher than minimum wage, plus tips. She said, "We'll determine your schedule based on whether or not I like your work. It may only be one day. How's that sound?"

Brett was somewhat surprised at the way the situation was unfolding. "That sounds great," she said. "I won't let you down."

Jimmy and Karen arrived for work. Hank introduced Brett, told them about Elaine's flu, and explained what Brett would be doing. They were welcoming, knowing that most of the time Hank had good instincts when it came to people who worked for her.

A little while later, Brett emerged having memorized the shorthand. Much of the coding was pretty standard. While she'd been busy in the back, Hank had filled in, helping Karen wait on customers. As soon as Brett started working, the restaurant settled down to a smooth flow, as was its normal state.

Karen said to Hank, "I'm impressed. She knows how to fan-carry multiple plates of food, and she moves with efficiency."

Hank said, "Yeah, almost too good to be true."

At the end of the day, Hank asked Brett, "How'd it go?"

"It was busy, but we were never slammed, so I could stay on top of things. I made a couple of mistakes, but Jimmy covered me with fast replacements."

"I noticed that. Can't expect absolute perfection the first day. What did you say to the customers? I had five regulars tell me that I should hire you. They were all men and rather enthusiastic with their recommendations."

Brett didn't respond to the implications of Hank's statement but said, "They just said things like, 'You're new here. Where's Marion and Elaine?' So I told them, and I said that I was auditioning for a job. I got some very nice tips today. I'm impressed with how much business your restaurant does. It's a cold winter day, you're not in a town, and yet we were busy."

"Part of it is location, location, location. We cater to three communities close by. There are a lot of people living in the mountains around here that you can't see just driving by, and we're on a main route. Gilson claims to be ten thousand people, but if you looked at an eight-mile radius around its center, there might be as many as forty-five to fifty thousand living within it. We get fly-fishermen, hikers, and bicyclists in the summer, skiers in the winter, commuters all year, retirees that like to hang out here, travelers passing through, contractors, ranchers, construction workers, and housewives. We used to get real estate brokers before the housing market collapsed. We've been here a long time and have a good reputation, so yes, we're busy…even on cold winter days. Can you work Tuesdays through Saturdays from six-fifteen to two-fifteen? That's a forty- hour week."

"Yes."

"Can I see some identification?"

Brett handed Hank her driver's license, which was, indeed, a New York license with her name and picture on it. Hank handed it back and said, "How come the Oregon plates on the van?"

"The van belongs to a friend. I've got to return it one of these days unless it breaks down. Then he told me to junk it. It's got 235,000 miles on it."

"You'll need to sign some papers and fill out a W-4. And over the next few days, I'd like to see if we can't find a better place for you live, close by."

"You don't have to do that, Hank."

"I know I don't. But I want to help you. And the age of that van you're driving has me a little worried about its reliability…and yours."

Chapter 74

Willie had shaved off his beard and gotten a decent haircut. When the four friends gathered for breakfast, the others marveled at Willie's cleaned-up appearance. It made a difference.

George said, "A new woman in your life, Willie?"

"Not yet, but I'm eyeing the new waitress."

Russ, who had been in Irvine for a week, asked who she was.

"You mean Karen hasn't told you?"

"No, I got home late last night, and I haven't talked to her."

"Her name is Brett Ashley. She was hired to replace Marion."

"How'd Hank find her?"

George said, "She showed up on Hank's doorstep at the right time… a stray."

"A very attractive stray." Willie nodded. "So, Russ, how was your trip?"

"I sometimes wonder why Dunstan pays me a consulting fee. As far as I'm concerned, they didn't need me to help them figure out their problem. They have good people that were on the right track, but senior management likes to have a so-called objective source review the process. So they pay people like me to say what the staff has been saying. Only I say it with more authority. Anyway, I'm glad to be back." Russ paused. "So, what do you know about this new girl?"

Pete said, "She's a nice kid, temporarily living in a motel on Colfax. Hank wants to find her a nicer place to live closer to the diner."

"I have a nice place." Willie grinned.

Pete said, "Willie, Willie, Willie. You need to keep your willie quiet for a while."

Karen arrived to take their orders—the usual again. Pete said to her in his best Paul Newman voice, "We're here admiring the beauty of the new waitress, Brett."

"Oh, you've noticed?"

"Hank does a very good job of hiring attractive waitresses," Russ said. "Is that by design?"

Karen blushed slightly, but no one noticed except Russ. "She's never admitted it. She's more interested in skills and their work ethic, but somehow, she finds good-looking ladies who have those traits. Brett needs a place to live, and I'm considering having her move in with me. I've got this finished downstairs. She could have her privacy down there and use the kitchen upstairs when she wants. I live entirely on the first floor, so it could work."

Russ said, "Do you know her well enough to do that?"

"I don't know her that well, but she seems very nice, and she really pitches in here. She's a hard worker. We get along great, and I don't get the sense that she's an axe murderer or the roommate from hell. Hank is high on her, which is a pretty good recommendation. I could always use the extra cash."

After Karen departed, the men nursed their coffee or tea, saying nothing.

Finally, Russ broke the silence. "Do you guys ever have dreams?"

Willie answered, "Sometimes."

Pete and George nodded.

"I seldom dream," said Russ. "And usually, I don't remember them when I do. Nonetheless, last night I had this vivid dream that is as clear in my mind as the conversation we've just had."

Willie asked, "Was the girl anyone we know? I assume there was some sexy woman in it."

Russ smiled. "I was in a play, and it was during the performance. I was off to the right side of the large stage, if one is looking out toward the audience. While I was *in* the play, I was more an observer of the action than a participant. Intuitively, I knew that the audience was large, but I couldn't see most of them because they were in the dark. Only once did I feel embarrassed or have a sense of stage fright, but it passed quickly as I reasoned there was no sense to fear the situation at hand.

"The set looked like an upscale, massive living room of an estate house, with expensive furnishings, high ceilings, and tall windows with elaborate drapes. The scene was a nineteen-forties cocktail party with tall men wearing World War II army uniforms. The women were well-dressed in period clothes holding cocktail glasses. It looked like a scene from the movie, *White Mischief*—an odd British film about the decadence of colonials in East Africa during the early forties. People were conversing with each other, but there was no real sound other than the multiple mumblings of people in quiet conversation.

"I knew of no plot or any real story being told, only the scene. I had the sense that I didn't know what was going on, or what was to happen next, and I was comfortable in my ignorance. I noticed a naked woman across the stage—"

"See, I told you!" Willie said.

They all chuckled as Russ continued. "She was at a distance, sitting on a padded stool with her back to me. She had shoulder-length, auburn-red hair, but didn't have the complexion of the typical redhead. Her skin was well-tanned and appeared smooth, without freckles or any blemish. Her perfect posture and positioning on the stool indicated that she had been trained as a model. Her thin waist and straight back were appealing. No one paid any attention to her, but my eyes were fixed on her. She changed the mood of my admiration when she reached down with her left hand, raised her left butt cheek, and scratched herself well underneath on the left side. The act exposed the nice line of her butt crack and the pleasant shape of her rear."

"Vivid description there, Russ." Willie grinned.

Russ shrugged. "Well, she did it elegantly, and it made me smile. I wanted to meet her, but kept my distance. After all, this was a performance.

No one else seemed to notice. People moved slowly on stage, and she continued to be ignored while I watched her, transfixed, wondering who she was.

"Time shifted. Now, she had on a light green, low-cut dress. Note the green dress with red hair…appropriate color coordination even in a dream. Anyway, she leaned back, and I could see down her dress. I got an eyeful of her well-proportioned breasts. She was half-sitting on another dressed woman, who was positioned on a long couch. Both women had cocktails in their hands. I wondered whether the two women were just being friendly, or whether there was more going on between them. Then the play ended to great applause. The curtain closed. There was no encore.

"I moved away from my location on the stage and was immediately confronted backstage by a toad-like fat man in a wheelchair who had been in the play dressed as an old woman. He was also the director. Somehow, I knew this, but had no memory of him directing anyone. He had two big goons with him, also participants in the play. As he was removing his wrap, wiping off his woman's makeup, he said to me in a threatening voice, 'I know you! I see what you're trying to do! You spend your time here being engaging, trying to be friendly with everyone, working you're way in!'

"I looked at him stoically, expressionless. Then he turned to the two thugs dressed in the military uniforms of the play and stated gruffly, 'Give him eleven thousand dollars so he can go out and have a good time.'

"A picture flashed before my eyes. I was walking around a large Midwestern city, late at night, with few people anywhere, not really knowing what to do. I had that eleven thousand dollars in my pocket. Then, I was backstage again, and asked the fat man, 'What's the money for?' He spoke in a voice like Orson Wells. 'Give him thirty thousand dollars.' Then he wheeled away angrily, leaving me with the two thugs. As one of them reached in his pocket, I said matter-of-factly, 'This isn't a gift, is it? It's a loan.'

"The big goon just smirked and pulled out a small, thick roll of what looked like coupons, not cash. I asked if it was the same as money. I asked if I could go into a bar, order a beer, and pay for it with that script as though it were cash. He said with assurance that it was as good as cash anywhere in town. I had the sense that there was something sinister going on, that I would be bound to the toad in some way I wouldn't like if I accepted the script. In a hard, bold voice, I said, 'I don't need your money.' A kind of fear stepped in as I said it. It struck me that I might be forced to take it. The mystery of the unknown consequences and the ultimate debt to be paid broke my concentration. I awoke with a start, wondering about the girl."

The men just stared at Russ. Then Willie said, "That's it?"

"Yes, that's it. And I haven't a clue what it means."

George said, "I'd say it means that you are very weird, Russ."

"I think it's very Freudian," said Willie. "But then, I would say that, wouldn't I?"

They all laughed, then Pete said, "You're an introvert, aren't you Russ?"

"Myers-Briggs tests showed that I am a flaming introvert."

Willie said, "But you're personable, engaging…you know how to talk to people."

"That's out of necessity. I've had to adapt to a world where, statistically, the majority of people are extroverts. I need my downtime to recharge my batteries. Small groups like this one, or one-on-one conversations, are best for me. I want to be invited to the party, but I don't want to go. Often, like Garbo, 'I vant to be alone.' I'm getting plenty of that lately."

Pete said, "Without thinking too deeply about it, it seems to me that in your dream, you depicted yourself as an observer of life. It's like you are on a ladder just watching, taking the scene in, above it all. It's understandable given what you've been through. Being a participant, boldly loving people like you did with your daughter and wife, then losing them, has made you gun-shy about making such commitments again. It is too painful. And it takes courage. The toady fat man? I don't know. Maybe his role involves some fear of entangling alliances. You remember the stress of being a driven businessman and what success in that arena entailed, so you are cautious about the future. Perhaps, dropping out has been very freeing for you. As for the woman, I'd say that it simply means that you are still a man. You aren't dead yet."

The others chewed their food, smiling over Pete's last comment as he continued. "I don't see this as too strange, really. We are all mostly spectators in life, entertained by powerful evocative images—eye candy—in a media-driven world. We are being led by breathless hyperbole, not reason. There are large parts of our culture out to win the crowd—get the amused mob to revere you, like the gladiators of ancient Rome. We're fascinated by the latest absurdity of celebrities, or their death, or by the latest shocking crime. We've had our share of shocking crimes in recent years right here in our back yard—Columbine and the killing of Emily Keyes at Platte Canyon High School. The nation was transfixed. We want to know all the gory details and there are plenty of willing providers. Which is to say, Russ, that in my opinion, your dream suggests that there is nothing wrong with you. But there is something wrong with the world we live in."

Chapter 75

Russ and Karen were having dinner at the Bella Bistro, an Italian restaurant in Arvada with a very eclectic menu that changed nightly. It was a converted gas station with beautiful stainless and glass doors that replaced the original garage doors. They would open these up in the summers for patio dining. It was Karen's favorite restaurant in all of Denver and when she told Russ about it, and the wonderful owners, he wanted to take her there. It was busy as usual—all the tables were full, and there were people waiting. The two sat at the granite counter over-looking the kitchen—Karen's favorite spot to sit—enjoying a forty-dollar bottle of Sicilian red wine, watching the owner and young chefs work magic as they prepared the patron's meals.

Russ asked, "So Brett's been living with you, what…two, three weeks? How's that working out?"

"She's really very nice. She keeps to herself downstairs, after work, reading…I think. And I have free long distance, so every couple days she asks to use the phone downstairs for an hour or so. I don't know who she's calling, but she makes lots of calls, which is all right with me. I don't get many calls on my land line, anyway, because I give my cell number to my friends. When we talk over dinner, or in the car—since we're riding together most days—she's engaging and funny. We talk about work, the customers, you, the news, or my daughter. She buys groceries and helps with the evening meals, and insists on doing the dishes. We mostly grab breakfast and lunch at Hank's. It's part of Hank's contri-bution to our lives."

"Does she talk about herself at all?"

"No, and that's the strangest thing. I went downstairs a few days ago to get a crescent wrench, and she was sitting on the couch, crying. I went over to her, asking her what's wrong, and she said, 'I can't talk about it.' Almost pleading, she said, 'Please don't ask me to talk.' I suggested she might want to visit with Pete, and she said, 'What's he going to do, suggest I pray with him?' I told her that he might, that he'd really helped me through my divorce and my situation at the Presbyterian church. Then I told her all about what had happened at the church, just to get her mind off her troubles. And I suggested that when she's ready, she might want to consider talking to Pete. He's a very good counselor. Since then, I've not probed into her personal life at all. There are some deep secrets there, though, and I'll try to help her, but she'll have to make the first move."

"You mentioned the Presbyterian church before, that you don't go there any more."

"I haven't told you about that, have I?"

"No."

"Well now, it's really not a long story. I was a regular attendee, and I went to Pastor Lawrence to have him help me through my divorce. I really unloaded, sharing all sorts of intimate things with him. After several sessions, he started telling me about his marriage and how his wife didn't understand him. Okay, so maybe he didn't come right out with that stupid line, but there was a lot of sympathy seeking going on. Then he started making advances."

"What kind?"

"Well, he didn't touch me. But he did ask me if we could meet under more private and loving circumstances. I simply said, 'No,' got up, and left. We've never spoken since. He's no longer the pastor there. I managed to get him fired."

"Which is why you don't go there anymore."

"Right. They have a very nice woman pastor now. I hear she's terrific. But too many people blamed me for Lawrence's departure. There was a faction in the church that thought I was lying, that Pastor Lawrence would never do such a thing. It became very uncomfortable for me to attend services there. Hank and many others—the majority—did believe me, so a committee was formed to find a new pastor."

"You've not attended anywhere else since?"

With a sardonic smile, she said, "No. I'm disillusioned with church, in the sense that one must be *illusioned* before being disillusioned. Pete helped me deal with the Pastor Lawrence thing, but I told him I'm staying away from churches for a while. I expect I'll come around someday. He tells me that he keeps praying for me."

She glanced around the restaurant for a moment. "Don't look now, but Shawn just walked in with the bimbo."

Not looking at anything except Karen, Russ said, "Does that make you uncomfortable?"

She reached over to him, smiled, and kissed his cheek. "No. They'll probably wait in the bar. The place is packed tonight. Let's change the subject. How have the breakfasts been going these few months?"

"Terrific. I'm enjoying the good-naturedness of it all. Sometimes strong statements are made, but nobody takes offense. Although we try to avoid politics, we sometimes drift there. I wonder about our discussions. I mean, who decides what the issues of the day are?"

"Our leadership in Washington, the media, and to an extent, academia. Academia is where all the 'studies' are done."

"Right. It's like we're being tugged or pushed by other people who have something to gain—keeping our minds focused either on trivial crap, like what celebrities do or think—or they're anxious meddling moralists yapping about the importance of their agenda as though it must be my agenda.

"You know, I've never hooked up Mrs. Robinson's TV to the cable system, and I quit getting the newspaper after a month's trial. I haven't been to a movie in three years. Occasionally, I'll get a movie and play it on the DVD player, but they're all old movies, classics, or something that I want to check out. If I don't like it, I'll turn it off and send it back to

Netflix. It's very freeing. I don't get the sense that I've missed anything important."

Enjoying herself, Karen said, "Not a bad approach. Brett and I only watch the educational programs, things like *Entertainment Tonight, Dancing with the Stars,* and *American Idol.*"

Russ laughed as Karen continued, laughing also. "No, we really don't watch much of anything. The TV is mostly background noise, and we listen to music when we're in the mood."

Russ said, "Another thing…we try to segregate mere opinions from convictions. We throw around a lot of opinions, but we know that's what they are. And we do talk about the big moral issues of the day. It's like that old joke about the married couple. He gets to decide all the important stuff—how to fix the economy, tax and social policy, the environment—and she decides all the trivial stuff—where they live, what kind of house they have, how to spend their earnings, how they spend their time. So we sit around making decisions about things where we have no control."

They both laughed again. After a long pause, Karen said in a tender and slightly nervous voice, "What's really important to you, Russ?"

Russ lowered his head a moment, then looked at her with a soft intensity she'd not seen before. He reached for her hand and rubbed it, saying, "Over these last three years, I became dead inside. What's important to me right now is restoring my soul. I'm no good to anybody if I'm not grounded. I came here to leave all that happened in California behind. To find peace, and new friends, and maybe someone to share my life with, and hopefully happiness. I'm glad we're seeing each other, Karen."

Karen squeezed Russ's hand and said, "I am, too."

Later, Shawn and the bimbo were seated and Russ received the bill. He placed his credit card with the check, excused himself, and went to the bathroom. Shawn took advantage of the moment and left his seat to visit Karen. He approached her and said, "Hello, Karen. Who is the guy?"

"A man I'm dating."

"A man you're dating. No details to offer?"

"No."

"Are you sleeping with him, yet?"

"As a matter of fact, I am. But why don't you just return to your little friend, and let me enjoy my evening without you."

"No problem. I just thought I'd try to be friendly."

"Okay. You were friendly. Goodbye."

"Touchy, aren't we?"

"We? No, you're just being crude and intrusive, and I'm not enjoying it."

"Have a nice evening, anyway."

In a short time, Russ returned and signed the merchant copy of the credit card receipt after applying a fat tip. On the trip home, half-way there, Karen told Russ of the conversation with Shawn. He said, "In other words, you lied."

"Yes, I did."

"Why?"

"I don't know."

Russ shut down, saying nothing.

After a period of silence, Karen said, "Is something wrong?"

Quietly, he said, "I don't think I like being used. I don't want to be a means for you to get back at your ex."

"When I told you what he said, I thought I was pointing out what a jerk he was, not that I was being a jerk. Is that what you think? That I only see you as a means to revenge?"

"No, I can see in the way you treat me that there's more than that between us. Your words just struck me badly."

"They struck you badly? Can't you tell how I feel about you? What do I have to do? You keep holding back. You say nice things, you treat me like a queen. And earlier tonight, you told me what you were doing here—trying to find happiness again. I would have done anything you wanted right then. Don't you know that I love you? Don't you think I know how hard it is for you to let go of Sara? You're afraid. And I'm not going to quit on you unless…unless you push me away because you don't want me."

Russ pulled the truck over to the parking area at the Genesee exit off I-70 and stopped. He unfastened his seatbelt and reached for her, kissing her face as tears rolled down her cheeks. They said nothing more, but they smiled as they kissed and rubbed each other's shoulders, back, head, and arms.

Russ wanted her. He said, "Let's go home and be with each other."

Chapter 76

Several days later, at about one-forty-five on a Friday afternoon, Russ stopped at Hank's for a late lunch. Karen had taken the day off to help Rebecca make curtains and decorate her new apartment near CSU. On this day, Brett served Russ. Noticing his Carhartt work pants, old checkered flannel shirt, and work boots, she said, "You look like you're in the middle of something."

He smiled at her. "Yeah, I'm working on a shelf-building project, and I'm on my way to Home Depot for some supplies. I hope I'm not too late for a BLT on wheat toast."

"No, I'll get it for you right away. Anything else?"

"No, that'll be it, and a glass of water." He watched her walk away, thinking how pretty and pleasant she was, but he also knew that she acted this way when she knew people were watching her. He'd also seen deep sadness in her eyes. Her face told stories without facts.

Minutes passed, and Russ finished his sandwich. It was closing time now.

Russ walked to the back of the restaurant, heading for the bathroom. Jimmy scrubbed the grill. Unseen and unheard, the dishwasher was in the back cleaning pots and pans. Elaine and Brett were finishing up with the tables.

Hank counted money at the cash register. She removed funds from the cash register three times a day, putting the bills in a big safe in her little back room office. The money she handled at the moment represented the diner's proceeds since noon.

The front door was unlocked. Usually, Hank didn't lock up until the waitresses left for the afternoon.

Two men entered, both dressed like young gang-bangers with big, oversized jackets. One was short and skinny. He held a gun, visible to all. In a loud voice, he said, "Everybody over by the cash register!"

The other man was about five-feet, nine-inches tall and probably weighed two hundred fifty pounds or more. He didn't appear to have a gun, but then, he looked like he didn't need one.

Hank noticed that they drove a Subaru Outback, but she couldn't see the license plate.

The little one said, "Get away from that cash register, old woman. And you"—he waved his gun at Brett—"you come over and get out the money."

Brett moved to the cash register. The drawer stood open, so she pulled all the paper money and handed it to him. He said, "That's all there is? What the fuck? That's it?" He stuffed the bills into his coat pocket, then pushed Brett, turning her around in front of the open drawer. He grabbed the back of her neck and stuck the pistol up her crotch, saying, "Lift out that drawer. You had better find more money in there, puta!"

Brett did what she was told, wincing. The gunman was hurting her. She showed him that there was no more money. Hank was about to tell them about the safe in her office, when they all heard a toilet flush. The robbers looked at each other and waited for whomever was in the bathroom to come out. In a moment, Russ appeared and stopped by the bathroom door, taking in the scene before him.

The little guy said to him, "Go stand over by the old woman. Anybody else in there?"

Russ said, "No."

"There better not be, asshole."

As Russ did what he was told, the big guy leaned against a counter stool, picking at something on his pants, looking bored with the whole thing. He appeared to be satisfied letting his partner do all the work. Then, he said in a matter-of-fact voice, "I think I heard a door close."

The little one said, "Shit, is anybody else here?"

Nobody answered for two seconds. He repeated the question, this time screaming it as he shook Brett by the neck and shoved the pistol harder up her crotch. She began to cry from fear and the pain.

Hank yelled, "Stop it."

Russ took two giant steps and reached for the gunman's shoulder, but the big guy was very quick. He grabbed Russ and threw him to the floor in one balletic movement. A large, make-my-day revolver materialized in his hand, and he stood over Russ, pointing it at Russ's head.

Russ stayed motionless, wondering where the hell that piece had come from.

Hank hollered, "Stop! Stop! You'd better go. That was my dishwasher you heard. He's gone out the back. He's probably called the sheriff already. And you won't find him, either. He's a runner, and those are thick woods back there."

The larger gunman said to his partner, "*Vamanos*," and started to leave. The smaller guy licked Brett's neck, made kissing sounds in her ear, fondled her breasts, and whispered something to her in Spanish.

Brett squirmed, facing the cash register, sobbing. She understood every disgusting word.

Then, he pulled the pistol away from her crotch and joined his partner. They were now gone.

Jimmy ran to the window to get their license plate number as the car kicked up snow and dirt, racing out of the parking lot, heading west. Hank and Elaine immediately went to Brett who had slumped to the floor.

Jimmy said, "Are you okay, Russ? Are you hurt anywhere?"

"No, I'm fine," he said, although he felt some pain in his shoulder, hip, and head, where the three had met the floor. "Where did that cannon come from?"

Reaching for the phone to call 911, Jimmy said, "It was stuffed inside his coat."

Elaine ran for some facial tissues, and Russ knelt with Hank to see if he could help Brett. Hank asked Russ, "Can we get hold of Pete? Pete needs to be here."

"He's in Virginia visiting family. He won't be back until Wednesday."

"Well, it's just us, then."

Elaine returned, dispensing tissues, and Russ got out of the way, reaching for his cell phone. He dialed Karen's number, but there was no answer. He left a message for her to call him as soon as possible.

When the sheriff arrived twenty minutes later, siren blaring, he apologized for taking so long. He had been in communication with his people, who had picked up the speeding Subaru south of Bailey. It was stolen.

The dishwasher heard the siren and emerged from the safety of the woods to join the group.

In short order, two other police cars arrived, and the interviewing began. The whole affair lasted almost two hours.

After the police left, Hank and Russ walked Brett to her van, both offering to take her home. She said, "That isn't necessary. I'm okay." She got into the van as Hank and Russ looked at each other with a knowing glance. She wasn't 'okay.'

Challenging her, Russ started to say bluntly, "Why are you—?" Then, he backed off, saying in a softer voice, "Look, let me take you home. We'll go in my truck." Brett tried to start the van but its engine wouldn't turn over. She kept trying to no avail. Russ opened the door as Brett gripped the wheel, shaking it violently in her anger and frustration.

Gently, he took her arm to help her out. "I'll drive you home, and I'll see what we can do about the van later." Standing by the truck, he reached for her and she allowed him to hold her in his arms until she was ready to step into his Ford.

Hank, stressed and tired, was relieved and thanked Russ for taking charge. As Brett and Russ pulled away in his truck, Hank walked up the hill to her house, slowly, her legs feeling like lead, and her mind awash in strained thoughts.

Chapter 77

Brett was quiet, just sitting there looking out the window in Russ's truck. She wondered if this was now her lot in life. What that horrible man did to her was almost like being raped again. She wanted to curl up in a fetal position but she couldn't with the seatbelt on. She also wanted to scream and lash out at a God she didn't believe in, knowing full well the incongruity of such a thought. How can you be mad at something if you've come to think it doesn't even exist? And she was angry with the world that seemed to be going against her. It was all getting to be too much. She'd never contemplated suicide. It wasn't in her, but why not? She thought, "I'm not doing what I know I should do to get past this. I used to be a fighter. I once knew how to work through my self-doubts and compete—gut it out. How did I let myself get into this downward spiral? I have to do something to break this self-loathing and fear of reaching out to the one thing that means everything to me." She curled up as best she could on the truck seat and couldn't contain it any longer. She bawled—huge sobbing cries as Russ, not knowing what to do, said, "Brett, please. It's going to be okay. We'll help you. We'll get you help." He reached over and patted her, saying nothing more as she let it all out.

After a minute, she asked Russ, "Do you have any tissues? Russ said, "sure" and opened the center console, handing her the box. He kept glancing at her while also needing to pay attention to his driving. She said, "I'm sorry, Russ."

"Brett, it's okay. I understand. It's going to be okay."

She said, "No, you don't understand." Russ, feeling very ill at ease, didn't know what to say as he pulled into Karen's driveway, parked the truck, and turned off the engine. Brett just sat there looking at her hands. She turned to him and said, "Please don't leave me alone this evening while I wait for Karen. Please Russ, stay with me. I really cannot be alone until Karen comes home."

"I'll stay with you, Brett," he said reassuringly. "I'm not going to leave."

They walked into the house and Russ said, "Brett, it might be a good idea for you to meet with Pete when he gets back. And you should have a good talk with Karen when she returns home this evening. I couldn't reach her earlier, and she hasn't called back. But I know she was planning on arriving by eight o'clock."

"It can't wait."

"What do you mean, 'it can't wait?'"

With an intensity Russ hadn't seen before she said, "I can't do this any longer. I am living a lie, and I do not like what it is doing to me. I keep fighting this despair and going deeper into a black hole. I should have listened to Trish and gotten help last November. I long for Cody, and I'm afraid to do what I want to do, what I know I must do if I'm going to find happiness." She shook her head and said, "I'm sorry. You don't know what I'm talking about."

Puzzled, Russ looked at her and gently said, "Let's go inside. Maybe you'd like to freshen up, and I can fix you something to drink."

They entered the house. Russ tried to call Karen again, and heard her phone ring on the kitchen counter top. "I guess we know why she hasn't called back. Do you want anything to eat? I'm not hungry, but what about you?"

Ignoring his comments about the phone and food, Brett stepped up to Russ and hugged him. Then she said nervously, "I've got to shower and I'll be right back. Please get me a cup of Chamomile tea. You know where it is?"

"Yes, I'll fix a pot and join you. Take your time. This has been a very tough day for you."

"There's more to it than that."

Chapter 78

Russ didn't know who Trish or Cody were or what this was all about, but he thought through her remark while he waited for her, "I'm afraid to do what I want to do, what I know I must do if I'm going to find happiness." He thought about his own situation with Karen and the aftermath of their evening at the Bella Bistro. He smiled inwardly thinking, "Nothing like a little fight to stimulate expressions of love." Karen had told him she loved him and he knew he was falling in love with her. He knew he had to do more, get out of his own passive funk, and take more of the initiative with Karen if he was ever going to be happy again. Their recent night of love-making was certainly a kind of commitment to each other, but he knew it would just become a crude interlude if he didn't act on his own feelings about her. He had a twinge of guilt about Sara in thinking these things, but he also thought, "Yes, time does heal wounds. I've got to move on."

Brett took a hot shower and put on loose comfy clothes. She joined Russ in Karen's living room, and she sat in a stuffed chair set at ninety degrees from a couch where Russ sat. She thanked Russ for fixing her tea. They both took sips and she said, "My name is not Brett Ashley. It's Zoë Valiente. My parents were both killed last July seventh in an auto accident while on vacation in Israel."

Russ was surprised and said. "Oh…I'm really sorry."

"It's only a part of what's happened to me."

Feeling uncomfortable, he said, "You don't have to tell me, if it's difficult for you."

"Yes I do. Karen told me about your life and I know what you've lost—your wife and daughter. Karen's in love with you and she knows how difficult it must be for you to love her back. You more than anyone may be the person I need to talk to, but it doesn't really matter because the important thing is I need to get it out *right now*."

Zoë told him about her background, her tennis career, her attendance at Columbia, her failed relationship with Darrel, the restaurant where they worked, and then her experiences in Wyoming. She talked about the friends she had made—Martin, Amanda, Jake, and others, and how she'd fallen in love with Cody, reluctantly at first, but then wholeheartedly. She told him more about the painful aftermath of her parents' deaths and her decision to honor their wishes to finish school at Columbia. She described the dinner she'd had with Lacy and Robert, and what had happened that night, including the people involved. And then she told him about the rape, the hospital, and the horror of the next few days alone in her apartment, her fake ID purchase, and her running away from New York into the unknown. Then, she fell silent, wondering if Russ had anything to say.

Russ was fascinated by her story, realizing that this girl had suffered greatly, but as he watched her talk, he also saw her strength of character emerging—how at ease she was as she unloaded her shocking news. She didn't appear to be holding back, and he thought it must have been cathartic for her to talk about it. He now understood the sadness in her eyes that he had seen at Hanks. But he still didn't know what he was supposed to do to help.

He simply said, "So, you went to Oregon? The plates on the van...."

"Yes, I went to Portland looking for Darrel. I thought I might find him by locating his friend, Gary, who works at Powell's Books. One day, I watched Gary leave the store, and I followed him home on the trolley, keeping my distance, wearing a hoodie. I verified the apartment number and left. The next morning, I was outside his building, watching him leave, trying to get a sense of his movements. I kept thinking I'd see Darrel around him. But, no Darrel."

"What were you going to do if Darrel had appeared?"

"Call the police. Or kill him. I'm not sure. After a few days of watching Gary, I saw him leave for work one morning and there was Gerty at the door with him, giving him a big, sexy, goodbye kiss. She'd been there all along, and I just hadn't seen her before. Gary's hands were all over her, inside her sweats fondling her. Eventually, he dashed off to work. And I'm thinking, 'What gives?'

"I waited a while, then said to myself, 'What the hell.' So I went up to the building and buzzed the apartment. Gerty answered. I said, 'Gerty, it's Zoë. Let me in.' There was no response, so I repeated my words. Then, I heard the door buzz open. It was a crummy building, and I was scared to death. But I went up there, and she let me in. She had this frightened look on her face. She said, 'My God, what are you doing here? And what happened to your hair?'

"I told her I was looking for Darrel, and she asked why. 'Help me first, Gerty,' I said. 'I thought he was packing up your things so the two of you could run off together after he murdered that guy. She said, yes, but that was before he changed his plans and well before she knew the man was dead."

"Gerty told me that she and Darrel had been planning to take off for Oregon, but he called her that morning telling her that he'd changed his mind, she should meet up with Gary and him at Nellie's Deli with Darrel's stuff. I said, 'I know. I heard the phone conversation.' What happened next?' She looked puzzled but told me the three of them met at noon as planned. They exchanged bags, and Darrel gave her one thousand dollars in cash. He told her to fly to Portland with Gary, that he'd catch up with them there. He had a plane ticket, but she didn't know where to—he wouldn't say—and he took a cab to LaGuardia. Evidently, he wanted to be far away from New York as soon as possible. Gerty said he was excited, nervous. She knew then the matter was serious, but Darrel wouldn't admit it. He just wanted to get away.

"I asked Gerty where Darrel was. She wanted to know why I was looking for him before she'd say anything else. I explained that I had found him in the apartment the morning they'd left town, packing her clothes. Then I told her about the rape, what Darrel had said to me, and how he had treated me like a thing. That hit her between the eyes. We talked about it all, and she told me horrid details of her experiences when she was thirteen, her infatuation with her gymnastics instructor that had turned into his rough, sexual abuse. He skipped the country, and she was left with a pornographic view of what love is. We just talked like real friends. And in that one moment, our relationship changed.

"Gerty told me she and Gary hadn't heard from Darrel in days. She said he had been on the move and that he was traveling under an assumed name. I said, 'Daniel Sterling,' and she confirmed the name, asking how I knew that. So I explained about buying the information from his source, the person who had sold me my fake ID.

"Gerty went on to say that that Darrel had called Mario, a guy who worked at Antonio's. Mario had warned him that he was in some deep trouble. Apparently, Antonio had been angry that I'd skipped work, and he couldn't locate me. But then, the police came and he heard what had happened and became distraught. Mario also said some guys from Wyoming had visited Antonio looking for information about me. Mario told Darrel that they were pretty upset.

"I asked if Darrel said anything about who the Wyoming guys were, and Gerty said no, there were no names mentioned. I then asked her if Darrel said where he was headed. But she didn't know, and expected to hear from him any time."

Russ asked, "How much time passed between when you left New York and when you met with Gerty in Oregon?"

"About six weeks. I took the first available long-distance bus out of New York, and it was going south. I didn't know what I wanted to do. I'd never been so confused in my life. I got to Atlanta and headed west, taking buses that landed me in Arizona with lots of stops in between. I ended up staying with a nice old couple—snowbirds from Canada—at a mobile home park in Quartzsite, Arizona. I played the lost homeless girl with a past and they took pity on me. In a way, I wasn't acting. The lady fixed my hair, cleaned up my crude scissor job. Finally, I decided I wanted to find Darrel before he found me. He scared me, and I wanted the fear to end. That's when I took a series of buses to Portland. I stayed various places along the way, spending Christmas in a small town in Northern California, feeling sorry for myself."

"How long were you in Portland?"

"Several weeks. Gerty said I could stay, and after we talked it through with Gary, he was okay with it."

"You trusted them that much? What if Darrel had just showed up?"

"Hmmm…yes, I did trust them. Gerty and I connected quickly when we shared the intimacies of our rapes. Up until today, and except for the people at the hospital, she's the only person on this earth whom I've talked to about it. We shared what our experiences had done to us— about the soul-destroying aspects, the loss of self-worth, the hurt, the guilt, and the terror." Zoë started to tear up and Russ patted her arm as she regained her composure.

"Gosh, Gerty had been just a kid, and that man had done awful things to her. I won't describe them. I felt so sorry for her. In the New York apartment, she never told me and our roommates what she told me in Portland. We knew about the episode, of course, but she'd glossed over it, never telling us how bad it really was. She told me she wanted to kill herself. It was devastating for her because the abuse had come from a person she trusted, a person she thought she loved, even if it was only a kid's love.

"And the other thing…I was pissed that she'd given Darrel a key to our apartment. But after we talked all this through, she felt terrible about that. She said he had insisted she turn over a key to him. Darrel told her that he could get in and out of the place more easily that way, and if I didn't like him being there, he'd just tell me to shut up. Gerty and I concluded that he didn't want the two of us talking about what had happened the night before when the guy landed on the stairs. The key thing bothered Gerty the whole time I stayed with her. She hated Darrel."

"What about Gary? You also concluded that he was trustworthy?"

"He's a very gentle man. Before I got to his place, I'd withdrawn inside myself. I wasn't the normal me at all. I'm still not. But Gary and Gerty were very supportive. Gerty kept telling me that none of this was my fault and I was beginning to see that, but that maybe seeking revenge on Darrel wasn't the best course of action. I wasn't so sure about that part."

Russ wondered why Zoë hadn't just called Cody, especially since Gerty had been helping her come around, but he decided to take the conversation in a different direction. "Why is it that you came here to Colorado?"

"Because Darrel is here."

"In the Gilson area?"

"No, he's in Denver somewhere. I'm guessing he's working as a waiter, probably using the name on his fake ID: Dan Sterling. So, I made lots of phone calls to restaurants on Karen's phone—she has free long distance—trying to track down a waiter named Dan Sterling."

"How do you know he's in Denver?"

"He called Gerty one night and told her he was settled in Denver and he planned to stay there. He gave no details. He didn't like the idea of being in Portland because he was afraid of being picked up. He wanted Gerty to come to him, but he thought it best that they stay separated a while longer since he thought the police were watching Gary and her. She never told him that she had no intention of going to him.

"Gerty, Gary, and I talked about it, and I thought I'd head in this direction. Since I was short on funds, Gary gave me the old van—just *gave* it to me—hoping I'd make it here. If it foundered on the road somewhere, well 'sorry.' We talked about the possibility of Darrel coming to Portland anyway, 'unannounced,' but Gerty and Gary didn't get the sense of that, given his prior conversations with them.

"Why don't you just call the police here?"

"What would I say? 'There's this guy who killed somebody and raped me in New York City last year, who is now using an alias, and he's somewhere in Denver. I'm guessing he's working as a waiter, so why don't you guys check every restaurant in Denver and find him.' Would they really be interested in that? No, I want to find him and then call the police."

"So, you're not planning on killing him, after all."

"No, it was never a real consideration, although I've imagined several satisfying mutilations and tortures. I haven't got it in me." She paused a moment and said, "Just before I left, Gerty gave me a big hug and said, 'Zoe, you need to think hard about what you are doing. Don't let Darrel take up permanent residence inside your head or you'll never get to the place where you need to be.'"

"That sounds like good advice."

"Yes, I think I'm beginning to get it."

Russ asked softly, "What about Cody?"

Zoë started to cry. "Oh Russ, I feel so terrible. These last few months, I kept asking myself, 'How can you go to him?' And as time moved on, it became even more of a troubling question. I'm afraid to go to him, yet I feel guilty for not doing so. I feel guilty for all sorts of things…for not asking for his forgiveness, for being afraid to go to him, for being ashamed. I'm afraid, Russ. I'm afraid he won't love me."

The tears flowed as Russ reached for her, consoling her, feeling awkward with his feeble attempts.

Chapter 79

Russ heard the automatic garage door lift and moments later he heard Karen come in. She walked into the kitchen, saw Russ with Brett in the distance and cheerfully said, "Hi, I got home a little early. What are you doing here, Russ? I thought...." As she approached them, Karen's happy expression changed. Russ was holding Brett's one hand as she was wiping the tears from her eyes with another. Karen asked, "What's going on here?" Russ looked at her pleadingly and said, "Please get yourself a tea cup and come sit next to me."

Karen dropped her coat and purse, found a cup, and sat next to Russ. He poured her some tea and pulled her close to him. She continued to look confused as Russ said, "There was a robbery at Hank's today and Brett was terrorized."

Karen looked at Brett and said, "Oh, no! You poor girl. What happened?"

Zoë just looked at Russ hoping he would intervene. He picked up the signal. "Karen, it's only part of what's happened. First of all, her name isn't Brett, it's Zoë. But we've been talking for almost an hour, and we're at a critical point, and I don't think we can ask Zoë to go through her story again, at least not right now. I'm going to ask that you to let us continue and we'll fill in the gaps later. Karen looked even more confused, but said, "okay." Russ kissed her, squeezed her hand, and didn't let it go.

There was a long period of silence among them. Zoë was thinking about Cody and what she wanted to know from Russ about coping with tragedies. She remembered Cody's comments last August about dealing with the bad things that happen and wondered why it hadn't been at the forefront of her thoughts. Russ was searching for a way to pick this conversation back up, wanting to help, but feeling uncomfortable about giving advice over matters he knew little about. He said, "Zoë, I think I understand your fear of reaching out to Cody, but how can I help?"

Haltingly, Zoë asked, "I want to know how you got over the loss of your daughter, Grace, and then your wife. I cannot imagine what losing a child must be like, yet you seem to be so in control. I lost my parents, but they were much older and, of course, they would be lost anyway at some point. I understand how that works. But your child? I lost other things too—my self-respect, my trust in humanity, my spirit, my courage; and I may have thrown away the thing I love most—Cody. How have you coped?"

Russ said, "It hasn't been easy, Zoë, and I'm not sure I've handled it as well as you think I have. I've gone through periods of depression. I know that I often behave passively, that I'm sometimes in a mental funk, not connecting with reality, and I fight it with activity. But the real help came, for me anyway, by making new friends, making a new life, finding Karen—slowly, those things begin to work."

Karen leaned close to Russ. Zoe was watching, listening as he continued, "Many years ago, when I still worked for my former employer, they sent me to one of those week-long leadership development programs with about twenty-five other rising stars. Near the end of the week, I spent two hours with a lady psychologist dissecting all that I'd learned about myself and how I relate to people. At one point, I asked her how people cope when a crisis hits. I told her I was thinking of an example in which there is a death in the family, or cancer. I never thought for one second that I was making a prophetic statement. I wondered out loud how she thought I'd handle a crisis. It was like looking for the evil eye or knocking on wood.

"The psychologist said the way I think, reflect on things, and mentally process, is a strength, not a handicap. It's where I get my certainty in life. And I would always be able to draw on that strength and on my stable background if something bad happened. I told her that in a crisis, I would probably say something like, "I don't like this at all. It's tearing me apart. But I'm going to learn to live with it, one way or another. I'll adapt…I'll find a way to nurture my soul."

"My point is that your upbringing, the values instilled in you, the grit and gumption you have at your core—like what it took for you to play a professional sport—and the people in your life who love you and are no doubt worried sick about you…if you can draw on all that…."

Zoë teared up again saying, "I know. My mind tells me that you are right, but it's like I've been paralyzed. I cannot seem to move. I'm in mental slow motion. For a long time, I kept feeling like I couldn't rely on my own judgment about who to love and who was the potential monster in my life. I once loved Darrel, and he became the monster. They kept telling me at the hospital that it wasn't my fault, that it was a choice Darrel made. For so long, I haven't even been able to think straight. Gerty and Gary helped with some of that. And the people I've met here have been so nice, but, I really need my Cody back, yet I'm afraid."

Russ paused, then said, "I went through some counseling with a minister friend in California, after Sara's death. He once paraphrased St. Augustine for me, as sort of a closing remark on my situation: 'God wants to give you something good in life, but he cannot do so if your hands are full.' I think he meant full of worry, full of doubt, full of fear, hanging onto the past. Love is there to be received, but you have to take the step. You have to accept it." And while he was saying this to Zoë, he also knew he was saying it to himself for the umpteenth time.

Karen hung onto him as soft tears appeared on her cheeks. Russ said no more. He just held Karen while Zoë was absorbed in thought.

Chapter 80

It was evening-time, but not too late. Zoë willed herself to dial the phone. Cody's cell rang and rang, and she left no message. She paced the room. Russ and Karen were there because she wanted them there—in case it turned into a disaster. She had to resolve again to dial the phone, this time, to Martin and Sylvia's home. Sylvia answered. Zoë said, "Sylvia?"

Recognizing the voice, Sylvia squeezed the phone in a death grip and with her other hand flailing, she motioned for Martin to pick up the other phone. She said, "Zoë? Is that you, Zoë?"

Martin was shocked to hear Sylvia's words. As he grabbed his phone, he heard her say, "Yes, it is. It's me and I'm okay…and I want to come home."

Sylvia went to Martin as he took over the conversation. "Oh Zoë, I cannot tell you how happy we are to hear from you. Where are you? Can we come and get you?"

"I'm in Gilson, Colorado, in the foothills just west of Denver. I tried to call Cody, but I got no answer. I didn't leave a message. Is he…does he…?" She was afraid to ask the question in her heart.

"Cody is in Alaska, but he'll be home late tomorrow night. I imagine you have lots to tell us, and I want to let you know, right up front, that Cody absolutely longs for you. He's been frantic with worry and yet he holds on to hope." Martin could hear her emotion at the other end of the phone and said, "I'm not telling this to you to make you feel bad, Zoë. I'm telling you this to let it know that it's going to be okay. Cody loves you no matter what. We all do. And we're thrilled that you're coming back."

"I am, too. It's taking away such a burden. But, I…I don't know how I'm going to get there."

Russ, standing in the kitchen with Karen at his side making more tea, said, "We'll get you there" at exactly the same time Martin said, "We'll come get you."

Martin heard the voice in the background and asked, "Are you with other people right now?"

"Yes, I'm with a man named Russ and his girlfriend, Karen. We're at her house. Martin, I don't want to hang up, but let me talk to the two of them for a few minutes and call you back. I don't think I can wait for Cody to get home late tomorrow and then expect you to come down here to get me. I have access to an old van, but I don't think it would make the trip. Let me figure out how I can get there. I'll call you right back. Okay? And Martin, thanks for being there for me."

"That's fine. Just call me back as soon as you can."

"I will, Martin. My love to you both, and we'll being seeing you real soon."

Chapter 81

It had been a rough Friday afternoon and evening, but Zoe was showing a new spark after her discussion with Russ and after talking to Martin, hearing his words about Cody. She went to bed early after taking some Ibuprofen.

Russ sat up with Karen until 2:00 while Russ explained everything he could remember. Karen was full of questions and he tried to answer them as best he could, but he hoped that Zoë would be willing to explain more of the details on Saturday. At one particular quiet moment, when both were getting sleepy, Russ said. "I love you, Karen." He stayed the night and left in the morning before Zoë emerged. Since they were leaving at 4:00 A.M. Sunday morning, he would be back to stay Saturday night also.

Russ, Karen, and Zoë left Sunday as planned. Russ drove Karen's SUV while, early on, both women slept. They found a place in Cheyenne for breakfast and for rest of the trip, Zoe told them all about the people they would meet, especially Cody. Russ and Karen laughed when hearing about Madge, Amanda's sense of humor, and Jake's preposterous story about Bigfoot. Both said they were looking forward to meeting everybody.

During a quiet time, Zoë thought about Cody and worried how he might react to her, in spite of what Martin had said. She even wondered how she would react to those first sexual advances that she knew would be coming. Would she be able to handle it? Would her animal instincts and her love for him usurp the psychological damage of her rape? Would he be afraid to touch her? She remembered how cautious he was when they were together in Jackson; and she knew he would be gentle, because he always was, but how would he feel now?

Around 8:00, she asked to borrow Russ's cell phone. She hadn't had one since Darrel had smashed hers in New York. She said, "I can't wait. I have to call Cody." Russ pulled over and stopped the car. He handed her his phone and said to Karen, "Let's step out and stretch our legs, give her some privacy."

As they could see, she connected with him. They couldn't hear what was being said, but Zoë looked extremely happy. Karen looked at Russ and said, "An amazing change of events since Friday, huh?" He embraced her, kissed her, and said, "Yes, and in a significant way, it's awakened me. I know it might be too early for this, and I don't know if I'll ever be totally ready—" Russ hesitated for just a second before blurting out, "Karen, will you marry me?"

She beamed and said, "Yes!" They embraced tightly and Russ twirled her around as they both giggled. Karen looked at him with a more serous face and said, "We probably shouldn't say anything to anybody for the next few days. I don't think it would be right to upstage Zoë's reunion."

"I was thinking the same thing."

Zoe jumped out of the car looking excited and said, "how fast can you drive?"

Chapter 82

It was beautiful day in April, the muddy season, and Russ, Karen, and Zoë pulled into the driveway of the Miller ranch mid-afternoon. Russ stopped the car and noticed a handsome young man walk onto the front porch from the door of the main house. He asked, "Is he your Cody?"

Zoë said, "Yes! Isn't he gorgeous?"

She jumped out and ran to him as he walked down the porch steps, leaping into his arms. Russ and Karen couldn't hear the words spoken between the reunited couple as they kissed and held each other.

Getting out of the car, Russ said, "They seem to like each other."

Karen joined him by the side of the SUV, laughing. "Yes, I think that's an understatement."

Walking toward the main house with Karen, Russ saw five people there gathering on the porch. Zoë and Cody joined Jake, Kay, Madge, Martin and Sylvia and everyone introduced themselves. Jake said, "come into the house and we'll get acquainted."

They visited with each other, somewhat awkwardly at first, because the Wyoming folks didn't quite know how to react to a rape victim. They didn't know where Zoë had been, and they weren't going to ask, even Madge. Cody appeared simply happy to have her there. Russ, having a sense of the social dynamics, said, "You know, I've only known Zoë a short time, but this is one remarkable young woman." That started an upbeat conversation—involving everyone—of Zoë as reporter, as horsewoman, as maker of raison cream pies, as waitress extraordinaire, as athlete, as nurse, as smart, as full of life, and as a friend. Nobody brought up anything that would possibly take the conversation to uncomfortable places. Russ's move was like magic. They all knew how to care for hurting people. And nobody reminded her that she looked like Halle Berry. It was an afternoon of new relationships, an afternoon of warmth, with people that know how to live and love.

Later, Cody led Zoë into the mobile home and said, "It hasn't changed, darling. It's still ugly."

"Today, it looks fabulous," said Zoë. "Oh, I am so happy to be with you, and I'm so sorry for what I've put you through."

"You're here. That's all that matters. I've missed you terribly, but having you with me again takes all the pain away."

They stood inside the door, holding each other. Cody was cautious, as she knew he would be. Zoë wasn't sure what to expect from her body or her psyche but she was beginning to realize that she wasn't impotent. She said, "Do you remember that first time I walked in here when you were cutting onions?"

Laughing, he said, "I certainly do…one of the best days of my life. I wanted you, and I was thinking that a relationship between us probably wouldn't go anywhere. You showed me I was wrong."

Zoë pushed him to the couch, and as they both plopped onto it, she said, "Kiss me and hold me and gently touch me like you did that day."

Chapter 83

Russ and Karen stayed over Sunday and Monday, spending their nights at Martin's ranch since he had better accommodations than the Miller's. They were planning to drive back to Colorado Tuesday morning, Karen feeling the need to get back to help Hank since the restaurant owner had just lost one of her good waitresses.

There was a small gathering at Martin's on Monday evening. Jake, Kay, and Madge were there, as well as Amanda and her son Davy. Cory was traveling with the rodeo circuit, and to Amanda's ultimate relief, was no longer a future consideration in her life. Cody and Zoë disclosed their plans to visit his family the following week, and her family in Florida in May. Zoë had talked to Lacy, Gerty, her rabbi uncle, Dr. Wilhelm, and members of her family in Palm Beach. Zoë and Amanda planned a day to themselves the following Saturday, a time for girl talk.

Cody liked Zoë's hair, but she was letting it grow out, figuring that as each inch grew, it would be a measure of the distance from that awful day in New York. Zoë had called the Denver police and given them the information they needed. Martin called the police at the Twenty-Fifth Precinct in New York City, telling them about Zoë's return, and learning that Darrel's whereabouts were still unknown.

During their drive back to Colorado on Tuesday, Karen said to Russ, "I really liked those people. I especially got a kick out of Amanda and

Madge. Just think, a few days ago, we didn't know they existed. That part of Wyoming has some beautiful country, too."

"Yes, Demming is a gorgeous spot. As for the people we met, they're very authentic, aren't they? Martin is an interesting guy—seems to me he could be very successful at a bigger newspaper, but he's at peace with himself in Demming. And Jake likes to play the crusty old man."

"Ah, but he's a *lovable*, crusty old man. Zoë told me we'd get invited to her wedding."

"Oh? When is it?"

"Not settled yet. She hasn't decided."

Russ laughed. "Doesn't Cody have something to say about it?"

Acting perky and with a twinkle in her eye, Karen said. "No."

It was the following Sunday in Demming. The ground was beginning to dry out, and there was a cool wind in the air. On this day, Zoë, Cody, Jake, Kay, and Madge were having a Sunday noon meal at the Miller ranch. After they'd washed and put away the last dish, Jake said, "Cody, you mind if I borrow Zoë for a while?"

"How long?"

"Well, you just let me worry about that. As long as I want, how's that?"

Cody laughed and said, "Okay, Jake. Where are you taking her?"

As Jake handed Zoë her coat and put on his, he said, "Sheesh, nosy aren't ya?"

The pair walked to the arena inside the main barn, Zoë's arm locked in his. Jake said, "I just want you to know how sorry I am for what you've been through, and I sure am glad you're here."

"Thank you, Jake. I'm glad I'm here also. It really feels good."

"I want to show you something. Don't move."

Zoë was at the outside edge of the arena near a gate as Jake walked over to Steely Dan's stall. Jake put a halter on the horse, clipped a lead to it, and led him to the open gate. "He's filled out some since you were here last."

"He's absolutely beautiful, Jake. Just look at that long mane and tail."

"He's frisky too. Watch."

Jake took off the lead and had Steely Dan run the circle of the arena. Keeping him moving wasn't difficult. The horse bucked, crow-hopped, snorted, and occasionally whinnied. He was enjoying himself, running fast, turning in the opposite direction when Jake commanded it. Steely Dan had stopped running and came up to them, agitated, still full of piss and vinegar. They both stroked and talked to the horse, calming him. Zoe stepped closer and the horse nuzzled her while she patted his neck. She said, "He's so spirited, so full of life. He's a beautiful horse, Jake—beautiful to look at and beautiful inside."

Jake said, "that's why you should have him."

"What are you saying, Jake? What do you mean?"

"I'm saying that I'm giving him to you. He's my present to you. In some ways, you two are alike. When I got him, he'd been through some rough spots in his life, but inside he had this spirit that wouldn't be destroyed. It just took some time, some patience, and some love to bring it out."

Zoë hugged Jake with tearing eyes. "I love you, Jake. Thank you. It's so generous of you. I cannot believe it. What a gift!"

"I've been riding him a little. With all the ground work we've done together, it's been an easy transition. He's got a nice smooth lope. A little more work, and he'll be finished. I'll keep him here for a while longer while I work him, but then he can go with you, wherever you end up…if it works out that way for you. He'll be a good riding horse and a stud that should command some nice fees, if you want to use him that way." Jake gave him a treat from his pocket, saying, "You know, Zoë, I was real worried that whole time you was missin', and I was worried about Cody, too. I just couldn't accept that I wasn't ever gonna see you again, before I'm gone."

"Oh, Jake, I am *so* sorry that I didn't return sooner—what I put you all through. I was hurt and miserable and angry at the world and scared." With tears and a tender smile, Zoë kissed his cheek and held him close. She said softly, "I'm sometimes a foolish young girl, you know…just trying to get a grip on life."

The End

Acknowledgements

Special thanks to Sarah Sailor, a former creative writing teacher who diligently helped me through two early edits of the content and structure of the novel; and to Laura Abbott, a professional editor who was my copy editor. Also, thanks to Dr. Patricia Ross, my editor and publisher who tirelessly helped me get the book into its final form, which you, the reader, are holding in your hands.

I want to thank Dr. Terry Vogt, a now retired emergency room surgeon of thirty years who instructed me on emergency room protocols regarding events described in the book. And thanks to Dr. Randy D. Whitesell, a clinical psychologist who explained the nature of sociopaths and the psychological damage affecting victims of a crime. And special thanks to Donna Brown who told me about life growing up on a Montana ranch. I also want to thank, Doug Bell, editor of *The Canyon Courier*, the weekly newspaper of our small Colorado community who taught me about the struggling newspaper business and guided me to books that taught me more. My apologies to all, if I have taken too many liberties with those things shared.

I also want to thank my ninety-seven year old mother, to whom this book is dedicated, for instilling in me the desire and the will to write. And to my wife Karen, I owe particular thanks for putting up with me during this long process, knowing full well that she'll have to further endure my need for quiet writing time as I continue to pursue the craft.

About the Author

Retired since 2005, James R Ament spent almost thirty-nine years working for a major aluminum company or its subsidiaries and successor companies. For the last twenty-three years, he was a senior sales and marketing executive with a global manufacturer of aluminum engineered specialty products, traveling the world extensively. He is now pleasantly situated on a quiet dirt road, 8000' in the Colorado Rockies, happily living in reasonable solitude within the silence of the mountains with his wife of forty-one years, Karen, and his children and grandchildren close by. He has an agreeable social life—not too much—enjoys skiing, bicycling, fly-fishing, reading, writing, and playing his guitar. He is working on his second book, a *noir* mystery, and regularly blogs at www.jamesrament.com.

A Reader's Guide

Questions and Topics for Group Discussion

1. This is arguably a novel about a person's ability (or inability) to "know thyself." Does Zoë know who she is? Is she in the process of finding out, and if so, how well is she doing?

2. There are various references to politics throughout the book. Do you think it is a political, apolitical or anti-political novel? Why?

3. There are those that say if you don't get involved in politics, then you leave the outcomes to those that do get involved. That may be true, but can a person be a good citizen without being "involved?" In what ways? What does the novel convey on this point?

4. Russ shares a past conversation with his mother where she tells him, "You are what you think." Is this true? There are also some references to passion throughout the book. Consider philosopher David Hume's provocative claim that reason is and always will be the slave of our passions.

5. The day after Zoë unloaded on Martin, he gives her a speech about self-righteousness and nurturing one's soul. What was he really saying? Do you agree or disagree with Martin's thinking here? Why?

6. Zoë and Amanda have a critical conversation about Cody after Zoë receives Cody's card. What did you think of Amanda's advice?

7. In another conversation between Amanda and Zoë, Amanda offers a theory about men and, at least for some, their reaction to feminism. What do you think about her idea?

8. Cody's sister-in-law and Zoë have a conversation dealing with this question: "What happens when you become something other than what other people thought you were going to be—when you change and you don't live up to their expectations?" How would you approach such a question?

9. What did you think of Pete's message to Russ: "One shouldn't die wondering what his convictions are." Was this a plea for certainty or was he suggesting something more profound?

10. Early in the book, Martin Coleman and Dr. Wilhelm discuss the newspaper business and politics in relation to Zoë's planned internship. Even if you don't know any professors of journalism, you read, see and hear the results of our various forms of media that provide the public information. Do you think that what Dr. Wilhelm described is what is being taught at universities today or is he an anomaly?

11. In speaking about Jake, Madge tells Zoë: "Like a lot of folks around here, he's indifferent to most human qualities other than endurance." Is this a good trait—higher than others? What other qualities must a person have in order to be able to endure, e.g. a disability, a life-long disease, unfair treatment in life, bad luck? Where do you place endurance on the scale of qualities of personality? Why?

12. Zoë described to Cody how her parents got along in spite of religious and political differences. Is that possible? How can that work?

13. There are several religious references throughout the book, but the main characters are not strongly committed to much of anything religious. And with many others, the subject isn't addressed or it's viewed negatively. What do you think the author was trying to convey?

14. There are occasional references to maintaining old friendships in spite of distances. In an age with almost instant communications, it seems more difficult today to maintain close connections with old friends than it did when people hand-wrote letters and transportation was extremely slow. If you agree with this observation, why do you think this is so?

15. Russ had to deal with real tragedy in his life. How do you think he handled it? What would it be like for you if such things occurred in your life? Or have they? Can you relate to Russ, his passivity, his inner struggles?

16. In spite of Zoë's resistance, Zoë and Cody's relationship evolves quickly. Is this realistic? Do such things happen?

17. Martin tells Zoë that he wants to hide the real story about Jake's accident, which is inconsistent with his earlier thoughts on *The New York Times*. How does that change the way you view Martin?

18. Why is Russ's sister Grace in the novel? She is a minor character, but why is she important?

19. In explaining her past relationships, Zoë leaves the impression that she adapts to the boyfriend of the moment, although she eventually figures out what is going on, and she is the one who

ends the relationships. Is there anything different about her relationship with Cody that suggests this won't be the same?

20. On the surface, the ending is a pleasant one. But consider all the loose ends, the unknowns. Do you think the novel ends ambiguously or not? Why?